D0282919

The Breached Wall

Also by Anita Burgh

Distinctions of Class
Love the Bright Foreigner
The Azure Bowl
The Golden Butterfly
The Stone Mistress
Advances
Overtures
Avarice
Lottery
Breeders
The Cult
On Call
The Family
Clare's War
Exiles
The House at Harcourt
The Visitor
The Broken Gate
The Heart's Citadel

As Annie Leith

Tales from Sarson Magna:
Book 1. Molly's Flashings
Book 2. Hector's Hobbies

The Cresswell Inheritance
BOOK THREE

The Breached Wall

Anita Burgh

First published in Great Britain in 2007 by Orion Books,
an imprint of The Orion Publishing Group Ltd
Orion House, 5 Upper Saint Martin's Lane
London WC2H 9EA

An Hachette Livre UK company

1 3 5 7 9 10 8 6 4 2

A CIP catalogue record for this book is
available from the British Library

ISBN (Hardback) 978 0 7528 6072 5
ISBN (Export Trade Paperback) 978 0 7528 7434 0

Typeset by Deltatype Ltd, Birkenhead, Merseyside

Printed in Great Britain by Mackays of Chatham plc, Chatham, Kent

The Orion Publishing Group's policy is to use papers that are natural,
renewable and recyclable products and made from wood grown in sustainable
forests. The logging and manufacturing processes are expected to
conform to the environment regulations of the country of origin.

www.orionbooks.co.uk

For my granddaughter, Poppy Leith, with love

Acknowledgements

I would like to thank my publishers, Orion, for their patience with me during a difficult year, especially my editor, Jane Wood, who has stood by me through thick and thin.

I would also like to thank my friends Ann and Andrew Johnston and Jane Collier for their kind permission to use an image of their Bibury Court Hotel on the cover of this book.

My heartfelt thanks to Mr Kirkpatrick, Mr Johnston and Mr Mohammad for restoring my sight. And to Dr Silva for keeping the Parkinson's 'shakes' at bay!

Love is a breach in the walls, a broken gate,
Where that comes in that shall not go again;
Love sells the proud heart's citadel to Fate.

Rupert Brooke 1887–1915
Collected Poems 1915

CHARACTERS

The Cresswell Family
Sir Mortimer (Mortie) Cresswell
Coral – his wife
Penelope – his mother
Morts – his son
Rowan – Morts' wife
Felix – his son
Lettice Hamilton – his daughter
Hugo Hamilton – her husband
Charlotte – her daughter
Georgia – her daughter
Hannah Cresswell – Mortie's sister
Agnes Beatty – Hannah's companion
Oliver Cresswell – Mortie's brother
Esmeralda – Oliver's wife
Marigold – their daughter

The Cresswell Family's Staff
Edward Whitaker – butler
Eve Gilroy – cook
Philomel Herbert – housekeeper
Nurse Winlock – nurse to Penelope
Willow Marshall – kitchen maid
Freddie – footman
Robert Robinson – head gardener
Fred Robertson – gardener
Sol Pepper – boiler man
Harold – coachman
Lavender Potts – Hannah's maid
Bridget – Esmeralda's maid
Gussie Fuller – Esmeralda's housekeeper
Milner – Esmeralda's butler

Other Characters

Stan Eldridge – Esmeralda's father
Zephaniah Topsham – owner of the Cresswell Arms
Dolly Topsham – his wife
Apollo – their son
Cordelia – their daughter
May Snodland – Dolly's employee
Ramsey Poldown – a neighbour
Petroc Cornish – Stan Eldridge's associate
George Meopham – customer at the inn
Reverend Samuel Plunkett – vicar
Sorrel – his wife
Sister Westall – Convalescent Home
Lady Sylvia Ferguson – VAD
Major Frobisher Fellowes – Medical Officer
Fanny Petty – orderly
Polly Pepper – orderly
Sergeant Bob Tanner – army cook
Bert Banks – patient
Flossie Marshall – cook at Cresswell Arms
Alf – her husband
Oak – her son

Animals

Cariad – Hannah's dog
Blossom – Esmeralda's dog

Chapter One

Spring 1915

1

Sitting in the church on her family's estate, Hannah Cresswell took a strange comfort in knowing that most of her ancestors were lying close by in the crypt below her feet. It emphasized a much-needed continuity in a frightening world. It was reassuring that, despite the havoc of the past year, some things never changed, and the peace she found simply in being here was one.

She glanced up at the fine stained-glass windows behind the marble and alabaster altar, each one in memory of a member of her family. In the Lady Chapel there was a beautiful tomb of two Cresswells who had lived and died in Queen Elizabeth's reign, husband and wife lying side by side, their hands folded in prayer, a faithful hound at their feet. As a child Hannah had cried incessantly for the dog until it was explained to her that he was not in the tomb with them.

On the wall opposite a brass plaque commemorated her father, old Sir Mortimer, who had asked for something simple. Despite that, twelve years ago Hannah had arranged for an avenue of horse-chestnuts to be planted because they had been a particular favourite of his. The trees were doing well and in fifty years would stand as a fine memorial to him.

She was early so she was alone in the church, apart from the verger who was scurrying about lighting the candles. She had not meant to be, but a trying altercation with her stepmother, Penelope, had made her hurry from the house – she needed to put distance between herself and the difficult woman.

Hannah was always regarded by those who knew her as patient. Little did they know how hard it was for her to contain herself when she was dealing with Penelope – she would find herself wishing the old woman dead and then suffer pangs of guilt. Something must be done about her, but what?

Penelope was bedridden and demanding – no matter how much the family pandered to her whims nothing was ever right for her. Hannah was sure that boredom was the prime cause of her discontent. There was nothing wrong with her, or so her myriad doctors had reported. So many physicians had been to see her that they were having to summon others from a hundred miles away – she had already consulted all those who practised nearer. All had said the same, Penelope needed to get up, eat less and move more. But, as Hannah knew, it would be easier to shift Calder's Hill than Penelope. She was now so large that it was a miracle her heart could pump blood to her extremities. When she died, it would be a difficult task to get her into a coffin. Hannah had mentioned this to her younger brother, Oliver, who, to her consternation, had laughed. She had said nothing to her other brother, Sir Mortie, because he was so squeamish about death and bodies.

Hannah sat rigidly upright in the family pew, which was set at a right angle to the body of the church. She noticed some dust in the ornately carved decoration and could not resist poking her grey-gloved hand into the aperture – such a fussy thing to do, she thought, and hoped no one had noticed. She was dressed entirely in a soft grey, which did not suit her because it was too close to the shade of her hair and drained what little colour she had from her face.

Slowly the church filled. As more people arrived the chatter increased. The atmosphere of excitement and anticipation was more in keeping with a celebration than a solemn service. Most of those present were not regular churchgoers. Still, who was she to criticize? Hannah had never felt the need to worship regularly but she enjoyed attending services occasionally, especially at Easter and Christmas.

From her handbag she took out a handkerchief drenched with her favourite lily-of-the-valley scent, and pressed it discreetly to her nose. It had been raining and the smell of damp clothes mixed with unwashed bodies was drifting to her. She was doing her best to promote the importance of personal hygiene by talking to the children at the school, with, it had to be admitted, only limited success. Miss Crick, their teacher, had pointed out to her that since few of the estate cottages had running water it was hard for the mothers, but Hannah couldn't understand why they didn't boil an extra kettle or two.

She looked about her as more piled in. Although most of the men were at the army training camp in Salisbury, there would soon be only standing room. These days, apart from weddings and funerals – those who lived on the estate set great store by a good funeral – it was rare to see such a large congregation. In her grandfather's time Sunday attendance by the servants and other workers had been obligatory; dismissal followed if his instructions were ignored. She remembered the boredom of those interminable Victorian sermons. In her father's time there had been a marked relaxation of the rules, especially since he was rarely here. Now her brother, Sir Mortie, had to be dragged to any service – in the family they joked that he wouldn't go to his own funeral.

She wondered if Oliver and his wife Esmeralda might attend. She was a sweet child and beautiful, but totally unsuitable, of course – her father was in trade. Hannah always thought her vacuous and not nearly intelligent enough for her brother, whom she considered clever. Esmeralda liked nothing better than to talk about clothes and shopping, and since Hannah had no interest in either, it made conversation between them rather stilted. Oliver had felt it necessary to marry her because she had run away to be with him, thereby irreparably damaging her reputation. Last Christmas, after years of barrenness, she had presented him with his daughter Marigold – it would have been hard to find a more doting father.

Perhaps it would be best if Oliver did not come. He had an unfortunate penchant for vicars' wives and she had heard that the new one was pretty. Some blamed him for the death of a previous incumbent's wife. This, in Hannah's opinion, was nonsense – the woman had been deranged, pure and simple. She straightened – just thinking about the whole sorry incident made her feel uncomfortable.

Several of the congregation, she saw, were on their knees and praying devoutly. They were from that small nucleus of people to whom the church was an oasis in their difficult lives, but they were of an older generation. The young did not appear to need spiritual comfort. Today, she was aware, nosiness had brought them here rather than religious fervour. This would be the Reverend Mr Plunkett's first sermon to his flock.

Hannah looked about her at the familiar faces. Many she had known all her life, many she had known all their lives, but these days there were many she knew hardly at all. Hannah had acknowledged the odd greeting with a dignified bow. How times had changed, she thought. No one would have behaved in such a relaxed manner when she was a child. She preferred this, she thought.

Every family from the estate appeared to be represented. There were a few Peppers, not the whole clan. They had worked for the Cresswells as far back as anyone could remember, supplying labourers, stokers and maids. The families' lives had been led side by side but their circumstances were so different. Perhaps it was because they lacked ambition, she thought.

Dolly Topsham – though Hannah always thought of her as Dolly Pepper – had taken her place in the Topsham pew, not with her family, which wouldn't endear her to them. They had decided Dolly thought herself too good for them now. She had done well to marry young Zephaniah Topsham – but her pregnancy had had a lot to do with it. Compared to most on the estate, the Topshams were well-to-do. Zeph, with his sister, Xenia, owned the Cresswell Arms, left to the family by Hannah's father – what ructions that had caused. She smiled to herself.

Such a lovely creature, Xenia, but she'd gone to London and no one heard of her now. Hannah had been told that Zeph meticulously banked his sister's share of the inn's takings, ready for the day when she returned. He was a good man.

Exotic names were a Topsham speciality. Zeph and Dolly's children were called Apollo and Cordelia – outlandish in Hannah's opinion. She didn't like Dolly very much. The woman was obsessed with money. She had once run a business in the local town, Barlton. What was the world coming to when former maids ran businesses? She understood that Dolly's in-laws had not been happy about the union. Zeph's grandfather had been the senior gamekeeper, a position of respect on the estate, compared to the stoker of the boiler. It amused Hannah to think how snobbish the working classes could be.

The wife of the estate carpenter, Rob Robertson, was there with their children, all heavy-boned and stout like their father. Rob and his brother, Fred, were at the camp. Fred was a good, competent gardener, and with spring coming the grounds would soon be in need of him, Hannah fretted. The Cresswell Manor gardens were her pride and joy.

The Marshall family took up a whole pew, Flossie getting bigger every year, which wasn't surprising when she was such a good cook. If she lived to seventy she'd have to be wheeled about, Hannah thought. Flossie's family sat beside her, such a jolly group who never stopped smiling. There was Oak, nearly a young man now, then the pretty daughters, Aspen, Maple, Acacia, Cherry and Holly – not that Hannah was ever sure which was which because they looked so alike. She hoped the family was complete – what other suitable tree names could there be? The two prettiest, Rowan and Willow, were not there. No doubt the latter was in the kitchen at the manor since she could see the cook, Eve Gilroy, sitting with the housekeeper, Philomel Herbert, and the butler, Whitaker.

Hannah and the cook acknowledged each other. She could not re-member when Eve had entered their employ, but she knew it would be a tragedy if she ever left them because she was the best cook they had ever had. Like so many of her profession, she had a fiery temper, which was completely at odds with her petite figure. She always reminded Hannah of a bird as she darted about the kitchen, especially with her fine angular nose, which was rather like that of a large eagle. Hannah had not known black eyes existed until she had met Eve, but hers were like jet and had the same sparkle. Once she had cooked for the family and the staff. Now, without complaint, she cooked for them, the patients and the medical staff who were billeted with them.

Hannah smoothed her skirt. She longed for this wretched war to be over. 'Finished by Christmas,' they had been assured, and for three months after that it had dragged on with no sign of abating. Only last week two footmen had enlisted, While she admired their patriotism, Hannah had been exasperated by their lack of consideration. Two fewer indoor servants put such a strain on the others and led to untold inconvenience.

There was still no sign of Rowan, but she would be helping with the patients. She hoped the girl would join her in the family pew now that she was a Cresswell – although that was still hard to accept. Hannah liked to think herself the least snobbish member of her family but it had been hard to adjust to a housemaid as her nephew's wife.

It saddened her that she was sitting here on her own. There had been a time, on special occasions such as this, when so many of the family had been with her that they were uncomfortably squashed. Of course, the women's clothes had not helped, being fuller and fussier than today's more austere fashions. That was one of the few good things about this wretched war – simpler clothes. Hannah had never been one for the ornate fashions of the past; today's trends were easier for her maid and, best of all, dressing did not take nearly so long.

From her copious bag, which was always with her, she took out a somewhat battered copy of *Hymns Ancient and Modern* and began to check which ones the new vicar had chosen. He seemed a pleasant enough man, a great improvement on the last, who had been overbearing and had had a superior manner. He was married with two children, who, hopefully, would make him agreeable and helpful.

The Reverend Samuel Plunkett's arrival was the reason Hannah was in church on this Sunday morning – she had felt she should represent her family at his first service. She didn't believe in God, and had questioned the hypocrisy of attending, but had decided eventually that such feelings should not preclude her from joining in the great festivals. She was aware that she was one of a growing number who felt like this. War, she had observed, made people either turn to the church for comfort or turn their backs on it in disgust.

When was the last time they had all been here as a family? It must have been the Christmas of 1913, she decided. By last Christmas the divisions between them had become pronounced.

Hannah sighed deeply as she thought of her youngest nephew, Felix, who, at barely fourteen, had run away last year to enlist as a soldier, lying to the recruiting officer about his age. The boy was a constant worry. When she heard or read of casualties, it was always Felix she thought of. At such times she thought what a solace faith must be.

His mother, Coral, blamed Hannah for his going. She was right – it had been Hannah's fault, if inadvertently. She had stupidly confided in another, whom she had thought she could trust, of indiscretions in Coral's past – kleptomania and a self-induced miscarriage. She shuddered. What a troublesome person Agnes Beatty had become. Anonymous letters about Coral had been sent to Felix – penned by Agnes, she was sure. The boy's pride and self-confidence had been destroyed and he had distanced himself from his family. Fortunately Felix had kept the contents to himself – only Hannah and Coral knew. If he were killed Hannah would never be able to face her family again. How could she live with the guilt?

She had invited Agnes to live with her and now when she thought about their relationship she was overcome with embarrassment. She had wanted to be loved, that was all. All her life she had dreamt of finding the right person. She had been at her lowest when she met Agnes and had mistaken their friendship for something deeper. Or, perhaps more accurate, Agnes had persuaded her it was love. But whichever way she looked at it she could never understand, or excuse, taking the woman into her bed. What a dreadful price she had paid! Agnes was evil and had thought nothing of blackmailing her.

These days, Coral could barely bring herself to speak to Hannah, and had banned her from the house – Hannah didn't blame her. Anyway, it had been no great hardship for she had built her own lovely home on the estate.

With the outbreak of war, though, Hannah had been appointed matron of the Cresswell Manor Officers' Convalescent Home and had returned – but if Coral chose to leave London, where she was now living, Hannah would have to make herself scarce. It was all so undignified.

There was a noisy rustle at the west door. Some of the manor patients were arriving. She could hear the squeaking of wheelchairs. She was sure, in years to come, when she heard such squeaks, she would be reminded of these troubled times. They had tried everything to get rid of the sound but the chairs creaked no matter how carefully they were handled. They were followed by the click and clatter of crutches on the stone-flagged floors as others, more mobile, followed them. She turned to smile encouragingly, for she knew what an effort it was for some to get this far. Her patients' courage frequently reduced her to tears, but she felt immense pride in them, too.

There was even more rustling and shuffling in the pews as room was made for the soldiers. She wished people wouldn't stare at the two who had suffered severe burns. It wasn't kind, and must add to their suffering. She wondered if there was anything she could say to the villagers to stop them doing it. But if she tried, they would resent it. Once they would have listened to her. How times changed … At that thought she nearly laughed. She must be getting old – too often, these days, she caught herself thinking in that way.

At the sight of Rowan she moved along the pew, but Rowan went to the main body of the church; she did not even look in Hannah's direction.

What a conundrum. Hannah had felt it was wrong for people to marry out of their class. From her experience it never worked. Differences in outlook, opinions and education were insurmountable. Admittedly, so far, Rowan had behaved impeccably in what was a tricky situation. Hannah was aware that she was not alone in feeling as she did – even some of the staff made things difficult for the girl.

Hannah was disappointed when Sister Westall and Nurse Ferguson joined her. She had been hoping that Major Frobisher Fellowes, the medical officer, would sit beside her. When he had first arrived she had taken to him immediately. He must once have been very handsome, but now, in his fifties, his hair grey, his features perhaps a little too filled out, he was less so. But Hannah was more interested in character than looks, and she admired his calm, resourceful and always pleasant disposition. How silly of her to be disappointed, she chided herself. She was like a child at a party wanting to sit beside her best friend.

Mrs Plunkett was scuttling into the church, her eyes fixed steadfastly on the floor, shepherding her children to the front pew reserved for the clergy's family. Hannah smiled in their direction. It could not be easy to join a new congregation.

The organ, badly in need of repair, wheezed into life and everyone stood as the new vicar entered.

As was customary after the service, everyone milled about the cemetery, talking.

'Thank you, Vicar. You gave a most interesting sermon.' Hannah shook his hand.

'I'm pleased you enjoyed it, Miss Cresswell. It was a fine turn-out.' He nodded towards the chatting groups.

'I fear that many came out of curiosity. I hope you won't be disappointed next Sunday when your congregation is smaller.'

'I'd thought as much. It's nearly always the same. I shall just have to persuade them.' He was laughing. Thank heaven he had a sense of humour, she thought.

Alf Marshall, Flossie's husband, had brought the ambulance as close to the church door as possible, the easier to get the most infirm men back into it. Hannah caught up with Rowan, who was pushing one of the wheelchairs. 'I'd hoped you'd join me in the family pew, Rowan. It's your place.'

'I was content where I was.'

'But you're part of the family now.'

'I think I should do things slowly – for everyone's sake, Miss Cresswell.'

'You've wisdom beyond your years, Rowan, which is most commendable.'

'Now, Captain Garside, if you could put your hand on my shoulder, I'll take your weight …' Rowan turned her attention to her patient.

Hannah watched with admiration as the girl supported the officer. How strong and patient she was. How skilfully she dealt with him. 'I trust you will join us at luncheon?'

'Thank you. I will, if I can be excused my duties,' she replied.

Captain Garside safely in the ambulance, Rowan went to help the next man. Feeling in the way, Hannah made her farewells and began to walk back to the manor.

It was impossible to ignore Rowan's studied distance. She understood it, but wished it wasn't so. Of course it was her fault – again. She could see now that she should never have interfered in Morts's affairs, trying to separate him from Rowan by hiding their letters to each other. Morts had told her it was none of her business whom he chose to marry. She had only been trying to protect him and, to a lesser extent, Rowan. Although she understood his reaction to what he saw as meddling, she was puzzled that he couldn't see she had acted with the best of intentions. She had apologized, so now all she could do was hope that when Morts returned from his training camp he would have forgiven her, and that time would make Rowan feel more kindly towards her. Once they had got on so well, but that was when Rowan had been the servant and Hannah the mistress. She must be patient.

2

The kitchens at Cresswell Manor were, as always, a hive of activity. The sound of clattering pots and pans soared to the soot-blackened ceiling high above. From a beam hung large hanks of dried herbs, which swayed in the heat rising from below. The click-clack of the cook's high-buttoned boots echoed on the ancient flagged floor. When the door of the vast range was opened for the fire to be replenished, the heat was like an impenetrable wall.

Eve Gilroy, cook for many years to the Cresswell family, never walked into a room. Rather, she bustled, as now. She was always on the trot as if she were late, which she never was. Her small stature belied the strength that a lifetime of hauling heavy saucepans had given her. Her dark hair, now scattered with grey, was tied in a severe bun, on top of which perched a white cap. Past her youth, she was a pleasant-looking woman who had missed being handsome by a whisker.

Eve's life was ruled by the clock. She knew to the second how long it would take to roast a joint, bake a souffle or prepare a meal for forty. She had a watch that she wore only on special occasions for, as she was fond of saying, she felt no need for it because she knew the minute of every hour. On the wall of the cavernous kitchen there was a large clock, which she claimed she never looked at, but all were in agreement that she must, even if no kitchenmaid had ever seen her glance at it.

Eve ruled her kitchen with a firm hand and a loud voice. It could never have been said that her bark was worse than her bite for she was prone to hurl a handy saucepan at any kitchen- or scullery-maid who had vexed her.

Even the large kitchen range, which stretched for a good fifteen feet along one wall, behaved for her but for no one else. Many maids had wept copious tears over its vagaries, but Eve would soon have it tamed with the deft opening of a draught here, the closing of a damper there. Capable of doing at least three things at once, and to perfection, she was held in awe by the staff and with gratitude by the family. She was content with her position and wanted for nothing – except love.

'Well, *he* was a disappointment, and no mistake,' she said, as she took off her coat, hung it on a hook on the door, and replaced it with a large, starched apron in one fluid movement.

'Would that be the new padre you're referring to?' asked Sergeant Bob Turner, a hefty, solidly built man who was so much her right hand that she couldn't imagine how she had managed before he came – seconded, last year, from the army. He was sitting in a wheelback chair, folding the newspaper he'd been reading, his feet up on the range, the only person in living memory whom Eve had allowed to do that. It was an indication of the favour she chose to bestow on him.

'Short and dull. I didn't like his voice one bit – droned, it did. I like a dose of fire and brimstone. There's some on this estate need a bit of fear putting in them.' She checked the large rib of beef she'd put into the oven before leaving for church, then riddled the fire, muttering to herself as she did so. Time was when such duties would have been beneath her but now, short-staffed as they were, she had to do it. 'Willow, have you filleted them fish?' she shouted, as she slammed the oven door shut, brushing a veil of sweat from her forehead. She did not wait for a reply but returned her attention to the sergeant. 'Been invited to luncheon, he has. As if I didn't have enough mouths to feed.' Eve sniffed. She had a fine range of sniffs that Whitaker claimed he could interpret to indicate what mood she was in – not that he had ever told her he could.

'You'll manage, Eve. There's no one copes like you do.'

Eve smiled at the compliment. 'But being taken for granted upsets me.'

'And quite right too.'

The man was a marvel, Eve thought, as she tossed the parboiled potatoes into a pan of hot dripping and slid them into another oven. She had two passions in life. The first was her cooking, in which she took great pride. The second was a secret, not even divulged to her best friend, Gussie Fuller. She longed for a man to sweep her into his arms and take her with unbridled desire. There were two males she hungered for and dreamed about in her chaste bed: Edward Whitaker, the widowed butler, who, despite the friendship they had built over the years, always behaved with frustrating correctness towards her. When she was honest with herself she admitted that it was hard to imagine him in the throes of rampant fervour with anyone. Then there was the sergeant, who flirted with her and appreciated her – but not in the way she longed for.

Of the two she felt Whitaker was the better catch and the more dignified but even though, at fifty-two, she was still a virgin she sensed that the sergeant would be the better lover.

'The trouble is, I don't think Miss Cresswell considers the likes of us,' she continued.

'Oh, I don't know. She seems fair to me. She's a bit on the cold side – no doubt needs a man to warm her up.' He laughed.

'Or *someone* …' Eve said significantly.

'What do you mean?'

'A new dog, that's what her needs. That Cariad's getting old and smelly,' she said hurriedly. She'd nearly slipped up there. If there was one thing Sergeant Bob didn't like, or so he claimed, it was gossip. That was sad for there was nothing Eve liked better. She would have loved to tell him of the disgusting relationship that Hannah Cresswell, for all her airs and graces, had had with that stuck-up Agnes Beatty. Unnatural, it had been and it was the talk of the neighbourhood for a good ten years. Still, the Beatty woman had gone, and just as well. She wasn't to be trusted.

'And what's the paper saying today?' Eve asked. With an adroit flick of her wrist, she began to whisk the cream for rhubarb fool.

'You don't want to bother yourself with it. All doom and gloom, the usual lies.' He laughed.

'What's tickling your fancy?'

'I dare not tell you.' He was grinning now.

'You've got to.'

'Then you'd better sit down.'

She did as he suggested. Bob coughed and rustled his newspaper. 'There's a register being compiled and requests have gone out for women to do more. There you go, Eve. You're not doing enough.'

'What?' She bristled, until she saw the twinkle in his eye. 'Oh, you.' She gave him a playful push. 'But what cheeky beggars – as if women don't have enough to do! I haven't time for any more, and what about the mothers with children? Who would look after the little ones?'

'Their grandmothers?' Bob suggested. 'Whichever way you look at it, it don't seem right. It's up to the men to do the work and the fighting.'

'I couldn't agree more,' said Eve, forgetting that she had been working since her fourteenth birthday. 'And what else do the papers say?'

'If you ask me, the situation gets worse not better. This venture into Gallipoli is madness.'

'With Lord Kitchener at the helm we can't but win.'

'I wish I shared your confidence.'

'He's a great man.'

'He might be, but I still think it's a mistake. The losses in France are too great for us to open up other fronts.'

'I thought the casualties were getting fewer.'

'That's what they want us to think. But you only have to talk to the patients, as I do, to learn the true facts. Lack of ammunition for one thing ...'

'I don't think them as are in authority would lie to us. And them soldiers upstairs shouldn't be spreading alarm and despondency.'

'Shouldn't they? Why would they lie?' He frowned, which made Eve feel flustered. Disagreeing, she knew, could lead to further argument, the last thing she wanted with Sergeant Rob.

'Willow – fish!' she shouted. 'Where's that dratted girl got to?' Boots click-clacking on the stone floor, starched apron cracking, she descended on the scullery. 'Willow!' She trod carefully over the damp floor – it was always awash and treacherous. She flung open the back door to find Willow sitting on the steps talking to Freddie, one of the footmen. 'What are you about? There's fish to do. Or have you forgotten?' Eve grabbed the kitchenmaid's collar and yanked her to her feet.

'It's my fault, Mrs Gilroy. I asked Willow to come outside.'

'Did you indeed?' Eve let go of Willow and swung round to face the young man. 'Don't you dare waste my maid's time, you whippersnapper!' So ferocious was her expression that Freddie backed down the steps, slipping on the last. 'And you should be ashamed of yourself! Why aren't you with the others at camp? Too frightened to go? Coward, are you?'

'Don't you dare call him that!' Willow interrupted.

'And don't you dare speak to me in that tone!'

'I'll speak as I find.' Willow stood firm, her hands on her hips. 'I'm tired of the way you talk to me. I hate this place and I hate you, too.'

Eve was taken aback, but pulled herself together quickly. 'You're dismissed,' she snapped.

'No, I'm not. I've already told Mrs Herbert I'm leaving. So there!'

'The housekeeper has no say over who I employ or not in my kitchen. You'll get no testimonial from me.'

Willow dug into her overall pocket and took out a piece of paper, which she waved provocatively at the cook. 'Mrs Herbert's already given me a character.' With this, she flicked back her hair, in a triumphant gesture, jumped down the steps, linked her arm in Freddie's and the two strode away across the stableyard.

'Well I never!' Eve was shocked to the core. She shook herself, rather like a horse before it bolts, and stormed back to the kitchen. 'Cheek!' she said, to no one in particular, as she swept past the sergeant.

She did not knock at the housekeeper's door but swept straight in to Mrs Herbert's sitting room. 'Out,' she said, to the startled housemaid standing in front of the desk. Needing no second bidding, the girl scurried away. 'How dare you?'

'Eve, dear, calm yourself, do.'

'Don't you "dear" me. And I would appreciate it if you did not interfere with my staff. I demand an explanation.'

'I presume you're referring to Willow Marshall. I tried to find you to tell you what action I had taken but, if you remember, you told me not to trouble you.'

'I remember no such thing.'

'Well, I do. I was aware it was irregular but I was acting on Miss Cresswell's instructions. Willow had seen her to say she was leaving and asked for a character to be written.'

'Then why didn't she come to me?'

Philomel Herbert looked uncomfortable and shuffled some papers that were lying on her desk.

'Why?' Eve repeated.

'She didn't think you'd let her go.'

'I can't wait to be rid of her. She's a lazy minx.'

'Then I don't understand your complaint, Eve.'

'There have always been conventions by which this household is ordered. Begin to break them and chaos will be the result.'

'I hardly think this incident will lead to the end of society as we know it.'

'Then you're even more stupid than I thought.' Eve turned on her heel and, still muttering, stalked out.

'Problems?' asked Whitaker, when she appeared in the kitchen.

Eve relayed to him the cause of her fury.

'I do sympathize. No wonder you're upset,' he said soothingly.

'A fuss about nothing is what it sounds like to me,' Sergeant Bob interjected.

Eve and Whitaker looked at him with astonishment.

'I beg your pardon?' Whitaker was at his most dignified.

'If the girl doesn't want to work here, why should she?'

'You miss the point, Sergeant. There are procedures. There always have been.'

He didn't look convinced.

'Where will she go?' asked Whitaker, 'With no recommendation from you, Eve, she's unlikely to find another place in a kitchen.'

'I've no idea, Edward. I'm not privy to her plans.'

'She's going to London to work in the armoury,' the sergeant said.

Eve and Whitaker were astounded.

'She told *you*?' Eve's voice brimmed with hurt, anger and bewilderment.

'Several weeks ago. Says she wants to do her bit. I shall miss her.'

'Well, I won't. Good riddance'. She bustled over to the oven and swung open the door. 'No!' she wailed. On top of everything else, and most unlike her, she had burnt the potatoes.

3

Before the war, and before the house had been converted into a convalescent home, the room Hannah entered now had been the estate office. She had chosen it not just for its convenient position within the house – just off the main hall and close to the main staircase – but for the desk, large as a table, that stood in the centre, with an old, well-worn but comfortable captain's chair behind it. Comfort was necessary, since Hannah spent many hours at her paperwork. The lighting was more practical than elegant, which suited her for this room had to be functional rather than pleasing to the eye. On the walls hung large maps of the estate, with ornate scrolled writing that testified to their great age. The bookcases were filled with ledgers stretching back two hundred years. Other documents from even earlier centuries were stored in a large strap-work iron chest, which stood under the window with a cushion on top. When she had time for a cup of coffee, Hannah liked to sit there, gazing out at the garden on which, until last year, she had lavished so much care.

When she had taken command as matron of the convalescent home she had tried to keep order but, she had quickly discovered, it was not to be easily achieved. As soon as she finished the latest clerical work, another pile of forms would arrive on her desk and further muddle would ensue. It was never explained to her why the War Office required everything in triplicate. In consequence, the room was stacked not only with files but also with odd pieces of equipment, which were awaiting removal or had been dumped there since no one knew where else to put them. A stack of washing-bowls and two artificial legs leant incongruously against the Gobelin tapestry in which Diana was shown hunting in a verdant forest. To one side there was a pile of books she had not had time to read and a bag containing the obligatory knitting of army socks that were never finished. Dealing with the British Army, she had rapidly learnt, was a nightmare to which there was no end in view.

'Was it a good service?' Major Frobisher Fellowes asked, from his position in front of the fire. He was puffing contentedly at a pipe – Hannah liked a man who smoked a pipe. He was so smart in his uniform, she thought, as she dealt with Cariad's enthusiastic welcome.

'It was a short sermon.' She removed her fine kid gloves, straightening the fingers as she did so.

'That would have suited me. I can't abide a long one, I suppose because I hate being lectured. I like to make up my own mind about things.'

'The sign of high intelligence,' she said, hoping she did not sound too admiring.

He ignored the compliment, but perhaps he had not heard it.

'Do you remember when we were children those interminable sermons that went on and on? My stomach always seemed to rumble at the worng time,' he said.

'I do. My father tended to nod off – on the rare occasions he attended.' She laughed at the memory.

'You miss him?'

'All the time. Not a day goes by when I don't think of him and wish he was here.'

'You were fortunate to have been so close to him. I didn't know mine.'

She would have liked to cross the room to comfort him – he looked so sad. 'May I ask what happened?'

'He was lost at sea when I was a baby. He was the captain of a clipper.'

'I always thought such ships sounded so romantic but, of course, they can be tragic too.' Immediately she was imagining him as a fatherless child. 'Is that why you joined the army?'

'You know, you may be right, I'd never thought of that before you mentioned it. You're perceptive, Hannah, are you not?'

'I can hardly say, can I?' She felt herself colour with pleasure. To cover her confusion she picked up a new stack of forms and pretended to look through them.

'But you are fortunate that you still have your mother.'

'Unfortunately she died in giving me life. So, like you, I have the sadness of no memories. Lady Cresswell is my stepmother,' she said, in a sharp tone that implied much – that she didn't like her and didn't wish to speak of her. 'I had hoped you would be at the service,' she said instead, neither flirtatiously nor accusingly, but as a statement of fact. It never failed to amaze her how straightforward she could be with this man. It was as if she had known him for years instead of barely three months. There was no intimacy between them other than a solid and building friendship – but that didn't stop Hannah hoping that this might change.

'I'm rather concerned for young Nigel Debden, I felt I shouldn't be too far away from him.'

'The congestion on his lungs is worse?'

'Yes it is, and I fear he won't be with us much longer.'

Hannah sighed. 'Poor man – but he's not even that, just a boy, at only nineteen.' She would have to deal with his grieving parents – a task she dreaded. Since this was a convalescent home and most of the patients were a long way towards full recovery, it was not a frequent occurrence but recently there had been a few deaths. Invariably the parents wished to see where their sons had died – it seemed to Hannah that they needed this to feel closer to them – but it was always too much for them. In such circumstances Hannah felt inadequate.

Still, she thought, young Nigel was not dead yet and it was her duty to maintain hope. She adjusted the silver buckle on her belt, which looked well against her navy uniform. She felt such a fraud in it because she was not a nurse, but both Oliver and Frobisher had said she should wear it since it gave the men confidence in her. Their counsel had helped – a little.

'Shall you be joining us for luncheon? I've invited the new vicar and his wife. They seem a pleasant couple.'

'But of course. Would I miss my luncheon?' They both laughed for Frobisher was famous for his appetite although he never put on weight, unlike Hannah's elder brother, Mortie, whose waistline bore witness to his love of food.

She glanced at her watch. 'I do believe we've time for sherry before the guests arrive,' she said.

Once Whitaker had announced that luncheon was served, Hannah led the vicar and his wife to the dining room.

As they progressed along the corridor, Mrs Plunkett paused to admire the paintings on the walls.

'You appreciate art, Mrs Plunkett?'

'It is of great interest to me, Miss Cresswell. You are fortunate to live with such beautiful pictures.'

'My grandfather was a collector and we have him to thank for them. So many people come here and walk this way but don't even notice them.'

'Then they must be spiritually blind.'

'Precisely.' Hannah warmed to the woman who, she judged, was in her early forties. A comfortable age, she always thought. No doubt she was settled in her life and had put her dreams and aspirations into context, yet was not afflicted with the physical blights of advancing age.

'Oh, such elegance,' Sorrel Plunkett clapped her hands and, Hannah noted, was rewarded with a frown from her husband. She liked the woman's spontaneity but wondered if the vicar might think it *infra dig*. 'I don't know why but I thought everything would be far more utilitarian.'

'This dining room is one of the few main rooms that have remained as they were pre-war. The drawing room and long gallery have been made into dormitories for the officers – I don't like to call them wards.'

'Quite,' Mrs Plunkett agreed.

'The library is now a recreation room and, of course, the billiards room has never seen so much activity.'

'It is highly commendable of your family, Miss Cresswell, to tolerate such intrusion,' the vicar put in.

'I don't see it in that way, Mr Plunkett. Rather, it is an honour. My brother and his wife are rarely here – they are not enamoured of the countryside so, really, it is just me … and Rowan, of course,' she added hurriedly, and took a sip of water to cover her confusion at such a lapse. 'I admit that I miss the library, which was a peaceful room, but now it is usually full of chatter and music from the phonograph I bought for the men. They enjoy it so.'

'How do you accommodate the doctor and nurses as well as your own staff?'

'It is a crush. The smaller drawing room is now the mess room and several of the bedrooms have been made into treatment rooms. There is a room for the nurses, one for the doctor and just recently we've had to find space for the man who has come to help those in need of artificial limbs.'

17

At this the vicar's wife gave a squeal, which Hannah found disappointing.

Hannah's guests were seated at either side of her while she was, as usual, at the head of the table – something else that Coral would not like. It was a good place to sit for she could observe everyone, which was particularly important where her patients were concerned.

The number at any sitting was never the same from day to day. Any of the many volunteer helpers could join them and on some days there were half a dozen, on others none. Women came from as far away as Barlton to read to the men and write letters for those whose hands were bandaged. They sat with any who were really poorly, which allowed the nurses to attend to other duties. They were a Godsend, everyone agreed.

Those officers who were ready to leave normally joined them, but she had noticed that some, as the day of departure and their return to the front approached, became quieter and tended to remain by themselves. That was one of the harder elements of her work. A young man would arrive wounded in body and mind, they would help him, heal him, and then he was sent back to risk death again. When he had initially gone to the front he had been enthusiastic and eager in his innocence. This time, returning, he knew what awaited him.

'Do you ever feel that all your skilful work is wasted?' she had asked Frobisher Fellowes one day.

He had laughed at her. 'I trust not.'

'Frobisher, you know what I mean.' She had pushed him playfully. 'You mend these dear men, then have to sign them as fit and send them back perhaps to be killed.'

'I sometimes wish I didn't have to send them back, but how can it be a waste to restore a man's health? If I thought that I could not continue.'

'Do you think the War Office is telling us the truth? The numbers coming here are increasing every week, so if it's the same at every hospital and convalescent home how many are being wounded?'

'When I went to London last week, I was talking to a fellow medical officer. He was just back from the front, and he was telling me that the field hospitals are inundated and cannot cope.'

'I pray that our estate workers aren't sent abroad. My brother, Oliver, is particularly anxious about them. You see, he organised them as a defence group, primarily to guard the families here. Now they have been summoned to the training camp – and it would appear that the next step is France.'

'He shouldn't feel guilty. Such groups would have had to be organised at some time or other. If this goes on, it is only a matter of time before conscription becomes necessary.'

She had been shocked at this. Surely he was wrong. Hundreds of thousands of men had volunteered to add to the standing army. But then she thought of the situation at Cresswell Manor. When they had set up last August they had expected to accommodate approximately six officers. Now they were up to twenty, sometimes more. How appalling if Frobisher proved correct.

Now he was sitting halfway down the table – there it was again, her childish longing to be beside him. 'We won't wait for Mrs Morts, Whitaker. She said it might be difficult for her to get away from the ward,' she said to the butler.

It was a shame Rowan hadn't come. She must be eating with the other nursing staff, not wanting her family connection to be construed as preferential treatment. Although this was commendable, she felt Rowan should have been there to meet the vicar – some duties could not be ignored.

'I trust you are enjoying Cresswell?' She concentrated on her guests.

'The local inhabitants have been most welcoming and helpful. We were both most impressed by Miss Crick at the school.'

Hannah beamed with pleasure. 'Shall you be sending your children there?'

'We have no son, Miss Cresswell. Miss Crick's village school will be sufficient for Dorothy and Janet.'

'I see.' Hannah was not impressed by this, and noticed that Mrs Plunkett looked uncomfortable. 'I have always thought that if I had been blessed with children I would have wanted sons and daughters to have the same education – dependent on their ability.' It was a subject she felt strongly about. She had been educated by governesses, some good, some bad, while her brothers had been sent away to school and university. The experience had not been wasted on Oliver, but Mortie, with his limited intelligence, had gained nothing from it. It was a constant sorrow to Hannah that she had not benefited from the same opportunities.

'Quite so.' The vicar paused to put more food into his mouth.

What was it about vicars that they needed to shovel it in as if they were afraid it would be their last meal for a month? she wondered.

'From your reaction, Miss Cresswell, am I to asume that you are in favour of women's suffrage?' he asked, between forkfuls.

'That is correct.' Try not to bristle, she told herself. After all, she had

had plenty of practice at dealing with such disapproval. She could not believe that he had been here a week and not been told that, just over eighteen months ago, she had been imprisoned for her belief that her sex should have the vote.

'I find violence distressing, especially in women.'

'As do I, Mr Plunkett. Is it simply the violence you object to or the belief?'

'I didn't say I objected.'

'There was no need, Mr Plunkett. The tone of your voice was sufficient.' Hannah smiled as she spoke, not wishing to offend him but not prepared to be a Judas to the cause. What a disappointment he was becoming. Mrs Plunkett was staring at her hands, which were restless on her lap. She wondered if the woman approved of her stance. 'Mrs Plunkett, since you are interested in art, perhaps, one afternoon, you would care to come to my house to see my paintings?'

'You don't live here?' She seemed surprised.

'I work at the manor, but my home is up by Maiden's Wood. I particularly enjoy the work of Burne-Jones.'

The vicar laid down his knife and fork with a clatter and coughed. 'I would rather my wife did not view such work.'

'Why ever not?' Hannah was surprised.

'You may have purchased the man's work, Miss Cresswell, but I, for one, would question your judgement.'

How unutterably rude, she thought. 'Then you are an art critic too?' With great self-control she still managed to smile. How mistaken she had been – probably because he was youngish and quite good-looking. She always had such faith in the young, especially if they were even moderately handsome. She should have learnt by now. But then, as Oliver had once said, some people were born middle-aged or even old. How could she have thought Mr Plunkett might be an asset to the estate? She wondered what he would make of the rest of her family. She turned back to his wife, needing to know if she'd misjudged her too.

4

Rowan Cresswell was on her hands and knees in front of a mahogany encased lavatory. She was diligently polishing the wood until she could see her face in it. The air in the room was heavy with the smell of beeswax and lavender. Dark red flock paper covered the walls, on which hung several oil paintings. Matching damask curtains were draped at the window, topped by an ornately swagged pelmet. In the corner an ornate jardiniere supported a flourishing aspidistra.

She picked up the tin of Brasso and began to rub the brass fitments. The pipes would be next – everything had to gleam in here, for a brigadier was about to join them. Once the brass was shining she dusted the books on the shelf. She had shrieked with laughter when she had first seen them – she'd never thought anyone would read in the lav.

She checked the Izal paper. Her life had changed so much, she thought. Cut-up newspaper hung on a string in the outside privy at her mother's cottage, but she was getting used to the luxury of special paper, even if it was on the harsh side compared with newsprint.

She brushed the lavatory pan with Jeyes fluid, then yanked at the handle and a waterfall gushed into it. At home they had a bucket of sand to sprinkle.

This particular lavatory had been old Sir Mortimer's; it was so grand that it made her think of a throne room. She wished she could show it to her sisters. They'd be amazed and would giggle over it long and loud. She also wished she had known the old man, for everyone said how kind he had been and easy to work for. Would he have accepted her as a member of his family? Probably not, she thought, as she sat back on her haunches to admire her handiwork. She was learning rapidly about this family. They might act in one way but they often thought the opposite. She was getting better at knowing when they did, but she wasn't always right.

Apart from her husband, Morts, the Cresswells constantly annoyed Rowan. She had noticed their arrogance. They behaved as if their standing in society gave them knowledge that was not shared by others, as if their opinion was the only one that mattered. Did they ever listen to anyone else? Did they ever think they might be wrong? It seemed to her that they felt they could do and say whatever they wanted and everyone else was duty-bound to accept it and not answer back, or be angry and hurt as she frequently was.

Hannah was such a one. She expected Rowan to fall in with everything she suggested and was puzzled when she didn't. Rowan had made a deliberate decision not to sit with her in church because she knew what others from the estate would have said if she had – that she was getting above herself, and worse. Had Morts been at home, she would have joined him in the pew, but that was different – then she would have been there as his wife, not as Rowan. There was the luncheon too. Did the woman not realize the resentment it would have caused among the other nursing staff if Rowan had taken up the invitation? If she could understand it, why couldn't Hannah? But there it was. It was what Hannah wanted, and therefore it was right.

It also angered Rowan that Hannah behaved as if nothing had happened between them. Had she forgotten that she had *stolen* Rowan's letters to and from Morts, before they were married? Rowan knew she herself would never forget and was having trouble forgiving. Morts had excused his aunt, which to Rowan was a betrayal. She understood his feelings for Hannah but that didn't stop her wishing he had stood firmer on her side.

Hannah had presumed that it was her right to interfere in others' lives – it had been a bald attempt to end their courtship. The thought of what the consequences might have been if the letters had not been found made her shudder. Morts had written regularly and when his letters had stopped arriving she had thought he no longer loved her, that he had found someone else. It frightened her to think of what she might have done. She knew that pride would have made her look for another boy to show Morts she didn't care. And where would that have left them?

Rowan was fully aware that some of the Cresswell family had been disappointed that Morts had chosen to marry her. Apart from the meddlesome Hannah, Morts's mother had fallen into an hysterical rage that had gained momentum until she had fainted and had had to be revived with *sal-volatile*. Later, when she had calmed down, Lady Coral had berated Rowan for ruining Morts's life with her *pursuit* of him. She had not argued. There had seemed no point. She had flinched when she was accused of being a gold-digger – and smiled inwardly now at the contradiction. She had refused the money Coral had offered her in ever-increasing amounts to walk out of their lives. She had been amazed the woman had been unable to grasp that Rowan couldn't deny her love for Morts.

His uncle Oliver had said nothing, which she had found ominous. She sensed he was not happy with the situation either. That was hypocritical, for she knew from gossip in the servants' hall that his family had disapproved of him marrying Esmeralda who, though rich, was also deemed not suitable since her father was in *trade*.

Morts's father had stood up for them valiantly but somehow she felt he had done so to annoy his wife.

Initially she hadn't blamed the Cresswells – she had thought she was unsuitable too. She hadn't needed anyone to point it out to her. But when Morts had proposed, her love for him had defeated her logic. They had married late in December, just before he was sent to Salisbury Plain to train as a soldier.

It had been neither the right time nor the right reason to marry, she knew. Alone at night, she often wondered if fear of death had made him rush her to the altar. If so, how would they fare when the war was over? How would she survive, watching him grow bored with her? She knew she would never change, that she would always love him – come what may.

Still, she was wasting time, thinking and worrying about things over which she had no control. She stood up and glanced once more at the shining surfaces. Even Sister Westall wouldn't be able to find fault with that. She collected her cleaning materials into the basket she carried and moved on to the next lavatory. Only another four to do – and none of the others was as elaborate as this one.

Since Morts had gone, it had been hard for her. In marrying him, she did not belong anywhere any more. She had become a Cresswell but she didn't feel like one. It had come as an even bigger shock to discover that although she had been a Marshall she no longer felt one of them either. Her family looked on her differently now. It was as if an invisible barrier had been erected between them.

'What did you expect?' Her mother had interrupted her pie-making when, a week ago, Rowan had asked her why she sensed this. 'It stands to reason. You're in a different world now, somewhere we don't belong and never will. And, no doubt, you won't neither.'

'Mother, how can you say that?'

'Because it's the truth. And I always says what I thinks. You and that Morts are chalk and cheese. His mother will never forgive you. She thinks you'll ruin his life and I fear he'll ruin yours.'

'He won't.'

'How can you know what'll happen?'

'And how can you? Why think the worst? Why not think we'll be happy?'

'Because I can't see as how you ever will be.'

'But I'm still *me*.'

'No, you're not. You're trying to be a Cresswell. You talk different. You *are* different. In time you'll be ashamed of us.'

'I never will. I love you.'

'I'm sure you do, but I'm not talking about loving, I'm talking about pride. You mark my words, young woman, a day will come when we'll be an embarrassment. But I'll tell you one thing. We shall always be here for you, come what may ...'

That conversation had hurt Rowan so much, and she had mulled over it again and again. She always came to the same conclusion – that her mother was wrong, and she would prove her so. But what she also couldn't understand was the feeling she had that her mother was cross with her too.

And it wasn't just the families who had reacted so. The Cresswell staff had become cold. The friendliness she was used to had gone and she felt isolated. If she went into the servants' hall and others were there, silence would descend. She was sure it wasn't her imagination.

'It's as if I've done something wrong when I haven't,' she confided in Fanny Petty, as they unpacked and folded a new supply of blankets. Fanny, like Rowan, was an orderly and helped with the nursing. She was the only one here who still treated Rowan as she always had.

'They're jealous of your good fortune.'

'I don't feel very fortunate.'

'Never having to worry about the bills again – that strikes me as lucky.'

'But money isn't important.'

Fanny smiled broadly. 'Only the young and them in love say that. You're wrong there, my dear Rowan. Money dominates most people's lives – or, rather, the lack of it! It's all my Brian and I talk about these days.'

'It shouldn't be important.'

'Lots of things shouldn't be but unfortunately they are.'

'I admit having nice things is a fine prospect, but if Morts had nothing I'd still love him. Everyone's against us – even my mother. I can't fight them all.'

'Flossie's afraid for you – she's not against you, don't even think it. She knows the Cresswells and how they can be.'

'It's Miss Cresswell who's hurt me most – I'd always thought she liked me. After all, Mrs Oliver and Miss Lettice tried to help, teaching me how to behave, what to do, how to speak, which words to use. But Miss Cresswell – she tried to stop us.'

'I'm not surprised. She's a nice woman, and can be kind, but she's one of *them*. She thinks she's modern and not a snob – but of course she is. Like the rest, she wants everything to stay the same. She's in for a shock, in my opinion. People won't put up with it much longer.'

For a second Rowan felt she should defend Hannah but she didn't. What Fanny had said was close to the truth.

One of the volunteer nurses – the VADs – had made the nastiest comments. Rowan wasn't surprised. It was what she would have expected from Lady Sylvia Ferguson who, after all, had been interested herself in Morts and had been so angry when she had discovered that Rowan was his sweetheart. 'You do realize you can't *become* a lady. You have to be *born* to such status.' Sylvia had chosen to say this on the day that Rowan had seen Morts off on the train to Salisbury Plain.

'Is that so? It didn't work with you, did it?' Rowan remarked, with a hint of triumph.

'Miaow.' Sylvia smirked. 'You'll never be accepted in society.'

'Perhaps I don't want to be accepted by anyone who thinks like you.'

'Brave words, but you'll learn. Picture your son at school – imagine the ragging he'll get. What will his fellow pupils have to say when they find out his father's married to a tweeny?' She laughed; she had a particularly pretty laugh, which sat oddly with such spite. Rowan longed to slap her face but knew that that was exactly what Sylvia wanted her to do. Then what a fuss she would make. Rowan stood up and left the room. She wouldn't give her the satisfation of seeing how angry she had made her.

'I've finished the lavatories, Sister Westall.'

'Take your break now, Cresswell. When you get back I want all the trolleys scrubbed.'

'Yes, Sister.'

Since she had come here, the more menial jobs had been hers. She had not minded – when she had volunteered as an orderly she had known what tasks she would be set. But she had worked hard so that after a couple of months she had been allowed to help with nursing the patients, giving them blanket baths, even changing the odd bandage. All had been basic duties, but she had been proud to do them. She had begun to believe that her dream to become a real nurse might come true. However, since her marriage, that had changed. Now her contact with the men was minimal and she spent her shifts scrubbing and cleaning. It was as if the sister, too, was punishing her for marrying Morts.

She made her way to the staff dining room. It had once been the servants' hall and she could remember the good times she'd had there when she had been a popular member of the staff. Now she avoided it as much as she could. From the empty room she collected an apple from the fruit bowl, some bread from the sideboard and a glass of milk, then made her way to the bachelors' corridor. She walked to the end and paused at a door. She looked right and left to check that she was alone, then pushed it open.

She stood in the doorway and inhaled deeply. It smelt of him. She crossed the room and pulled back the curtains, allowing the weak sunshine to filter in. Spring was late this year, she thought, as she gazed out at the bare trees in the garden. Then turned and looked about her, taking in the position of every object that was his. The walls were covered with photographs of school teams and Morts was in every one, apparently the captain – cricket, rugby, tennis and fencing. His handsome, smiling face beamed out at the world. Just looking at them, she felt so proud.

Also on the wall were a couple of épées and an oar – he had never said anything about rowing and since there was no photograph of him with a crew perhaps he hadn't been so successful at that. She hoped that was the case. No one should be perfect at everything.

On the dressing-table there was a photograph of Clemmie, Morts's first wife, who had died having his baby. Rowan studied the solemn-faced young woman who, elegantly dressed with beautiful posture, stared back at her. She wasn't pretty, but she wasn't ugly either. She held herself with a pride that Rowan knew she herself lacked.

He had loved her deeply. Had Clemmie loved him too? Rowan was sure she could not have loved him more than she did. She was not jealous of her – how could she be when Clemmie was dead? What bothered her was that she had been the first – the first engagement, the first marriage, the first setting-up home, the first baby … With Rowan, Morts would be doing everything for the second time – and she feared being second in his heart. '*Second best*,' was what Sylvia had called her, when the news of her marriage had filtered through. She put the photograph back. But Clemmie was dead and she was alive.

She sat on the bed – his bed – and began to eat her dinner. *Luncheon*, she corrected herself, which made her smile.

She felt so much closer to Morts when she was in this room and on her own. It was almost as if she could touch him. She sometimes thought that if she longed for him hard enough he would appear in the flesh.

Loving him was wonderful but with it had come something new to her – worry. Until now all she had had to worry about was whether she was late, whether the housekeeper would disapprove of her dusting, whether Sister Westall would be cross with her. Now she woke with worry bordering on fear that stayed with her all day long. Terror that he might come to harm in his training – she had learnt it was tough for the men. She was disgusted with herself that, several times, she had thought that if he was hurt, just a little, the army might say they didn't want him. But how could she want the love of her life to be injured in any way? And over all these fears was the dreadful one that he would write to say he was off to France. Worse, that he would go and never come back.

She stood up abruptly. She was doing herself no good, mooning about like this. She crossed to the wardrobe – she always left this treat until last. She opened the door and breathed deeply. She closed her eyes, transfixed, as she smelt him and felt him even closer.

She had to hope. She had to believe in their future or there might not be one. She concentrated all her thoughts, channelling them into optimism, willing him to come back safe to her. Then she opened her eyes. Time to go, she told herself.

She closed the door and walked quickly back along the corridor. She felt rejuvenated – she always did when she had been in his room.

'Good afternoon, Mrs Herbert,' she said, on meeting the housekeeper in the hall.

'Rowan ... I mean, Mrs Morts, were you looking for something?'

'No, just taking my break.' She wondered if Philomel Herbert had muddled her name on purpose. It was a small triumph that the woman she had once been afraid of didn't frighten her any more.

She was running up the stairs so she did not see that the minute she was out of sight the housekeeper bustled along the corridor to Morts Cresswell's room to check nothing had been taken.

5

An ornately draped bassinette stood in the centre of the overheated room. Esmeralda Cresswell was bent over it, fussing over her baby, Marigold, who lay sleeping contentedly. The nanny stood to one side, her hands neatly clasped over her crisp white apron. She wore an expression of bored resignation, as if she was used to this scene.

'Nanny, are you sure Marigold should be making that strange snuffling noise?'

'It's normal, Mrs Oliver.'

'But how can you be sure she's not ill?'

'Experience, Mrs Oliver. She's in a deep sleep. Babies often snore.'

'Snoring?' Esmeralda looked at her with astonishment. 'Surely she wouldn't do anything so vulgar.'

The nanny smiled. 'Babies do, Mrs Oliver. There's no need to worry.'

'Perhaps I should call the doctor. What do you think?'

'As you wish, Mrs Oliver, but I can assure you he will say the same as I have.'

Marigold was four months old. She was developing at the normal rate, eating and sleeping well. She had no rashes, no infections – but no amount of reassurance could soothe Esmeralda's concerns.

'You think I'm being silly, don't you?'

'No, Mrs Oliver. Your anxieties are those of any new mother.'

Esmeralda stepped back. 'Well, if you're sure ...' With a distracted air she wandered out of the room and made her way to her boudoir. She rang the bell to summon the housekeeper.

'And how's dear Marigold, this morning, Mrs Oliver?' Gussie Fuller asked, the minute she walked in.

'Do you think Nanny Martin is competent, Mrs Fuller?'

'She came to us highly recommended, Mrs Oliver. I've no reason to think her inept. Also, she is well thought of by the other staff. Are you concerned, Mrs Oliver?'

'Marigold is making the most horrible noise. Nanny said she was snoring, but I'm worried. Old men snore, not babies.'

'Really, Mrs Oliver, you worry too much.' Gussie coughed, placing her hand in front of her mouth, so that Esmeralda couldn't see that she was smiling.

'You think so?'

'I do.'

'Well, yes ...' Esmeralda resisted the temptation to argue for her relationship with her housekeeper was not an easy one. Mrs Fuller could be kind and understanding one day, but the next her irritation was plain to see. There were moments when Esmeralda determined to dismiss her but within the hour she had changed her mind. She had always been indecisive but, rather than acknowledge it, she would tell herself that Mrs Fuller was an excellent housekeeper – and where would she find another? In any case a replacement might be even worse.

'Is that all you wanted to see me about, Mrs Oliver?'

'Oh, no. Silly me! I've received a telegram from my husband. He is returning this weekend with a guest. I suggest we put Mr Poldown in the blue room. And when you've arranged that perhaps you could send the cook up. It would be nice to have a dinner party on Saturday. And could you ask Bridget to come to me? I think that's all …' She turned back to her desk took out a sheet of headed writing-paper and began to pen a note.

When Bridget appeared, she handed it to her. 'Please take this to the doctor and ask him to come as soon as he can,' she ordered, and felt a little calmer to have made that decision.

The cook was dealt with, and then Esmeralda returned to worrying. Before Marigold had been born she had hardly worried about anything but now her life was filled with anxiety. She crossed the room to the Chippendale mirror and peered at her face, but saw only a blur. From her pocket she took a small pair of *pince-nez*, placed them on her nose and tried again. She studied her dark hair, to make sure there was no grey. Her eyes, she was pleased to see, were still dark brown; she'd watched her father's fine dark eyes become lighter with age and dreaded that happening for she was proud of hers. Her cheeks and chin were still sharply sculpted, and her upper lip was still full – too often she remembered her grandmother's wizened one. She touched her face gently, searching for lines that as yet could not be seen. Every day she studied herself intently, often several times. She feared losing her looks for she was convinced that her beauty was all she had to commend her. And if she became wrinkled and ugly, her husband would surely look elsewhere.

She pulled her hair back, wondered if it suited her better and decided against it. There was so much she wished she could change. Oliver was so clever and she was so stupid. She had tried to read books he would approve of, but never finished them because she found them dull. Each new year she vowed to study *The Times* every day so that she could talk to him intelligently about current affairs – her resolution rarely lasted the first week of January. Politics had to be the most tedious subject in the world.

She didn't want to bore her husband – she was familiar with boredom and knew how uncomfortable it could be for the spirit. There were times when she saw exasperation cross his face and wanted to cry out to him to give her time. But how much did she need? They had been married for fourteen years. It was a miracle he hadn't tired of her already.

And then there was the problem … She looked at the image in the mirror and watched as her face reflected the fear that was now as big a part of her as breathing. She was doomed to carry the burden with her to the grave. For Esmeralda, who adored her husband and should have been carefree and happy, was haunted with the dread that Marigold was not his.

She put her arms about her and hugged herself, then turned from the mirror, moved wearily across the room to sink with a sigh into her favourite chair. Whenever she allowed that thought to worm into her mind the horror of the violation she had endured returned with it.

Esmeralda knew she would waste time thinking *what-if* and *if-only* – which was totally pointless. *If only* she had not gone to Buxton to take the waters on her own. *If only* she had not booked into the Palace Hotel out of the many in the town. *If only* she had not met her father there. *If only* his friend Petroc Cornish had not appeared. *If only* she had not been so stupid as to flirt with him. *What if* she hadn't gone on that walk? *What if* Bridget had not been ill … ?

As if aware that she was sad, Blossom, her Pekinese, jumped on to her lap and licked her cheek. 'Oh, Blossom. I've been so foolish.' The dog had been a gift from her tormentor and a constant reminder but Esmeralda cherished her – what had happened had not been the dog's fault. 'Who do *you* think she looks like, my darling?' Blossom wagged her plumed tail.

Esmeralda spent hours beside her child longing to see a likeness to Oliver in the baby's face. She prayed with fervour that Marigold would grow up to look like him so that then she would know for sure. If only there was someone to whom she could unburden herself. Sometimes the weight of this knowledge was too much for her to bear.

Lettice, her niece by marriage, was the only person she had confided in but she was no longer here. Esmeralda had been on the point of telling Oliver but Lettice had counselled her, almost begged her, not to. What Oliver did not know could not hurt him, she had reasoned. So Esmeralda had kept her silence.

It was wrong. That was the problem. It was wrong to deceive him. He was a good man, a caring man. And she was living a lie with him. Had he not the right to be told? He loved the child intensely. Should he not be the one to decide if he should continue to do so?

When he left to go to training camp with the men of the Territorials he commanded, she had nearly told him. But then she had reasoned that it was not the right time, for even if he, at forty-five, was too old to be sent to fight he was still responsible for many other men. Or perhaps she had used the war as an excuse. On top of everything else she knew she was a coward.

She picked up the telegram she had received from Oliver that morning. She had been surprised that he had invited Ramsey Poldown to stay. His niece, Lettice, had had an unfortunate relationship with the man. It had been quite wrong of her, of course, married as she was, but her husband, Hugo Hamilton, was a horrible man and unkind to her, so Esmeralda understood why she had been drawn to him. Lettice had wanted to stay with Ramsey but Hugo had threatened to take her children from her, so she had returned to the marital home. It was all so unfair. Ramsey and she hadn't meant to fall in love—and Oliver had not approved yet now he had invited the man here.

'Dr Greenslade, madam,' Milner, the butler, announced, making Esmeralda jump half out of her skin.

She was immediately on her feet and gracefully moving towards the visitor, her hands outstretched in greeting. 'How kind of you to come so quickly, Doctor.'

'And what is the matter today?' He smiled as he took the seat she had indicated, then listened to her report of her baby's health.

'I am sure the nanny is correct,' he said, when she had finished.

'You think I'm worrying needlessly, don't you?'

'I think you're as all mothers, full of concern and rightly so. But I shall, of course, examine the child, now that I'm here.' He opened his commodious black leather bag and removed a small brown bottle. 'I would hazard that you're not sleeping well. You have a strained look about the eyes.'

Esmeralda's hand shot to her face, as if to explore it for the sign he had seen.

'A teaspoon of this might help.' He handed her the bottle. 'One teaspoon, mind, no more.'

'Thank you, Doctor. As it happens, I'm not sleeping at all well. There is so much to worry about, I find – managing my husband's affairs while he is away … the war … And I am so afraid he might be injured. There are so many guns where he is and the soldiers are not trained. Accidents happen …'

'Is anything else troubling you?'

'Good gracious, no. Isn't that enough?' She laughed, in a strained manner, but inside she was screaming, *He knows*!

6

There were never enough hours in the day for Dolly Topsham, landlady of the Cresswell Arms, situated by the harbour of Cress-by-the-Sea. From six in the morning until midnight she was always on the run, attending to her numerous tasks, trying to catch up with herself and never achieving her goal. With her husband Zephaniah away at the war there was no one to help her.

'Not now, Del, I've not got the time,' she said to her daughter, who was asking for help with a poem she had to learn for school the next day.

'That's what you always say.' Cordelia slammed the poetry book shut.

'Because that's how it always is.' She knew she had snapped, that she had hurt the girl's feelings. Can't be helped, she told herself, as she bustled off to make sure that the drayman wasn't cheating her.

His bill was satisfactory, though he scowled at the time she took to check it. She didn't mind what he thought of her – no one was going to cheat her. As a woman running the business alone, she was aware that some had tried. Once the barrels were stored to her satisfaction, the empties removed, she sampled the beer and pulled a face. That men drank it for pleasure had always been a mystery to her. When she saw the state of the floor she swept it like greased lightning, then ran up the rickety stairs from the cellar. Halfway she had to grab the banister as a tread creaked ominously and shifted under her weight. The steps were dangerous and might give way at any time. She had to have them seen to, but by whom? If he hadn't been away with the Territorials she'd have asked Rob Robertson, the estate carpenter, who would do most repairs for a pint or two. This wretched war was making life so difficult for her – although she worked all hours, there was never enough money for maintenance. With so many of the young men away her takings were sorely depleted.

She shouldn't be in this position, she thought. She knew her husband had been left an annuity when his mother died and they should have been secure, but they weren't. Zeph insisted on two-thirds of it being put into a bank account to which she had no access; the accumulating money was for his sister Xenia, and his younger brother Timmy – a wastrel and deserter, long gone from these shores.

'He's probably dead,' she'd argued with her husband, before he went away.

'You can't know that and I'd prefer you did not say such things about him.'

'And who helped him escape?'

'You did, for which I'm grateful, but since you did, there is less reason for you to judge him.'

How he exasperated her when he argued with such logic. She had tossed her head as if to erase the truth. 'As for Xenia, what need does she have of your money? She's all right, from what I hear.'

'And what does that mean?'

'In London. Very successful, some say.' She folded a napkin, 'Though I've never liked to ask how.'

'Take care what you say, Dolly.' He looked furious – or as cross as someone so mild-mannered could look. The gossip never stopped about Xenia, whom they never saw and with whom they did not communicate. What was the point of all that money mouldering in the bank when they could use it? And what did he do with his third? He saved it, that was what. 'We don't know what the future holds for us,' he said, until she wanted to throttle him. Money! She hated it – but loved it too. Worse, Zeph had insisted they move here from Barlton to run the inn when he knew she didn't want to leave the town. He thought only of himself, never of her.

In the kitchen she wrote out the grocery order, making as many economies as she could without upsetting Flossie Marshall, who did the cooking. Then she had to race upstairs to reassure herself that the chambermaid had cleaned the guest bedrooms to her high standard. Only then did she return to the small family sitting room behind the bar.

'Now, Del, which poem was it you wanted me to hear?' Even as she spoke she was dusting the rather cluttered sideboard. Dolly rarely sat, and if she did, her hands were never idle.

'It doesn't matter any more.'

'Of course it matters. You want to get good marks at school, don't you? We can't have Miss Crick thinking you don't care about your work, can we?'

'I don't care what she thinks. And *you* don't bloody care about me neither.'

Dolly slapped Cordelia's cheek, knocking her off-balance. She clutched her face, trying not to cry, anger and hurt in her eyes. 'Use language like that again and I'll scrub your mouth out with soap and water!' Dolly wagged a finger at her daughter. 'And you can wipe that nasty expression off your face or I'll do it for you.'

Cordelia twirled round and flounced out of the room. Dolly allowed herself to sit down for a minute. She and Cordelia argued too often and it wasn't right. She pulled her sewing-basket to her and searched for the wooden mushroom she needed to darn Apollo's sock. As she did so she paused to study her hands, which seemed to sum up the state of her life. They were chapped, rough to the touch, and her nails were split. She gazed at them with a rueful smile. Such dreams she had once had for herself and her children. These hands were supposed to be soft and milky white, the nails buffed to a pink shine. Still, she told herself, there was no point in thinking of what might have been. It wasn't, and that was that. She positioned the mushroom under the hole in the heavy grey sock – what did Apollo *do* with his feet?

So many things had happened to her in the past year. Once she had been a woman of means with her own business. She'd sat behind a desk and organised an army of cleaning women. Now she was reduced to doing the cleaning herself. She had tried to keep the agency going but eventually she had been forced to close it. That business had been her pride and joy. She had set it up against all the odds, no experience, little money and a husband who did not approve. But she had made it a success – to everyone's surprise. But Dolly had always known she would succeed.

Had it not been for the war … That was what she told everyone. She had explained that servants were going to fight so the agency had struggled from lack of cleaners, not clients. However, the truth was that if she had been free to run it personally it would have survived. Instead she'd employed May Snodland. And she was not about to confess she'd made a mistake, Dolly would never do that.

Just thinking of May made her shudder. Both May and Zeph had been surprised when Dolly had asked May to run the office for her – May, with whom Zephaniah had been unfaithful last year. Dolly had been cut to the quick by both of them, and especially when she had found out *after* they had moved here. She often wondered what the outcome would have been had she discovered the truth while they were still in Barlton.

She had buried her hurt and resentment for, above all, Dolly was a businesswoman; May, she had thought, would be ideal to run the office for her. She was wrong. The takings slipped and there were many complaints. The day had dawned when Dolly realized she had to choose – and the inn won. So here she was, trapped and struggling to make ends meet.

Was she the only woman who had thought herself happily married only to find that her husband was cheating with a woman she had trusted? She doubted it, but that did not lessen her pain.

He had forsworn May, asked for forgiveness, and Dolly had taken him back into her bed. She had tried, but the humiliation was too deep and she could not forget his infidelity. In bed with Zeph, she would find herself wondering what he had been like with May. She hated May and wished her dead. She had longed for her life to be as it once was. Now she knew that going back was the stuff of dreams. Her trust in Zeph had died and her happiness with it.

The return to Cress-by-the-Sea had been a step back, not forward. She'd spent her life on the estate and knew how enclosed and restrictive life could be, every move watched by others. But when her mother-in-law became ill and died, Dolly had known she had to come. And where was her husband when she needed him? Enlisted. Everyone said how noble of him it was, how patriotic, but she knew better. He'd done it because he was unhappy. As hurt gnawed at Dolly, guilt gnawed at Zeph and, if the truth were told, he had gone to get away from her.

Often she thought that if he hadn't gone they might have solved their problems. Perhaps he hadn't wanted to marry her in the first place and this was her punishment for letting him have his way with her, Apollo being the result.

Dolly was a strong person so she had weathered it all – or she thought she had. But she was honest too, and she knew that her resentment would never leave her. She did not like it, she wished it would go away, but it stuck with her, like a shadow.

There was another companion who never left her side – loneliness. At night when the children were in bed, when the last customers had gone, the desolation of being on her own swamped her. That was when she had a brandy or two.

What if? she would catch herself thinking half a dozen times a day. *What if* she had never employed that sly minx May Snodland? *What if* she had seen she was setting her cap at Zephaniah? *What if* the war hadn't started?

She laid down the sock. It was pointless to think like that. She had somehow to forget, to think of her future and shed the past.

But the past stayed relentlessly with her. And the present was hard. She had too much to do. She had no time for herself and her family. She was becoming a nag; she didn't show her children enough love. She could no longer remember what it was like not to feel tired.

Dolly loved her children, lived for them, and worked as hard as she did for them. They were her life – and she couldn't let them know it. She had long been aware that she was not an affectionate person; she sometimes wondered if her inability to show Zeph affection was partly why he had sought solace in May's arms. Now she was doing it again with her children. Unless she hugged them, unless she told them she loved them, they might turn their backs on her too.

'That's a big sigh.'

Dolly looked up and smiled as Flossie Marshall bounded into the kitchen. She always exploded into a room. She was a large and capable woman who was usually good-natured, but when she wasn't everyone ran for cover.

The smile did not last long for Dolly knew she was going to have to dismiss Flossie. What else was she to do with money so tight? She intended to speak to her today. She was aware that Flossie still had five of her eight children at home and would be hard hit if she let her go – but she couldn't help that. She had to think of herself first. 'I've just had words with Del,' she said. 'All she wanted was for me to listen to her recite her poem but …' she shrugged, '… I didn't have time.'

Flossie sat down on the other side of the table. 'You should make time. I know it's hard and you've too much on your plate, but she'll be away and married before you know where you are and then you'll regret it.'

'You can't just make time.'

'Well, let things slide a bit. You're too fussy for your own good. I doubt the customers notice when the runners on the chairs haven't been dusted. They wouldn't do it in their cottages.' Flossie laughed.

'I sometimes think I do it to stop me thinking too much.'

'You can never escape a worry. I've always found problems should be faced head on or they have a nasty habit of getting worse.'

'If only it was that easy. How can I when the main problem is away at this wretched war?'

'It could be worse. Mabel Stills – you know, lives in the end cottage of Fisherman's Row – her son's been killed. She got a letter from his mate yesterday, saying how sorry he was, like.'

'The poor woman. But it's not official yet?'

Flossie snorted in disdain. 'You could wait for hell to freeze before you'd hear from the powers-that-be. She's the third one I've heard of what's been told by letter from a friend. The War Office managed it three weeks later.'

'It's not right.'

'There's a lot that's not right.'

'News like that makes you look at your own problems differently, though. Poor woman, I must go and see her.'

'She'd appreciate that. Miss Cresswell's been already.'

'She's a good woman.'

'She's two-faced.'

'Miss Cresswell?' Dolly was surprised. It was rare for anyone to speak ill of Hannah Cresswell. She leant forward, sensing gossip.

'She's stuck-up. She pretends she isn't, lets everyone think how much she cares for them, and then she dismisses my Alf when he's done nothing.'

'Why on earth did she do that?'

'Because of Rowan.'

'What's Rowan done?'

'Married Mr Morts, that's what. Miss Cresswell said as how it didn't seem right to have Alf as her chauffeur when he was almost related to her. Cheek!'

'Well, I suppose it might be difficult. I mean, how can she tell him what to do – in the circumstances?'

'Why punish him for what his daughter's done?'

'But she hasn't done anything wrong. She's got married, and a nicer man she couldn't have picked.'

'Fish and fowl. It never works. Best to know your place and keep to it. I warned her it'd be difficult but you know the young, she wouldn't listen.'

'Then why didn't you stop her?'

'She wound her father round her little finger, didn't she? He's always weak where his daughters are concerned. He'd given his permission before they plucked up the courage to tell me – I'd have put a stop to it. And now Willow's off. Walked out on Mrs Gilroy without a by-your-leave.'

'Going to nurse, like Rowan?'

'No, she's always been the difficult one. She's off to London. Wants to work in munitions, she says. The truth, more like, is her Freddie's gone that way.'

'Flossie, no! You must be so worried. A munitions factory! That could be dangerous.'

'I know. But what does she care? When I told her I'd worry she just laughed and said I was a fussy old hen, that she'd be fine, the authorities looked after them ...' And to Dolly's horror Flossie began to cry.

Dolly was unsure what to do. She had never seen Flossie like this. Flossie was a strong, positive woman. 'Flossie ...' she said, but the other woman did not hear her.

She waited for her to calm down. At least Flossie had taught her something, Dolly might think her life was hard but it was as nothing to Flossie's. The dismissal would have to wait.

7

A year ago, had anyone told Eve Gilroy that she would now be cooking for up to forty people nearly every day with just one helper, she would have said, in no uncertain terms, that she wasn't anyone's slave, that she needed at least one scullery-maid, two kitchenmaids and a pastry-cook. But here she was, with the pastry-cook dead, the kitchenmaids long since left to work in the blanket factory at Barlton and now Willow Marshall gone too.

Consequently Eve had prepared the vegetables herself, then made the pastry for the umpteenth steak and kidney pie and was singing 'The Church's One Foundation' at the top of her voice. She was not a religious woman, but she enjoyed singing hymns. When those who knew her, heard her fine contralto, they winked at each other for it indicated that the tempestuous little woman, whose uncertain temperament could strike fear in the most stalwart of men, was happy.

'If Lady Coral could see the menus these days she'd have the vapours and no mistake.' Vigorously, she sprinkled flour on to the marble slab on the table, ready to roll the pastry. 'I mean, she'd faint at the vulgar idea of soup for luncheon.'

'Needs must when the devil drives.' Sergeant Bob was mixing a cake – he was a born baker.

'Not that she'd see it like that.' She laughed. 'I enjoy a bowl of soup myself.' With a flick of a knife she trimmed the sheet of shortcrust. With the sergeant there, she did not mind the loss of her kitchen- and scullery-maids nearly as much as she might have done. And now the last thing she wanted was a pretty, flighty maid about: men could never be trusted with nubile young women around the place.

'What's she like – her nibs, I mean?'

'Haven't you met her? Well, aren't you the lucky one? Like most of her kind, she's selfish and very difficult – wouldn't you say, Edward?' she asked, as the butler entered the kitchen.

'And who might *she* be?'

'Lady Coral. We all know about Lady Penelope – she's in a class of meanness all her own.'

'Neither lady is the *easiest* of persons with whom to deal. But then, on the other hand, Lady Coral has high standards, as one would expect from one of her exalted status. She demands that all is shipshape, and who can blame her?'

'And what's so exalted about her?' Bob asked.

'Her father is an *earl*.' He spoke as if he were referring to the Second Coming, so in awe of the aristocracy was he.

'No doubt she still has need of the thunderbox.'

Eve shrieked with laughter, but Whitaker turned away his head with an expression of disgust. Eve quietened, not wishing to offend him, of all people. 'There is a war on, or has no one told her?' She allowed herself a little laugh as she trotted out the platitude that was a constant in their lives now. She was feeling particularly skittish today. Nothing pleased her more than to have the men in her kitchen at the same time. Her life now was a whirl of indecision – which did she prefer?

'It seems strange to me to own a large place like this and never visit. If the manor were mine I'd never want to leave it, that's for sure,' opined the sergeant.

'I'd agree, but there's no accounting for taste. Sir Mortie and his wife have a busy social life in London.'

'I bet the war's put the kybosh on that.'

'Do you think so? From what I hear there's more entertaining, not less. Just like the Romans.' Whitaker was full of doom.

'And what have they got to do with it?' asked Sergeant Bob.

'It seems to me that even in this day and age too many fiddle while Rome burns.'

'Careful, Edward. Sounds to me like you're criticizing your betters.' The sergeant was grinning broadly, Whitaker looked put out.

'For some life barely changes. It's so unfair, isn't it?' Eve accompanied this remark with a sniff to mark her disapproval of such shenanigans.

'Certainly, times are different. I was speaking on the telephone only yesterday with the London butler. He told me that some of the people they entertain wouldn't have got past the door before the start of hostilities.' Whitaker looked mournful as he imparted this information. 'It becomes more difficult to maintain the old standards. Any riff-raff seem to think they've a right to use the front door, I've just packed off a telegraph boy round to the back. Of course, he knew where he should go, he was simply trying to annoy me with his impertinence. It'll be the doctor thinking he's the right if this continues.'

'Does it matter which door they use?'

Whitaker looked at Sergeant Bob with astonishment. 'I presume you are making a joke, Sergeant?' The butler spoke in what, to Eve, was an admirably controlled tone. She often wished she could master it. It was a prime example of the muddle in which she had frequently found herself since Sergeant Bob's arrival – she agreed with both men but didn't want to risk offending either by saying the wrong thing.

'Well, as Eve here says, there is a war on.' Sergeant Bob burst out laughing but Whitaker ignored him. He was irritable, these days, and Eve wondered if he was jealous at the attention she paid the soldier. How exciting that would be! How perfect!

'I heard you singing, Eve. A joyous sound.'

'She's a lovely voice, hasn't she?' Sergeant Bob said – a mite quickly, Eve thought.

'Why thank you, Bob and Edward. It has been commented on before.' She smiled coquettishly. Sergeant Bob had tried to kiss her last night. She had, of course, repulsed him, but it had made her happy even though it had been marred by a whiff of alcohol. She would love her best friend Gussie Fuller to know about it, but was that wise? Better to wait until she was more sure of where she stood. She didn't want Gussie taking a shine to him or, worse, Bob showing an interest in her. And Eve knew Gussie: she'd be attracted like a bee to a flower.

'I've a message from Lady Cresswell's maid. Her ladyship wants some oxtail soup.'

'Then she can want. I haven't time to do that – it takes hours to cook. She can have celery like everyone else.'

'Perhaps you could prepare it for tomorrow,' Whitaker suggested diplomatically.

'I don't see the point. She'll have changed her mind by then and be wanting something else.' She was now wielding the rolling-pin some-what aggressively.

'You know best, Eve.' Whitaker had sensed that Eve's good mood was slipping away. 'Well, I must stop chattering, I have duties to perform.' And he walked, dignified and ponderous as ever, out of the kitchen.

'He's a pleasant enough man but a shade pompous, don't you think?' Sergeant Bob returned to his cake mix.

'Pompous?' Now, here was a quandary, Eve thought. How could she deny Edward by agreeing with Sergeant Bob – even though secretly she thought he was right? But if she argued the point with him she might offend him. Best not to say anything, she decided.

'I heard he was a widower. Unusual, isn't it, a married butler?'

'This is a progressive house,' she replied, neatly covering the pain she had suffered when Edward had suddenly married Hilda. 'Had she not insisted on deserting her husband and going to Whitby she'd still be alive. She was killed in the shelling last December.' She thought that must have sounded rather cold, so she added, 'Poor soul,' which wasn't what she had thought at all.

'Pastry-cook, wasn't she?'

'So she said.' This was accompanied by a dismissive sniff.

In fact, Hilda had been an excellent cook. When she had been killed, Eve had worried about the desserts and puddings. While she herself was a genius with meat and savouries, she had never been confident of her capabilities as a cake-maker – not that she had ever admitted it. But Sergeant Bob, it had transpired, could bake anything; biscuits and cakes were now his domain. Eve declared that she had never tasted a sponge as light as his – of course, she had not said so in front of Edward. She was only tactless if she chose to be.

'Tell me, Lady Cresswell is her proper title, why do people call her Lady Penelope?'

'With so many Cresswells here it's become a bit of a tradition. Now, if no more guests arrive I might have made enough pies to last us.' She stood back, hands on hips, to admire her handiwork.

'They look good enough to eat!'

'Oh, Sergeant Bob,' she giggled, 'you are a card.'

'You know what impresses me most about you, Eve? If things go wrong, or too much is put upon you, you always cope so good-naturedly.'

If Eve had still had the ability to blush she would have been scarlet. She had never heard a more untrue statement.

'I fear I get a little heated at times.' This, she knew, was a gross under-statement for she lost her fearsome temper too easily; until now she had had no intention of controlling it. It was a compliment to Sergeant Bob that, with him in her kitchen, she lost it less frequently.

'That is the privilege of a cook of your standing, Eve.'

'You say the nicest things. Now, the junkets. Miss Cresswell is ada-mant we have them ready every day since they're easy for the sickest soldiers to digest.' She bustled off to the dairy for the rennet. There she did not even notice the chill; a glow of happiness warmed her. It was obvious that Bob liked her – where would it lead?

Upon her return to the main kitchen Rowan was sitting at the table, a tray of feeding cups in front of her, chatting to him. Eve felt an unpleasant stab of jealousy. The girl might be newly married but she was too attractive to be around *her* Bob.

'Ah, Mrs Gilroy, there you are. Sister Westall wondered if you had any Bengers. We've run out.'

'Inefficient of her, isn't it?'

'Yes, but we've been very busy. We've had some badly wounded arrive this week.'

'And you don't think we've been busy? We never stop.'

'I didn't mean that, not at all. Everyone knows how hard you work.' Rowan had flushed.

'I haven't got any Bengers. Give them Bovril.'

'We've run out of that too.'

'Oh, really!' With a well-planned flounce Eve clattered across the kitchen to her dry-goods storeroom.

'I've upset her,' Rowan said, when she had gone.

'No, Eve takes a lot of upsetting.'

Rowan looked at the soldier as if he had lost his wits. But there was no time to respond as Eve came back with a large jar of Bovril. 'Tell Sister Westall I want it replaced. What if I run out of ingredients? You'd all starve.'

'Yes, Mrs Gilroy, I will ...'

Sergeant Bob watched her as she left the kitchen. 'What a lovely creature she is.' Admiration lingered on his face.

'Um,' was Eve's noncommittal reply.

'I feel sorry for her. She seems lonely.'

'She should have given more thought to what she was doing.'

'A lot to expect from one so young. When love comes in the window, sense flies out the door, doesn't it? Or it always has in my experience.'

'Have you a saying for everything?' She was finding it hard to keep her temper. He was just like the rest. Show him a pretty face and his wits deserted him. And what experience? Was he boasting to her? How unfeeling.

'I'm sorry.'

'What about?'

'Annoying you.'

'Tsk – of course you're not. But I've watched that child grow up and she's not as innocent as she appears, you know. She's quite aware of the effect she has on men.'

Eve decided to make some bread. Kneading dough violently always made her feel better.

Chapter Two

Spring–Summer 1915

1

'You must be happy to have Oliver home safe and sound,' Hannah said, as she kissed Esmeralda in the spacious and elegant hall at Lees Court.

'I'm delirious. He seems to have been away for years rather than just a few months. Now *he* can deal with the estate problems, instead of silly me. The worry's given me beastly headaches – the bills and wages are very hard, Hannah. I hate sums.' Esmeralda, a picture in blue silk, fluttered about her guest.

'I'm sure you managed perfectly well.' Hannah handed her coat to the butler. 'Are you well, Milner?'

'Very, thank you, Miss Cresswell.'

'The war isn't impinging too much upon you?'

'We have our staff problems like everyone else, Miss Cresswell.'

'It's a wretched nuisance, isn't it? And, Mrs Fuller, I trust all is well with you?'

Gussie Fuller bobbed and beamed.

Esmeralda envied Hannah's easy manner with the staff. It was evident that they respected her but the same could not be said about their attitude to herself. After all these years she still felt uncomfortable with them – as she did with most of the Cresswells.

She was aware that Oliver's family felt she had not been and never would be good enough for him. Oliver constantly tried to reassure her but Esmeralda felt they were right in their assessment of her. It wouldn't matter how many years passed, she would never truly be one of them. It was one of the reasons she felt such sympathy for Rowan, whose situation was even worse than her own. 'Shall we …?'

Following Esmeralda, they proceeded into the drawing room, which, like every room in the house, was large, with long, casement windows that flooded the interior with light even on a dull day such as this. Everything in the room had been chosen with meticulous attention to detail. There was not a piece of furniture that jarred or was not of the right period for the noble Georgian house. The lighting was discreet and flattering. The curtains at the windows were of rich brocade and fabulously wrought. Unable to find a carpet she liked, Esmeralda had had one woven to her own design in muted beige, pale blue and the softest green. Many had admired it but none had ever commented – it was considered ill-mannered to do so. In consequence Esmeralda often worried that it was an example of poor taste, or vulgar. Whenever she suggested to her husband that perhaps they should change it he refused point-blank but never said he loved it and was proud of her skill.

Once he had served the sherry, Milner bowed himself out of the room.

'The men were away at camp for much longer than we had anticipated.'

Esmeralda laughed. 'Oliver says they were so bad at learning their drill they were kept longer than any of the others.'

'Really?' Hannah's voice sounded as if she was not reassured.

'It made me worry so. There is gossip on the estate that they were being prepared for extra duties, which could only mean one thing, France.'

'If that were so I'm sure Oliver would have said.' Again Esmeralda heard the doubt. She knew she was the last person to whom Oliver would give bad news and had hoped to find out more from Hannah, but such was her reputation as a worrier that she doubted her sister-in-law would tell her either.

'There is such bad news in the papers.' Hannah sipped her sherry.

'I don't read them. It's all too ghastly. What I don't know I can't worry about, can I?'

Although Hannah smiled, Esmeralda regretted her words. Did they not make her sound stupid and empty-headed? So often she regretted things she had said the minute they had left her mouth. 'Oliver will be here in five minutes,' she added. 'He sends his apologies. He was delayed on one of the farms.'

'Is there a problem?'

'It's the lack of men. Too many have enlisted. Oliver tried to persuade them to wait and join the Territorials with the Cresswell men, but the blacksmith is rather a hot-head and he urged them to go. I think he wanted to get away from his wife. She's *huge* and very frightening ...' Esmeralda held her hands wide apart.

'Oh, Esmeralda, you're so funny. Blacksmiths are always fine figures of men – the last to be afraid of anyone.' Hannah chuckled.

'You've never met Bunty Ball. Even the horses shy away from her!'

Esmeralda giggled. 'Now I hear there's talk of employing women to work the land.'

'Good gracious, whatever next?'

'I'd have thought you, of all people, with your passion for gardening and your little landscape business, would approve, Hannah.' It always puzzled Esmeralda why it was accepted that Hannah could have a business and not be looked down on but that her own father was beyond the pale.

'You're teasing me.'

'Just a little.' Esmeralda was glad Hannah couldn't read her thoughts.

'If I think about it, however, I begin to see that it's actually a good idea. After all, I know from personal experience that it can work. Emily Sprite, whom I employ, is a wonderful gardener – even if now, of necessity, she is concentrating on vegetables rather than flowers. As for the others, provided they are not exploited and are paid the same as the men, I can only agree.'

'I don't think that would be fair, Hannah. They won't be able to do as much work as the men so they won't deserve as much money.'

'But I'm sure they will. Even the heavy work.' The door opened and Hannah turned. 'Ah, here's my dear niece, Marigold,' she cooed, as the nanny entered, carrying the baby, dressed in a long, frilled lace dress. 'Oh, may I hold her?' She put up her arms to take the child. 'What a pretty little creature she is. Is she not five months already? How time flies. Now, who do you favour? Your mama, or your papa?'

Esmeralda clasped her hands together, unaware that she was holding her breath while Hannah studied the baby's face.

'You know, Esmeralda, I can't see either of you in her. She's herself – aren't you, my angel?' With the child in the crook of her arm, Hannah opened her bag and from it removed a small jewel case, which she handed to Esmeralda. 'A little present.' She kissed Marigold's forehead.

'Oh, Hannah, you're so generous to her.' Esmeralda flicked open the leather case. 'It's beautiful. Adorable.' She admired the small brooch in the shape of a butterfly, the wings studded with emeralds and rubies. 'Too lovely.'

'I'm pleased you like it. It belonged to my mother.'

'Then it's doubly precious.' She swooped down to kiss Hannah.

'It's been such an age since my dear little great-nieces, Georgia and Charlotte, were here to indulge so please bear with me if I pamper dearest Marigold.' They fussed over the child, with Hannah having constantly to reassure Esmeralda that, in her opinion, Marigold was in the best of health. Eventually the baby became restless with all the attention and Hannah handed her back to the waiting nanny.

'Have you news of dear Lettice?' Hannah asked, once the nanny had left and they had settled again.

'No, I haven't, and it worries me. I write but she doesn't reply. I have telephoned and asked to speak with her but the butler always says she is not available. I've even sent telegrams, but there is never a response. I begin to doubt she receives them. I'm sure that Hugo has stopped her having any contact with us.'

'He *is* a bully and, to our shame, we took too long to realize it. Superficial charm can be so dangerous. I find myself quite perplexed by the situation. I sympathize with poor Lettice, of course, but one cannot forget that she behaved abominably with the wretched Ramsey. And how wrong we were about him!' Hannah pursed her lips. 'We thought him charming, too, when Morts introduced him to the family. Instead he is a duplicitous adulterer.'

A frown crossed Esmeralda's face. 'But, Hannah dear, that's so harsh. Lettice was in love and I'm convinced Ramsey loved her too. He was kind to her and she needed that kindness badly.'

'I'm afraid that is no excuse for such appalling behaviour.'

'But when her husband is so cruel, isn't it understandable that she would be more susceptible to someone compassionate?'

'I understand what you say but I cannot agree. She's a married woman and nothing can alter that. She made her vows, and to deceive her husband ... I can hardly bring myself to think of my niece's downfall.' Hannah was agitated.

'But with all your support for women I would have thought you might be more understanding.' Esmeralda had surprised herself. She was not normally so forthright with her sister-in-law.

'The women's suffrage movement has never countenanced sin,' she replied sharply. How pompous, thought Esmeralda. 'Though I have doubts about Hugo's treatment of her – too unkind – I can understand that no man would permit another to usurp his position with his children. It was not right for Charlotte and Georgia to be with them, was it?'

'Perhaps not ...' Esmeralda agreed grudgingly. 'But Lettice told me she was discreet.' And what would you know about living with a difficult husband? she thought.

'How can you be sure? You were not there and, of course, that is what Lettice would say.' Hannah spoke even more sharply, which made Esmeralda feel wretched, but out of loyalty to Lettice she had to persist.

'Hugo never noticed them, never showed them any affection. He told her he did not want them, that he would have preferred a boy.'

'Many men might say such things, but it does not mean that they are happy for another man to take their place.'

'It worries me that he keeps her a virtual prisoner.'

'We don't know that, Esmeralda. Perhaps she no longer wishes to have contact with us ...'

Esmeralda stood up, her colour high. She could hardly believe she had heard Hannah judge Lettice so harshly. Perhaps it's her age, she thought.

'How is your father?' Evidently Hannah had sensed hostility building and had chosen to change the subject.

Esmeralda felt hot. She hated discussing her father with the Cresswells. 'I rarely see him,' she said tightly.

'You were once so close. It seems a shame.'

'He annoys my husband, and Oliver annoys him. It is better this way.' It was Esmeralda's turn to sound short. 'I had hoped you were going to bring Rowan with you.' She wanted to get the conversation back on safer ground.

Hannah sighed again. 'It is so distressing. She avoids me.'

'Surely not.'

'Oh, yes, I fear it is so. Whatever I suggest, she does the opposite. Today is an example of such. She said she would try to come but that is what she always says, and she never does.'

'Why do you think that is?'

'I have no idea.'

Esmeralda would have liked to contradict her, certain that Hannah was fully aware of why Rowan avoided her. 'We need to help her more,' she said. 'She is a dear girl and, after all, she's Morts's choice.'

'Now let me guess. You were talking of Rowan?' Oliver Cresswell strode into the room. A tall, upright man with a fine figure, whose hair, even though he was still in his forties, was almost white; it gave him an even greater air of distinction. How handsome he is, Esmeralda thought, as she always did when she saw him even if he had been away from her only an hour, as now.

'Oliver, what joy to see you. And looking so well too.' Hannah accepted his kiss.

'I'm glad I do, for I thought the training would kill me. There were days when I felt far too old for the regime we were put through. My feet thought so especially.' He grinned.

'Your feet?'

'Route marches, every day …'

'Officers too? How shocking.'

'We have to be fit and I felt it was wrong to expect the men to do something I would not.'

'How commendable of you, Oliver.'

'I'll tell you a secret, Hannah. He loved every minute of it!' Esmeralda laughed. 'And what he failed to add was that he didn't carry the sixty pounds of equipment the men did.'

'I'm not insane, you know!' Oliver poured himself a drink. 'Did I hear you ask for Rowan? She's here. She's just popped along to see Mrs Fuller.'

'How rude,' said Hannah.

'She asked me if she might. They are old friends, it seems.'

'Hardly. Gussie Fuller had left our employ long before Rowan joined the staff.'

'Does it matter?' Esmeralda could feel herself becoming irritated again and her protective instinct rising. 'She probably knows her from living on the estate.'

'I'm glad she has come. And Esmeralda is right. She needs our help.' Oliver squirted soda into his whisky.

'I have somehow to make friends with her, haven't I?'

'Yes, Hannah, you must.'

'But I thought you didn't approve of the marriage either, Oliver.'

'I didn't, but it's done and we would be wise to accept it. Also, we owe it to Morts to help her. It will be hard enough for the poor child when Coral comes.'

'That doesn't bear thinking about.' Hannah shuddered. 'But Morts is not with you?'

'No, he comes tomorrow – but it's a secret. He wants to surprise Rowan.'

'And this wretched war, Oliver. What is to happen to us all?'

'You're not to worry, sister dear.'

'But I do. I hear such dreadful things from my patients.'

'That is in France, not here. We're safe, unless the Germans invade us …' At this Esmeralda gave a little scream. Oliver patted her hand. 'I shouldn't have said that, frightening you. It won't happen. We shall win this war. And even if they did come, Esmeralda my dear, they would have us to contend with. We will defend you stalwartly. Why, you should see the Robinson brothers' skill with a bayonet.'

'So you don't believe you will be sent to France, which is what every-one thinks?' Hannah asked.

'The first problem with war is rumour. No, we shall remain here.'

'Thanks be for that,' Hannah said, with marked relief.

Esmeralda wished she could believe it.

'Miss Cresswell, Mrs Oliver.' A diffident Rowan was standing by the door as if unsure whether to enter. She looked as if she would prefer to escape. She was dressed in a drab black skirt and white blouse, both of which had seen better days. But her clothes could not disguise her blonde, blue-eyed beauty.

'Rowan, how kind of you to come when you're so busy.' Esmeralda rustled swiftly over to her and kissed her firmly on both cheeks. 'Oh, but your poor hands. They're so rough.' She peered at them myopically. Rowan blushed and Esmeralda clapped a palm across her mouth, but it was too late.

'They get chapped in the cold ...' Rowan said lamely.

'Of course they do, Esmeralda. Rowan works hard.'

At the implied criticism from Oliver, she felt wretched. 'I didn't mean to be rude, Rowan.' She flapped her own hands, which, since they were pale and beautifully manicured, only added to her confusion. She put them behind her back.

'I know you didn't, Mrs Oliver.' Rowan smiled at her.

'Oh, please, do call me Esmeralda. Now, a drink for you. Perhaps a little sherry?' She guided Rowan purposefully into the room.

'That would be lovely.'

'Come and sit beside me, Rowan dear.' Hannah patted the cushion on the sofa. Reluctantly, it appeared to Esmeralda, Rowan sat.

'You are enjoying your duties as a nurse, Rowan?'

'Thank you, yes, Mr Oliver.'

'Is Nurse Ferguson being kinder to you?' Hannah asked.

'No, she isn't. But I ignore her. She doesn't matter to me.'

'It's surprising that she's unkind, given her background.'

'Perhaps she is because of it,' Rowan said, quite sharply.

Esmeralda regarded her with admiration.

'I'll have a word with her.'

'I rather you didn't, Miss Cresswell. It would make matters worse.'

'Well, if you're sure ...'

A silence descended. No one seemed to know what else to say and all were relieved when luncheon was announced. Passing through to the dining room and the fuss when they were seated covered up the lack of conversation for a few minutes. But, napkins unfolded, cutlery fiddled with, they were faced with the problem again.

'How many patients –' Oliver began.

'The garden is looking –' Hannah said.

'What lovely weather –' Esmeralda chimed in. Then they laughed at their gaucheness while Rowan stared at the napkin on her lap.

'What do you mean, Esmeralda? It's raining,' Oliver spoke with a mix of exasperation and amusement, but Esmeralda heard only annoyance.

'Is it?' she said, blushing a pretty pink.

'It was better earlier,' Rowan offered.

'Thank you, Rowan, I thought so.'

The butler began to serve the first course. 'Why has that place setting not been removed, Milner?'

'I wasn't informed, sir.'

'It's my fault. I forgot to tell him.' Esmeralda was even more flustered now. 'If you wouldn't mind, Milner?'

The placement was removed.

'Were you expecting a friend?' Hannah asked.

'He had some business to see to and had to excuse himself.' Oliver fingered his collar.

'Are we to know who it is? Or is it a secret?' Hannah laughed.

'You would not be pleased if you knew the name of our guest.'

'I'd rather be the judge of that, Oliver dear. Now you've intrigued me.'

'Very well … It's Ramsey Poldown.'

Hannah's fork clattered on to her plate. 'Oliver! How could you? He's the last person who should be welcome in a Cresswell home.'

'I beg to differ, Hannah. The Cresswells have caused him enough trouble as it is.' Oliver concentrated on his salmon mousse rather than look at her.

'And what has he done to poor Lettice?' Hannah was red with indignation. 'He seduced her, a married woman – excuse my mentioning such a delicate subject, but it is the sad truth. Her reputation is in tatters. Consequently she has lost contact with her family. No doubt her life is very sad now. And whose fault is that? Ramsey Poldown's.'

'Lettice has some responsibility too, Hannah. It was she who went to him, she who ran away. He took her in. What else was he to do?'

'Send her packing, which is what any true gentleman would do. Of course it's his fault. And how you could put me in such a compromising position? I don't understand, Oliver.'

'He's not here.'

'No, but he might appear. I might bump into him.'

Rowan was looking from one to the other. 'You can't help who you fall in love with,' she ventured timidly.

'Quite so.' Esmeralda smiled encouragingly at her.

'What love?' Hannah sounded quite waspish. 'Had he really loved Lettice he would never have put her in such a position. A position that has ruined her life. No, he cannot have loved her. True love calls for sacrifice. No one who really loved would create difficulties for their loved one.'

At this Rowan blushed.

Esmeralda felt a spurt of anger on her behalf. 'That is very harsh, Hannah.'

'It might sound so, Esmeralda, but it is how I, and many, feel.'

'I thought long and hard before I invited him here, Hannah. He is, after all, Morts's friend, not mine, but during the camp I got to know and appreciate his sincerity. I asked him not to take luncheon with us, since I was concerned for your position, Hannah. You might be interested to know that the business he has had to address is that his house has been burnt to the ground.'

'Oh, no! Poor Ramsey!' Esmeralda cried. 'What happened?'

'At first, of course, it was thought to have been an accident, but some of his livestock have been slaughtered.'

'Dear God!' Hannah exclaimed.

'That's barbaric.'

'Yes, Esmeralda, it is. And the finger of suspicion, of course, points directly at Hugo Hamilton. Not only did he want Lettice back with him, but he is evidently intent on ruining Ramsey.'

'Is Lettice safe with her husband?' Rowan asked. 'It seems to me that rather than criticize, perhaps she should be rescued from such as he.' With that she blushed an even deeper red.

2

Because she was overworked and lacked sleep, Rowan was tired. Worry kept her awake at night, and now she had a fresh anxiety. Why had Morts not come back with Oliver and the other estate workers? Where was he? Yesterday, at luncheon, she had wanted to ask

Oliver why her husband was not with them, but she had stopped herself, knowing it would make her seem stupid and, worse, pathetic. During the night, however, she wished she had put pride in her pocket and asked. On reflection she realized she had been stupid – everyone else would know he had not returned. There would have been a gathering at the Cresswell Arms last night that would have gone on until late. She could imagine them gossiping about her, that although Oliver had come home with them, Morts had not. She put the pillow over her head in mortification.

One particular thought made her sit bolt upright. What if he had been there and was hiding from her? Then she decided that if he had someone would have gone out of their way to tell her.

During the night her fears grew apace until, by three, she had convinced herself that, while he had been away from her, Morts had realized their marriage was a grave mistake and that not coming home immediately was his way of telling her so. By four she knew for certain that he had left her for ever, having met another, more suitable, woman.

These worries were fuelled by her constantly repeating to herself Hannah's words, from the day before: 'No one who really loved would create difficulties for their loved one.' She loved Morts, but if Hannah was right, how much did she love him? Was her love selfish? His family's disapproval would get worse as time passed, so to protect him from them, their disapproval and the complications that would ensue, should she not leave him and prove her love to everyone – especially to him?

That thought made her turn her pillow yet again and thump it hard, the idea frightened her so. How could she turn her back on him? She'd rather die. She would fade away without him. Did that mean she didn't love him as much as she thought she did? That she loved herself more?

By five she was bathing her eyes with cold water to reduce the puffiness; she was determined that no one must know how she felt, she envisaged them agreeing on how right they had been, what a mismatch she and Morts were, how it was all a blessing in disguise ...

By six she was piling the washing-bowls on to a trolley to take to the men.

'Have you caught a chill, Cresswell?' Ella Shipley, a new VAD, asked kindly.

'I think I'm starting one.' Rowan sniffed.

'You don't look top notch. Why not go back to bed? I'll tell Sister you're unwell.'

'And have me shot at dawn?' Despite her misery she was able to laugh at this idea. 'She told me if I was ever sick it would be my own fault, that it was simply not allowed. She said I owed it to my patients to stay healthy.'

'How stupid. How can anyone help being poorly?'

'That's what I thought too – not that I dared point it out to her.'

'She never said anything like that to me.'

'She wouldn't dare. You're a VAD. She respects you and loathes me.'

'She should respect you especially. I've watched you working. You do far more than Ferguson and me put together – and the men adore you.' Ella began to pull clean towels from an upper shelf. 'Let me help you with the washing. I'll give these out.'

Rowan began to add the tin toothmugs, each labelled with a patient's name, to her trolley. She had liked Ella the minute she had joined them two weeks ago. She pulled her weight and was always on duty early, while Ferguson was always late. Sister never told her off – it was if she was under her spell or, rather, as Fanny Petty had pointed out, that she was sucking up to her because she had a title. 'Just like you'll have one day,' Fanny had said, with pride. Rowan had been horrified by the idea.

Although Ella, like Ferguson, was attractive and although she wore the same bespoke uniform, which showed her fine figure, and although she had the same accent, she was as different from Ferguson as could be. She was friendly, helpful and, most importantly, Rowan did not feel threatened by her where Morts was concerned.

Soon after Ella had arrived she had asked Rowan about her marriage – not in a prying manner but in a natural, friendly way so Rowan told her. No sooner had she started than she had regretted it, certain that Ella, knowing about her, would disapprove like everyone else – but for some reason she found she could not stop. And she had been wrong. Ella had stood in the midst of all the bottles and bedpans that Rowan was cleaning, clenched her fists and said, 'That is the most romantic and beautiful story I've ever heard.' Rowan was convinced there had been tears in her eyes. They had been firm friends ever since. She wished she could talk to her now, unburden herself, but she could not quite bring herself to confide in Ella her latest fears.

Voices and accents fascinated Rowan. She had never taken much notice of them before, apart from thinking how hoity-toity some of the Cresswells sounded. But now she was learning to differentiate between them. She realized that Sister Westall's accent was false: every so often the cut-glass vowels would slip and another, rather ugly, note would slip in. Hannah's voice was clipped, like Lettice's, but Morts and Esmeralda sounded different. As hard as she listened to the latter two, she could not detect any accent. The butler spoke with a rigid one, as if afraid that another might escape. Mrs Gilroy's, she had learnt, was Cockney. She herself had a West Country accent, which was not as strong as it had once been – or so her sisters were keen to point out to her. They sneered at her because of it, accusing her of trying to be something she wasn't, but she hadn't changed it on purpose. Since she had been with Morts it had changed by itself, as if she was absorbing everything about him, including the way he spoke. She had noticed, though, that on her rare visits home there was soon no difference in the way she and her sisters sounded. It was all very strange.

Rowan pushed the trolley on to the ward. Half of the men were awake and the others were still asleep, or pretending to be. Her first task was to carry the screens, stored at the end of the room, then place them round the beds. They were heavy, made of wood and canvas. If a soldier was fit enough he would help her but this morning there was no one she could ask. She had overheard one of the officers telling Sister they didn't need them.

'After all, Sister, there was no privacy in the trenches. It doesn't bother us if we see each other washing.'

'You're not in the trenches now, Lieutenant. You're on my ward and standards will be maintained.' Sister had summarily rejected the suggestion.

'But poor Nurse Cresswell. They're far too heavy for her.'

'Nonsense! She's as strong as an ox.'

So Rowan had been left with the daily screen battle.

'Let me help you.' It was Ella. But they had only had time to place one before she was called away.

'I'll take that end.' Captain Taylor, newly allowed out of bed, took hold of the screen.

'Thank you, Captain, but I don't think you should,' Rowan protested.

'It's my pleasure.' He lifted his end. 'Golly, they're heavy. I'd no idea ...' They carried the unwieldy object the length of the ward, wobbling alarmingly as they did so until eventually they were both laughing and dropped the screen with an almighty clatter. Those soldiers still sleeping woke up, and it was as well that Rowan had become immune to their language.

'What's going on?' Ferguson appeared in the doorway. 'Cresswell, what on earth are you thinking of?' she snapped. 'Dear me. You are a naughty captain ...' Her voice had altered in a flash to a coo that reminded Rowan of doves. She fluttered down the ward towards them. 'You will harm yourself.' She caught hold of the captain's arm. 'What were you doing, Cresswell? The captain isn't fit enough to do your work for you.'

'Nurse Ferguson, I assure you I volunteered. Those wretched screens are far too heavy for her.'

'I wouldn't hear of it. Now, you come back to bed. Let Nurse Ferguson help you.' She fussed over him.

Rowan continued with the screen. Why didn't people see Ferguson for the two-faced person she was? Rowan had noticed that she was only sweet to those officers who were handsome and who, she assessed, came from good families with, most importantly, money. From Ella she had learnt that, for all her airs and graces, Ferguson's family was on its uppers because of her father's gambling. Normally she would have felt sorry for someone in such a pickle but, secretly, she was rather pleased and, what was more, it explained why Ferguson had made such an obvious play for Morts. This didn't make Rowan feel particularly proud of herself but, she reasoned, Ferguson had brought it on herself with her spite.

Rowan lugged the screens, distributed the bowls, the soap, then had to carry round the heavy jugs of water and give out the flannels and towels. Last of all she passed round the toothmugs, checking the names on them so that they each received the correct one.

'You haven't given Captain Callow and those three officers their bowls.' Ferguson had reappeared.

'Because they're able to go to the bathrooms,' Rowan explained.

'And I think they shouldn't.'

'They prefer to go. It makes them feel better.'

'Did you not hear what I said?'

'I did.'

'Then do it!'

'No. If you want them to stay in bed, you take them the flaming screens and bowls.' Rowan turned on her heel.

'Stop. How dare you speak to me in that manner? You listen to me. I'm senior to you. You will obey my orders.'

Rowan swung round. 'And you can boil your head! You can't tell me what to do.' Ferguson opened her mouth to shout at her, but several of the men were applauding.

Rowan felt herself blush.

'You'll regret this, Cresswell.'

'You won't order me about any more, Ferguson, or it'll be you doing the regretting.' And with that she stormed out of the ward. After the night she had endured, and with all her worries, Ferguson had been the last straw.

'Good for you. It was about time you stood up for yourself,' Ella said. To her consternation, Rowan burst into tears. Ella moved towards her to comfort her.

'No, please, don't!' Rowan ran into the linen room and curled up on the floor in the space between the shelves and the window. She hated them. She hated being here. She'd had enough. And where was Morts?

'Sister Westall wants to see you.' Fanny Petty had put her head round the door. It was an hour later: the sister must just have come on duty. 'Don't let her bully you – Ella told me what happened. It was time you put a stop to it.'

But Sister Westall was incapable of not bullying. Rowan stood in front of her and tried to think of something else to distract herself from the grating voice that went on and on. She had, apparently, endangered the health of the patients; she had been seen to flirt with them; her work was not up to standard ... On and on she went. The voice stopped. Thinking she might have paused for breath Rowan waited, but when nothing else followed she realized she was supposed to say something. 'Is that all?' she asked.

'You need not be impertinent.'

'I was simply asking. So you wish me to leave?'

'I did not say that.'

'You did not need to. If, as you say, I am so bad at my work, it would be better if I left, wouldn't it?' Anger gave Rowan the courage that she had lacked.

Sister Westall spluttered – she was searching for words now.

'I'm not happy here. I'm expected to do too much. I thought I was helping but evidently I'm not so it's best that I go.'

She left the room, but had the satisfaction of hearing Westall run after her. 'Cresswell! Listen! There's no need to lose your temper with me.'

'But I haven't. I'm weary of being treated as I am by you and Ferguson. I shall go and see Miss Cresswell and let her know ...'

'Rowan, you are needed. Please come back ...'

She looked at the older woman with dawning surprise. Sister was scared of Hannah Cresswell, she thought. Having spoken her mind, she felt quite light-headed with relief. 'You chose the wrong day to reprimand me, Sister. I've decided I will not accept any more unpleasantness.'

Rowan was running down the main staircase to find Hannah when the front door opened. There stood Morts, handsome in his officer's uniform.

'Morts! You're here!'

'Of course I am. Where else would I be?' He scooped her into his arms, swung her round and kissed her lips, then put her down. 'I was so fed up yesterday. Everyone else had left and I had to take a report to Exeter. I was so angry ... Uncle Oliver told you?'

'No, he didn't.'

'Good – I asked him not to. I wanted it to be a surprise.'

'Morts, how could you? I've been imagining all sorts of things.' She felt foolish now.

'Morts! I thought I heard you!' Hannah came bustling out of her office. 'Wasn't that a lovely surprise for you, Rowan dear?'

'You knew too?'

'My brother swore us to secrecy. Such fun!'

Rowan said nothing. She thought it had been thoughtless of them all. But a drab and miserable day had suddenly become a happy one and she saw that the sun was shining.

3

The early-morning light filtering through a gap in the curtains woke Rowan, who lay curled tightly in Morts's arms – like a winkle in its shell, she thought. She snuggled closer, relishing the warmth of his body. She had missed awakening to this when he was away.

He had changed physically. He felt harder and fitter from his time at the camp. Moving even closer to him she remembered their lovemaking of the night. How wonderful it had been, how miraculous that it had become more passionate, more tender ... more sublime. *Sublime*. It was a lovely word that she had learnt only recently.

Even as she savoured her memories of the night, Rowan was fretting with a new anxiety: how could she contemplate doing any work today with Morts in the house? She had calmed down from yesterday and knew she could not leave because she was needed, but, if only, just for a few days, she could be permitted to do nothing ... When Morts had been away in training she had thought of him constantly, but had managed to do her work. Now … Rowan knew that her job, menial though it was, had importance but wanted to spend every second with her husband.

She listened to him breathing. She would have liked to watch him as he slept but she did not dare move for fear of waking him. The bed was so narrow that they lay like spoons in a cutlery drawer – the notion made her smile.

His arm, flung over her, was becoming heavy. Stoically she made herself lie still. But then the tip of her nose tickled – she tried to make herself think of something else but it was no good. Gingerly she moved her hand to scratch it.

'Hello, wife,' he said and, from his tone, she knew he was smiling.

'Good morning, husband.' She began to sit up, the better to see him. Far from being sleepy he was wide awake. 'I didn't dare move for fear of waking you.'

'Me too. I didn't want to disturb you – especially when I'd deprived you of so much sleep.'

'I was happy to oblige.' She giggled. 'Wasn't the night wonderful?' She stretched like a contented cat.

He was grinning as he sat up, ruffling his hair. 'We need a bigger bed,' he announced. 'I'll get Whitaker to arrange it.'

'You can't ask him!' She pulled her cotton nightdress across her bare breasts.

'Why ever not?'

'I'd be embarrassed. You simply mustn't. Then he'd know what we do!'

He laughed at her horrified expression. 'We can't continue sleeping like this, can we? And what is there to be embarrassed about? We're married – or have you forgotten?' He pulled her to him. 'What if I asked them to move us to a different room, a larger one, and don't mention the bed?'

'That would be even worse!' She covered her face to hide her confusion. 'Then everybody would know!'

'That we make love? They know that already, silly.' He kissed her neck. 'Ah, you smell of love …' He inhaled deeply. 'We need a room with a big bed in it, one we need never leave.'

'Morts, I've been thinking. There are so many cottages on the estate, could we not move into one and have a place of our own?' It was a tentative question since she did not know what was possible, how much money Morts had, what rights. She knew nothing of his affairs.

'But this is my home,' he answered. But not mine, nor will it ever be, she thought, but did not say. 'I couldn't live in a cottage. Whatever next? What would people think?' He laughed at the very idea.

But I would love nothing more, she thought.

He took her into his arms again and began to kiss her with greater intensity.

Later he asked, 'Do you think we made a baby?'

'Is that what you would like?'

'How can you ask it? Our child! I dream of it. A boy or a girl, I don't mind which, though an heir would be nice.'

'I didn't know you thought about babies.'

'I'm your husband, of course I do ... And the sooner the better.'

Rowan had been happy at this turn in the conversation, but his last remark pulled her down. 'Don't say that,' she said sharply. He looked at her quizzically. '"The sooner the better." You meant in case you're killed, didn't you?'

He laughed. 'How dramatic you are, my sweet. I wasn't thinking that at all. In any case, as I keep telling you, I won't be sent away to fight. We'll be used for defence.'

'I don't believe it. No one does. We all think you'll be sent to France. I've heard the men talking on the wards. They say that losses at the front are heavier, that conscription is only a matter of time.'

'What rubbish! You shouldn't listen to such uninformed gossip.'

Rowan didn't respond. He was wrong. The men were informed. Who would know better than those who had been at the front? He hadn't. But she didn't want to argue with him. It wouldn't be right. He was her husband, and she must respect his opinions.

'When I said goodbye to you at the railway station in January, I was convinced you wouldn't come back, that that was where you were going ...' Tears welled in her eyes, her fears returning. 'You don't understand how afraid for you I am.'

He leant towards her and kissed her. 'Ssh ...' he said. 'If you listen to rumours you'll die of fright. There's a lot of nonsense talked and you must learn to ignore it.'

'A lot of sense is talked too ... We aren't stupid.' Maybe she shouldn't have said that. 'And there's the officers' terrible wounds that we treat. When I began the men were recovering but now they come with dreadful injuries. I know how terrible it's all becoming and I don't want you to be part of it.'

'You look so sad, my sweet one.'

'I am. It's such a muddle, Morts. One minute I'm beside myself with happiness, the next I'm in despair. I feel joy one moment, fear the next.'

'My poor darling.'

'And just a moment ago, when you were talking about having babies, I suddenly realized there's so many other things I don't know about you … What you like, how you think.' She frowned. 'That's wrong. We should know everything about each other.'

He laughed. 'I doubt my parents do.'

'We're not your parents,' she said, with quiet dignity. 'If I compare us to my parents, why, it seems sometimes they know what the other one is thinking. They even finish each other's sentences. That's what I want us to be like.'

He sat up. 'They've had a long time to learn about each other. But your parents are fortunate to have such a marriage. Let's hope we're as lucky.' He put his hands behind his head, which she knew meant he was thinking deeply. She'd seen him do it before.

'I'm sorry to disappoint you, my love, but there's not an awful lot to know about me,' he said eventually. 'First and most important, I love you. I've eyes only for you.' He paused. 'That, of course, is not strictly true.' Rowan's heart plummeted. 'You see, you have a rival …' Now her heart lurched. She had been right all along. She steeled herself. 'I am, of course, madly in love with my new motor-car!' He grinned at her and she felt like slapping him, but she smiled, pretending she didn't mind the tease.

'I like to hunt, but I don't *live* to hunt as some of my friends do. I enjoy my work and I like making money – I could never be like my father and do nothing.'

Still his hands were at the back of his head but he was serious now. 'I think this war is necessary and at the same time I hate it. I loathed the training, which made me see I'd make a hopeless soldier. I'd like to live the rest of my life here at Cresswell with you and at least six children. There!'

'Six!' It was her turn to laugh.

'Fewer than your mother!'

'You're teasing me.' She must learn to understand when he was. She mustn't be so sensitive all the time. 'But what about your favourite colour – and food? Do you like chocolate? Do you believe in God or heaven? See? Lots of things.'

'Let me see … I love yellow, the colour of hope. I like roast beef, Mrs

Gilroy's steak and kidney pudding, never pie. I drink too much claret. I hate chocolate. I most certainly believe in heaven – being with you here is Paradise.' He was grinning again.

'You see? Still you tease me.'

Suddenly he was serious again. 'If it's important to you, my darling. Yes, I believe … though, I have to be honest, I've given it little thought – it's just one of those things, like the King is on the throne, so God is in heaven and I'm sure he wears white tie and tails and went to Eton …'

She pushed him as she laughed. 'Now you're being silly. You should be careful – He might hear!'

'But you're wrong, Rowan. If you think about it you know a lot about me. We share a love of Keats and Tennyson. You know I'm interested in painting and music, you know my dreams …'

'Am I being silly? I'm sorry, Morts.'

'You never call me "darling".'

'It's not a word I'm used to.' She clambered over him.

'Where are you going?'

'To work, of course.'

'But you can't! I'm here.'

'You tell Sister Westall. I wouldn't dare.' She was laughing now as she searched the room for her clothes, which she had abandoned in haste the night before.

'Then I shall.' He swung his legs over the side of the bed.

'I didn't mean it. I was joking. I can't not go – the others depend on me.'

'Then I'll have a word with my aunt.'

She put out her hand. 'No. Please. I'm serious about what I do. I don't want any special treatment.'

'You're afraid of them?'

'No, you weren't listening. I don't want it to seem as if I'm playing at this work. I want to do some good. It's my duty but I like it.' Despite the problems she had, it was true that she enjoyed working with the officers. There was no greater pleasure than watching them leave, upright and healed. It was a wonderful feeling.

'Beautiful and a paragon …'

'Don't use words I don't know the meaning of.'

'I'm sorry. It means you're a shining example to us all.'

'You're laughing at me.' She was upset and turned away so that he couldn't see her expression.

'My darling, I'm not.' He crossed the room to her, stood behind her, put his arms about her and nuzzled her neck. 'You're too sensitive,' he chided gently.

'How could I be any other way?'

'What do you mean?'

'Nothing.' She concentrated on clipping her belt into place.

'There is something. Has someone upset you? Tell me.'

She did not answer. What would be the point? If she told him of the slights and sneers they would sound petty. She knew they would because she had practised saying them out loud and she could hear how trivial they might appear to someone else. He had to *be* her, be in her skin, to know how the words, the attitudes, hurt, how her self-confidence was being chipped away.

'I must go.' She turned and, standing on tiptoe, kissed him, then slipped from the room before he could stop her.

As she skimmed along the corridors and up the main staircase, Rowan was lecturing herself. She must stop reacting in the way she did. She knew she got too upset before she had thought things through. Morts was being kind to her. If she continued to be as sharp with him as she had just been she would annoy him, and then where would she be?

However, Morts's presence had made a difference to her, which was apparent from the minute she arrived on the ward. Even though she was more than half an hour late, nothing was said, and Polly Pepper, a young girl from the village, was waiting for her.

'No doubt you know our new volunteer, Cresswell? Show Pepper how we do things here. Then you can help the nurses with the blanket baths,' Sister Westall ordered, before bustling off self-importantly, leaving Rowan astonished. There was nothing she would like more than to help the nurses.

'You're very welcome, Pepper.' She turned to the nervous-looking girl. 'I've been worked off my feet and needing help for ages. Here's my little empire.' She opened the door to the large bathroom, which had been made into a sluice room for the two main wards.

'Cor ... What's them?' Polly pointed to the row of glass bottles.

'They're for the gents to piddle into. We have to keep them clean – they get smoked up and then Sister comes roaring down the warpath. Over here I've got some shot. You put a couple of spoonfuls in, like this ...' she demonstrated the technique '... then shake it about a bit and it cleans the sides. Tip the shot out, then rinse it like this ...' She held the bottle under the bath tap.

'Well I never. Where did you learn to do that?'

'I once saw one of the footmen cleaning the crystal decanters. I wondered if it would work on these – after all, they're glass too – and it did. Now, these are the bedpans. We scrub them out with this mixture of Lysol and water after every use. Try not to get it on your hands – it hurts.' She pulled one of the trolleys towards her. 'We wash these with this diluted phenol mixture. When the bloodied bandages come back from the wards put them in cold water in these buckets with a couple of heaped tablespoons of salt in it.' She showed Polly the salt jar. 'Leave them to soak, then take them to the laundry and ask for Maggie. She boils them for us – I'm supposed to do them here but it takes too long on a Primus stove. When they're dry we roll them up. Do it slowly – it's the only time we're allowed to sit down, except when we make cotton-wool balls. Sister Westall's a bit of an old Tartar.'

'I thought we were doing them a favour.'

Rowan laughed. 'I don't think *she* sees it that way, Pepper. Now where was I? Ah, yes. We clean all these instruments, then we boil them for five minutes – no less – in these saucepans. We store them in these little trays with pure Lysol covering them.'

'Sounds a lot of trouble.'

'You can't be sloppy with it, Pepper. It's very important that we do it properly. The doctor, Major Fellowes, gave us a long talk about it. It stops the soldiers' wounds getting worse. If we don't do things right they might be ill for longer.'

'There's lots of stuff, isn't there?' She indicated the pile of scissors and scalpels that awaited Rowan's attention.

'A lot of what we do seems silly, Pepper, like the way we have to wash the beds after every patient, but it's all important. That's what I think about when I'm getting tired. Mind you, I'm not sure how having all the bed wheels pointing the same way helps their recovery ...'

'Why don't you call me Polly any more? We've known each other all our lives.'

'It's another of their rules. We must only use surnames – it's to do with discipline. If I call you Pepper all the time, even when we're alone, I won't slip up and call you Polly. If I did it in front of Westall, she'd have my guts for garters. We aren't supposed to chatter either but here, alone ...' She shrugged. 'How's Dolly?'

'I never see her, these days. You'd never think she was my sister – she's got so stuck-up. I asked for a job at the inn but she turned me down. Too grand for the rest of us now.'

'I wouldn't have thought it of her.'

'Then you don't know her. She's always thought herself a cut above the rest of us. Can't think why. You haven't gone all hoity-toity like her and you've married someone a lot posher than Zeph Topsham.'

'And I hope I never will. I wouldn't know where to start! Now, will you help me with these bottles?'

As they worked Rowan watched carefully. As time wore on she allowed herself to relax. Polly was going to be fine.

Later she was allowed, once more, to bath four of the patients and was filled with purpose and a happiness that had been missing for some time now. Just to make one of the officers more comfortable gave her a satisfaction that went some way to dissipating the weariness and aching feet, while Ferguson and Sister paled into insignificance.

Today Rowan changed her routine and ate in the staff dining room, determined to show the others that she wasn't expecting special treatment even though Morts was at home. She ignored a remark from Sylvia Ferguson about her accompanying Morts to his bed; for the first time she could look at her and think what a vulgar, ridiculous woman she was, despite her airs and graces.

By half past eight in the evening, she was finished. She raced to Morts's room but he wasn't there. She began to worry. Where was he and who was he talking to? 'Stop it!' she ordered herself. She collected her soap and towel, had a long soak in the bath, which made her aching feet feel much better and calmed her down.

She changed into her one good dress and peeped tentatively into the family sitting room.

'There she is!' Morts was racing across the room towards her. 'I was just saying to Aunt Hannah that they work you too hard. The hours are too long.'

'It's what we all do. You get used to it.'

'Come with me ... We'll be back, Aunt.' Without giving her time to say anything to Hannah, he grabbed her hand and pulled her out of the door into the hall, up the stairs and along the upper corridor. He opened a door with a flourish, then bent down, picked her up – she squealed with delight – and carried her into the room.

'Oh, Morts!

Before her, in the light from a dozen candles, was one of the best bedrooms in the house. She knew it well from her days of cleaning it, but not like this. Every surface was covered with pots of white narcissi, their scent filling the air. A nightdress and peignoir, a cloud of cream silk and lace, had been laid on the bed. On the dressing-table there were shining bottles of perfume and creams. An ornate powder bowl, the largest she had ever seen, stood in the centre, and beside it a swansdown puff.

'Morts! For me?'

'You need spoiling. I've been so thoughtless. I want you to have all the best things in life. I've arranged for Esmeralda to introduce you to her dressmaker.'

'You're so good to me ...' She stood tall to kiss him, as he held her tight.

'Let me see you in my present ...' he whispered in her ear, his voice husky with longing.

Shyly she took off her clothes. She could not believe the softness of the silk as it settled over her flesh. 'It feels wonderful. Thank you for spoiling me ...'

He took her in his arms. They did not return to the family sitting room and Hannah.

4

In the two weeks since Morts's return, he and Rowan had settled into a routine. Despite her protesting that she did not want to be treated differently from the others, her hours of work had been changed. She now worked from eight in the morning until six at night and every Sunday was free.

'Don't be daffy, Rowan. You need time with your husband. No one else is complaining – just you,' Ella Shipley had told her, as Fanny Petty nodded in agreement. 'Pepper has settled in well and is quite capable of doing the early-morning shift.'

'I can imagine what Ferguson had to say.' Rowan pulled a rueful face.

'No one listens to her.' Ella gave her a hug.

Despite Rowan's persistent feeling of guilt, the new arrangement worked well. Morts was busy with the estate's affairs because his uncle Oliver, who had managed it previously, had returned to sort out the chaos on his own estate. Esmeralda had been right. She had indeed made a muddle. This meant Morts had less time to go to London to his brokerage firm, which was now managed by his partner and friend, Alkie Sommerton. Morts planned to go to London once a month for two days, but so far he had not gone. For now, at least, there would be no more farewells.

Within a few days Rowan was enjoying her new regime. Finishing her shift earlier, she had time for a relaxing bath and to pretty herself before she joined Morts for dinner. She loved the bathroom. As a child, she had bathed once a month in a large bowl in front of the fire in her parents' cottage. As a maid at Cresswell, she'd been rationed to one a week. When she had worked for the former vicar she had not been allowed one at all. Now she bathed every day and would have done so twice, if not three times.

Rowan needed time to relax each evening because the prospect of the formal dinner she was expected to attend always made her nervous. She was never sure who would be there. If she was lucky Hannah would have decided to return to her own home – she could not feel at ease in the older woman's company and began to wonder if she ever would. When Hannah was there, the medical officer, Frobisher Fellowes, would join them. Their friendship had caused much gossip not only on the wards but among the servants. Although Rowan had not forgiven Hannah for trying to stop Morts courting her, she hoped romance would blossom for her. In love herself, she wanted everyone to enjoy the same happiness as she.

There were usually two or three recuperating officers at the table – those who were almost fit. They didn't frighten her because she knew them and they liked her. It was an ordeal, though, when the volunteer helpers chose to join them. For the main part they were haughty, unfriendly, smug women, who said barely a word to her but seemed to watch her all the time, hoping to catch her out. Worst of all was when Sylvia Ferguson had been invited. Then Rowan's stomach churned throughout the meal. She had reached the sad conclusion that it tended to be women who stood in judgement over her while the men were kind and understanding. She wondered why that should be.

The work was becoming harder as more officers arrived and, of necessity, the convalescence of some was curtailed to make room for the new intake. When Rowan had first worked there the men were all local. Now they came from all over the country; they'd had officers from the Black Watch Regiment, several Welsh and even a few Canadians.

'Seems to me when another poor bugger arrives at a hospital in need of patching up then them as have been there some time gets booted out and have to go wherever there's room for them. That's us, and it don't matter how far away from their families they are,' said Fanny Petty, as they stole a five-minute break.

'I feel sorry for those who never have visitors. It's hard for them at a time when they need their family most,' Rowan said.

'Ferguson makes up for it.' Fanny gave a mightily disapproving sniff.

'Only if they're handsome,' Polly Pepper added.

'Not always. I saw her talking for hours to that truly ugly major.' Rowan wasn't sure why she was defending her.

'Then he must be rich.' This time Fanny's sniff was awe-inspiring.

The day had started much like any other.

'Cresswell, you're to help Lady Cresswell's maid. Her nurse has fallen and twisted her ankle – stupid woman.' Sister Westall was irritated. 'As if I don't need every pair of hands here.'

'Isn't there anyone else you can send?'

'Are you questioning my decisions, Cresswell?'

'Well, no, but it's difficult ...'

'That's your problem, not mine.'

Rowan had never met Penelope Cresswell, who was permanently tucked away in her suite of rooms, and had hoped she never would. She had heard enough about the woman to know that she was truculent, a bully, and upset everyone who came into contact with her. No one, including Morts, had suggested she should meet her. She presumed they had their reasons, but how could she tell the sister that? Lady Cresswell was Morts's grandmother and Rowan wondered if he was protecting her – if so many disapproved of their union, an old lady such as she was even more likely to.

Her heart was thudding as she tapped on the door to the suite of rooms in which the bedridden woman lived, like a spider in the centre of a web. She had heard that Lady Cresswell, despite her disabilities, still tried to control her family.

The door was opened by the French maid, Colette. The household agreed that she had the patience of a saint – even Mrs Gilroy, who loathed the woman's entire nation, had conceded that.

'I've been sent to help,' Rowan said, her voice betraying her nerves.

'We're in a bad mood today, I should warn you,' the maid whispered. 'The best thing is to ignore what she says and not to let her hurt your feelings.'

'I hear she does it on purpose,' Rowan whispered back.

'She suffers greatly from *ennui*.' Colette waved her hands dramatically.

Rowan, not knowing the word, presumed it was an illness she had not come across. 'Really? How does it affect her?'

'Her head, it is full of nonsense ...' Colette's accent was so pronounced that Rowan had to concentrate hard on what she was saying. 'But, as you English say, her bite is worse than her bark.'

Rowan was about to correct her, then thought it might be rude.

'Who's that?' an imperious but rather beautiful voice asked. 'Why are you whispering? Come in this moment.'

'She's woken up. Come, do not fear ...'

Rowan took a deep breath and entered the hot, crowded, over-scented bedroom. In a large four-poster bed lay a woman of gargantuan proportions. She did not have a double chin but rather four or five – it was impossible to say for sure. Her eyes were like black dots in her face. Her cheeks were rouged, which made her look like a badly painted doll, but her white hair was beautifully dressed. On her fingers, ears and round her neck she wore some of the most wonderful jewellery Rowan had ever seen.

'Who are you?'

'Rowan, milady.' She bobbed. She thought it best not to say Cresswell. As far as she knew, the woman might be ignorant of her existence. Best not to make trouble.

'Well, you're a pretty one, aren't you?'

Rowan said nothing.

'Answer me. Aren't you?'

'I don't think it's for me to say, milady.'

'Don't be stupid – you've got eyes. You're lovely, and you know you are. At least I shall enjoy looking at you. I'm bored with Colette's ugliness.'

'That's not a very nice thing to say.' Rowan had spoken before she thought. Colette, out of the old woman's sight, was frantically shaking her head, a finger pressed to her lips.

Penelope Cresswell stared at Rowan with such intensity that she was sure her legs would give way. 'I'm not a nice person – but, no doubt, you've already heard that.'

'No, milady.'

'Don't lie to me. If there's one thing I can't stand it's a liar.'

'Yes, milady.'

'So?'

She took a deep breath. 'I'd heard you were difficult.'

'Then why didn't you say so?'

'Because I thought it would be rude.' Lady Cresswell snorted. 'And, in any case, I didn't want to be shouted at.'

Penelope had been wafting an ornate ivory fan. Slowly she laid it on the bedcovers. Rowan stood rigid, barely breathing. Suddenly Penelope threw back her head and laughed. As she did so, her superfluous flesh rippled. She laughed for so long and so loudly that eventually she choked.

'See what you have done!' Colette rushed to her mistress, pushed her forward and banged her on the back. 'There, there, milady ...'

She coughed and spluttered, waving her fat hands in the air. Finally she wiped away a tear with a delicate lace handkerchief. Rowan was unsure what to do, but wished she could run away.

'Stop fussing, Colette. Leave us.'

Convinced she was about to be shouted at or worse, Rowan watched Colette's retreating back.

'Well, what a surprise! I like you.' Lady Penelope smiled and her eyes disappeared into her fleshy face.

'You do?' Rowan stood astonished. Then she smiled too.

'I can't remember the last time anyone answered me back.'

'I wasn't ... I was just saying how I felt.'

'Don't spoil it for me. I liked it. I'm so bored with everyone agreeing with me, I know why they do and it irritates me.' She flapped her hand in the direction of a glass on the bedside table. 'Get me a whisky and soda. It's over there in that cupboard.'

'Should you?'

'No, of course not. But I'll have it anyway.' Rowan was very conscious of Lady Cresswell watching her as she crossed the room, she felt awkward. 'You're Morts's new wife, aren't you?'

Rowan nearly dropped the glass. 'Yes.'

'I can see why he chose you. Such beauty ...' Rowan blushed. 'You must learn to accept a compliment graciously.'

'I know I'm not ugly, but I couldn't say if I was lovely. Still, it's nice to hear you say it, even if it makes me blush.'

'Are people horrible to you?'

Rowan did not answer immediately but her mind raced. She had heard so much about this woman and wondered if she could trust her. 'Nothing has been said that I can't deal with.' She returned the bottle of whisky to the cupboard so that she didn't have to look at the woman as she spoke.

69

'And Lady Coral?'

'She's not happy.' At the inadequacy, in the circumstances, of this comment she could not stop herself laughing. 'The truth is, she had hysterics and fainted when Morts told her.'

'Good.' Lady Penelope clapped. 'How satisfying that you should upset her. Mind you, I expect she was pretending to faint – she does that, you know. And why have you not been to see me sooner?'

'I presumed you didn't know about me, that the family thought it was better you didn't. I believe they thought you'd be so upset if you met me that you might do yourself an injury.'

Penelope thumped the bedcovers. 'That is the sort of thing which makes me so angry. How dare people presume to know how I think? Do you want to know my opinion?'

'Not really.' Rowan grinned.

'I shall tell you anyway. I like your looks and your spirit. Some beauty in this family will not go amiss.'

Rowan bent down to pick up a book that had slid off the bed so that she did not have to answer.

'Of course you're not suitable, that goes without saying. Marriages across the classes rarely succeed. But you have spirit so you may surmount the criticism. But you must be willing to learn. By the way, your shoes are disgusting. You can always judge a person by their shoes.'

'They're the only pair I have.' She supposed she should be upset but instead she appreciated the old woman's honesty.

'That's ridiculous. A lady needs mountains of shoes. What is Morts thinking of?'

'He's a man – he wouldn't think, would he?'

'Then it's up to you to train him to do so. Whatever next?'

'He has arranged for Esmeralda to take me to her dressmaker but I think she's forgotten.'

'Typical. She's a stylish creature but has little brain, unfortunately. I can't think why my son married her. And have you met her dreadful father? A true mountebank, if ever I met one.'

'She loves him.'

'Which only proves how stupid she is.'

'Don't you think it would be a good idea if you got out of bed for a while?' Rowan changed the subject deliberately. She didn't want to be disloyal to Esmeralda, who had always been kind to her. 'It would be best for you. My mother always says you feel better if you're up.'

'How can I? Look at me.' She indicated her flesh. 'I was lovely once.'

'So I've been told,' Rowan said. 'I'm sure we can manage to get you out of bed. I'm stronger than I look.'

An hour later, an amazed Colette returned to find Lady Cresswell seated in an armchair with Rowan sitting on the floor in front of her, the two in animated conversation.

5

The walk from the manor to Hannah's house near Maiden's Wood was no hardship. It was a lovely day and Rowan had a free afternoon. She had been torn between spending her time with Morts or going to Barlton with Esmeralda on the promised visit to the dressmaker. In the end she had no need to choose since Morts had insisted she go to buy frocks.

She thought it strange that Esmeralda wanted to meet her at Hannah's, but the chance to fill her lungs with fresh air and admire the swathes of blossom on the trees in the park was irresistible.

Hannah's house looked lovely, and Rowan had always admired it. From a distance it appeared to be more glass than bricks. Built on a small hill, shrubs planted right to the walls, it appeared to float out of the greenery. She wished she and Morts could live in such a house. While it was big in contrast to the cottages she was used to, it was small compared to the manor, and thus in her eyes, preferable to that intimidating mansion.

As she climbed the steps to the front door, she admired the pieces of sculpture Hannah had placed on them. She'd do that one day, when she had a home of her own. As she rang the bell she thought she'd never get used to using the front rather than the back door.

'Hello, Rowan. You're looking well.'

'I could say the same of you, Sally,' Rowan replied. She was quietly satisfied to find Sally Pepper there. She had complained about the surliness of the last maid but had never expected Hannah to listen to her.

'How's our Polly?' Sally enquired.

'She's doing well. I don't know what I'd do without her now.'

'You wouldn't get me helping with all that blood and gore.'

'It's not that bad and the soldiers need looking after. Has she got someone with her?' Rowan asked, as voices floated out of the drawing room.

'The vicar's wife, Mrs Plunkett. Bit snooty, she seems to me.'

'Then I'll wait here for Mrs Oliver.' She moved towards a hall chair.

'No, you'd best go in. She's got ears like a bat and she'll have heard the bell.' Sally Pepper crossed to the double doors, opened them. 'Rowan's here, Miss Cresswell,' she announced.

'Really, Sally! Mrs Cresswell or Mrs Morts to you. Whatever next?' Hannah laughed, but Rowan, in the hall, could hear her embarrassment. Hannah's Westie, Cariad, raced over to welcome her, claws clicking on the shiny parquet floor. Rowan bent down to pat her; she was glad of the distraction after Sally's mistake.

Hannah swept towards her and kissed the air by her cheek, which Rowan always thought a silly gesture. She only kissed people she loved; but then, since it wasn't a proper kiss, perhaps it didn't count as such.

'Mrs Plunkett, have you met my *dear* niece, Mrs Morts?'

'No, but I saw you in church a few weeks ago. How do you do?' As they shook hands Rowan detected a supercilious air about Sorrel Plunkett, but she dismissed the thought. She was being over-sensitive again, imagining slights.

'Are you enjoying living here, Mrs Plunkett?' she asked politely.

Hannah beamed at her as she poured sherry – she must have said the right thing. 'I'm pleased you're visiting me at last, Rowan.'

Rowan stiffened. Was that a criticism?

But Hannah looked as if she regretted what she had said. 'You're so busy these days,' she added, as if to make amends. She handed the glass to her. 'It's sherry,' she said, as Rowan hesitated. She didn't want a drink, not at this time of day. 'Your coat, Rowan, give it to Sally.'

For a second Rowan was confused, not sure how to handle glass and coat. 'I'm not staying, Miss Cresswell.' Hannah seemed bemused. 'It was Mrs Oliver's suggestion that we should meet here.' Rowan took a dainty sip of the sherry. 'She is taking me to her dressmaker's.'

'How exciting for you. New clothes are always such a joy.'

'Aren't they? And Mrs Oliver has such wonderful taste.' Rowan smoothed her skirt, conscious of how drab she must seem – but not for much longer, she thought. She couldn't remember ever having new shop-bought clothes, apart from her wedding dress, which dear Esmeralda had insisted on buying for her.

'I don't think I've met a Mrs Oliver,' Sorrel Plunkett said, in a voice that was little more than a whisper.

'No doubt because she lives over at Lees Court – a lovely house, three miles from here. She's my sister-in-law, married to my brother Oliver and a dear sweet person. A great beauty, of course ...'

72

'The Cresswell men have good taste,' Sorrel said, but Rowan felt her response had been automatic, rather than genuine. 'You nurse at the convalescent home, so I've heard, Mrs Morts?' Sorrel Plunkett continued.

'I'm not a nurse, I'm an orderly.'

'One of those wonderful voluntary girls – VADs, are they not called?'

'No, I'm simply an orderly.'

'I think you should say you're a nurse, Rowan dear ...' Hannah interrupted. Again she looked as if she wished she hadn't spoken.

'Why? It wouldn't be true.'

'No, of course, but ... Would you like to see my house? I'm inordinately proud of it.'

'It's so lovely, Miss Cresswell. And you planned it all yourself?' Sorrel Plunkett asked, in her soft little voice.

Rowan wished she would speak up.

'With help, of course. I sketched out what I wanted and a young architect from Barlton – John Snape – drew the plans for the builders. So, yes, it is my concept and his expertise.'

'Is he the architect you worked for?' Rowan began.

'You *worked*?' Sorrel Plunkett leant forward, her face alight with interest. Rowan noticed that her voice was suddenly almost normal.

'I hardly *worked* for him, Rowan dear.'

'I'm sorry. I thought you planned the gardens for the villas he built in Barlton,' Rowan ploughed on, sensing she had made an error but not sure what it was or how to make matters better.

'I made suggestion to him out of gratitude for the work he had done here, nothing more.' Hannah laughed, but seemed even more flustered.

'And do you still *help* this young man?' Mrs Plunkett asked.

'Good gracious, no. Mr Snape was one of the first to enlist, brave man that he is. And in times of war the designing of gardens does not have the same degree of importance it once had.'

'We still need beautiful things around us,' Sorrel Plunkett answered, 'and you must miss *helping*.'

Rowan felt uneasy at her tone, neither did she like the somewhat sly expression that flitted across her face. She was dressed in a dowdy suit of indeterminate green, with an unbecoming hat, but they were unable to eclipse her natural prettiness and peaches-and-cream colouring. For all that, though, Rowan did not like her.

'I so admire this modern style of architecture and furnishing – so new and clean, rather than musty and old.'

Rowan wondered if she spoke so softly to ensure that she had everyone's attention.

'Just look at the fine carving on this chair. It matches that on the mantelshelf,' she went on.

'Not many people notice such fine detail.' Hannah smiled at her guest, and Rowan wished she could think of suitable things to say. 'I've always been a great enthusiast for the work of the late Mr Morris, and dear Mr Gillow is a great devotee also, in homage to the master. Many of the designs are echoed throughout the house. And the fabrics and furnishings sit so well with my paintings.'

Rowan trailed in their wake, having no idea who Mr Morris and Mr Gillow were.

'See here.' Hannah opened the double doors with their beautiful engraved glass, and showed her guests into the dining room. 'I find myself in quite a dilemma for I sometimes think this is my favourite room and then I change my mind and think, no. It has to be the drawing room.'

'So understandable ...' At least, that was what Rowan thought Sorrel Plunkett had said. 'What a wonderful painting.' They had paused in front of a large oil. It was of a young woman, with long, flowing hair, her clothes of another age but matching, and somehow becoming part of, the landscape in which she had been portrayed. It was so exquisitely executed that it seemed one might pick the wild flowers from the canvas. Rowan had been about to say how much she liked it but Sorrel Plunkett beat her to it. The woman clasped her hands, as if in prayer, which to Rowan looked false. 'Oh, Miss Cresswell, how fortunate you are to possess an object of such beauty.'

'I was shocked that your husband seemed to regard Mr Burne-Jones's pictures as rubbish.'

She waved a hand dismissively. 'I sometimes think he says things for effect rather than because he believes them, to make himself appear assertive.'

Rowan thought she should not say things like that about her husband to strangers, and liked her even less. She realized that the woman's voice rose quite considerably when she was animated, as now.

'What refreshing candour,' said Hannah. 'And is he? Assertive, I mean.'

Sorrel Plunkett laughed gaily. 'Good gracious me, no. He's a dear.' She stopped again. 'Oh, and this one?'

'That's a portrait of Cariad, which I commissioned. It's such a likeness, don't you think?' Cariad sat down to look at herself. 'Have you ever seen such a smug expression on a dog's face?' Hannah beamed down indulgently at her pet. The Westie seemed to be smiling at her portrait. 'My friend, Agnes, thought me mad to have it made.'

Rowan noticed that Hannah looked sad as she mentioned that name. Perhaps she was hoping to find a replacement in Mrs Plunkett. She hoped not. She wouldn't trust her either.

'Why shouldn't you have a portrait of your dog? It's your house, after all.'

'And Cariad is my best friend.'

'I love dogs, but Samuel won't permit me to have one.'

'How assertive!' Both women swayed with laughter but Rowan couldn't see why.

'Was that a motor I heard?' Hannah led them back to the drawing room.

Esmeralda, Rowan realized, as she watched her with admiration, never simply entered a room but swept in in a whirl of silk, satin and scarves, with clouds of perfume wafting about her. Kisses and introductions over, she sat elegantly, refusing sherry. 'No, we haven't time, Hannah. We have so much shopping to do.' She clapped her hands in joyful anticipation. How like a little girl she is, thought Rowan, yet she must be at least eight years older than me.

'Well, it will make you happy, Esmeralda.'

It was Esmeralda's turn to look downcast.

'Oh, my goodness!' Hannah exclaimed. 'I must apologize. That sounded as if I was criticizing when I meant what fun it would be for both of you.' But the more Hannah explained, the more flummoxed she became.

Esmeralda laughed. 'Oh, I thought you were going to give me a lecture on my spending, like Oliver does – all the time! So boring.' She spied a bronze and was quickly on her feet. 'Is it a leopard? Oh, how lovely it is. I do envy you – is it French?' The questions tumbled out of her.

Rowan was bewildered. Hadn't Esmeralda told her it was rude to admire others' possessions?

Esmeralda stopped swooping about the room. 'Glory be! I've just remembered. Oliver said I was to apologize for not telephoning to warn you that we would descend on you.'

'My dear Esmeralda, it's a pleasure to have you here.'

'Oliver will be along in a minute. He wanted to see your Alf.'

'Alf? But he doesn't work here any more. I enjoy driving so much that I don't need a chauffeur.' Now Hannah appeared to be avoiding Rowan's eye.

Rowan was shocked at this news of her father. She'd had no idea.

'Oh, bother. Oliver wanted him to drive Rowan and me back from Barlton since he has to go to Exeter.' Esmeralda frowned as she searched for a solution. 'I know. We could stay the night. Oh, yes, Rowan, wouldn't that be fun? We could stay at the Victoria Hotel. Perhaps have an adventure!' Esmeralda was alight with pleasure at the prospect. All Rowan could think was that she did not want to spend the night away from Morts.

'You'd stay in a *hotel*?' Sorrel Plunkett's voice echoed her astonishment.

'The Victoria is a very respectable establishment.' Esmeralda's response was quite short. Normally she was so charming. 'Still, perhaps we should try to get home. Only I'm always so bored when Oliver has to go away and I'm left on my own. Could we not stay here?'

In Rowan's opinion this idea was even worse. She most certainly did not want to stay at Hannah's house, nice though it was. In any case, rumour had it that Hannah had invited the major to dinner so she would not want them anyway. But further discussion ceased as Oliver strode into the room.

'Good afternoon, Hannah.' He crossed the room to kiss his sister.

'Oliver, I'm sorry, you've had a wasted journey. Alf no longer works here, Hannah tells us. How are we to get back? We must make other arrangements ...'

'So I gather. The maid told me – I presumed to use your telephone, Hannah. I trust you do not mind? All is arranged. Morts will pick you up from Barlton at seven – I've suggested the ...' Oliver stopped. 'I'm so sorry, I didn't know you had a guest. I must apologize, madam.'

'This is Mrs Plunkett, the new vicar's wife,' Hannah explained as she introduced them. Oliver took her hand in greeting and bowed.

That was not unusual but Rowan felt uneasy. From where she was sitting, she could see his enchantment written on his face, and Sorrel Plunkett was batting her eyelashes provocatively. She hoped Esmeralda hadn't seen.

6

At every bump in the road the occupants of the motor-car were thrown back and forth. At every corner they almost fell on top of each other.

Rowan was in the back of Oliver's car with Esmeralda beside her. Their knees were covered with a silky fur rug, which Rowan couldn't stop stroking. Her other hand was holding the leather strap that hung at the side in a futile attempt to stop herself colliding with Esmeralda as the car rocked from side to side. Rowan was surprised that Oliver was driving so fast and recklessly; she had thought him the sort of man to do everything perfectly and sedately.

'How I miss our chauffeur,' Esmeralda said to her loudly, so that she could be heard over the clatter of the engine. She laughed as she spoke. Yet again they were thrown together.

Esmeralda seemed to be enjoying herself, but Rowan wasn't so sure. 'Where is he?' she raised her voice too.

'Enlisted, wretched man. So selfish.'

Rowan let this pass. What an odd mixture Esmeralda was. She could be so kind and thoughtful, then say something as unthinkable as that. Still, she thought, weren't all the Cresswells the same? Except Morts, she added. 'Do you know why my father's no longer driving for Miss Cresswell?' she asked.

Esmeralda cupped her ear. Rowan repeated her question, shouting this time.

'She explained – she likes to drive herself.' Esmeralda was taking a particular interest in her gloves.

'I think there's something else.'

'Do you?'

Esmeralda looked surprised, but Rowan thought she was acting. 'Yes.' And it's probably to do with me.

'Oh, look at those people! Don't they look funny, all wrapped up and shapeless?' Esmeralda deflected the conversation.

Oliver cursed mildly as he swerved to avoid the couple walking along the road. Rowan, looking out of the side window of the vehicle, saw that it was Maggie Burrows, wife of one of the woodmen, and her daughter. She turned her head abruptly, afraid they might recognize her; she felt ashamed to be bowling along in such comfort while they had to trudge. And she hated the way that Esmeralda had referred to them. It was not kind ... or was that how she truly saw them? Only a few months ago Rowan would have been traipsing along the pot-holed, muddy lane, cursing the inconsiderate driver of a car that covered her with mud. And now ... How confusing and difficult it all was!

Rowan was glad that the car was so noisy for they had had to stop trying to communicate. It was tiring to shout. It wasn't that she found talking to Esmeralda difficult – she was one of the easiest people to be with – it was that she didn't want to do so in front of Oliver.

Rowan was not sure what Oliver thought of her. At one moment he was pleasant and relaxed, at another he was distant. Some time ago she had decided he did not approve of her but she wondered if he was trying to make the best of a bad job. When she had first married Morts she had tended to agree with his family about her suitability but now their attitude angered her.

What gave them the right to judge her? It wasn't as if she was a bad person who had done wicked things – then they would have had good reason to disapprove. What gave them the right to think they were superior to her because they knew which knife and fork to use, which words were correct, and they could make polite conversation? Just recently she'd listened to them with greater attention, hoping to discover the secret, and she couldn't understand why she found it so difficult since they never said anything of note. She had concluded that it was the way in which they said everything that intimidated her.

'You're miles away. Penny for them?' Esmeralda asked.

'Oh, nothing, I was just dreaming.' If only she knew.

At last Oliver drew up in front of a small shop, discreetly tucked away in a Barlton side-street. Rowan had seen it before. It was painted grey with 'Le Puy Modes' in scrolling gold letters. The window had always puzzled her – there was only ever one dress on display with a vase of flowers beside it. An odd way to entice customers, Rowan thought. She remembered the small haberdashery in Cress whose windows were so cluttered with items for sale that they couldn't have squeezed another in.

It was not yet two and she wondered aloud if the shop wouldn't be still closed for lunch.

'Of course it's open. Madame Le Puy will see us at any time,' said Esmeralda, as they tripped up the steps.

'Why is Morts coming so late? Surely we won't need so much time?'

'My dear Rowan. In five hours, we might just have finished what we need to do.'

Here was another change. She had never shopped for clothes before because her mother had made everything she wore or she had had hand-me-downs. She followed, distinctly nervous, as the bell over the door tinkled, announcing them.

Upon entering Rowan decided that this was not a shop. She'd never seen anything less like one. It was more a boudoir, with its comfortable chairs, discreet lighting and elaborate flower arrangements. The air was heavy with their perfume, which Rowan found odd because the blooms were out of season. When she touched one she understood. It was made of silk and no doubt drenched in scent. Extraordinary. She wondered what sort of person would prefer them to real flowers. She soon found out. A curtain at the back of the shop parted with a dramatic flourish and Madame appeared, a tiny creature dressed in black, with sharp features, beady eyes and hair that looked suspiciously dark for one of her age.

The introductions made, she appraised Rowan with such a penetrating stare that she felt uncomfortable – it was as if her eyes could see her body beneath her coat. How rude, she thought.

'*Elle est belle, exceptionelle!*' she clasped her hands together.

'Do you speak French, Rowan?'

'No,' she answered shortly. Esmeralda must know she didn't. Why, even her English needed correcting.

'Madame Le Puy says you are exceptionally beautiful, which of course is the truth.' Esmeralda beamed at her.

'Champagne?' Madame clicked her fingers and an even smaller woman appeared, with a marked resemblance to a rabbit. There was much ceremony over opening the bottle and at the pop of the cork Madame and Esmeralda clapped and oohed.

Rowan sat on the sofa, sipping her drink. Madame Le Puy spoke to her in a garbled way that Rowan presumed was French until Esmeralda, giggling helplessly, assured her it was English. 'She needs to measure you,' she spluttered, then turned to the woman and, speaking rapidly in French, evidently apologized for her mirth. Madame found it funny too, but Rowan thought Esmeralda was being most discourteous.

Time sped past as they studied patterns and fabrics, agreeing, disagreeing, selecting, rejecting, then finally settled on the cloth and trims for two dinner and two tea gowns, two tweed suits, a cloak, an overcoat and, finally, two ball gowns.

'Why do I need so many frocks? I never go anywhere,' Rowan had pointed out at the beginning.

'So many! My dear friend, this is the bare minimum. In any case, Cinderella shall go to the ball!' was Esmeralda's response.

'But the expense,' Rowan had objected halfway through their deliberations.

'That's Morts's responsibility, not yours.' Esmeralda dismissed Rowan's concerns with an airy wave.

Three hours later Rowan was happily choosing scarves, several hats,, and had been measured for footwear by the shoemaker who had arrived, summoned by Madame Le Puy. The hats, scarves, and bags were carefully wrapped and boxed. Rowan had insisted on taking them with her – she couldn't wait for them to be delivered.

Esmeralda peered at her watch. 'I can't see the time – I've something in my eye ...' She held out her watch on its gold chain to Rowan, who blushed deeper than the red silk they had rejected as unsuitable.

'I can't. I don't know how to tell the time ...' she said, as quietly as she could, not wanting to share her shame with the dressmaker.

'How quaint! I wish I couldn't. I always have to chase myself to keep up with time, such a bore but Oliver's a stickler for punctuality. Oh, well, if we're late we're late, and nothing can be done about it.'

Gushing farewells were said, arrangements were made for the corsetière to visit Rowan at Cresswell Manor and then, followed by the little assistant laden with bags and boxes, the two young women clattered into the street. 'Oh, listen!' Esmeralda stopped dead in her tracks. 'The church clock! It's just chimed five. We've plenty of time to go to the Emporium.' With astonishing speed, she turned and they made their way to the high street and the large department store Rowan had seen on a previous visit to Barlton but had never dared enter. There, after long consideration, they purchased handkerchiefs, nightdresses, petticoats and knickers of silk and lace, all so lovely they made Rowan blush at the thought of wearing them.

The packaging complete, they were now joined by another young assistant, equally laden with bags and boxes. They raced from the shop and up the slight hill to Gold Street and the Victoria Hotel where they were to meet Morts.

Already Rowan was worrying at the extent of the bills she must have run up and how her husband would react to such extravagance. She estimated that several families could exist for a year on what Esmeralda had insisted she spend.

As they entered the building Rowan felt she would always cherish this hotel more than any other for it was there that she had spent her wedding night and where her new life had begun. She loved its bustle and ornateness. She wished she could live there, rather than at Cresswell Manor. Then she would be away from the disapproval that hung about her like fog.

'Shall we have some more champagne while we wait for Morts? There's a dear little sitting room upstairs that I have used in the past.' Esmeralda gave the order and Rowan was impressed by the easy manner in which she did so. Esmeralda began to mount the stairs, Rowan following in her wake. They had almost reached the top when a loud voice called, 'Esmeralda!'

At the sound of her name her face changed. The smile disappeared, her colour, always pale, became ashen. Her mouth opened as if she was about to say something. Her hand clutched at her chest. 'Petroc!' she whispered. She swayed, her hand feeling feebly for the banister as she fainted and tumbled head over heels down the magnificent staircase.

7

Esmeralda sprawled at the bottom, lying ominously still. Rooted to the spot, their faces etched with horror, Madame Le Puy's assistant and the shop girl were still clutching the parcels and bags of shopping. People were emerging from all sides, clustering round the prostrate form. By the time Rowan reached her, they had become a gawping crowd. Of necessity she shoved her way through using her elbows without apology.

The man who had instigated her fall was already beside Esmeralda. Rowan joined him, kneeling down, taking her hand, chafing it, calling her name, ignoring him. There was no response.

'Speak to me! Esmeralda, please!' She looked up at the curious faces. 'Has anyone sent for the doctor?' No one answered. 'For God's sake, do so!' She was unaware that she was shouting but she felt sick with fear.

'Esmeralda! My dear one ...' The man grasped Esmeralda's hand pushing Rowan's away. Then, using his bulk, he tried to shuffle her out of the way.

Rowan was having none of it. 'Here, do you mind?' she protested, manoeuvring herself back into position. 'Get out of my way.'

'How dare you?'

He was angry but for once she was not afraid. Concern for her friend swamped all timidity. 'You caused her to fall. This is your fault.'

'What a ridiculous thing to say. I did not. I called her name. I didn't expect her to slip. I'm mortified if I've hurt her. She must have been taken by surprise.'

'Surprise!' Rowan's voice was shrill. 'You frightened her.'

The man looked at her. 'Are you her maid? Where's Bridget?'

'I'm Mrs Cresswell's niece, and who might you be?'

He laughed unpleasantly. 'You! Related to her? Oh, yes, and I'm the Tsar of Russia.'

For good measure, Rowan gave him another shove and had the satisfaction of catching him off-balance.

'The doctor has been summoned. He's on his way.' Dulcie Prestwick, the owner of the hotel, had joined them. 'Rowan, what's happened?' Too large to join them on the floor since it was doubtful that she could get up again, Dulcie loomed above them.

'She fell down the stairs, Lady Prestwick, from top to bottom. This man startled her.' She pointed a finger at him accusingly. 'I feared she had broken her neck but she's breathing. I can't wake her, though ...' Rowan wanted to cry and fought back the tears.

'I don't think we should move her. It's best we wait for the doctor to arrive. I'll send for *sal-volatile*.' Dulcie turned her attention to the group around them. 'I'd be most grateful if everyone would move away. Everything is under control.' Dulcie had a natural air of authority and, albeit reluctantly, the crowd fell back, except the man who had caused Esmeralda's accident. 'And you are, sir?' Dulcie focused on him.

'Petroc Cornish. I'm an old friend of Mrs Cresswell. Indeed, I fear I startled her.'

Rowan regarded him cynically. He was pretending to take the blame and now she registered that his cuffs were frayed and his shoes scuffed. He was not so high and mighty, after all.

Suddenly Esmeralda stirred and gave a weak sigh.

'Esmeralda, I'm here! Wake up ...' Rowan begged.

Slowly her eyelids fluttered open. 'Rowan,' she said weakly. 'What happened? Where am I?'

'You fell down the stairs. From the top to the bottom. Does it hurt anywhere? The doctor's coming ...'

Esmeralda struggled to sit up.

'It's best if you lie quietly, my dear.' Dulcie handed Rowan a cushion to place under Esmeralda's head.

Esmeralda put a hand to her forehead. 'Am I bleeding?' They reassured her that she wasn't. 'I don't know ... Silly me ...' She attempted to laugh. She began to look about her. On seeing the man kneeling beside her she gasped and shrank away from him. She was holding Rowan's hand so tightly that it hurt.

'It would be better if you left us alone. You're upsetting her,' Rowan said firmly to him.

'But I'm her friend.'

'As you keep saying. If you are, why is she afraid of you? Lady Prest-wick, this gentleman caused her to fall and now his presence is distressing her. Would you please ask him to go?'

'Perhaps in the circumstances it would be for the best, Mr Cornish. We shall remain with her.' Although Dulcie spoke pleasantly enough, her tone indicated that she would not be disobeyed. To Rowan's intense relief he stood up and went into the bar. 'There, my dear Esmeralda, he's gone.'

'Don't let him come back.'

'Who is he, Esmeralda?' Dulcie asked.

'I don't know him,' she said, in a rush. 'What is he doing here?' she asked, adding to everyone's confusion.

'He booked into the hotel this afternoon. But if he concerns you so, I shall ask him to leave. There! Does that make you feel better?' Dulcie smiled kindly.

'I hate him ...' Esmeralda began to sob.

It was fortunate that at this moment the doctor arrived. There were questions Rowan wanted to ask but felt she could not. Something bad was afoot here, she thought, and instinct told her that she didn't want to know what it was.

Two of the porters, on the doctor's instructions, lifted Esmeralda gently and carried her into a small sitting room that Dulcie had cleared of residents. The doctor's examination was swift. Nothing was broken, but she was bruised and shocked. 'Perhaps if Mrs Cresswell stayed here overnight, Lady Prestwick?'

'No,' Esmeralda protested. 'I want to go home.'

After a flurry of arguments, the doctor reluctantly agreed. From his large leather bag he gave Rowan a small bottle of sleeping draught and some pills for the pain. 'I fear, Mrs Cresswell, that you will ache badly tomorrow. I recommend several hot baths and that you should remain in bed for at least a week.'

Esmeralda agreed to his instructions with such alacrity that Rowan was sure she would not take his advice. Dulcie ushered him out, telling Rowan to ring the bell if she was at all concerned.

Rowan pulled a low chair up to the sofa on which Esmeralda was lying. 'You poor dear,' she said, then wished she hadn't sounded so sympathetic for Esmeralda began to cry again. 'Please don't upset yourself. The doctor said you must remain quiet.'

'Oh, Rowan, you don't understand. I'm so unhappy ...'

'I'm not surprised. You took a nasty tumble. But you did it very elegantly. You have no cause for embarrassment. Had that been me I'd have made a right rumble.' She was trying and failing to make Esmeralda laugh. She was also delaying the confidence she feared was coming.

'Has he gone?'

'The Petroc man? He's in the bar.'

'Oh, no!' The weeping began again.

'But Lady Prestwick's going to ask him to leave. You've nothing to fear. I won't let him in here.'

'If only you knew, Rowan ...'

'Would you like some tea?' she asked, a mite too brightly.

'I knew he'd come. I knew it was only a matter of time. I've been living in dread of this moment,' Esmeralda said. 'He has come to ruin me, I know it. He is evil ...'

'There, there,' Rowan said, knowing that, in the face of such emotion, it was inadequate.

'If I tell you ... If I confide in you ...' She stopped as if she was trying to make up her mind. Rowan said nothing but was praying she would not continue. 'Please, I beg you, don't tell a living soul ... Not even Morts.'

'How can I promise that?'

'Because you are my dear friend and I need to tell you. I fear if I don't I shall go mad. You must promise.'

Something in her voice told Rowan that this was no false claim. She did not want to keep secrets from her husband, just to be safely at home with him. 'I promise,' she said. What else could she say?

'You're a good friend. Rowan, I do know him. I met him in Buxton. I went on my own and met my father there. I had to keep it secret – Oliver would have been furious if he'd known that I'd seen my father. They're not friends ...'

Rowan relaxed. This wasn't too serious: everyone knew that Oliver and his father-in-law were enemies.

'Petroc is a friend of my papa's. I was stupid, silly. It was my fault. I flirted, I can't help myself, I always flirt ...'

Rowan's sense of security deepened. 'Oliver knows what a flirt you are. We all do. It's hardly a secret.'

'I have always been flirtatious. What I mean is I used to be but not any more ...'

That was a relief, Rowan thought, and wondered what the fuss was about.

Esmeralda was crying again. Not desperately, but in a soft, almost resigned way. She felt for Rowan's hand and gazed up at her, with despair and a strange hope, as if she was praying for Rowan's understanding. Rowan felt anxious for her again.

'He violated me!'

Rowan hoped that she had misheard. Her hand shot to her mouth to halt the cry she knew she was about to make. 'He ... violated ... you?' She found it difficult even to say the word. 'You poor dear.' She sat beside her and took her in her arms to comfort her.

As the sorry tale unfolded, Rowan listened in disbelief. Her mind was shrieking for her friend to stop. She longed to tell her she did not want to know how he had tricked her, forced himself upon her. How she had begged and he had laughed. She wanted to tell her that she must keep her secrets to herself. But there was no stopping Esmeralda. Out poured the horror. It became worse as she voiced her fear about the identity of Marigold's father. These were secrets no one should be told. These were secrets Rowan would have to keep. Esmeralda's burden had been transferred to her.

Oliver was still in Exeter when Morts halted the car in the driveway at Lees Court. Rowan had hoped that on the journey, Esmeralda, especially since Morts was with them, would compose herself. But most of the way she had sobbed, which had been heartbreaking. It was a relief that Oliver was not there for Esmeralda was in no fit state to see her husband who would, no doubt, at the sight of her tear-stained face, have bombarded her with questions.

Instead Bridget, her maid, took control. She insisted that Esmeralda should have some tea, a bath and then go to bed. As Rowan said goodnight to her, Esmeralda grabbed her hand. 'You promise?' she whispered, since her maid was in the bedroom with them.

'Whatever happened to her?' Bridget asked Rowan, once they had settled Esmeralda and were outside her room, standing in the corridor. 'Were you there? Did you see what happened, Mrs Morts?'

'Mrs Oliver fell from the top to the bottom of a very steep staircase. We were both tired. We'd had a busy afternoon shopping. I think she must have caught her shoe in her hem ...' That, she thought, was the first lie she would tell for Esmeralda.

'Then it's my fault.' Bridget was distressed. 'I'm sure that skirt was sound this morning. I always check everything ... But it can't have been!'

'I doubt Mrs Oliver will blame you. It was an accident pure and simple.' Second lie. How easy it was, she discovered.

Sitting beside Morts in the car as they headed for home, Rowan went over the evening's events. It was an horrific story. Why had Esmeralda not told anyone of her distress at the time? After all, as she herself knew, if problems were not dealt with immediately they usually grew in intensity. It was not Esmeralda's fault that that evil man had attacked her so why had she not sought help? But even as she thought this she knew the answer.

If, God forbid, the same had happened to her – the idea made her shudder – would she have kept it secret from Morts? Would it have changed how he felt about her? Surely not. But then … men were different. If another touched her, would Morts cast her aside? Had Esmeralda not dared confess for fear that Oliver would turn against her?

Then she remembered village gossip when it was rumoured that a girl had been attacked. 'Brought it on herself!' she'd heard one woman say. 'Flaunting herself,' said another. That Esmeralda was a woman of position rather than a village girl made not a jot of difference. Society would blame her, not the man. It always did. Perhaps her position would make matters even worse for her.

But Rowan could have gone to her father and told him. Surely he would have kept her secret. He, of all people, would have made sure that Petroc was punished. Why had not Esmeralda gone to her own father? Rowan had heard he was a hard man. Perhaps she was afraid of what he would do, and the problems that would have ensued.

Towards the end of their conversation Esmeralda had said she was going to have to tell Oliver. Rowan was not sure if this was because Petroc had appeared or because she could no longer keep her secret from her husband. She found herself wondering if this was wise. Any man would wonder why she had delayed so long in telling him.

What would Rowan do if she were ever in the same circumstances? Would she tell Morts? Those words would be hard to say. *I'm not sure that the child is yours.* At that thought she pulled her coat closer round her. How could any woman say that to her man? It was not surprising that Esmeralda had not.

In a way she understood. The officers often flirted with her but she had learnt how to deal with them, chiding them in a light-hearted way that usually stopped them. But one day she had been cornered in the linen room by a particularly persistent captain who had tried to kiss her. Had she told Morts? No. And why not? She hadn't wanted to worry him, or have him storm off, find the man and hit him. It was simply a matter of degree, she reasoned.

And what would be the point of Esmeralda's telling Oliver now? What good would it do? What if Oliver turned against the child he doted on, threw Marigold and her mother out of their home, even depriving the little girl of his love? After all, she thought, it was hardly Marigold's fault.

'That was a heavy sigh.'

She felt Morts searching for her hand in the dark. She took his, and squeezed it. As always when he touched her she felt a pleasant jolt go through her. 'Did I?'

'As if you had all the troubles of the world on your little shoulders. What's happened?'

'Nothing. I wasn't aware I sighed.' She felt flustered and was sure she sounded it.

'There is something.' He steered the car into a gateway, stopped, then faced her. 'I think you should tell me.'

Rowan looked at her hands because she couldn't meet his eye. She wanted to tell him, needed to confide in him, and felt wretched that she had promised not to.

'I'm worried about the amount of money I spent today because you might be cross.' She was shocked by how easily the lies tripped out.

'I won't be. I want you to look pretty. Again he took her hand. 'Look at me …'

She forced herself to turn her head and even tried to smile.

'That's not the problem, is it?'

She didn't answer.

'Is it?' he persisted.

Steadfastly she stared at her hands, as if they might solve her problem. 'I'm sorry, Morts, I can't tell you,' she said.

'You have secrets from me?'

'No, of course not.'

'Then why can't you tell me?'

'Because it's not my secret to tell.'

'I don't think we should have confidences we cannot share.'

'I agree. But I gave my word.'

'I'm afraid I don't understand, my darling. You promised not to tell me?'

'Not you in particular. I just promised not to tell anyone.'

'So you agreed to listen to something that you knew you couldn't tell me? I find that hurtful.'

'I didn't want to … I wasn't thinking properly. Esmeralda was in such a state I feared for her so I let her tell me.'

'I'm your husband. I have a right to know everything that affects you.'

'I gave my word.'

'And you gave me yours. You vowed to obey me and now it appears that you didn't mean it – or, rather, that you would obey me only when it suited you.'

'Why are you being so horrible to me? It's not my fault.' She felt a flash of anger. He was not being fair.

'It is very much your fault. You should never have promised, let alone listened.'

'I'm sure you have secrets. I'm sure there are things you keep to yourself. You didn't tell me you were being sent away for training.'

'I was protecting you.'

'I'm sure there are other things. You never talk of other loves you've had. That's keeping secrets.'

'That is the past and has nothing to do with our present.'

'I can't agree. You know everything about me and I have a right to know everything about you.' She was angry now. It had been a dreadful finish to what should have been a happy day. She wished she had never gone.

'Is she betraying my uncle?' he asked, without warning.

'I told you, I can't say anything. I wish you would stop this.'

'Then she is. I'm disappointed in you, Rowan. I thought you would have more loyalty to your new family than this.' He climbed out of the car and swung the starting-handle angrily. They rode the rest of the way home in silence.

That night Rowan cried herself to sleep. She waited for Morts to come but he didn't so she lay in the dark in her fine new bed in her fine new room, tossing and turning, regretting going to Barlton. Regretting promises made. It was so unfair. But what could she do? This secret was so enormous and the consequences of her telling so potentially severe that there was nothing she could do.

When she awoke in the morning, she found that Morts had not come to her but had slept elsewhere.

Chapter Three

Summer 1915

1

A week later Rowan was in a slough of despair from which she was sure she would never emerge. Morts was barely speaking to her. Apart from the normal courtesies, all he said was that she should tell him what she knew of Esmeralda. Stubbornly she refused to betray her friend; stubbornly he badgered her to do so. The more she said, 'No,' the more determined he became. They were in a vicious circle from which she could see no escape.

And there was not only the misery of his not speaking to her. Instead of searching him out and feeling her heart lift when she saw him, she hid from him and her pulse raced with apprehension rather than pleasure at the sight of him.

He had returned to her bed, but since that awful day they had not made love and she missed him. Her body ached for him. He would say, 'Good night,' coldly, as if to a stranger, and she would reply in the same vein. They would lie, their backs turned to each other, rigid with hurt and indignation, instead of curled in each other's arms. She would lie in the dark, fretting and wondering what she should do. Sleep was a long time in coming so that each morning when she woke it was as if she had not slept.

'You look so tired, Cresswell. Not sleeping?' Ella Shipley asked one morning as, together, they served the officers their breakfast.

'I had indigestion last night,' she lied. All she seemed to do these days was lie, then had to remember what she had said.

'When do you receive the clothes you ordered from the dressmaker?'

'I'm not sure. I need several fittings but I don't know how to go about making the appointments. Mrs Oliver has not been in touch with me – she had a funny turn when we were in Barlton.' That was an over-simplification but she congratulated herself on how neatly she had explained the problem.

'If she is unwell I could always go with you. I need to find a good seamstress.'

'That would be kind of you.' As Rowan smiled in gratitude, she realized it was the first time she had done so in more than a week.

'If Esmeralda is poorly, why not go and see her?'

'Perhaps I will,' she said, but did not see why she should. She felt quite cross with her friend, who had not seen fit to send her a note to let her know how she was. It had been left to Bridget to tell her that, after a night's sleep, her mistress was fully recovered. This struck Rowan as unfair – the cause of her problems with Morts was well again while she was in misery. Perhaps Esmeralda had not contacted her because she was ashamed. There was only one thing for it, she supposed. She'd have to go and see her but if she did, and Morts found out, he would be even crosser with her. How complicated it was.

'I'm thinking of going to see her myself. If you could give me the address?' Ella said, now that breakfast was over and they were in the sluice room preparing the trolleys for the dressings round.

'Sorry, whose address?'

'The dressmaker, silly. If you don't want to go with me I'll go by myself. My, you are in a doze,' Ella teased. Then she leant forward, having glanced over her shoulder to ensure they were alone. 'If I tell you, don't let on, will you?' she whispered.

Rowan was aghast. The last thing she wanted was to be burdened with anyone else's secrets. She was about to say no but Ella pre-empted her. 'Major Treadwell has invited me to meet his parents when the doctor discharges him.'

'Ella, that's wonderful. He's such a nice man.'

'Isn't he?' Ella's face was dreamy. 'But, for heaven's sake, please don't say a dicky-bird – if Sister found out I'd be on the mat.'

'I promise.' Now that was a secret she could promise to keep. And Ella was right – if Sister Westall found out there would be trouble. There was a strict rule of non-fraternization, unless you happened to be Sylvia Ferguson. At the thought of her Rowan, despite everything, smiled. Sylvia would be furious with Ella. Major Michael Treadwell was not only handsome, debonair and brave, he was titled and rich – everything Sylvia was searching for. Perhaps, she thought, Sylvia tried too hard and that was why she ended up with no one. It was sad, really.

Halfway through the morning Rowan was summoned to Sister's office. As always, she set off with a thudding heart and a sense of foreboding, wondering what she had done wrong this time. She need not have worried. She was informed that she was to go off duty immediately to sleep since she was to start night duty. Fanny Petty was ill and would not be back for at least a week.

This came as a shock. She knew that on night duty she would be alone with the men and she feared that she lacked the knowledge and experience to care for them. She knew that if anything happened to worry her she had permission to fetch a senior nurse, but what if she woke the woman unnecessarily? There would be recriminations.

It was not just this that bothered her. Perhaps Morts had arranged it. Perhaps he was using night duty to tell her he no longer wished to share her bed. Logic told her not to be silly, that he could not have controlled the onset of Fanny's illness. But then, she thought, as she walked back to her room, he might have bribed her to say she was sick. Ridiculous! But, like many thoughts these days, no matter how often she told herself she was being foolish, the idea would not go away.

Watched by a gaggle of fascinated boys, the group of estate workers, supervised by Sergeant Bob Turner and resplendent in their new khaki uniforms, were lined up in fours on the flat lawn that, prior to the war, had been used for croquet at Cresswell Manor.

'Attention!' Rob Robertson, the estate carpenter, roared. He'd been promoted to corporal, not just because he was the largest but because he had the loudest voice. On command, the men wheeled to the left, then to the right, watched intently by Sergeant Bob. The commands echoed against the ancient walls of the house. At an upstairs window, partly concealed by the curtain, Eve Gilroy watched him admiringly. Further along, at another window, some nurses were peering at them.

'To the *left*, quick march!' As one they swung round. 'To the *right!*' Back and forth they went, heads high. One or two had army rifles slung over their shoulders, while others carried their shotguns, arms swinging as they marched.

'They've improved since the last time we saw them. A bit out of step, weren't they?' Ella commented.

'If this is what we have to depend on in the event of an invasion, God help us,' Sylvia Ferguson sneered.

'Do you never see anything good in anyone?' Ella asked her, in a reasonable tone.

'How offensive you are!' Sylvia flounced off.

'You've done it now,' one of the others said to Ella.

She shrugged her shoulders. 'I'm sorry, but these men have worked so hard. They deserve praise.' There was a murmur of agreement. 'Oh, do look, everyone!'

The young village boys were now marching behind the amateur soldiers, pieces of wood slung over their shoulders, just like the men, just as proud. From the nurses there was a combined 'Aaah!'

There was even more fun when the men raced towards sheaves of hay and plunged their bayonets into them. 'Bloody Hun!' they shouted, with suitable venom. If anything the yells of malevolence from the children were even louder.

By now a group of proud women and a throng of girls had gathered to shout their encouragement and smile proudly at the men and boys. Then Sergeant Bob called them back together, told them to take a half-hour break and to return for their weekly route march. There was a communal groan. No one liked the seven-mile tramp he insisted upon.

Gussie Fuller was visiting from Lees Court. She had not been invited for a couple of months and suspicion had brought her over on her afternoon off. If invitations were not forthcoming it meant that her friend, Eve Gilroy, was up to no good.

'Well, this is a surprise. We don't see much of you these days, Gussie. Look who's here, Edward.' Eve acted astonished. 'We thought you'd forgotten us,' she added, for good measure. She was rewarded with a cynical little smile.

'And how are you this fine summer's day, Gussie?' Whitaker intoned.

'I thought I'd come to see that all was well with you since I never see hide nor hair of anyone.'

'We're too busy, Gussie, and that's the truth. Run off our feet, aren't we, Edward? As to an afternoon off, I've forgotten such luxury.' She managed to convey disdain and martyrdom in one sentence.

'How many patients have you got, then?' Gussie sat down and looked about her hopefully for signs that tea was being made.

'Twenty-five. Packed in like sardines, they are.'

'Can't be healthy for them, can it?'

'In fact, Gussie, they never complain. An example to us all.' Whitaker evidently hadn't liked the implied criticism. 'After the conditions they've experienced, this is luxury. Any tea on the go, Eve?'

With alacrity, Eve rushed to put the kettle on. 'All right for some,' Gussie muttered. 'We've lost our scullery- and kitchenmaids and the cook's in high dudgeon. But there are no replacements to be had for love nor money.'

'It's the same here. I was reduced to scouring the pots myself. Can you imagine? Me! But Sergeant Bob insisted we had a private give a hand. I don't know where I'd be without him.' She spoke as the gentleman in question entered the kitchen. 'Tea, Sergeant Bob?' From the corner of her eye, she observed Gussie stiffen her posture, lick her lips and pat her hair. She'd been right. Gussie would have to be watched.

'Need you ask, Eve?'

Gussie sat smiling, waiting to be introduced.

'I was just saying to my friend, Gussie, what a Godsend you are to me—' Eve began.

'So you're the famous Mrs Fuller. How do you do?' He stood to attention and saluted. Gussie glowed, which annoyed Eve so much that she spilt some tea.

'Pleased, I'm sure ...' Formally, they shook hands.

'Don't you two know each other?' Eve asked, with arch false innocence. She had done everything in her power to prevent such a meeting.

'Unfortunately, no,' Gussie said, looking angrily at her.

'Everyone talks about you with nostalgia, Mrs Fuller. It seems that Mrs Herbert has never managed to fill your housekeeping shoes to everyone's satisfaction.'

'Well, that's nice to hear, I'm sure.' Her expression was supposed to convey modesty but it failed miserably for she inflated with pride. 'But I'd be wrong to believe you, Sergeant. I'm sure you flatter me. Mrs Herbert is well qualified to replace me.'

'You work for Mrs Oliver, don't you, Mrs Fuller?'

'I do, but even after all these years I still miss the camaraderie we had here. It's a much smaller establishment, and there are days when I feel lonely ...'

'That will never do, Mrs Fuller. We must have you over more often, mustn't we, Eve, Edward?'

Whitaker readily agreed, but Eve plonked the teapot on the table with such force that tea spurted out of the spout.

'Excuse me,' a sleepy-eyed Rowan appeared. 'I wonder if I could have some hot chocolate, Mrs Gilroy? Only I can't sleep ...'

'Sleep at this time of day? Whatever next?' Eve scowled.

'I've been put on night duty and I'm supposed to be in bed now but there's so much noise outside my window.'

'Sorry, Mrs Morts. That was us, drilling the group. We've finished now so you can nod off at your leisure,' Sergeant Bob explained.

Reluctantly Eve made Rowan the hot chocolate. 'You want a little whisky in it, Mrs Morts. That'll soon send you off.'

The assembled group sat in silence as they watched Rowan leave the room. 'How's she getting on?' Gussie asked.

'Patchy,' Eve answered. 'She should thank her lucky stars her mother-in-law isn't here.'

'Poor little thing.'

'Gold-digger, if you ask me.'

'Come, Eve. That's hardly fair,' Whitaker remonstrated.

'I speaks as I find.'

'What's Lady Cresswell think of her?' Gussie asked.

'That's the strangest thing. They get on like a house on fire,' Whitaker observed.

'Well I never! Who'd have thought such a thing?' Gussie took a dainty sip of her tea and looked pointedly at the whisky bottle, but no one offered her a dram. 'I was wondering if you knew anything about my Mrs Oliver? Has anybody said anything? A few days back she came over all odd, she did, and fell down the stairs at the Victoria.'

'Too much champagne?' Eve asked, but was silenced by a furious glance from Gussie.

'Rowan and Mr Morts brought her home. Funny business altogether. Rowan said as she'd tripped on her hem. Well, her Bridget was annoyed because it meant she hadn't been caring for her clothes proper, like. And how could she have caught her heel what with the short skirts, these days …' Gussie sniffed in disparagement of such apparel.

'Oh, I don't know. I rather like them.' Sergeant Bob grinned.

'Oh, Bob, you are a one!' And Eve pushed him in a proprietary manner, with a sly glance at Gussie. 'Nothing's been said here, Gussie. Have you heard anything, Edward?'

'Not a word. However, if you ask me, all is not well between Mr and Mrs Morts. A slight frisson, if you ask me.'

'What over?'

'I fear I know nothing. Just an atmosphere I've detected.'

'You always were a sensitive man, Edward,' Gussie said.

Eve looked as if she would like to slap the simpering smile off her face. 'And how's your lot over there? Trouble, you said?' She nodded in the direction of Lees Court.

'I said no such thing. If you must know, everything's much better since the baby. Less coolness, if you know what I mean. It's wonderful what a baby can do for a marriage, isn't it?'

2

All the worries Rowan had acquired over her ability to work alone at night had been for nothing. To her surprise she found she enjoyed it far more than working in the daytime, which was a bonus.

Being on her own had many advantages. She could organise her work as she liked with no sister checking on her and no Ferguson making snide remarks. She could study the notes left by the nurses and doctors and learn a lot about medical matters. She was responsible for writing up the nightly report, which made her feel important. If the doctor came to see a patient it was her duty to accompany him, like a proper nurse.

However, the biggest advantage was the men themselves. During the day there was never time to sit and talk to them. Sister would have had apoplexy had she seen her doing so. Rowan had always regretted this, and even more so in the last month. The number of patients and the speed at which they were treated meant that they were quickly back at the front. No sooner had the soldiers arrived than they left to make room for others. She barely knew them and they certainly didn't know her.

The nights, however, were different for she had that valuable commodity – time. There were men who, during the day, showed great courage and never complained. Those who met them acknowledged their pluck – it was a rare person who thought that they, in similar circumstances, would be as brave. But at night those men changed. Maybe darkness freed them to cry out and admit their pain, their fears. Many would confess to her how afraid they had been, what cowards they were, how guilty they felt that they were alive when their friends had died. She would sit on their beds, hold their hands and listen. They spoke about their hatred of war, the pitilessness they had witnessed. They confessed how they dreaded returning to the battlefield. Sometimes they told her of their sweethearts, of their dreams for the future. At others they wept because they felt they had no future, that the war would always be with them.

For Rowan the worst was when one of the men, without warning, would suddenly begin to tremble, then quake violently. Others went into cataclysmic shaking. Their beds rattled so noisily that others woke. Some shouted at them to be quiet, which only added to their distress. There was little she could do but sit beside them and talk softly to them, trying to calm them. But she soon learnt that nothing could stop the fearful tremors and that patience was the only thing she could offer them.

Sometimes the nights were disturbed by shouts and screams as the soldiers relived their experiences in hideous nightmares. Then they would sit upright their faces distorted with fear. She, a mere slip of a girl, would hold them, comfort and reassure them that *she* would keep them safe.

She knew she was growing up fast, too fast. But she took pride in this and knew that what she did was important, that she was helping the men in ways that could not be quantified but were very real.

Mercifully she was kept so busy that she was able to forget, if temporarily, her own problems.

One morning, off duty, she had gone in search of Hannah. She was not sure if her idea might be regarded as presumption but she knew she was right and that the well-being of the men was more important than how Hannah thought of her.

'Miss Cresswell, if I might make a suggestion?' she said, once the greetings were over and she had reassured Hannah that she enjoyed working at night. 'I've been thinking that perhaps the men should be divided into different rooms.'

'Different rooms?' Hannah sat down at her desk, her interest apparent.

'Yes. Some have the most dreadful nightmares and they are liable to shout and scream. There are those who are so shocked that their beds rattle. The noise can be quite deafening and they wake others, who become angry.'

'I often have to deal with complaints of noise when I do my daily round. It's a difficult situation.'

'You see, Miss Cresswell, the noise is getting louder because, I think, the fighting is worse and the damage to their poor minds increases.'

'So you suggest we segregate them into one of the other bedrooms. I'm not sure if my brother would approve ...' while Hannah wondered what Sir Mortie would think, Rowan stood with her hands folded in front of her clean white apron, her lovely face serious as she waited for Hannah's decision.

'How thoughtful of you, Rowan. It's a very sensible suggestion. After all, we don't want those who are nearly recovered to be set back by lack of sleep. I shall discuss it with Major Fellowes. You realize that he must be consulted on any decision about the patients?'

'There's something else. It seems to me that the nightmares the men suffer aren't taken seriously enough, Miss Cresswell. I've checked back and there's no record of them in the night nurses' reports. I think it is something that needs observation and perhaps they could be treated in some way.' She sounded vague for she had no idea what could be done and she was surprised by her temerity in speaking out. She hadn't intended to raise this last point.

'I agree. I wonder why nothing *is* done. It sounds as if they need a strong sleeping draught.' Hannah made a note on her pad. 'Tell me, have you discussed this with Sister Westall?'

'No, I haven't.'

'I think you should have, don't you?'

'I thought about mentioning it to her but I felt if I said anything it would be ignored. She doesn't like me.'

'Who could dislike you, Rowan?' Hannah smiled.

Rowan made no response. She thought Hannah was just saying those words and did not mean them. In any case she knew the problems Rowan had with some of the nursing staff. 'I think it would be best if you didn't mention my name to her. You should tell her it was your idea,' she said.

'As you wish. Are you well, my dear? You say you enjoy your night duty, but is it proving too much responsibility for you? You look worried. Is something bothering you? Anything I can help you with?'

'No, thank you. There's nothing.' She was having difficulty in controlling the tears that, these days, were never far from the surface. If she told Hannah that Morts was barely speaking to her, no doubt she would be overjoyed.

'I haven't seen Morts the last couple of days. Is he well?'

'Yes. He has had to go to Exeter.'

'Really? What for?'

Rowan blushed. 'I don't know. He didn't say. Something to do with the Territorials, I expect.'

'How strange.' Hannah was busily scribbling notes when she looked up to find herself alone. Rowan had left. 'Even stranger,' she said aloud, to the empty room.

After luncheon Hannah asked the major to join her in the office. Once she had poured him his usual brandy and soda, which, he assured her, was to aid his digestion, Hannah explained to him, at length, Rowan's suggestions for the patients. 'I think she has a good idea, don't you? She is such a caring girl.'

'In principle, yes, but it may lead to even more bad feeling among the men.'

'How could that be?'

'There are many who think that the dramatic behaviour of some is a sign of weakness. Sister Westall would agree with them. It would be interpreted that they are receiving preferential treatment.'

'I can't believe that. Why, they can't help having nightmares. Nor can they help themselves when they shake uncontrollably.'

'Can't they?'

Hannah leant back in her chair, unable to comprehend what she was hearing, might she have imagined it? 'But only the other day I was walking in the garden with Captain Jones and, without warning, he began to shake in the most alarming manner. He could barely stand. I had to support him and it was most distressing.'

'How convenient for him that you were there to observe it,' he said, as he began painstakingly to fill his pipe.

'But, Frobisher, you can't mean ... You don't think for one minute he was acting?'

'No, I don't say that is certainly the case, but he may be. There are those who would act for their own gain. You must realize that most of the men here would like to be declared unfit to return to active service. Not something I can approve of.'

'I'm sure that Captain Jones had no control whatsoever over his actions,' she said stiltedly. She was still reeling from shock at what he had said.

'You think so?' he asked cynically.

Hannah did not like what she had heard. 'I do,' she replied, as firmly as she could.

'There are many cowards about.' He did not look at her as he said this, intent on tending his pipe. She was becoming aware that he always did that when she disagreed with him.

His lack of sympathy for the men was a revelation to her. She felt deep disappointment in him, and found she was regarding him in a new light.

'If some are noisier than others at night, it would seem logical to put them elsewhere.' She had decided to pursue this idea, for she knew, with building conviction, that he was wrong. 'We could utilize my sister-in-law's sitting room. In fact, the work has already started. Immediately after I had seen Rowan, I ordered that Coral's possessions be packed up and stored for safety.'

'Then why bother me when you have obviously made up your mind?'

'Because I didn't for one minute think you would object.'

'Then you were wrong.'

How self-satisfied he was, she thought, and became even more determined to continue with her plan. 'Perhaps if we say we need another ward because of the overcrowding.' He made no objection. 'And I think it best that we don't mention Rowan's involvement to Sister.'

'Very wise. She would automatically reject the idea if she thought young Rowan was involved. Not the easiest of women, in my opinion.'

'I'm worried about Rowan. I'm sure that something is troubling her.'

'My dear lady, if Rowan wishes you to know she will tell you.'

'Of course you're right, Frobisher.'

My dear lady. Only yesterday she would have grasped those words and held them to her, as she had whenever he had shown her any warmth. But today was different. She was not thrilled.

How could he regard any of those brave men as cowards?

3

'Morts, we cannot continue in this way.' It was eight in the evening and Rowan was dressing in her uniform for she was still working at night. She was holding her chemise to her, looking anxiously at her husband who was lying on the bed where they had just made love. To Rowan, it had been a poor substitute for their normal passion.

'I know.' He put his hands behind his head to prop it up so that he could see her better.

'We had something so wonderful and I feel it is slipping through our fingers. I don't want it to slither away.'

'I know.'

She wished he would stop saying that – it wasn't helping her. 'Is that all you can say?' She bent to pull up her thick, serviceable black stockings. Once, dressing in front of him had been an embarrassment. Now she didn't think anything of it, unless, like now, the atmosphere between them made her remember. She turned her back on him as she felt for her garters.

'The solution is yours,' he said, almost as if the problem was no concern of his, which pained her. It made her think he no longer cared.

Her stockings in place, she slipped on her shoes, lowered her skirts, and as she put on her crisply starched apron, she turned to him. 'Do you want me to leave?' It was hard to say the words and her heart was pounding so hard that the blood was thudding in her ears.

He sat up straight. '*No!* Whatever makes you think that? I need you.'

'It doesn't seem that you do, and that is why I feel you no longer want me here.'

'I love you, but I'm angry. You know why. The solution to this problem between us remains with you.'

She sighed. 'I love you too,' she said, her voice heavy with sadness and longing.

She left him. They were going round in circles and would continue to do so with no answer in sight.

Two hours later, nearing ten, Whitaker appeared on the ward. It was unusual for any of the household staff to venture there. The two sides of the household kept very much to their own parts of the house. He tiptoed up to the desk where she sat, the lamp shaded by a cloth draped over it. 'I'm sorry to bother you, Mrs Morts, but Lady Cresswell wishes to see you immediately.'

'Impossible, Mr Whitaker. I can't leave the patients.'

'But her ladyship was adamant.'

'Did you not explain to her that I cannot desert my post? I have a particularly restless officer whom the doctor is worried about.'

'I did, Mrs Morts, but unfortunately her ladyship was in no mood to listen to me. I took the liberty of suggesting that her nurse replace you temporarily but Nurse Winlock insists she must finish her hot chocolate first.'

'I'll wait for her.'

Whitaker was agitated. 'Her ladyship cannot be left, Mrs Morts, not for a minute. Nurse Winlock was adamant.'

'Thank you, Mr Whitaker, I understand,' she said, though she did not. Who was more vulnerable? The captain or the old lady? 'I doubt that five minutes will harm her. I'll leave instructions for Nurse Winlock with the new young VAD. She will then know what to do.' As she spoke, she did not notice her new confidence. A few weeks ago she would have deferred to the VAD, no matter how inexperienced she was, not the other way round.

As she had expected, the new girl, Beryl, made a fuss at being left alone, if only for a few minutes, and she couldn't blame her. This was her first night duty, working with Rowan – an influx of wounded had meant she needed help – and Rowan knew how frightening the ward could be at night. She steeled her heart to Beryl's tearful pleas. When Penelope Cresswell ordered, everyone jumped.

As she raced along the dimly lit corridor she thought how ridiculous it was that Lady Cresswell had a trained nurse to care for her while the officers were left to the tender mercies of orderlies such as her. Still, she thought, that was what wealth made possible. It was unfair but then, she was learning, so much was.

Nurse Winlock, new to the position, was waiting in the sitting room for her. 'I hope you have better luck with the old trout than I have. A more difficult patient it would be hard to find.'

'She can be truculent,' said Rowan, and hid a smile. Winlock had no idea who she was. She felt proud to have used the new word she had learnt – *truculent*.

'At least I shall be able to do some proper nursing tonight.'

'We've twenty-eight men, and I'm particularly worried about Captain Hilbert. His wound is giving him much pain, and it's infected so he has a fever. There's a brigadier in the blue bedroom, and four are restless, suffering from shock. They need comforting.'

'Comforting! Backbone, more like.' And with that she bustled off. Such callousness made Rowan worry for her soldiers, but she knocked on the door, pushed it open and entered the overheated, musty-smelling room.

'You took your time getting here.' Lady Cresswell was slumped on her pillows, neither sitting up nor lying down.

'I came as quickly as I could. I have responsibility to others, you know. We *are* very busy.'

'And I don't matter?' Penelope Cresswell looked tearful.

Rowan doubted it was genuine. 'Of course you do. I came, didn't I?' Rowan picked up several books that lay on the floor and a handful of discarded handkerchiefs. It was as if a child had dropped them. She crossed the room and opened a window.

'I shall get a chill,' the patient complained.

'No, you won't. It's stuffy in here.' She resisted the temptation to add that the room smelt of old ladies, which it did. 'Let's get you up the bed a bit.' She entwined her arm in one of Lady Cresswell's and, holding the head of the bed with the other, hauled at the woman, who remained in the same position. 'You'll have to help. Push your heels in hard.'

'I can't.'

'Of course you can.'

As it had in the past, her no-nonsense approach worked and, with much huffing and puffing on both sides, she was able to get the old lady into a more comfortable position. Once she had shaken her pillows and rearranged them, Penelope lay back with a contented sigh. 'You see why I had to call for you? You're the only one who can make me comfortable.'

'That's not true.' Rowan was smoothing the bedcover. The clock on the side table chimed the half-hour. The night was speeding past and she had hardly scratched the surface of her duties.

'Winlock will have to go. She's too rough for one as sensitive as I am.'

'How can you even think such a thing? It took Miss Cresswell weeks to find her. You've no idea how fortunate you are to have a trained nurse. We'd give anything to have her on the wards.'

Penelope regarded her slyly. 'That's exactly what I've been thinking. The men should have the advantage of a proper nurse, and since you aren't one you could care for me and she for the men.' She was smiling broadly now, evidently delighted with her own cleverness.

'I wouldn't want to do that. I'm happy working with the officers.'

'So you would not be happy caring for me?'

'Yes.'

'You're very rude.'

'No, I'm being honest.'

'People say they're honest simply to disguise their rudeness.'

'Perhaps they do. But I spoke the truth. I don't want to look after you because I like you ...'

'Do you?' Penelope sounded surprised.

'Yes. But if I looked after you all the time you would annoy me and I might end up not liking you.'

Penelope banged her hand on the counterpane, threw back her head and laughed. Rowan did not join in. She had little to laugh about, these days. 'Oh, I like you so very much, Rowan. You're like a breath of fresh air to me. How did I manage before you came into my life? I get so lonely ...' The tears in her eyes were genuine this time, but so were those in Rowan's as she was reminded of her own present loneliness. 'My dear, what is it? Why are you so sad? What has happened? Is it Morts?'

At the mention of his name tears rolled down Rowan's cheeks. She brushed them away, but still they fell. She nodded. Penelope patted the bed. 'Tell me.'

'I can't.'

'Of course you can, and if you won't I shall summon Morts and get to the bottom of this.'

It took time since the secrets were firmly bottled and she chose her words carefully so that she made no betrayal of Esmeralda.

'Now, have I understood correctly? You have a friend who has sworn you to total secrecy, and Morts is suspicious, demanding you expose your friend. Well, I *am* surprised. You should be commended for your steadfastness, not made so miserable. Really! The stupid boy!'

'He's not!' Rowan jumped to Morts's defence. 'He's hurt.'

Penelope needed a chocolate to help her think. Rowan found the box amid the muddle on the night table. It took two before Penelope was able to proclaim the obvious. 'This is your friend's fault. I presume it's a woman. Only women make such stupid stipulations. Those who demand secrecy over a confidence are selfish. They do not think of the consequences to the other person. You must go and see your friend and ask – no, you must *demand* that she sees Morts and explains everything to him. Threaten her with exposure, if necessary. This is so unfair.'

'She won't do that.'

'Then, in my opinion, you can tell him yourself.'

'I couldn't.'

Penelope shrugged her massive shoulders. 'So you will have to resign yourself to a petulant husband and, on second thoughts, I cannot blame him. The poor boy has, no doubt, been thinking the worst ... Of course, there is another solution. You make up a story about this friend. Palm him off with that.'

'But then I would be lying.'

'My dear Rowan, you have too many principles for your own good.'

For the rest of the night Rowan thought of little else. Once she was back on the ward, racing hither and thither, busier even than usual, she was still mulling over what Lady Cresswell had said. It affected her concentration so badly that she nearly gave the wrong medicine to the wrong officer. And she woke one poor man twice to give him his. He was not grateful.

Once work was finished and she had taken a hurried breakfast, she threw on her cape and made for the stables where she asked for the governess cart to be harnessed. She climbed into the little yellow carriage and picked up the reins, feeling rather sick. She had never driven a pony before. She had ridden in traps and observed, though, so perhaps she knew enough to get by. She need not have been afraid – the pony knew exactly what to do and she had only to hold the reins lightly for him to go where she wanted.

Soon she was sitting in the hall at Lees Court, waiting to see Esmeralda and praying that Oliver would not appear. What would she do if Esmeralda refused to help? She couldn't imagine betraying her ...

Eventually she was shown into the boudoir where Esmeralda was drinking tea, still in her peignoir, and Bridget was brushing her hair.

'Dear Rowan, how smart you look in your uniform. Come, sit with me. Bridget, a chair for Mrs Morts. And something to refresh you?' Esmeralda sounded strained.

'No, thank you.' She slipped her cape off her shoulders. 'I need to talk to you, Esmeralda.'

'It must be important for you to call so early. After eleven would be a better time to come, my dear.' She laughed a shade nervously. 'And you should have visiting cards. Has no one told you?'

After all that had happened, Esmeralda was worried about etiquette! Rowan felt like leaving. How could her friend criticize her – in front of her maid too? 'I have to sleep later this morning. I've been working all night.' Her voice showed her irritation.

'Of course. Silly me. You were saying?'

'I must speak to you in private.'

'Bridget is the soul of discretion and knows everything about me.' It was almost, Rowan thought, as if Esmeralda didn't want to be alone with her. Perhaps she was afraid of what Rowan would say.

Bridget continued brushing the long dark hair.

'It was Lady Penelope suggested I come to you. I will continue, if you wish.' Rowan felt uncomfortable. She was virtually threatening Esmeralda, who, she could see, had blanched.

'Well, perhaps it would be better if you left us, Bridget, since Mrs Morts is so insistent.'

As soon as the maid had left, Esmeralda grabbed Rowan's wrist. 'You've been talking about me to that old crow?'

'Yes.'

'How could you? I never imagined you would betray me.' Esmeralda began to cry, but Rowan ignored the tears.

'I haven't. I referred to a friend. And you're hurting my arm.'

'You told her the circumstances?' She let go of Rowan's wrist and fell to pleating the fabric of her *négligée*, stroking her hair or rearranging the objects on her dressing-table.

'Of course not. I'm here because I need your help ...' She knew she was close to tears.

'Oh, my darling, you should have explained. I'll always help you, you know I will.' Esmeralda bestowed her lovely smile on Rowan.

'You must explain something to Morts.'

'I can't do that! He'd tell Oliver!'

'He thinks you're having an assignation and threatens to talk to your husband. But the real reason I'm here is because I am in despair. He's so angry with me that he barely speaks to me. I fear our marriage is damaged and will never be the same.'

'Well, I don't know what I can do. I can't tell him *all*, can I? It's not my fault if he's cross with you.'

'Of course it's your fault. Every day he insists I tell him.'

'You shouldn't have told him we had a secret.'

'I had no choice. He feels that my loyalty should be to him, not to you.'

'What a grumpy young man he is.'

'He's honourable and expects it in others.'

'Then he should congratulate you on being so resolute in your loyalty to me.'

'I haven't come here to argue with you, Esmeralda, but to ask for your assistance. If you refuse it, my obligation to you is at an end and I shall tell Morts all I know.'

'You can't! You promised!' Esmeralda shrieked.

'I know I did. But I never asked to be told your awful secret. You made me listen. And my marriage is more important to me than anything else.' She stood up and put on her cape. 'It's for you to decide. I shall give you until tomorrow afternoon. I'm sorry, but I have no choice, and I am even sorrier that this, no doubt, means the end of our friendship for I have enjoyed your company and appreciated your advice.'

With that she swung on her heel, and, although she could hear Esmeralda calling her, marched out of the room and the house.

4

'Rowan, wake up!'

She opened her eyes to see Esmeralda beside her bed. Immediately she was wide awake and sat up.

'Put on your clothes and come with me,' Esmeralda said, in a dramatic whisper.

'Have you spoken to Morts yet?'

'No. I've been waiting in the drawing room for you. Then I came to find you.'

'But I was asleep.'

'Lazybones …'

Rowan felt a jolt of annoyance but knew there was little point in showing it. She pushed back the covers and began to get up. 'I have to sleep in the day since I work all night,' she said patiently, as if she were speaking to a child. She washed and put on her uniform, chivvied all the while by Esmeralda, who was roaming the room, picking up the objects in it to inspect them.

They had reached the hall as Hannah appeared with a sheaf of papers, looking even more harassed than usual. Once the flurry of kisses was over, Hannah said, 'I know you should be asleep, Rowan, my dear, and please forgive me, but there has been a crisis. One of the lieutenants has collapsed and half of the staff are indisposed, it seems. Would you see if you can help?'

Rowan looked at Esmeralda, not sure what to do.

'You can't ask that of her, Hannah. I need her.'

'Not as desperately as the men on the ward. I'm sorry, Esmeralda.' Hannah spoke sharply.

'I'll go immediately.' In a way Rowan was relieved that she wouldn't be with Esmeralda when she confessed her secret to Morts. She didn't want to see the horror on his face, the worry that would surely follow.

The next three hours passed in a blur for Hannah had not exaggerated. They were frantic with work on the ward. Sadly the young lieutenant died. The doctor had done everything he could for him but could not save him. His face purple, the young man had shouted and screamed, his body twisting in agony.

Later, Rowan washed him, her tears mingling with the water. She wept for him but also for all the other young men she had helped and those she had not whose lives had been so cruelly taken. The lieutenant's face was serene now, which made her sob harder.

'Now, Cresswell, this is not the sort of behaviour I expect.' Sister Westall had come in behind her. 'Pull yourself together. You'll upset the patients.'

'Yes, Sister.'

Each death affected the other men, but in this case the lieutenant had been on the mend after an operation on his leg. He had been due to go home next week before he was sent back to the front. Apparently he had been standing talking to a friend when he had collapsed, writhing, his face turning from pink to puce, then purple, verging on black.

'Was it his heart, sir?' his friend had asked the doctor.

'I fear not. More likely a blockage in his lungs.' The doctor had hurried from the ward, as he always did, Rowan had noticed, when one of his patients died.

Tenderly she dressed the lieutenant in pyjamas. She always thought they made the men look childlike and vulnerable. When she had finished she left the screens round the bed, and hauled others round the beds that were occupied. Quietly she requested that those men who were up and about should go outside or into the games room so they would not witness the body being taken away. It was odd, she thought, the way they protected them from death when they had come from a place where hideous death was commonplace. Once the ward was ready, she reported to Sister that the men could come to remove the body, then went to the sluice room. There she allowed herself to cry properly, for herself and the muddle she was in, as well as the dead man.

From there she heard the trundle and the squeaking wheel of the mortuary trolley – somebody should see to that. It wasn't right that its presence should be made so obvious. It was an ordinary trolley but Rob Robertson had made a cover for it, of purple felt with a large gold cross. It gave a measure of dignity to the body. From the ward it would be transferred to a tack room by the stables, which Hannah had had whitewashed. She had hung purple velvet on the walls and lit it with oil lamps. Flowers stood on a makeshift altar and the incense sticks would be smouldering. Despite that, though, Rowan could still smell polish, leather and horses.

It was another hour before Rowan could leave the ward. She felt so tired, and the chiming of the stables clock told her that, if she was lucky, she might get three hours' sleep. On the top landing she met Whitaker, who was bringing her a message from Lady Cresswell.

'Mr Whitaker, I can't see her. I simply have to sleep.' The butler's face bore a pained expression. 'I'm sorry. Tell her I'll see her during my break tonight.' She wondered if she would get one, and if she would find the energy to sit with Penelope.

When she reached her room she threw herself on to the bed without bothering to undress. As she lay waiting for sleep she thought over the day. She had not minded working the extra hours, she was glad to be of help, but she resented Esmeralda's and Lady Penelope's cavalier attitude towards her. Did neither of them realize that she might need to sleep?

Perhaps they felt it didn't matter if she was woken early. They really were selfish, free to disturb her because she had once been their servant. She hoped she would never become so thoughtless.

It was dark, and she was sure the door opening had woken her. 'Is there anyone there?' she called.

'Sorry. I didn't want to wake you. I'd just popped in to see if you were still sleeping.' It was Morts.

'What's the time?'

'Nine. You've missed your supper.'

'Why wasn't I woken? I shall be in such trouble!'

'No, you won't. You've been given the night off. Aunt Hannah had a word with Sister and arranged it. Then, to make matters even better, Fanny Petty returned to work this evening.'

Rowan flopped back on the bed with relief. 'How wonderful. I think I could sleep for days.' She moved over so that Morts could sit on the bed beside her.

He caressed her face. 'I saw Esmeralda.'

'Did you?' She knew she sounded guarded.

'You are a silly goose, causing all those problems for such an unimportant matter.'

'Am I?'

'Yes. Esmeralda told me she asked you not to tell as a joke. She never thought you'd safeguard her confidence to the extent that it would cause all this trouble.'

Rowan sat up. 'Did she?'

'The matter of her father was unimportant. My uncle knows she steals away to Barlton to visit him. He thinks it perfectly natural she should want to see her father. He told me so years ago.'

'Did he?'

Morts stood up and began to pace the room. They were interrupted by a tap at the door. A maid entered with a tray. When Rowan saw the bowl of soup and the glistening omelette, she realized she was very hungry. Once the maid had left them she set to with enthusiasm.

'As for the money, I shan't even bother to tell Oliver. That's what women do, isn't it?'

'What exactly?'

'Run up fearful dressmaking bills.' He was laughing as he told her. She tried to join in but found it difficult. She had not known what she had expected Esmeralda to say to him. She supposed she had hoped she would tell the truth and, in so doing, share her burden with him. In retrospect, that had been stupid. It would have put Morts into an even worse position than herself. After all, he was related to Oliver.

'Let me take that dismal dress off you ...' His voice was thick with longing. 'When we have finished, you must put on one of your new dresses. That is, if we bother to get up!'

Everything was as it had once been, but as Rowan lay in the dark after they had made love, listening to his rhythmic breathing, she realized he had not said he was sorry for being so cross with her over nothing. The sadness crept back.

That which had been perfect was now damaged. It was as if a crack had appeared in the lovely façade of their love and she feared it would never be mended.

5

For once Esmeralda was relaxed. She had not been so happy for some time. She felt as if everything had been resolved – and yet it wasn't. For the first time she had lied about her intolerable predicament – she did not count the frequent lies she told her husband. She thought of them as 'white lies' and chose to ignore the potentially enormous deception – the baby.

To her surprise she had found 'fibbing' to Morts easy. He hadn't looked the least bit suspicious, even though she was sure he must have been able to hear her heart thudding. He had accepted her explanation without the merest sign of disbelief. He had even laughed at the silliness of it all and she had joined in.

Of course, it had been much easier for her without Rowan present. When Rowan had been called away she had been distressed, but had soon realized it was the best thing that could have happened. As Rowan knew the truth, it would have been harder for Esmeralda to spin her tale in front of her. She would have been sure to throw her disapproving looks as she often did. She wondered if Rowan was aware of it and if, perhaps, she should have a word with her. After all, who is Rowan, a former housemaid, to disapprove of me? She looked at herself in the mirror. What an ignoble thought. Rowan had been loyal to her.

Esmeralda felt as if she had emerged from a dense forest – she had been lost in the dark and come into the light. It was as if a huge shadow had floated away and she was happy again, perhaps not as happy as she had been before but better than she had been since the … She picked up a powder-puff, shuddering. She was unable even to think the word. However, she knew she had gained strength from her awful experience. She had resolved never to tell anyone *ever* again of what had befallen her – Rowan had made such a dreadful fuss. She knew now it had been silly even to contemplate telling Oliver. What purpose would it serve? At last the decision that had haunted her was taken. Rowan had forced her hand.

With the matter determined, she found she had more energy than she had had for months and she made plans to change how she lived.

She *must not* allow the past to dictate the present. It was destructive.

She *must* make friends with her father again. Now that she was calmer, she was ashamed that she could have thought he had been involved with Petroc and the attack – she shuddered again. Her father adored her, he always had, and now she had Marigold she could better understand that love.

She *must* find the courage to speak to Oliver of her feeling for her father.

Perhaps most important of all she *must* rid herself of the feelings of inadequacy and failure that had plagued her for years. She *must* stop being intimidated by her staff. She was beginning to grasp that all this had been caused and nurtured by the knowledge that she came from the wrong stratum of society. No matter what she did, her husband's family would never accept her; her servants would always know. Since there was nothing she could do about who she was, she must cease worrying about what they thought of her. It was another subject she *must* discuss with Oliver.

She made a list of these topics. Writing them down made her feel she was more likely to do something about them. They became less airy thoughts and more real.

'I've never heard such nonsense,' Oliver declared, as they sat at the dinner table, the servants having been dismissed. 'My family are very fond of you – especially Hannah.'

'I expected you to say that. And I like to think Hannah is not in-cluded – though I fear she thinks me rather silly at times, which I am, it is true. But your mother and sister-in-law have never fully accepted me.'

He laughed, which she did not like. He was not taking her seriously. 'I wouldn't let their opinions bother you. Mother approves of no one and

Coral is the most crashing snob I've ever met. She thinks anyone who lacks a title is beneath her.'

'You don't have one and she's always nice to you.'

'But I am a man. It is for women that she saves the greatest opprobrium.' She did not mind his laugh this time. He might have been right. Coral was invariably more cutting with her own sex.

'I fear for poor Rowan if Coral comes here.'

'She won't. She's too fond of her life in London.'

'But someone was telling me that the zeppelin raids are becoming worse, which must frighten her.'

'The Germans wouldn't dare bomb Coral.' He laughed at his own joke. 'If they go anywhere it will be to her father's estate, which is far grander than Cresswell. But you're right about Rowan. She has to deal with real condemnation.'

'Your mother likes her.'

'Does she? How surprising.'

'Isn't it? I think it's because Rowan isn't afraid of her, or so her maid told me. She stands up to her when the rest of us have always quaked. Who'd have thought it of little Rowan?'

'If she gets all the Cresswell jewellery, Coral will like her even less.'

'What a horrible idea.'

'Not really. It might happen.' He crossed the room and kissed the tip of her nose. She liked it when he did that. 'But, my dear Esmeralda, you should not be so fearful. You're a great heiress and there is nothing society likes more than the very rich in its midst.'

'You're horrible and cynical too,' she teased him. She looked at her fine hands, wondering if this might be the right moment. 'I've been thinking about Papa. He is getting so old ...'

'He can't be much more than fifty-four!' He laughed again.

'So much time has passed. He would like to know Marigold and to see more of me.'

'You are suggesting?'

'That we – or, rather, I – should see more of him.'

'What? More than you have in the past?' He grinned at her and she panicked, wondering if he knew she had lied about how often she saw him.

'I hardly visit him, these days.'

'I know, and I've been wondering why. Have you two fallen out?'

'Good gracious, what a ridiculous notion. Of course not.' What did Oliver know? She felt her new confidence seeping away.

'Are you all right, my love? You're suddenly pale.'

'It must be the light.' She dabbed her forehead with her handkerchief. 'As you say I am an heiress – frivolous little me!' She made herself laugh. 'And when Papa dies everything will be mine and the land you argued about will come back to you. It seems so stupid to continue the feud over a few acres.'

'Near enough a thousand. And I don't think it was just the land. Your father was always jealous of me.'

'Papa jealous? I never heard such an absurd thing.' She laughed and at last she wasn't pretending. That laugh was genuine. 'You must understand what I mean. As I get older I feel guilty about him … And there's Marigold …'

He sat for some time gazing into the distance, frowning. Then stood up and walked to the window, which overlooked his grounds. 'Very well. You may invite him to dinner. I shall welcome him.'

Esmeralda rushed across the room and hurled herself into his arms, raining kisses on him until he was laughing and pushing her away in mock-horror.

'And, no doubt you're missing the money he used to give you secretly.' He kissed the tip of her nose again.

She felt the blood drain from her face. What else did he know?

Before she had determined to change her ways, Esmeralda would have worried about her husband's words, but this time she didn't. Instead she evaluated the scene: Oliver had been smiling, he had kissed her as if he was teasing her, and that night they had made love. She put the incident behind her and concentrated on her list of changes.

She began by taking more interest in her house. She made plans to redecorate her suite. She annoyed Mrs Fuller by insisting on doing an inventory of the linen; the housekeeper, unfortunately, took this as a criticism and Esmeralda, to her astonishment, heard herself telling the woman not to be so sensitive. In contrast, the cook was overjoyed to have her showing more interest in the kitchen.

Esmeralda decided she must take on more responsibilities, given her position in society. She would do more charitable things. At the outbreak of war she had planned to start a knitting and sewing bee but her initial enthusiasm had faded. Now she resurrected the group, even though it meant learning to knit, and wrote to all those she thought might join.

What was more, she promised herself she would learn to paint and would practise the piano every day. All this activity, she found, made her much happier and more content.

Her father accepted the invitation to dine and arrived as she had known he would, laden with presents for her and Marigold.

'Papa, you shouldn't!'

'You know you don't mean that,' he said. 'How disappointed you would have been if I'd come with nothing.'

His excitement at being welcomed back was touching to see. He and her husband shook hands and were coldly civil to each other, so it was not the easiest of evenings, but Esmeralda tried valiantly to keep the conversation alive. Still, she hoped the next time would be better and that gradually they would warm to each other. Despite the coolness, though, the occasion passed without a cross word and with no reference to any land which had been one of the causes of their arguing. As for herself, with her new-found happiness, she felt complete with the three to love.

She enjoyed the sewing and knitting bee more than she had expected. She liked the harmless gossip and chat that accompanied its sessions, and was proud that the women were so keen to attend. Why, Sorrel Plunkett went to all the trouble of travelling from Cresswell to be there. Such a charming woman, she thought.

From doing good works she found she was making new friends. She had already made several calls, which had been returned.

She was now involved in a far more active way with the estate school. She enjoyed being with the children so much that she could not imagine why she hadn't bothered to do so before.

When she thought about it, her life had improved immeasurably and all because she had told Morts a few little fibs.

The day was hot and Esmeralda had ordered tea to be served beneath the cedar and that Marigold be brought down to join her. She arranged a parasol so that the child was shaded from the sun, and watched, a tender smile on her face, as her chubby little girl kicked and cooed on the rug. She had dismissed the nanny, preferring to enjoy this time alone with her child.

Blossom, the Pekinese, was snuffling happily in the nearby grass when she suddenly whined. 'Blossom,' Esmeralda called, but the little dog was racing for the house, her tail firmly between her legs, as if she was being chased by demons.

'Such a pretty picture you make, dear Esmeralda.'

Esmeralda needed to shade her eyes to see the man standing before her. She feared she recognized the voice. 'Petroc!' was all she said, but she began agitatedly to fan herself.

'Did I make you jump? Forgive me.' He sank on to the rug beside Marigold. 'What a delightful child – but, then, you would have a beauty, wouldn't you?'

'Don't touch her,' she almost shouted.

'Why not? I would never harm her.'

'I want you gone.'

'But I've only just arrived.' He was smiling in a self-satisfied way that enraged her. Languidly, he helped himself to a cucumber sandwich. 'I hope you don't mind.' He waved it in the air. 'Why do you want me gone? I thought you would be pleased to see an old friend.'

'You know why. How dare you come here disturbing me? Creeping up on me like the evil man you are.' At least she was reacting with spirit this time, not fainting as she had last time. She felt quite pleased with herself. She stilled the fanning, sat upright and stared at him. It would be weak and, she sensed, dangerous for her to show him she was afraid.

He laughed, slapping his thigh. 'So, you think I'm evil. I don't. The last time I saw you, you fainted. Now you look like a frightened doe – I find it charming.' He took another sandwich. She watched as he ate it, noticing that the stuff of his suit was shiny and misshapen. His appearance put her on her guard.

'So, how old is the child?'

'A year.'

His insufferable laugh rang out. 'As a mere male I cannot claim to be an expert on babies, but I would lay a wager it's more like nine months. And if you add another nine months, why, I do believe ...' He stuffed the sandwich whole into his mouth and gave her a smile that, chillingly, was not reflected in his eyes.

'My husband will be joining me shortly.' It was a miracle she could speak at all, her heart was pounding at such a rate.

'Then why is there only one cup?'

'He does not drink tea.'

'You lie. He is not here. I watched him leave – and such a fine motor he has. You don't think I'm stupid enough to risk meeting him when there has been such passion between us?'

'You violated me.'

'You wanted me to.'

'How can you say so?'

114

'Because it is the truth and, no doubt, you hoped I would impregnate you since your husband had failed so dismally. Isn't that so?'

Esmeralda stood. 'Go.' Perhaps it was the alarm in her voice but Marigold, who had been content, began to cry.

'Not yet.'

As she bent to pick up the baby he grabbed her wrist and twisted it painfully, making her yelp. 'Not so fast, my dear. We have matters to discuss.'

'I have nothing to say to you ... Let go – you're hurting me.'

'But you like pain. I saw it in your eyes at Buxton. And I have plenty to say to you. Unless you give me two hundred pounds – I have some pressing bills – I shall talk to your husband about you.' At no point was his voice raised. He spoke in a normal tone as if he was having an ordinary conversation. It was unnerving.

'He would kill you.'

'I very much doubt it. A cold fish, your husband, with his penchant for vicars' wives.'

'You are insufferable. That was years ago.'

'Was it?' He studied his nails. Her wrist now free, Esmeralda scrambled to her feet. With one bound he was standing beside her.

'This is blackmail.'

'Unfortunately for you, yes, it is.'

'I don't have that amount of money.'

'Not on your person. I didn't expect you would. But I'm sure you have access to it.'

How could he be behaving in such an atrocious manner and still smile? 'I don't.'

'My dear Mrs Cresswell, I am sure you do. Otherwise ... I warn you I have every intention of ... How shall I put it? Spilling the beans. Such a shame for poor Marigold to be labelled a bastard. She'd never marry well, would she?'

All courage had seeped away from her. 'Please,' she begged, tears tumbling.

'You cry so prettily.'

'But if I give you this money, how will I know that you won't come back for more?'

'You will not. And I probably shall. I've always thought it unfair that some have so much when others have little. Much better that you share yours with an old friend. And you'd be protecting little Marigold from scandal, wouldn't you?'

'How do you know her name?' With a shock she realized she had not mentioned it.

'I make it my business to know many things. Now. I suggest you get this money, place it in a black bag and leave it here – you can trust these people.' He handed her a slip of paper on which was written an address in Barlton.

'I will get you the money—'

'Good girl.'

'But I will not leave it with a third party. They would soon be black-mailing me, too.'

'Clever. I didn't think that would occur to you. Very well. Where do you suggest?'

She thought for a minute. 'There's an empty house on the back drive – the North Gate, as it's called. I'll meet you there in three days' time – it will take me that long to raise so much money.' She felt oddly calm now and in control.

'At night? So much more exciting.'

'At noon.'

'If you're thinking of playing any tricks, don't. If you betray me and come with others, I shall kill your child. Is that understood?'

Since she was holding Marigold it took all her will-power not to collapse at this threat. She had no doubt he meant what he said. But as he strode back across the lawn towards the drive, Esmeralda had to sit down to prevent herself falling.

6

Everything had been so right and now everything was so wrong.

'You don't seem to have been listening to me,' Oliver said, across the dining-table.

'I'm so sorry. You were saying?' Esmeralda feared she must look guilty.

'The North Gate house …'

It was almost as if the glass of wine had tipped itself over. She had no recollection of her hand moving towards it but it must have. Hurriedly she stood, ineffectually dabbing at the winestain creeping across the highly polished table.

'I'll ring for Milner. Sit down – you're making it worse.'

Unusually for her, since she normally had perfect posture, Esmeralda slumped in her chair while the servants rearranged her place setting. This gave her time to think but not, unfortunately, to come up with an explanation that might satisfy her husband. Was it her imagination that he was looking at her with suspicion?

'There, that's better. Now, perhaps, we can finish our dinner and you can explain why you're so edgy, my love.'

Esmeralda put her hand to her head as if warding off a headache. 'I don't know what's wrong with me. I feel shivery ...' To justify the words she shook herself. 'Perhaps I've caught a chill. The breeze this afternoon was cool ...' She stood up. 'If you will excuse me, I shall retire.'

'Perhaps that would be for the best. I'll sleep in the dressing room so I don't disturb you.'

Esmeralda fled up the stairs towards the sanctuary of her room. There, she upset Bridget by snapping at her, but found she couldn't apologize because her irritation was worsening. Alone at last, she lay on her bed wanting to scream with frustration and anger. At one point she hid her head under the pillow in case she did. Her moods were like quicksilver as she moved from anger to self-pity to fear, then back again as she fretted the night away.

In the morning, if anything, she was worse. Not only did she feel sick with apprehension but her hands were shaking. Bridget was silent and resentful as she attended to her. Esmeralda delayed as long as possible so that she would avoid seeing Oliver – she couldn't face him in such a state. She went to visit Marigold and held the child so tightly that she made her cry and had to flee the nursery in case she broke down in front of the nanny.

In the middle of the night, when her fears were at their peak, she'd been thinking about Marigold when she realized, to her horror, that she resented her baby – everything had been all right until she was conceived. The idea had appalled her – the child was her life, how could she think of her so?

From worrying about this she began to mull over what Petroc had meant when he had said that Oliver liked vicars' wives. It had been spiteful of him. Oliver's unfortunate liaison had happened years before they were married, and the only one they knew now was Sorrel Plunkett, whom Oliver had met only once. There was no doubt that Petroc was an evil man.

She refused breakfast, and after Oliver had departed on his early-morning inspection of the estate she ordered the trap to be harnessed.

It would have been quicker to ride but, these days, she was not fit enough.

She was annoyed to have to wait for the trap to be made ready.

'I'm sorry, ma'am.' The coachman was flustered.

'I ordered it an hour ago.'

'I haven't the men, ma'am.'

'Then employ more.' She was jigging from foot to foot with impatience.

'There are none, ma'am. Most have gone to the war.'

Esmeralda frowned. The war! It added to her difficulties time and time again. She felt as if everything and everyone was conspiring to obstruct her. This morning she had taken a difficult decision and did not want to be left with time to change her mind. As the minutes ticked by she was losing her determination to see this through.

The trap was finally ready. She leapt in, picked up the reins and, with a crack of the whip, began to drive too fast across the park.

Her father was not at home, his butler informed her, and invited her in, but without a word she ran down the steps and climbed back into the trap. She turned towards Barlton even though the pony was already showing signs of exhaustion. She could not give up.

In the small town she had to ask directions to the factory. There, she called to a boy sweeping the yard to care for the pony, giving him money to ensure that he did so. The animal was sweating and she felt guilty.

As she had taken no interest in her father's affairs she had never been to the factory and her father had never suggested she should visit. Now she was astonished by how large and noisy it was. As she entered the building she could feel it vibrate, from the power of the looms, she presumed. The air was full of dust from the wool that made her sneeze. She had to skirt large bales of blankets, all in uniform grey, until she saw a pile of scarlet ones and admired the colour.

She saw an office and entered, to find a clerk sitting at a desk. She had to shout to be heard above the machinery.

'I'm not sure that Mr Eldridge is available.'

She had almost to run to keep up with the man. It was still strange to hear her father referred to as Eldridge. To Esmeralda he'd always been 'von Ehrlich'. She wouldn't have changed her name because it sounded too German. Not that it had seemed to bother him – but, then, it had not been his real name. He'd wanted to make himself sound exotic and mysterious, he'd once told her. Such a card, her father. She was shown into an anteroom while the clerk went to announce her.

'Esmeralda, what a wonderful surprise. I'd hoped one day you would come to see my little enterprise.'

She smiled at his modesty. 'Hardly "little". Papa. How many people work here?'

'More than five hundred. We are having to expand and build more premises.'

'I'm so proud of you, Papa.' She leant forward to kiss him. In her eyes he was an amazing man and, she thought, did not look anywhere near his age – she was unsure exactly how old he was. He was as secretive about that as he was about so many things. She shook away the thought. She did not like to think of his age because it reminded her that one day he would die.

'Are you cold?'

'No, Papa, I am fine.'

'Some tea or chocolate?'

She said she preferred lemonade, and was ushered into his office. With his handkerchief he unnecessarily dusted an immaculate leather chair for her to sit on. She looked about her at the grand surroundings he had created for himself.

'This is a lovely room. Such a fine view.' The large bow window gave on to a wooded meadow with the fast-running river Barl rippling through it. 'And a portrait.' She jumped up the better to inspect it. 'It's a fine likeness.'

'By Dulcie Prestwick's son. You gave me that miniature of yourself he had painted. You should sit for him again, a full-length portrait this time, and perhaps one of Marigold. I shall arrange it. I can't think why your husband hasn't done so already. You must feel rather hurt.'

'How kind of you. He's a fine artist.' She smiled at him, thinking how perceptive he was. That Oliver had not arranged a sitting for her had upset her, not that she had ever mentioned it – but her father knew.

'It makes me happy that you and Oliver are friends again.'

'I fear the word "friend" is something of an exaggeration. However, it is better this way. For you we can manage an hour or two of politeness. Which reminds me, when are you available to dine with me?'

'I meant to speak to you about that. It's most embarrassing but Oliver will not come if Agnes Beatty is there out of loyalty to his sister, Hannah. She treated her so badly before she ran to your protection.'

'Agnes would say the opposite.'

'Then Agnes would be wrong,' she said, with a firmness that surprised her father.

119

'I'm sure you are right. Then she must go. In any case, I have tired of her.' He leant forward conspiratorially. 'She's a nag.'

Esmeralda laughed. Should she feel sorry for Agnes? She wondered for a split second, then decided she need not. 'Though I hope you won't leave her destitute,' she said.

'You are so considerate. Never fear, I shall pension her off. But to what do I owe this honour?'

'It is highly confidential, Papa. I'd rather wait until our refreshments have been brought. I cannot be overheard by anyone.'

They talked of Marigold but Esmeralda was constantly twiddling a loose strand of hair, rearranging her skirt, touching her face, and although she talked to him it was as if she was not really listening to what he was saying.

'Now, tell me, my dear one. What is it that agitates you so?' he said, the minute the maid had left the room. He had issued instructions that he was not to be disturbed under any circumstances.

'I don't know where to begin. But, Papa, I'm so afraid.' She was close to tears.

He pulled up a chair, sat opposite her and took her hand. 'I normally find the beginning is a good place to start,' he said gently.

'Well ...' She took a deep breath and clung to his hand. 'You remember when you and I were in Buxton that you introduced me to your friend Petroc Cornish? Well ...'

With agonizing slowness she told her story. She left nothing out, even though she blushed deeply when she told him of the violation she had endured, and confessed her fears for Marigold's parentage. When she had finished she realized he was crushing her hand in his, yet she felt no pain.

The silence that descended was cloying. She looked anxiously at his face. What did it mean? Was he angry with her? Was he going to throw her out and not help her?

'I will see that he is paid,' he said eventually, but he sounded as if he was having difficulty in speaking.

'I can find the money.'

'The money is unimportant. I have to ensure that this is the one and only time he is paid.'

'He told me he would probably ask for more.'

'Then he will come back until he has bled you dry. If he knows that I am aware of everything, he will not return. The gatehouse on the north drive, you said?'

'But, Papa, you can't go there. You must not. I have to do this alone. He was adamant.'

'Then I don't understand. If you have the money and you are willing to go to this rendezvous on your own, why did you come to me?'

'Because I can no longer live with this dreadful secret, Papa. I had to tell someone – I felt I was going mad. And you are the only person I can trust. Before he came I had been so happy. I thought I could deal with the problem – I was learning to forget my worries. Then he appeared and ruined everything for me – again.'

'Have you told anyone else?'

'No, Papa. Who could I burden with this hideous tale?' She burrowed in her small bag for her handkerchief, giving herself time. This, of course, was not true. Lettice and Rowan knew, and her father was the third person in whom she had confided, but she must not let him know that. She had come because although she could pay Petroc this time she would need her father's wealth if he continued to blackmail her. Was that wrong?

'At least let me accompany you.'

'No, no!' She jumped up in her agitation. 'You must not. He has threatened to harm Marigold if I am not alone. He said he would kill her.'

'This is insupportable.' He stood up and paced the floor, his hands behind his back, deep in thought. 'What sort of monster can threaten the child?' His dark eyes were black with anger.

At the thought of her little girl, Esmeralda wept, dabbing her eyes with her handkerchief. Now she panicked. How stupid she had been! She should have told the nanny to take special care. But if she had, questions would have been asked.

'Do you know where he lodges?'

'I'm not sure I can tell you.' She clutched her bag to her.

'You have his address there?'

'At first he wanted me to go to a house in Barlton to give the money to another but I refused.'

'Very wise. So you are not sure he lodges there?'

'No.'

'Then there is no harm in giving me the address.' He held out his hand. Reluctantly she handed over the slip of paper. He placed it on his desk and sat down. 'Try to calm yourself, my dear. Emotion clouds the judgement. I have evolved a plan and you must listen.'

Esmeralda relaxed. She might have known her father would solve everything for her.

'Very well, I agree you are wise to follow his instructions. You should give him the first payment, but you should not visit him alone. Take your maid with you. After that I will pay him a visit.' He raised his hand to silence her as she opened her mouth to protest. 'I shall offer him a large sum of money to go away and not bother you again. I shall make him sign a confession of his bestial actions. That will protect you. If he returns to bother you I shall go to the police and have him charged.'

'Oh, Papa. You're so clever. I wish I had come to you long ago.'

'I wish you had too. I'm puzzled that you did not.'

She did not respond. She couldn't. She felt uncomfortable under the intensity of his gaze.

'Did you think I had arranged for him to attack you? How could you imagine I would stoop so low? Is that why I've hardly seen you this past year?'

'No, Papa. I would never think that.'

'You need not lie to me, my sweet.'

'I was angry with you for I felt you had arranged that we should meet. And I was angry that you wished to destroy my marriage. Was that wrong?' She looked woebegone.

'Then I will confess. Yes, I planned for you to meet him – he can be charming. A mild flirtation, that was all. You know how I feel about your husband and the way he has taken you from me. His bitterness towards me continues.'

Esmeralda was appalled to hear this but, for the first time ever, she saw her father contrite.

'I cannot apologise enough. It was wrong of me. I know that now. It seemed a harmless game. I wanted to hurt Oliver, not you. Had I any idea ...' He beat the palm of one hand with the fist of the other. 'To think I, of all people, could cause you such pain!' He put out his arms and she rushed into the security of his embrace.

He poured them both a glass of Madeira. 'I think you need this,' he said, proffering the glass.

'What should I do about Marigold, Papa? Should I tell Oliver of my fears?'

He nearly broke his glass as he slammed it on to the desk. 'Are you insane? What would such a confession achieve? Of course you must not tell Oliver anything about this catastrophe.'

Still she was doubtful.

'But in any case, my sweet one, you have nothing to fear. Marigold is Oliver's. The likeness is there for all to see ...'

'You think so? Oh, Papa, you have made me far happier than you realize.'

On the appointed day, the money was safely in a brown envelope – she liked that touch. It was how her father always paid his workers. It was a fine day so she walked to the gatehouse taking Blossom with her and, for security, Nadger, Oliver's gun dog. He would bite anyone who tried to harm her. She had thought about bringing Bridget, too, but had decided against it: she could not risk annoying him.

Her nerves were taut as she approached the empty lodge.

She waited for more than an hour but Petroc did not come.

Chapter Four

Autumn 1915

1

'It's thirsty work, this soldiering is.' Rob Robertson lifted his tankard and downed the cider in one. The bar of the Cresswell Arms was crowded, the men having returned from an enforced twenty-mile march. Dolly watched with a supercilious expression as the men's faces were hidden behind tankards and glasses as they quaffed noisily.

'You can say that again.' Sol Pepper wiped his mouth with the back of his hand, banged down his tankard on the wooden bar and demanded a refill.

'Ever heard the word "please"?' Dolly snapped at her brother, as she replenished his drink. Sol ignored her.

'I've got a bloody great blister,' Fred Robertson complained, slipping off his boot and sock to inspect his heel. Loud but good-natured banter followed, mainly about feet and cheese.

'You know what Mum told us – that we were to soak our feet in potassium pomegranate. A good half-hour steep, her said, toughen 'em up. It's your own fault if you didn't,' Rob lectured his younger brother.

'I couldn't remember what it was her said, what I was supposed to get. Long-fangled word like that, how'm I supposed to remember it? And there ain't much point in putting your feet in fruit, if you asks me. Didn't do yours much good, did it?'

Sol spluttered into his cider, some of which went up his nose. '*Permanganate*! That's what your mum said. T'other's the fruit, you fool.'

'That one what's full of pips?' Dolly asked.

'That's the one,' Sol began to laugh, then Fred joined in, but he was holding his sides, pointing at his brother, incapable of speech. Rob looked from one to the other with a puzzled expression. Then he allowed himself a small laugh that, given his good nature, grew in volume even though he wasn't sure what he was laughing at.

'He's been complaining about the pips getting between his toes,' Fred finally managed.

'Where did you get a pomegranate at this time of year? You don't see them until winter,' Dolly said.

Rob, having twigged what everyone was talking about, was shame-faced as he pointed at Fred. 'The hothouse,' he explained.

'I'd try the chemist in Barlton next time, if I were you. But watch it, them crystals make your feet go brown.'

So much laughing had made them all thirsty again, and a long row of tankards lined up on the bar.

'You shouldn't laugh so much, and then you wouldn't have such a thirst on you,' Dolly said as, rapidly and expertly, she drew the pints.

'Don't stop you taking our pennies, though, do it? Doing you's a favour and no mistake.' Sol Pepper sounded angry, but he invariably was when he spoke to his sister.

'It's more the hard work than the fun, Dolly,' Rob explained, in his serious voice. 'Them marches take it out of a man.'

'You lot don't know what hard work is,' Dolly ventured. 'A gentle stroll through the countryside – call that work?'

'I'll have you know …' Rob began, but then, realizing she might be teasing them, he laughed.

From her position behind the bar, Dolly watched them, pretending to laugh with them, making the odd comment but all the time aware that she was not one of them, that they kept her at a distance. She knew they still missed her mother-in-law, Melanie, and regarded Dolly as a poor substitute. She had tried to make them like her but she didn't have the right touch. Too often, if she tried to make light banter it was misinterpreted. They resented her too. She was one of them by birth but no longer by position. She often thought they begrudged her taking their money. Perhaps they thought she should give them their ale for nothing. She was sure that a day didn't go by when they wished Melanie was here rather than her. Still, it was time they woke up, she thought, as she cleared up the spillage. Melanie was dead.

It was hard, though, running the inn. It was hard to stand here and not be a part of the group. She was often lonely and, when the bar was full, as it was now, the loneliness was at its worst.

'Heard from Zeph recently, Dolly?' Sol asked.

'Yes,' she replied, though it was more than a month since she'd had a letter. She wasn't about to admit that to her brother, though. She knew some members of her family were waiting for her and her husband to separate and for her to end on her uppers.

How would they react if they knew that Zeph was a liar and a cheat?

Thinking of her husband's infidelity made her polish the pumps vigorously.

When the letter had come, she'd been pleased to see it, but it was short and, as always, unaffectionate. Zeph had written only that he was safe in France. That had struck her as a stupid word – how could anyone be *safe* there? She'd no idea where he was but, then, she didn't want to know. In the same way she'd no desire to look at the newspapers – they were only full of bad news. Some women devoured them each day, desperate for news, but not Dolly. The truth was, since the letter's arrival, she'd wanted to know even less. He had not even signed off 'with love', just 'yours.' It was as if she was an acquaintance, not his wronged wife, or as if she was the one who had committed adultery, not him.

Everything was so unfair.

'They say as there's stalemate on the Western Front,' Rob said.

'Do they?' She would have liked to ignore him.

'I was talking to someone in the know.' He tapped the side of his nose. 'He said more than three hundred thousand Tommies are dead. If you think about it, that's at least all the people who live in three Exeters.'

'Four, more like,' Sol suggested.

'They don't tell us, though, do they?'

'Don't dare. We'd all run away.'

'Speak for yourself, Sol. I'd think it an honour to serve.'

'We couldn't run, now the government has us all registered,' Fred pointed out.

'Did Zeph say where he is?'

'No, Rob. But he wouldn't. He's protecting me.' She busied herself with polishing glasses. 'And I wish you'd all stop talking about war and death. I don't like it.'

'And neither do we, Dolly, but some things have to be faced.' Rob was so reasonable that she wanted to hit him.

The glasses were already gleaming but she had to keep busy. She didn't like dwelling on how hard-done-by she felt, and she didn't want to be angry. It was a waste of energy and she needed every ounce she could muster to carry on at the inn.

'Polish that glass any more and it'll disappear,' said an unfamiliar voice.

'I have to do something.' Dolly smiled at the stranger standing at the bar. In his thirties, she assessed. Smart-suited, prosperous-looking.

'To allay the boredom?' He grinned.

'Perhaps.' She nodded towards her regulars. 'They seem to have the same conversation every day. So, yes, it gets wearisome. Still, I suppose I shouldn't say that, should I? It's disloyal.'

'Honesty never did anyone any harm. I don't think I'd last a week in your job, having to be pleasant to strangers and folk you wouldn't normally wish to spend time with.'

Dolly studied him with more interest. He was not very tall and of a slight build. He had a plain face, which changed when he smiled, as he did now. What perfect teeth, she found herself thinking. You could always tell a gentleman by his teeth. How nice to meet someone who apparently understood the tedium of her life.

'What can I get you, sir?'

'George Meopham.' He held out his hand to shake hers. She took it, surprised by the courtesy. 'If I might have a whisky and soda and perhaps a snack – a sandwich will do. I was also wondering if you have a room. I need one for at least a couple of weeks. I've business here.'

'Of course.' Her spirits lifted. Business? She wondered what sort and how profitable it was. There had been a time when more than half of the rooms were booked every night, but since last August business had been intermittent. She had hoped that the parents of the officers who were at the manor would come here, but they had not. The inn must be too simple for them. Instead, they stayed at the Victoria in Barlton. She was already working out what two weeks' bed and breakfast would bring in. 'Would you like to see the room now or whisky first?'

'The room, if it's not too inconvenient a time for you.'

'Of course not. Rob, would you keep an eye on the bar for me?' She led the way.

'Can you trust them?'

'Rob is as honest as the day is long. This way.' She went ahead of him on the stairs, conscious of him behind her. It was a strange feeling, but pleasant. She knew he was watching her and, to her surprise, she found she liked it and swayed her hips.

Dolly showed him her best room, then she moved along the corridor to the bathroom. Eventually, she left him to unpack his bags and went back downstairs.

In the bar she poured Mr Meopham's drink and asked Rob to point it out to him when he came down. She had to pop behind the scenes for a minute, she explained. 'Serve yourselves while I'm gone,' she added. She did not understand why, but suddenly she felt enough confidence for the task she had put off too long.

'Flossie, a word, if you've time,' she said, as she entered the kitchen where Flossie was sipping tea. She felt a spurt of irritation. It was all right for her, lolling about while Dolly worked like a navvy.

'I'm not exactly rushed off my feet.' Flossie grinned. 'Would you like a cup?' She lifted the teapot.

'No, thanks.' Dolly sat down, her confidence already seeping away.

'I hear we've a guest.' Flossie helped herself to a piece of cake. Dolly's cake.

'Yes, I have one,' she said sharply, and knew she had to act quickly.

Flossie sat up straight, carefully replacing her cup on the saucer and stared at her. 'Oh, yes? And what does that mean?'

'I'm sorry, Flossie, but I have to let you go. There isn't the trade for me to keep you on.' She said it in a rush.

Flossie sat as still as a statue, then took a deep breath. 'I see.' She paused for a long time. 'I've been loyal to this family ...' Her voice faded away.

'I know you have, and we've appreciated it.'

'This would never have happened if Melanie was here. She understood loyalty. Zeph, too. He won't like it.'

'But they're not here, are they? I am. It's my decision.'

They sat opposite each other, a barrier of resentment building on both sides.

'I'm racked with worries,' Dolly went on. 'There isn't enough money for me to pay you.'

'But you know Alf has lost his job too!'

'I give him work when I can, don't I? In any case he's Miss Cresswell's responsibility, not mine.'

'You call him in when you want heavy work done if you can't persuade one of the customers to do it for nothing.'

'I hoped you'd understand – and that it's a temporary problem. That when the war's over, we'll get back to normal ...'

'And the cottage?'

Dolly couldn't look at her. She fixed her eyes on the wall. 'Well, of course, if you're no longer working here I'll expect you to leave it.'

'So you can rent it out?'

'What I do with it is my business.' Dolly was irritable because she felt guilty. She didn't want to dismiss Flossie but she had no choice. Why couldn't the woman see that?

'Where's my family to go?'

Oh, no, thought Dolly. She's going to cry. If there was one thing she couldn't stand it was having to deal with a weeping woman. 'I really don't know. I suggest you ask your rich daughter for help.' With that she stood up and left the room.

2

It was hard to sleep at night knowing that just along the corridor George Meopham lay alone. She liked him, and as the days passed she liked him even more. He was always courteous to her – a true gentleman – and there were times when she caught him looking at her in such a lustful way that her innards clenched with excitement. Then he said and did nothing, which drove her mad.

Night after night Dolly tossed and turned in a lather of longing. She dickered with the idea of going to his room and offering herself to him, but pride prevented her. It was not in her nature to beg. Neither could she face the humiliation if he refused her.

When he had arrived, she had sensed his interest in her, but she had not intended to pursue it – she was, after all, a married woman.

She was not sure what had made her change her mind. Perhaps the note she had received from Zeph had galvanized her. He hadn't even troubled to write her a letter this time. What was more, she became aware of comments in the bar. Evidently some thought she had already clambered into George's bed. So, if her reputation was already damned, she might as well do as she liked. And then there was the fact that she was bored with her life, feeling sorry for herself, and wanted some excitement.

Now the decision was made. She was about to know another man carnally. She had considered Zeph's reaction, but only briefly. Why should he know? She would be discreet. She concluded that by sleeping with George she would be doing her husband a favour. In becoming an adulteress she would make them equal and then, she was sure, she would at last forgive him so that when he returned they would be able to get on with their life together.

Such plans she'd had. But nothing had happened. He continued to treat her with exaggerated politeness, which was flattering. He continued to flirt with her, which was also flattering. But that was all. Dolly's body ached with tension.

She did what she always did when faced with a problem. She worked even harder and nagged her children.

'Put that away.'

'Take that out.'

'Stop that noise.'

'Don't sulk.'

'Go to bed.'

'How dare you speak to me ...'

'After all I do for you ...'

These words rang round the inn in a seemingly endless stream. For the most part Apollo and Cordelia ignored her, unless they sensed she was about to clip them round the ear. Then they pretended to listen. In the privacy of their rooms they made endless plans to run away.

The inn was not a happy place to reside.

Rowan was crossing the park on the way to her parents' cottage. She hadn't visited them for several weeks. She had intended to but her work kept her so busy that there was never enough time – not that she thought Flossie and Alf would believe that.

She was not looking forward to seeing them. The easy camaraderie they had once enjoyed had gone. She didn't know why. She had racked her brains but could think of nothing she had done to warrant this distance.

She reached the ha-ha, clambered down the bank and up the other side, taking a short-cut. Before her marriage this route would have been forbidden to her. She took a perverse pleasure in using it.

A frown flitted across her face. As if she didn't have problems enough without her parents' displeasure. The conclusion she had reached was that in marrying Morts she had offended them. She was sure she hadn't changed, but her family plainly thought she had.

Before setting off she had wondered if she should bring something with her – a cake, some fruit, a ham – but had decided against it. She could just hear one of her sisters accusing her of acting like the lady of the manor, while her mother would bridle and announce that she accepted charity from no one. As she walked she clutched the bunch of chrysanthemums she had decided on instead.

The saddest thing of all was the change in her mother. Flossie had once been so happy and jolly, only ever seeing the best in everyone. Slowly, insidiously, she had become miserable, bad-tempered and suspicious.

It had begun when Melanie Topsham, the previous landlady of the Cresswell Arms, had died. And, Rowan had to be honest, her wedding had been the final straw.

Getting anywhere on the estate always took longer than she had planned. She knew everyone and each person she met would want to stop and chatter. While this was touching, it was also frustrating. She had planned to be away from the manor for two hours and had already lost thirty minutes, talking to neighbours.

At the cottage, she paused in the lane. It was not the home in which she had spent her childhood but one that Dolly Topsham had offered them when Alf had ceased to work for the Cresswells. Since Flossie was her cook, it was rent-free, a big consideration. She noticed that the window-frames needed painting. It was unlike her father not to attend immediately to repairs.

It was a pretty cottage, covered with a prolific rambling rose that would look lovely in the summer. The small latticed windows kept out the cold in winter and the heat in summer, but unfortunately precluded the light too.

As she pushed open the gate it wavered drunkenly on its hinges. Rowan caught it as it was about to fall and hitched it back. As she walked up the path she felt a surge of guilt. It was wrong that her family should live in a place like this when she lived in such luxury.

Two large galvanized buckets stood by the door. Used as she was to running hot water, she realized she had forgotten the sheer hard work of collecting water from the communal well. Hot work in summer, bitterly cold in winter. She had never been able to decide which was worst. Just thinking about it made her shoulders ache.

None of the Cresswell Manor cottages had running water either, she knew – and Hannah had started a crusade for the villagers to wash more, which showed how ignorant she was. How could she know what it was like to have a strip-wash in a chilly scullery with half a dozen others queuing up outside to take your place. Oliver had installed water in his cottages, but the other Cresswells had good ideas and never put them into practice.

This cottage might look pretty but she knew from her days of living in one that they were not comfortable. Damp was a constant problem and battling the musty smell was never-ending. The stairs were narrow and rickety and many were the tumbles down them. There was one room downstairs, with a large temperamental range that was likely to send out billows of acrid black smoke.

At the back, the scullery, with a sink in a wooden surround, was a breeding ground for silverfish and peabodies. Holly, the youngest, was terrified of them and had hysterics whenever she saw one. The family, with only four of the eight children still at home, were still squashed and uncomfortable. Sometimes, at night, alone on the ward, Rowan would think about her situation, and know that guilt was the main reason she rarely visited them. Perhaps she thought that if she didn't go she would forget, but of course she never had.

Feeling down already, she pushed open the door. 'It's only me,' she called. As she entered she noticed the dense smell of boiling washing. That meant her mother was at the copper in the corner of the scullery and wouldn't be in the sunniest of moods – yet only a short time ago she'd have been singing as she went about her tasks.

She was surprised, therefore, to find her mother sitting in the one comfortable chair. Then she spied Acacia through the scullery door doing the washing.

'That's good of you, Acacia. Mum needs a helping hand,' she said.

'They say steam's good for the complexion.' Acacia popped her head into the room. She was plump, golden-haired, pretty, and grinned good-naturedly. 'Tea?'

'That would be lovely. Here, Mum. I persuaded Fred Robertson to let me have these from the greenhouse.' She proffered the bunch of flowers.

Her mother looked at them in a perfunctory manner. 'They won't miss them. They've got so many.'

Rowan hid the dismay she felt at the bitterness in her mother's voice and sat on the rickety chair, whose rush seat needed repairing. It looked as if rats had been gnawing it, and pricked her through her skirt. 'Hello, you lot,' she said, to her other sisters, Cherry and Holly. There was no sign of her brother Oak. They muttered a welcome, but it wasn't the exuberant one she'd wanted. They were unusually subdued.

'Have you heard from Willow?'

'She sent a letter – if you could call it that – last week.' Flossie stood up and, from behind the Staffordshire figure of the Duke of Wellington that Rowan had given her for Christmas, she took a single sheet of paper. The writing was unformed – Willow had always had difficulty with reading and writing. She'd been too busy laughing and having fun to study. The note said little, only that she was well and happy – which, to Rowan, implied that Freddie, the ex footman, was still her love, not that she was going to mention him to her mother and put her in a state.

'She sounds happy enough.'

'No doubt there's a man in tow.'

'She's pretty. She'll be getting married before you know where you are.'

Flossie didn't respond.

'Mum worries about the zeppelins,' Holly said.

'We all worry about them, nasty things,' Rowan replied.

'Do you? I'm surprised you find the time.'

Rowan did not know how to reply to this. It had made her feel as if the raids were her fault. To distract her mother she began to talk about her patients, but within a minute it was obvious that Flossie was not interested in her news either. 'Mum,' she said, after a pause, 'have I done something to annoy you?' She felt nervous, as she had as a small child. She had always hated upsetting her mother, whom she adored.

'*Me, me, me.* All you ever think about is yourself!'

A lump formed in Rowan's throat. What on earth had she done? She gnawed at her lower lip to stop herself crying. 'I'm sorry. I don't understand what you mean.' Her mother said nothing. 'I think about you all the time.'

'You don't show your face very often.'

'Because I'm so busy ...' There she was again, making excuses. 'But what's the point in my coming if this is the welcome I get?' There. She'd said it. Her mother remained silent. Rowan leant forward, the chair wobbling alarmingly. 'What's happened, mother?'

'Nothing.'

'Something has.'

'She's been given the boot by that cow Dolly Topsham.' Acacia had come into the room, but Rowan's other sisters had disappeared.

'Good,' said Rowan.

'What's good about it?' her mother snapped, furious now.

'You work too hard. It's time you gave up and rested more. You've enough to do with the family to care for. Let Dolly stew without you. She'll miss you more than you'll miss her.'

'And what are we to live on? Fresh air? Don't forget Miss Cresswell saw fit to give your father notice. But you've probably forgotten that.'

'No, I hadn't. I had no part in Hannah Cresswell's decision. It was unfair of her to do what she did, but in a silly way, she probably thought she was doing the right thing.' Flossie snorted, as Rowan went on, 'She's never explained herself to me but I honestly think that's so. She felt it was difficult in the circumstances for Dad to be employed by a Cresswell. Now maybe you'll let me help you.'

'Good for you, Rowan.' Acacia smiled at her sister.

'We accept charity from no one,' Flossie said, as she had said so often in the past.

'This isn't charity. I'm your daughter, for God's sake. How do you think I feel? I worry about you all the time.'

Flossie sat rigidly upright, a sign of her inflexible pride. She turned to her daughter. Rowan was shocked by the coldness in her mother's eyes. 'When you went against my wishes and married Mr Morts I warned you there would be problems. I said you were making a foolish mistake. And I'm right. Look what your actions have led to.'

'My marrying Morts had nothing to do with Dolly's decision.' Rowan clasped her hands together as if to control herself. She was beginning to feel angry. Why was she so often put in the wrong?

'Oh, no? And who had to move out of the cottage we'd lived in all our married life?'

'You didn't have to move. Oliver Cresswell said you could stay.'

'And pay the sort of rents they ask? Where would the money for *that* have come from?'

'You wouldn't have had to, not in the circumstances.'

'And what circumstances might they be? Oh, I understand. Charity because of you. No, thank you.'

'But when you moved you said this cottage was more convenient because it was nearer the inn.'

Her mother thought. For a moment Rowan believed she had won the argument.

'We have a month to get out. A month!'

'Then let me help.'

'No.'

'Where will you go?'

'Only the Lord knows that. But don't offer again. I want nothing from that family.'

'They're my family, too, now.'

'Do you think I need reminding? We'll manage somehow. Your father's thinking of enlisting.'

'No!' Rowan's hand shot to her mouth. 'He's too old.'

'He can lie. I'm warning you now, Rowan, if he goes and he's killed, I shall blame you.'

3

Rowan raced from her mother's cottage, white-faced with shock, and in a jumble of emotions of which incomprehension predominated. It was unbelievable that her mother could say such cruel words to her. It was as if she was in a bad dream. She stumbled on the path as she wrenched open the gate. Without shutting it, she sped down the lane.

'Rowan, wait!'

She hurried on. She didn't want to speak to anyone, not even her sister. Too much had been said, and the hurt was too deep. She was sure she would never forgive. And she would never go back to the cottage.

'Rowan! Wait for me!'

She glanced over her shoulder. Acacia was running down the lane after her. 'Please, don't go! Come back!'

Rowan stopped so abruptly that Acacia nearly crashed into her.

'Why should I? How could mother say such things? How could she be so cruel? What have I done?' She was surprised she wasn't crying, she felt so unhappy, but she was angry, too, and anger stemmed tears more effectively than anything else.

A cluster of neighbours had gathered at the sound of shouting and doors slamming. 'Seen enough?' Acacia shouted at them. 'Go and gawp at someone else.' For good measure she poked out her tongue at them.

'Oh, Acacia, don't.' But she had to smile at her sister's spirit.

'Nosy old crows. Dad says if he farts they pop their heads out the door.'

'He never did!'

Suddenly serious, Acacia took her hand. 'She shouldn't have said what she did. That was horrible ... Come on.' She led Rowan down the hill towards the harbour. 'Here, we'll sit behind these bushes, then no one can spy on us.'

Rowan sank on to the scrubby grass and pulled her coat round her. Suddenly she felt chilled. 'What's made her like this?'

'Worry.'

'But I can help her – help all of you. I'm sure Morts would be willing.'

'She won't accept it, though.'

'Why is she so against me and Morts?'

'She's afraid of losing you.'

At this Rowan laughed humourlessly. 'Then why be so horrible to me?'

'She didn't want you to change.'

'I don't think I have.'

'Oh, come on, love. You must know you're different. Look at the clothes you wear, all soft and silky. And you talk like they do. And you're so confident.'

'Confident? Me? Oh, if only you knew, Acacia. I'm afraid all the time. Each day I live in fear of doing or saying something wrong. Upsetting people.'

'Then you should have gone on the stage. You don't seem afraid to me.'

'I'm resented everywhere. I get horrible remarks at work, some of Morts's family hate me and then my own mother turns against me.'

'It's more than that with Mum. She's worried about money and she does blame you, I know. And it's wrong. But she gets at all of us, even Dad. I think it's the change of life and she's gone a bit mad.'

'The change? But she's only forty.'

'Sue Robertson had it early too. Anyway, that's what Dad thinks. And I'll tell you something else if you promise not to breathe a word.' She looked at Rowan, who nodded. 'Dad's talking of enlisting so he can get away from her. Honest.'

'But he can't. That'd be dreadful.'

'He's determined to go. They need drivers and he can earn six shillings a day. Imagine all that money! The other soldiers only get a shilling.'

'They must pay the drivers so much because it's dangerous.'

'I don't think so. Of course it's dangerous but it's really because they don't have enough. He says he wants to drive an ambulance.'

'I'll fear for him.'

'We all will. But, Rowan, he's looking forward to it, so don't feel guilty about him.'

'I don't know. If I do something it's wrong, and if I don't, that's wrong too.' She sighed, then gave herself a little shake, as if to rid herself of her perplexity. 'How are you? We've only been talking about me.'

'Oh, I do what I can and keep out of Mother's way. And I'm seeing Jim …' She blushed prettily.

'Jim Robertson? How old is he, then?'

'Sixteen, same as me. He says he loves me.'

'That's nice. Don't do anything silly, will you?'

'I'm not daft.' Acacia pushed her playfully.

They sat for half an hour, chatting, until Acacia said she should get back. She'd promised to do the tea for Holly and Cherry.

Rowan was deep in thought as she made her way home. She had enjoyed talking to her sister who, she saw now, was wiser than her years. How quickly she had grown up in the past few months. But then she'd had to. I must see more of them all, Rowan vowed. But not her mother ... She walked on, deep in thought. 'Of course,' she said aloud, and turned back.

Dolly Topsham's welcome was far from warm. 'I can't keep your mother on. I can't afford her any more. Business is bad ...' she said, before Rowan had had a chance even to greet her.

'I haven't come here to ask you to. I appreciate times are hard – and, in any case, I'm glad she's lost her job. She's always worked too much.'

'Oh, well ... You'd best come through to the back. I'll make us some tea.'

Rowan followed Dolly into the kitchen. She'd been here so many times in the past, watching her mother cook. That had been in Melanie's time. None of this would have happened if she had still been alive. Melanie had known hard times too; she doubted that Dolly had.

'I've come to see you about the cottage. I want to sort out a way for my family to stay there, inadequate though it is.'

'What's inadequate about it? It's a nice cottage.' Dolly slammed the teapot on to the table.

'It's not big enough, it's damp, it needs water laid on and a lick of paint.'

'And you expect me to lay out the money for that?' Dolly snorted with derision. 'I suggest you ask your rich husband to house his in-laws.'

'He would. My mother won't let him. Dolly, I haven't come here to argue about your cottage but to find a solution.'

'Then don't criticize it.'

'I apologize, I shouldn't have. But I've an idea ...'

Dolly's curiosity was aroused as Rowan had known it would be.

'Is there some way I can pay the rent and for a few improvements without my mother knowing it's me? If you'd go and see her and tell her you've changed your mind and she can stay on ...'

Dolly's eyes lit up. She did not respond immediately but sat deep in thought, probably working out if this was truly to her advantage. 'I'd be happy to,' she said eventually. 'Only trouble is, would she believe me?'

'I've thought of that. If she's suspicious you could say you know Melanie would have been furious if she was still alive ... and that's why you want them to stay. You'd make it sound better if you apologized for having to let her go.'

'Why should I apologize for anything?'

'Because you'd be doing me a favour.'

'Pity the family you married into doesn't do the Topshams more favours. We're all related, aren't we?'

Rowan had heard the rumours that Zeph was her father-in-law's son but she'd also heard he was old Sir Mortimer's. Morts had never said anything about it to her. Since she had been the victim of gossip, she did not enjoy listening to it and was not about to start now. So she said nothing.

'That, of course, makes my Zeph the eldest son, by rights, doesn't it?'

'But about my mother?' She ignored Dolly's claim.

'Water and damp, you said. I'd have to have the money before I do anything.'

'Of course. If you can let me know the cost I'll make sure you get it.' Rowan stood up. 'I'm sorry, I don't have time for tea. I'll be late on duty.'

Dolly accompanied her to the door. 'In fact, Rowan, you've done *me* a favour. Your mother's been on my conscience.'

'I'm glad to have helped.' Rowan hoped her face didn't show her cynicism. She doubted that Dolly had a conscience. More likely it was the idea of having her cottage improved for nothing.

There was one problem. Now she had to explain to Morts that she needed money. She hoped he'd agree. If not she'd have to sell the pretty opal brooch Hannah had given her.

4

For the last fifteen minutes Rowan had been walking Penelope Cresswell about her bedroom. Not that her ladyship was doing so willingly.

'I'm tired. I want to sit down,' she whined.

'The exercise is doing you good.' Rowan guided her along the uncluttered path she had made from the bed to the door, having pushed the furniture out of the way. Every step they took was accompanied by a litany of complaint but Rowan felt that the older woman knew it was helping her. When she called a halt it was difficult to decide who was the most exhausted – Penelope, unused to any activity, or Rowan who had to support her weight. She had to stand with her legs apart, bracing herself to lowering the other woman into the wing-chair she had placed by the open window.

'I'll catch a chill.' Penelope sank with gratitude on to the cushion that Rowan had put at the small of her back.

'It's quite warm in here.'

'No, it's not. It's cold.'

'Then why are you sweating?'

'Whatever next, Rowan? What a thing to say. We ladies glow, men perspire and horses sweat. Never forget that.'

'It looks like sweat to me,' she persisted – but she made a mental note. Something else she'd learnt.

'I hate to admit this, Rowan – it's not like me to be proved wrong – but our little perambulations are helping. I feel better for them. Such a shame it's not summer. Then I could go outside and take the air.'

Rowan could have hugged her. That response was what she had been hoping for. 'If we get another day like today we could still go out into the garden,' she ventured.

'With this chill in the air? Are you trying to kill me?'

Rowan turned so that Penelope could not see her smile. She mustn't rush her. She busied herself pulling the curtains further back. Perhaps she should shut the window now. The last thing they needed was for her to get a cold and perhaps pneumonia.

'Why don't you change duties with Winlock? I can't stand the woman,' Penelope wheedled.

'You're always suggesting that. The answer is still the same.'

'If you don't ask you don't get. That's what I've learnt.'

'You pay me a great compliment but it would not be a good idea. She's an excellent nurse.'

'Not as good as you.'

'Flattery will get you nowhere.' She grinned at Penelope, completely relaxed with her.

'For me.' The wheedling continued.

'I like it as it is, you and me good friends.' She was busily replacing the furniture, dragging an intricate marquetry card-table back to its normal place. 'All you do is moan about anyone who cares for you. And I'm happy with what I do.'

'Like the men, do you?'

'That's a spiteful thing to say.' Rowan was now heaving a large Queen Anne chair into place.

'You're brittle this morning. What's bothering you?'

'Nothing. Which book do you want close by?'

'I'm not in the mood to read.'

'Which book? You know what you're like. The minute I've turned my back, you'll be bored and asking for it.' Rowan looked sternly at her, which didn't quite work.

'There you are, being offensive to me again.'

'It's the only language you understand!'

'Cheeky!' Penelope chuckled. 'Give me that copy of *Titbits*. Books are not nearly as good as they were in my youth.'

'That's because everything in the past always seems better,' she said wistfully.

'You can't think like that – you're still young,' she said sharply. 'And, like all the young, you haven't the sense to appreciate what you have. Do you read?'

'I never have time.'

'You should make time. You have to keep an alert and interested mind for your husband's sake.'

'Morts hardly ever reads either.'

'We are not talking about Morts. We are talking about you.'

'But if I should read, so should he.'

'Nonsense. Your role is to please him. He should be pleasure enough for you as he is.'

Rowan had to tidy the dressing-table to stop herself answering this. From what she had heard, her grandmother-in-law's treatment of her husband had hardly been that of the dutiful wife.

'And wash your private parts before he beds you.'

At this Rowan could not suppress a small shriek.

'Has your friend solved her problems?' Penelope asked without warning.

'Yes, thank you.' She felt uncomfortable, not wishing to talk about Esmeralda.

'But you still have them – problems, I mean.'

Again Rowan had to busy herself so that Penelope couldn't see her embarrassment. The old woman had a disconcerting habit of hitting the nail on the head.

'This secret you won't tell me about will eventually come out into the open. A secret once imparted is no longer a secret.'

'I'll never tell.'

'You don't imagine she's confided only in you? I'd wager you're not alone.'

To Rowan this was a horrifying idea. If Penelope was right and the truth eventually emerged, what would Morts think of her?

'So, what *is* bothering you this morning? Is it Morts again? Are you keeping more secrets from him?'

'Nothing's bothering me.'

'That's not true. Tell me. You know I'm your friend.'

It was true, unbelievable though it seemed. Rowan felt that Penelope Cresswell really was her friend. She was prepared to change her mind in a flash but it would make her sad if she had to. Maybe Penelope could advise her. What could be wrong about telling her?

'It's my parents. They've lost their employment or, rather ...' She sat down '... I've arranged with Dolly Topsham that I will pay the rent on their cottage and for some repairs. The trouble is – and before you say anything, I know it was stupid of me – I've no money and I hate troubling Morts.'

'Why?'

Rowan felt foolish as she confessed that she had no idea how much money her husband had at his disposal.

'Then ask him.'

'I couldn't do that. It's not my business.'

'You'd be well advised to make it so. Men are notorious for keeping their affairs secret. I've often wondered why. But I shouldn't worry, if I were you. The rental will hardly break the bank. And he's related to your family by marriage now. Why not ask him to house them on the estate?'

'My mother would refuse. She would regard it as charity.'

'Why on earth are the poor so inconsiderate? Pride is such a tiresome characteristic. And it spoils it so for the giver ...'

'I don't think my mother's tiresome,' Rowan said defensively.

'Oh, don't you be idiotic as well. Of course she is. But in marrying you Morts has taken on responsibility for and a duty to his in-laws ... even if they're not what was expected.' She said this in a much lower voice so that Rowan, tidying across the room, should not hear.

'I heard what you said, Lady Penelope, and I know what you mean. It's all my fault.' She felt close to tears.

'Don't turn on the tap. I hate blubbing.' Penelope looked anxious, and Rowan blew her nose.

'I'm sorry but no one seems to approve of my marrying Morts. I didn't think that included you.'

'I like you, Rowan, and you're making the best of a difficult situation.

You were too young to understand the problems that were likely to face you by marrying out of your class.'

'It didn't seem important to us.'

'Ah, but there's the rub. You're taking on English society, and I doubt you can win.'

'It's wrong.'

'I agree. It's your personality that should matter, not who your parents are. But it's always been so, and you and Morts will never change it. I commend you for trying, though.'

'Poor Morts. I wonder if he thinks like you – that I'm a problem. When he married me I shouldn't think he realized he was marrying my whole family.'

'There are rather a lot of them.' Penelope laughed and Rowan, used to jokes about the size of her family, smiled. 'It's strange when you come from such a fecund family that you're not with child yourself.'

'If I knew what *fecund* meant, I might be able to explain. It sounds rude to me.'

Penelope slapped her ample thigh. 'You're so droll, Rowan. I do delight in you.' She rummaged in the muddle on her side-table. 'Here.' She handed Rowan a key. 'Open the middle drawer of my bureau and bring me the red silk purse.'

Rowan did as she was told. Penelope, the diamonds in her rings flashing in a shaft of bright sunlight, untied the ribbons that held the purse shut and shook out on to her lap a pile of sovereigns. 'Take these.'

'I can't.'

'Oh, for the sake of the Almighty, don't argue. Just take them.' She waved at the coins. 'Take them and stop whining.'

'I'm not.'

'In my opinion you are. Now, see that wretched Dolly, give her the money and let's have done with it.'

'But what if Morts finds out?'

'Why should he? I won't tell. Unlike some, I'm good at keeping secrets.' She placed a fat finger over her lips. 'If you'll take my advice you'll be wary of Dolly Topsham. I can see her making difficulty for this family if that Zeph of hers gets himself killed. He can be trusted, but she can't.'

'Why should she do that?'

'You've heard the rumours?'

'What rumours?'

'Don't be coy. Everyone on this estate has talked of little else for decades. The rumour that Zeph is my son's bastard.'

Rowan found herself blushing again. 'Oh, that. I don't believe it.'

'Then you should. It's true. As with everything else, they tried to keep it from me but when they accused my husband of being the father – *my husband*, no less – I had to find out the truth. Which I did. I expect Dolly lies awake at night, wondering how she can cash in on the knowledge. Well, they've been handsomely paid off. Don't you ever forget it. You're too soft for your own good. Now, do you know what I fancy? A nice cup of tea.' She held up a hand. 'Can you change the position of this chair? I like to watch the young officers cavorting on the lawns.' She exhaled a monumental sigh. 'Sadly, that's all I'm good for these days, watching the delightful creatures.'

Rowan moved the chair with great difficulty. Sometimes Penelope was too shocking – that was no way for her to speak of the men. The very idea of someone so old lusting after them was too disgusting to contemplate.

Rowan left the room, her head in a whirl. She had the money, but in taking it she had yet another secret from Morts. And Zeph really was Morts's half-brother, even if from the wrong side of the blanket. And she was certain he didn't know, so there was another confidence she couldn't share with him. And it was all very well for Lady Cresswell to say *she* was good at keeping secrets when she had just divulged such a big one to Rowan.

She sighed as she swept along the corridor towards the kitchens. Her life had once been so simple but now every week she encountered another complication.

5

'You seem very thoughtful, Rowan. Anything wrong?' Eve Gilroy asked, as Rowan, staring into space, stood by the range waiting for the kettle to boil. 'You know what they say about watched pots.'

Across the kitchen Whitaker was frowning at her and shaking his head. She knew why. He thought she was being over-familiar, that she should treat Rowan as they did the other gentry. Well, she wasn't going to. Ridiculous idea! She'd known Rowan since she was a baby and to Eve it didn't matter whom she'd married. Gentry Rowan would never be.

On the other hand, Whitaker had been reading the paper but stood to attention the minute Rowan had walked in. Even more ridiculous! Eve performed one of her more impressive sniffs to show him that she had noticed his warning and had no intention of complying with it.

'Do I? Can't think why. There's nothing in my head.' Rowan laughed. 'That's how I usually am – empty-headed.' She laughed some more.

'How's her ladyship this morning?'

'She's doing very well. I persuade her to walk for a little bit longer each day and she's moving a lot better. She asked me to fetch her some tea.'

'She'll never walk properly until she gets rid of some of that blubber. Eating herself to death, she is.'

'Eve!' Whitaker remonstrated.

'She told me the other day that she wants to live to be ninety,' Rowan said.

'Bah! Have you ever seen a fat eighty-year-old? Makes me laugh, she does. Seen her order for her luncheon? Braised steak with suet dumplings. I ask you! A bit of banting wouldn't go amiss, in my opinion.'

'We're here to serve, not to question our betters' dietary requirements, Eve,' Whitaker admonished her.

'Mrs Gilroy is correct, Mr Whitaker. Lady Penelope does eat too much and she loves food that's far too heavy. But, then, it gives her pleasure and what else has she got to look forward to?' The kettle whistled. Rowan turned her attention to heating the pot.

'Why are you caring for her today?'

'Nurse Winlock had to go and see her sister at Tavistock. Seems she's poorly.'

This time Eve's sniff was of genuine disapproval. 'Gracious me! That woman has the most sickly family I've ever heard of. I suppose her grandmother's had the misfortune to die at least twice so that she can sneak a day off.'

'Really, Eve.'

Whitaker, she saw, was looking even more distressed. 'I speak as I find.'

'Yes, and one day it will get you into trouble. If you will excuse me, Mrs Morts, I have duties.' He bowed.

Such an elegant man, Eve thought. She might be annoyed with him but that didn't stop her admiring him. 'Don't you listen to him,' she told Rowan. 'He's an old fusspot.' She spoke quickly, suddenly aware that she had been looking at him in a way that might show her true feelings.

'But he's very kind.'

'Oh, I agree. Any chance of a cup for us?' Eve was always ready for tea, and she wanted to take this opportunity for a chat with Rowan. They were rarely alone. She sat down at the pine table. 'Everyone says you get on well with her ladyship.'

'I like her.'

'You must be the only one. Why, even her children can't be doing with her.' Eve was certain that Rowan had meant what she said. She had heard the sincerity in her voice.

'That's so sad. Imagine having children and loving them, then finding they don't care.'

'People reap what they sow,' Eve said enigmatically. 'I hear your mother's no longer at the Cresswell Arms. That must have been hard for her.'

'I'm pleased she's finished there. It's time she took it easy.'

'I was wondering if she could give me a hand here.'

'I don't think that would be a good idea, do you?' Rowan said, with dignity.

'Perhaps not. It was just I could have done with another pair of hands.' Eve was too thick-skinned to feel awkward.

'It's very kind of you to think of her, Mrs Gilroy. I'll remember that.' Eve beamed with pleasure. She could hardly wait to tell Whitaker, especially when he deemed her over-familiar. Rowan placed a teapot on the table with one cup and saucer.

'Aren't you going to join me?'

'No, I'd better get back or her ladyship will send out a search party for me.' The tea tray neatly set, she carried it from the kitchen.

If there was one thing Eve disliked it was being alone. It made her think and, as her old grandfather had been fond of saying, that never helped a body.

To her the bustle of a busy kitchen, the comings and going, and everyone deferring to her, for she was certainly the queen in her domain, was a joy. It wasn't like that any more. The kitchen was busy certainly, busier than ever, but there was a sombreness now that hadn't been there before. 'This wretched war spoils everything,' she said aloud.

As she sipped her tea from the fine bone-china cup she always used, she remembered times past. The huge lunches, the imaginative picnics for shooting parties, the ornate dinners with endless courses. She had been masterly in their preparation and indispensable, as she had known. 'Those were the days,' she said, as she drained the cup. Then she sharpened her knife with professional expertise and pulled a large piece of beef towards her, trimmed it and cut it into neat, uniform cubes.

Everything had changed. Would they ever get back to how it had once been? There were days when she feared that the old world had disappeared for ever; yet on others she was sure the war would soon be over and it was only a matter of time before everyone was back in their appointed place.

With no kitchenmaids and only male helpers, she missed female companionship – even though she had spent most of her time shouting at her girls. Perhaps that was why she had asked about Flossie Marshall – a hard-working family, they were. It would have been nice to have Flossie join her, but perhaps Rowan had been right. And who was to say that Flossie hadn't ideas above her station too, now.

Eve began to sauté the meat in goose fat. Good job Christmas was coming – she was running out of it. As she watched the meat she thought of her menus. They had changed too. This beef was a prime example – such a cut would never have been served in the family dining room, only the best for them. Once it had been fit only for below-stairs or a nice beef broth. And now she was preparing a stew – before the war the Cresswells would never have eaten anything so vulgar. Why, these days, she'd even made soup. Lady Coral would have had the vapours at the very idea of *soup* for luncheon – but, then, she was true gentry, with her father an earl. Breeding always showed, in Eve's opinion.

Cooking was a challenge now. Hannah had restricted her spending and supplies were becoming scarce. It was only a matter of time, Whitaker had said, until rationing was introduced.

'It's quantity not quality we'll be needing,' Sergeant Bob had said to her, when he had first arrived. She had managed the quantity, but Eve would not allow the quality to slip. Despite the shortage of help and the extra care she had to take to ensure that cheap cuts tasted expensive, quality had to be maintained. She'd learnt to disguise the new dishes in more ways than one. 'Stew' appeared on the menus as *ragout*, while *galantine* covered a multitude of sins. And she found *mélange* useful to disguise the bits and bobs, which, of necessity, she mixed together. Even Eve admitted that the French had a way with words.

As the number of patients increased and the work became harder, Bob had acquired a private to help her, but although at first pleased, Eve had soon discovered he was worse than useless. She could not rely on him even to peel the potatoes. She'd never known anyone who could reduce a stone to a mere couple of pounds – at least the pigs were happy with the thick peelings. Instead she had set him to do the heavy cleaning and peeled the vegetables herself. If it weren't for Bob, she'd be in a sorry state, which made her wonder where he was. He was never late. Perhaps he was unwell. She shook away the thought. Surely not – a tough, upstanding man like him? Just thinking of his physique made her come over queer.

She looked up as Whitaker returned to the kitchen. 'Mrs Morts has returned to her duties, then?'

'Yes, she couldn't even stay for a cup of tea. She's a good worker, is our Rowan.'

He coughed discreetly. 'I really do think, Eve, that you should begin to treat her with the respect her position calls for.'

'She doesn't mind.'

'Perhaps not now. She's still finding her feet. But the day will come when she will resent such familiarity.'

'Bah! Not Rowan.'

'Never forget that the day will dawn when that young woman will be *Lady* Cresswell. You should get used to the idea now, Eve.'

At the very idea of Rowan with a title, Eve burst out laughing. 'That'll be strange, I must say. But, no matter what, she'll always be Rowan to me. You worry too much, Edward.'

'Because I care about you, Eve.'

Eve had to hold the edge of the table to steady herself. What a lovely thing to say, she thought, her heart thudding. 'That's very kind of you, Edward.' She was so touched that she forgot to be coy. But, oh, what a flutter she was feeling somewhere between her heart and her stomach. 'Do you know where Sergeant Bob's got to? It's not like him to be late,' she said, to cover her confusion and began on the vegetables, thinly slicing the onions.

'He was called away to Tavistock. His grandmother's been taken poorly.'

Eve dropped her paring knife. 'Has he now?' she said, hoping her voice wasn't quavering as much as she thought it was. She started again, slashing at the onions now. 'I'd have thought she died a long time ago.' It was just as well she was working on the onions for if she cried, and she felt like it, Whitaker would think her tears were because of them.

'Perhaps he comes from a long-lived family,' he said, undoubtedly trying to be helpful.

'And don't you think it odd that Lady Cresswell's nurse has a poorly relation in Tavistock too?' Eve was fuming now but hoped she had disguised it.

The bell rang for Whitaker. Just as well, she thought, as it was now the carrots' turn to suffer an assault.

The sneak! The rotter! Still – she paused in her task – Edward *cared* for her. Hadn't he just said so?

When the butler returned, he was wan and sad.

'Dearie me, Edward, what's happened?' She stopped what she was doing and pulled out a chair for him. 'You'd better sit down before those pins of yours give way.' She patted the cushion.

'Sorrowful news, Eve. It was Miss Cresswell who summoned me.'

'Not Master Felix?' It was her turn to sit. There wasn't a day when she didn't think of that hare-brained young man, the younger son of the household, who had run away to war. Her hand shot to her mouth to suppress the cry she had thought was inevitable.

'No, thank God, but grave news. The Germans have shot Nurse Cavell,' he intoned.

'They never have? The barbarians! And her a woman.'

'They are no better than savages. Of course, this will give our men a greater impetus to slay the Boches.'

'Dreadful times we live in, Edward,' she said. It had been a bit stupid of the woman to hide those soldiers. What had she thought the Germans would do when they found out? Make her a cup of tea? Of course she would never say so, certainly not to Edward, who looked close to tears.

6

The hill to the cottage where the Marshall family were lodging was particularly steep. Dolly was walking as quickly as she could, despite the incline. She was in a hurry. She trusted the men enough to leave them in the bar for five minutes but she wasn't sure that they could resist temptation for half an hour. She missed Flossie for many reasons but especially when she had to leave the inn unattended. When Flossie had been there she had never needed to worry that she was being cheated out of a measure or a farthing.

Despite the autumnal crispness in the air she was hot as she toiled up the rise, and paused halfway up Trotters Hill for a rest. Far below her the bustling harbour looked pretty; closer to, it stank of fish. The people pottering about were like ants. The sun was shimmering on the sea, which was placid today but often a noisy tyrant. From here it was a lovely view, she thought, well worth the clamber. And being so high she felt a wonderful feeling of detachment.

In the opposite direction, at the top of the hill, stood a fine mansion that Dolly had often admired. To live in such a house, at the highest point of the town, away from the noise and riff-raff, would give one such a wonderful feeling of superiority – and rightly so, she decided. Only those of exceptional station could afford to own such an outstanding property.

Looking at her watch she saw she had little time to dawdle. She pressed on until she reached the cottage in a row of several similar ones of which the Topshams owned four. Melanie had bought them, years ago. The plan was eventually to own all of them – or, rather, that was Zeph's plan. Dolly thought it would be better to own one prestigious house, rather than a lot of run-down hovels.

The gate swung drunkenly on its hinges. Really! Why hadn't Alf mended it? She already knew the answer to that. She was aware of how a failure like Alf thought – it's not mine so why should I do anything to it? That summed up the difference between them. When she had rented a house in Barlton, she'd kept it immaculate. There was no question that she would live in anything less than perfect because she paid rent for it. When Zeph had insisted they move back to Cress, she had negotiated compensation from the landlord for, as she had pointed out to him, she was returning the house to him in a far better state than it had been in when she had taken up the lease.

There was no knocker so she rapped on the door with her knuckles. It was opened by a girl, she'd no idea which one. The Marshall children all looked the same to her. Eight children were far too many; it was so irresponsible of Alf and Flossie when they never had enough money. Alf should have controlled himself.

'Is your mother here? If so, you can tell her Mrs Topsham would like a word.'

'She won't want to see you, that's for sure.'

'I'll have none of your cheek. Go and tell your mother I'm here.'

With a look of venom that made Dolly shiver, the girl turned and shouted, 'Mum, that Topsham woman's here.' At this rudeness, Dolly experienced an almost overwhelming longing to slap the girl's face.

From the gloom within Flossie appeared. Dolly was shocked by her appearance; she had aged ten years. Well, Flossie should stop feeling sorry for herself and pull herself together.

'What do you want?' Flossie's arms were crossed over her ample

149

bosom, and the fabric of her blouse strained tight over her upper arms.

'I come bearing an olive branch.' Dolly smiled. 'I've a plan that is to your advantage. Might I come in rather than discussing our business on the doorstep for all to hear?' With an air of reluctance, Flossie held open the door.

The conditions inside horrified Dolly. She'd never inspected the cottages before – why should she when there was always a queue of people willing to rent them? Although it was tidy and Flossie had obviously tried to make the room comfortable, the musty smell of damp pervaded the atmosphere. As if to confirm the unhealthy conditions, the last child, Holly – Dolly remembered her name – who looked younger than her thirteen years, was huddled in the corner, sniffling into a rag and wheezing.

'I hope she's not infectious – is she all right?'

'What do you think? She had a cold and it's gone to her chest. It always does.'

'I suppose she didn't wrap up warm enough outside – I know what these young girls are like.' Dolly was immediately on the defensive since she knew how Flossie would answer.

'It's not that, it's the damp in here, as well you know. And nothing's been done about it, although my Alf's mentioned it to you times without number.'

'Flossie, don't be angry with me.'

'Why not? What do you expect?'

'I know, and I'm sorry I've given you such worry. I've thought about it and I've decided I acted too hastily. I want to make amends.'

Flossie looked at her with astonishment and a large dash of cynicism as they stood in the centre of the tiny room.

'I do have serious financial problems. I didn't make that up just to be difficult.' Dolly glanced about for somewhere to sit but, on seeing the state of most of the chairs, decided to continue standing. 'I'm sorry, I cannot afford to continue as we were. But …' she paused for dramatic effect. It was fascinating to watch Flossie's face. At one minute she looked confused, at the next hopeful and then, with Dolly's last sentence, her whole body had sagged. 'I cannot afford to pay you a wage, but if you returned to work for me I would allow you and your family to remain in this cottage. In other words your wage would be your rent. What do you say?' Dolly smiled benevolently, very much as she remembered Hannah Cresswell had when Dolly's mother had been ill and she had brought round baskets of food.

'How long for? No wages, I mean.'

This was not the answer Dolly had expected. Ungrateful slut, she thought. 'Until business perks up and I'm back on an even keel. And I'll get a builder in to see if we can do anything about the damp and get rid of the smell.'

Flossie sat down. 'I have no choice, do I?'

'It's up to you, of course.' Dolly was trying to sound nonchalant when in fact she was praying that Flossie would agree. Running the inn on her own was far harder than she had imagined. She knew, without the customers' comments, that her cooking was not nearly as good as Flossie's, and since Flossie had gone she'd had no time to herself.

'Very well. I'll be there in the morning.'

'That's very sensible of you. That child should be in bed. I'll see you tomorrow, then.' Dolly escaped as quickly as she could. She wanted to dance with glee in the lane but controlled herself in case Flossie was watching. What a coup! The rent safely paid by Rowan – a whole year in one lump sum – and Flossie working for the same thing. The idea had come to her last night when, as was normal now, she couldn't sleep. Then she had thought it a brilliant idea. Now she knew it was.

Guilt was not an emotion with which Dolly was familiar so she could see no wrong in what she was doing. If anything, she thought, it served Rowan right. She'd too much of everything and that rent money would mean nothing to her – but it meant a lot to Dolly. Already she was planning the new clothes she would buy this autumn. In any case, she'd only taken what was rightfully theirs, what with Zeph being related to them. Not that he would ever do anything about it, such a coward he was.

Delighted though she was with her own cleverness, she did not want to go back just yet, despite her worries about the bar. She felt like celebrating. There was another reason too. As she had been serving breakfast she had overheard Mr Meopham talking to one of the travelling salesmen about Trotters Mount, the house Dolly admired. She decided to climb to the top of the hill. She pretended she wanted to admire the view but, really, she just had to have another peep at the house. Also, George might be there.

At the top she stopped dead in her tracks. It seemed today that all her wishes were coming true. For, outside the house, looking up at the roof was George Meopham.

'Why, Mr Meopham, this is a surprise!' She was glad she had put on her best new serge skirt and her smartest coat with one of her more stylish hats. She knew she looked smart and could smile at him with confidence.

'Mrs Topsham.' He doffed his hat at her. 'What a pleasant surprise. And there I was thinking you never left your hostelry.'

What a melodious voice he had, and so well spoken. He was educated, she was sure, and Dolly set store by that. She batted her eyelashes so that he knew it was an agreeable surprise for her too. 'I'm here to admire the view. I always do when I come this way – that is, if I can spare the time.'

'I've been admiring this house. A fine property, is it not?'

Dolly looked up at the gabled red-brick house with its many balconies and large casement windows. 'It is. I have a high regard for it.' She was pleased with that last expression. It made her sound sophisticated, she thought.

'Then you should buy it, Mrs Topsham.'

'Me? La, I fear it might be too expensive.' If he only knew the half of it, she thought. 'I had no idea it was for sale.'

'It isn't yet. A death in the family. You knew Mrs Tyler-Fanshaw?'

'Unfortunately I never had that honour.' Hardly surprising, when the woman was famed for thinking herself grander than the Cresswells. She was the last person who would have acknowledged someone like Dolly. Dolly loathed such people, and smarted at their arrogance.

'Mrs Tyler-Fanshaw was my great-aunt.'

There! She had known all along that he was quality. She wondered if he was as rich as his aunt had been. Thank heavens she hadn't said anything bad about her.

'You must know that she died last month.'

'My condolences,' she said, in a suitably lugubrious manner. 'It was a fine funeral, well attended,' she lied. She had no idea how many people had attended, other than that the bar was crowded afterwards. 'So, is her daughter to live here now?'

'Not only did my cousin lose her mother last month but her son was killed at Gallipoli. He was her only child and she was widowed last year.'

'How sad for her.' It was strange that she had not heard about this – but, then, it wasn't *that* surprising since she only ever listened with half an ear to the gossip in the bar. 'I'm so sorry.'

'No need. I couldn't abide any of them. My great-aunt was a crashing snob, my cousin took after her, and John was one of the most idiotic people it's ever been my misfortune to know. The world will be a merrier place without them.'

Dolly was aghast, unsure if he meant it or if he was joking. Then she saw merriment in his eyes and clapped her gloved hand over her mouth. She always feared her breath might be tainted. 'Mr Meopham, tut-tut. You shouldn't speak ill of the dead,' she said archly, laughing.

'Why not? They never spoke well of me.'

This made her laugh even more. 'I never heard such naughtiness,' she pretended to chide him. 'So, who owns this lovely house now? Her daughter?'

'No, it seems they had a falling-out and it has been left to a distant cousin of ours. He lives in Australia, has no interest in the property and has asked me to sell it for him.'

'And you weren't left it?'

'Unfortunately, no. I would have loved to live there. I was left a portrait – not a particularly good one. Who it is of, God only knows.'

'Mr Meopham, you're so funny!'

'I wish you'd call me George,' he said, in such a soft, seductive way that her knees felt weak.

'Then George it is. That is, if you will call me Dolly.' She batted her eyelashes again. 'Is that why you are here?'

'Only partly. I had business with a Mr Eldridge – are you acquainted with him?'

'He's popular in the area. He's given many much-needed employment. I've only met him a couple of times. An intriguing man.'

'Not too intriguing, I hope. He's a hard man to do business with.'

'I can imagine he is. I wonder …' She managed to look coy.

'Whether you could see inside the house?'

'Why, George, you read my mind.'

'I do hope so.' There was that tone again. He could make the simplest sentence sound captivating.

'How kind you are – George.'

Half an hour later Dolly had fallen in love. The house was everything she had ever wanted or dreamt of. The views from all the main rooms were staggering. Each was huge, and as she wandered about she was already planning how she would furnish it if it were hers.

'How much is the vendor expecting?' she asked, out of curiosity, knowing full well it would be far too much for her to pay. He told her. 'That's a huge amount of money.' She didn't know why she should be so disappointed but she was.

'It's a bargain. Especially when you think that all the furniture is included.'

'Everything? Lock, stock and barrel?' Her eyes were greedy with longing.

'All you see. I've often thought, given the wonderful position, that it would make a fine hotel.'

'Wouldn't it?'

'Better than running an inn.'

'You never said a truer word.' She was coveting the heavy damask curtains, the twinkling chandelier, and the fine rosewood piano.

'Let's sit a moment and talk. From your expression it would seem to me that you would love to own this house. Perhaps we could find a way.'

'George, this is very kind of you but it simply prolongs my agony.' She tried to laugh but her yearning for the house, and the impossibility of acquiring it, had made her sad.

'Nothing, dear Dolly, is impossible. How much could you afford?'

'Half the sum you quoted.'

'Would the bank not help you?'

'Banks! The last time I tried they refused me because I'm a woman.'

'But times are changing. With this war, women are being treated with far more seriousness and respect than before.'

'You think so?' She wasn't convinced. 'Of course I have several properties I could sell ...' Her heart was racing now; she had smelt business, which always excited her. She could sell the cottages – not that they would raise much but it would help. She had the right to do so since Zeph had left her in full control of the business when he had left, and there was something in what George had just said. The manager at the bank was indeed politer to her than he used to be.

'I've just had an idea. My cousin is a wealthy man. I'm sure we could negotiate a satisfactory price for you. I could telegraph him. And he is in no hurry for the money. You could buy it over several years. What about that?' He beamed at her.

Now her heart was pounding and her cheeks were scarlet with exhilaration.

They went on a second tour, planning how best to utilize the space, and it was in the main bedroom suite that he kissed her.

7

The negotiations for Trotters Mount were protracted. 'Since we are accepting terms over a five-year period – obliging you to an astonishing degree, I might add – that must be reflected in the price. There has to be an adjustment,' said George Meopham as, with a gesture of his hand, he asked Dolly's permission to pour himself another glass of wine.

'Please do.' Dolly smiled, she hoped graciously, and declined one herself, she trusted with equal poise. 'I fail to see why the price should rise.'

'Really, you surprise me, Dolly, an intelligent woman such as you.' He was twisting the large signet ring on his little finger. What fine hands he had. How delightful it would be to have them run over her naked body. He was a frustrating enigma. Since that first wonderful kiss in the house, he had made no further advances, and she longed for him to do so.

Such thoughts were not helping her in these discussions. She must concentrate. She shifted on the hard chair she had chosen to sit on. She had not wished to be too comfortable while they bargained. She knew from experience that comfort dulled the mind so she had made sure he sat on the one with cushions. She had noted the twisting of the ring – a sign of tension, she was sure.

'But then, George, if you're willing to give me such favourable terms then to do so would imply that you're not certain of a quick sale or of getting the price you're asking.' She laid her hands on the chenille cover on the table, forcing herself not to fidget.

'Dolly, you wound me.' He laid a hand over his heart. 'I was trying to help you ...'

'And I'm greatly obliged.' The smile flashed again. 'But surely you're aware that with this war and the uncertain times we live in it is not the best time to be *trying* to sell property ...' There were times when Dolly amazed herself with her cleverness.

And so the argument batted back and forth. She enjoyed the sallies and was quietly confident. That morning she had been to see the bank manager. She was pleased with the manner of his greeting, and had proceeded to lie, assuring the man that she had written to Zeph for his permission. She had taken the precaution of forging a letter from him – it had taken her some time to copy his handwriting to her satisfaction. She wrote that he was enthusiastic about her plans and gave his permission to continue – masterly, she thought. However, to her surprise and not a little chagrin, the man gave it a cursory glance, accepting it without question to be in Zeph's hand. He knew the house and, although he voiced his surprise at the generous terms George had offered, he agreed it was too good an opportunity to miss.

'And how are you to meet these annual payments on the purchase? I see you are to pay a year in advance.'

'Well, Mr Bottomly, I trust you will help me to pay this year's instalment.' She gave him a little wink, then licked her bottom lip with the tip of her tongue and saw him change position in his chair. She despised men.

'And the year after?' The manager found it necessary to shuffle his papers and cough.

'By then the business will be established. I have no concerns about that.' She hoped she had spoken with sufficient confidence.

'Of course, as the war has affected property prices it has also affected business. I see from your books that the inn's takings are considerably lower than last year's.'

She had prepared for this objection. 'The war continues and, sadly, gets worse.' She composed her face in a suitably sober expression and crossed her fingers under the desk – she certainly hoped that would be the case. 'There will be more patients at Cresswell Manor. At the moment the relatives of the poor officers have to stay in Barlton when visiting their loved ones since there is nowhere suitable here. I intend to change that arrangement and make the Topsham Manor Hotel the best and most luxurious in the area,' she announced with pride. One of her first decisions had been to change the name – who would want to stay in Trotters Mount? A manor was what the Cresswells had, so why not the Topshams? 'Of course, to do that I shall need your assistance ... I couldn't do it on my own.' She smiled winsomely at the bank manager, who was so overcome that this time he had to concentrate on his ruler.

The silence in the room drew out. Dolly listened to the ticking of the large clock, the rattle of traffic in the street, the clip-clopping of horses' hoofs. Why did the man need so long to make a simple decision?

'You do realize that it is only because your husband agrees with this venture ...'

'But of course. As a woman, I know my limitations.' God, how it offended her to speak thus.

'I need your husband's signature.'

Dolly snapped open her bag and took out a document. 'I have the paper my husband arranged before he went to war. It gives me the right to sign for him ...'

Another long pause. 'Very well. I will propose a loan but only on the grounds that the asking price is dropped by at least one hundred pounds.'

'I'm sure that will be possible.' The idiot! She could have hit him.

And here she was, several hours later with just a hundred pounds between her and her dream. If only George would take her to his bed. There, she knew she would succeed.

Noting that the bottle was nearly empty, she stood up and fetched another. Perhaps if she got him drunk? Another hour passed. Dolly controlled her impatience with difficulty.

'Very well!' he said finally. 'As you wish. Who am I, a mere man, to argue with clever Dolly Topsham? Let's sign the papers.' He was smiling at her but suddenly stood up and moved round the table. He kissed her, placed his hands on her breasts and began to knead them. The sudden-ness of the action, the arrogance of his roughness, excited her beyond her dreams.

A week later Dolly, after yet another lust-filled night with George, was sure that she must look different – that everyone knew she was an adulteress. She peered at herself in the mirror, certain her sins were written on her face. But she was the same as ever. To her surprise, she was disappointed.

'Hussy!' She giggled.

She stretched her arms over her head. George was everything she wanted in a man. He was decisive, considerate, complimentary. Their relationship, which had started so suddenly, was deepening. Last night, fortified by a good claret, she had found the courage to tell him she wanted him to move into Topsham Manor with her.

'I need you, George. I want us to be together.'

'I have some money, not enough. I could never be a kept man.'

'Nor would I wish you to be. We could work together.'

He had taken her hand and kissed it tenderly. 'Thank you, my love. You're allowing me to have everything I have ever wished for. The house and you ...'

Now she had all she wanted. It was then that she had crossed the room to the old bread oven where, behind the black metal door, she kept important things. She returned to the table and handed him the first of the money. The deal was complete.

She sighed happily as she remembered the scene. It had been so romantic. Every night with him was special, but last night had been exceptional. To celebrate completion of the sale she had opened a bottle of champagne. Dolly rarely drank but that night she allowed herself to become gloriously tipsy. What few inhibitions she had were banished and she had given herself to him in total wantonness. She should have felt dreadful but she didn't. The excesses she had enjoyed had left her renewed.

As she was dressing she noticed a bruise on her breast. It was a good thing Zeph was away. How would she have explained it? She sat on the edge of her bed. How different the two men were. There had been times at night when she had felt afraid of George and his control of her. But then she experienced a new stirring in her loins. Zeph had never made her feel like this.

George made her feel like a woman. 'God, you're a true woman,' he had said to her. How many times had he taken her? She'd lost count.

Zeph took her gently, his kisses tender. He'd never bruised her and if he had he would have been contrite. But she didn't want apologies, she wanted to feel possessed. George was a real man, Zeph an apology for one. She could see that now.

She had expected to feel guilty but she didn't. After all, Zeph had been unfaithful first, and what was sauce for the gander ... If she had done wrong, it was Zeph's fault. If he had not strayed, she would have remained his dutiful wife – albeit one who would have spent the rest of her life wondering how different things might have been.

She was glad this had happened. If it hadn't, she would never have known the ecstasy and trepidation of these past nights. 'That would have been a tragedy,' she said aloud. She would not have missed this awakening for anything.

Now that she knew what she had been missing she realized she had been cheated for years. If she hadn't been so happy she'd have been angry.

'Come on, you two, you'll be late for school,' she called to Apollo and Cordelia. But her voice was happy, without the shrill nagging note of the past.

She was singing as she prepared their breakfast. Her children looked at each other with astonishment, as they had every morning since George had entered her life.

'You're always happy now, mother,' Cordelia ventured, as Dolly brushed her long blonde hair. Unusually she was gentle. Normally she tugged at the tangles and it invariably ended in tears.

'We're moving.'

'Moving?' The children were downcast.

'Don't fret. We're staying in Cress but we shall be living at the top of Trotters Hill. I signed the final papers yesterday. That's why I'm happy. But let's keep it a secret for the moment.' She was packing their lunch as she spoke. 'Off you go.' She kissed the tops of their heads, which only added to their confusion since she was usually in too much of a temper to do so.

Dolly flew round the bar clearing up the debris from last night. She opened the windows to air the room. She would normally have opened the door, too, since she was never closed, but today it remained bolted. Today she would celebrate and she had given Flossie the day off.

She tidied the snug that was their private sitting room and her office. The children's possessions lying about from the evening before would normally have annoyed her but this morning she just put them away. A pile of correspondence lay on her desk, but she put a paperweight on top of it. It could wait. She was usually up to date with her accounts but there were more important things in life than paperwork.

In the kitchen she cooked bacon, eggs and sausage, filled the teapot and placed everything on a tray with her best embroidered tray-cloth. She checked herself in the mirror, patted her hair, pinched her cheeks, licked her lips and then, with the tray aloft, she climbed the stairs to her guest's room – they were careful to make sure he was back in his own quarters before the children were awake.

She tapped lightly on the door but there was no response so, gingerly, she opened it and tiptoed into the room. She put the tray on the dressing-table. 'George,' she whispered. 'I thought I'd best waken you. I didn't know if you had matters to attend to today.' Secretly she was hoping he hadn't. She was looking forward to spending the day in bed with him. 'George!' Poor man, she had exhausted him. She crossed to the window and pulled back the curtains.

Had she been holding the tray she would have dropped it at the sight of the unused bed. 'Oh, no!' She raced along the corridor to the bathroom. It was empty. Back in the bedroom she inspected the wardrobe. His clothes had gone. Panic rose in her as if a flock of ravens were wakening. There had to be an explanation. But if there were, he would have given it. What had she done?

The money! She'd given him the first year's payment last night! She sank on to the edge of the bed, nauseous with fear. What had she done? She stood up abruptly. Calm down, she told herself. Think sensibly.

They'd signed the papers – Flossie and Rob had witnessed them. She sat again, holding her stomach, trying to calm the churning in her guts.

Just as she had grasped happiness it was to be torn from her. No. He would be back. He would! She pushed her hair off her face. She knew she was lying to herself. Once again she tried to be optimistic. She failed. She was devastated ...

She slumped, then sat bolt upright. The takings!

Dolly normally moved with speed but this morning she excelled herself as she ran down the stairs and back into the snug. What a fool she was! He'd have seen her last night as she put the money into the hidey-hole at the side of the fireplace. Her hands were shaking as she opened the old bread-oven door. With relief she saw that the metal box and its contents were still there.

'Put it down to experience,' she told herself, but she knew she was bluffing.

8

Unable to face the idea that George Meopham had left her Dolly decided to refer to his 'disappearance'. Had she not, she was sure her pride would never recover.

That first night, she had found sleep impossible, then again on the next and the next. She missed George with a physical pain. She feared that a good night's rest was to become something she remembered with fondness. Whatever she tried to induce sleep – a hot drink, lavender under her pillow, clean linen, opening the window, closing it – it failed. Rather than toss and turn she flitted about the inn at night, sorting and packing her possessions ready for the move in a week's time. Her clothes were hanging off her since she couldn't eat. Food made her feel sick. Always slim, she was now painfully thin.

The move was proving a Godsend. She was busy organising and planning so she could blot out the anger she felt at George's *disappearance* and forget the pain of his betrayal.

When he had first *disappeared* she was afraid he had in some way cheated her out of the house. But she calmed down when she had thought it through. There was no need to worry because she had the deeds – or, rather, the bank did. She had no fears since everything had been arranged and drawn up by a solicitor.

Dolly's own solicitor's offices were in Barlton but George had suggested she should use a friend of his who had just moved to Cress-by-the-Sea. In any case, the less the Barlton man knew the better because he was Zeph's solicitor too.

George had introduced her to James Gilbert, who was a charming and efficient man. She had been rather taken aback by the sparseness of the furnishings in his office but he had explained that he was still setting up and that, in fact, she was his first client there. He had, he told her, taken the liberty of purchasing champagne to celebrate. She was touched by his thoughtfulness.

Compared to her other solicitor, who was old and dull, this man was a gem. He had explained everything to her in minute detail, warning her that if she defaulted on one of her yearly payments the property would revert to the present owner. She had signed everything confidently, convinced that the business would be a great success. She had happily paid over the first instalment – nearly one hundred pounds, courtesy of the bank.

So impressed was she with the young man that she promised him all her future business. That he was slim and handsome, with a twinkle in his eye, helped her decision.

Just as she was leaving she paused in the doorway. 'Have you heard from George?' she asked, as nonchalantly as she could.

'Why, yes, he had some family matters to resolve. He should be back soon.'

'He mentioned something about it in his letter ...' she lied, through her teeth. What a relief.

The day arrived when she was to take possession of the house. As arranged, she made her way to James Gilbert's office to pick up the keys.

It was bare. The desk, the chairs, the books had gone. She nearly fainted. Mr Gilbert, the disgruntled landlord told her, had disappeared in the night. Panic mounted, but she managed to hide it from the man – it would do her standing in the community no good if others knew of this. She was not surprised to learn that he had left no forwarding address and, to make matters worse, his rent had not been paid. First George, now James.

'But he left this for you.' The man handed her a package. When she opened it and saw the keys to the new house inside it she could have wept with relief. There was a note. 'I enjoyed meeting you.' What a cheeky rascal he was, she thought. And what a roller-coaster this business was.

One minute she was terrified, the next certain that all would be well.

Outside again, Dolly pulled her coat close against the chill. The two of them *disappearing* was too much of a coincidence. Should she report their behaviour to the police? She hurried along the quay towards the local station, keeping her head low. She was in no mood to talk to anyone. Halfway there she stopped. The woman following her cannoned into her. Dolly made no apology but turned on her heel and walked back the way she had come. What if George returned with a reasonable explanation? What if Gilbert was the crook? Perhaps he had taken her money. She wouldn't report it yet.

Her next decision was to visit the bank. She hurried back along the quay, oblivious to others' greetings. At the impressive front door she paused. This, she decided, was not a good idea either. If she told the manager what would he do? He would cancel the arrangements, demand the first payment back, and then he would go to the police.

She raced back to the inn, her mind a whirl of plans, ideas and strategy. But underneath she detected an ominous sense of doom. Even though she had the keys to the property, logic told her that all was not as it should have been.

The shock of finding James Gilbert gone had had a salutary effect on her. She needed to clear her head and think. Quickly she decided what she must do. Once Dolly had made a decision she always felt better. This time, though, she could not shed the anxiety.

'Occupation is nine-tenths of the law,' she repeated to herself. She would move in as quickly as she could. Once there, it would be impossible for anyone to get her out. She would refuse to go. Whatever was afoot would be vanquished. Now she felt *much* better.

'You're busy. Are you throwing all this stuff away? If you are, might I sift through it first?' Flossie stood in the doorway of the snug, as Dolly emptied the drawers of her desk.

'No, I'm keeping it all.' Dolly sat back on her haunches and looked up at the other woman. So far she had not told Flossie of her plans, only her children, and she had sworn them to secrecy.

'I'm moving house.' There. She had said it. She smiled, but stopped when she saw Flossie sway and hold on to the door to stop herself falling.

'When?'

'Tomorrow.'

'So soon ...' Flossie stumbled across to the table and sank down on the first available chair.

'I'm selling the cottages.'

'Oh, Dolly, no!' Flossie's face was etched with anxiety.

Dolly leapt to her feet and sat down opposite her. 'There's no need to look so worried. I've a plan for you, Flossie Marshall.' She was enjoying this interview and the feeling of power it gave her. 'I was wondering if you'd consider moving in here and running the place for me.' She smiled her best Lady Bountiful smile – *whether she'd consider*. It made her want to laugh.

'Run the Cresswell Arms?' Flossie was astounded.

'Of course, you'd have to put the children in one room – we couldn't spare more for them—'

'No, of course not.' Flossie agreed, with alacrity.

'As you know, times are hard. I couldn't afford to pay you but you can feed yourselves.'

'Not pay me?'

'Well, of course, it's up to you. If you don't want the position I'm sure many would.' Dolly stood up.

'No, no! Please! I didn't mean that ...' Flossie trailed off.

Dolly sat down and studied her hands. She knew Flossie would accept – what choice did she have? No doubt she would steal from her and that would be her wage.

'It's very kind of you, Dolly. I accept.'

'Don't you want to discuss it with Alf?'

'He'll agree.'

Of course he will, Dolly thought with glee.

The following day, in the hall of the new house, Dolly waited impatiently for the carter to arrive with her personal possessions and the few pieces of furniture she had decided to bring with her from the inn. She wasn't sure why – compared with the furnishings in this house, they were rubbish. But they were the first things she had bought when she was newly married and renting a house in Barlton. Another lifetime ago, she thought, as she looked about her at the fine furniture in the hallway of Topsham Manor. She picked up the small ivory pad that hung on the chatelaine she had purchased for her new position as mistress of this grand house. On it she scribbled, 'name board'.

She stepped out on to the top step. Far below the sea shimmered in the autumn sunshine, as if someone had sprinkled the waves with mercury. Watching the inhabitants of Cress as they scuttled about their lives, Dolly thought, condescendingly, of how well she had done. Who would recognize Dolly Pepper, no shoes on her feet and hand-me-down clothes, now? She had always feared that a time might come when she would have to revert to such a life … but no longer.

The carter clattered up and the men began to unload the boxes and cases. Dolly watched every movement with an eagle eye. 'Careful,' she ordered, as the younger of the two men leapt off the back of the cart with her whatnot. 'You damage anything and I'll dock it from your fee.'

She was distracted by the sound of a motor-car on the driveway. She couldn't see who it was since the enormous rhododendron bushes hid them from view. She shaded her eyes the better to see, hoping it was a neighbour come to welcome her.

The chauffeur leapt out and, standing smartly to attention, held open the door. As Stan Eldridge descended from the car, Dolly swept down her front steps, in what she hoped was an elegantly welcoming manner. What an honour! What could he want? Then, to her even greater excitement, she saw Esmeralda get out on the opposite side. She did not notice the fourth person.

'Mrs Topsham.' Eldridge doffed his top hat.

'It's an honour to see you, Mr Eldridge.' She gave a bob and was then annoyed with herself. Why should she curtsy to them? Was she not their equal now that she owned this fine mansion? He was not smiling. Oh, Lord, she thought. She hoped he hadn't come to ask for the money he had loaned her to help Timmy, her brother-in-law flee and in return she should have spied on his daughter for him which she'd never done, nor repaid a penny.

'And Mrs Oliver too …' To her even greater annoyance she found herself curtsying to the woman, who acknowledged her so haughtily that she would have liked to slap her. She didn't even shake Dolly's outstretched hand.

'I fear we have a problem, Mrs Topsham.'

'I'm so sorry. Is there anything I can do to help?'

'Yes, Mrs Topsham. You can vacate my property.'

9

Had Dolly been the type of woman to faint she might have done so at Stan Eldridge's bald statement. But she wasn't. She blinked, swallowed hard, and asked him to repeat what he had said. Then she stood, feet wide apart, as if to protect the house from invaders. Unaware of what she was doing she folded her arms across her chest.

'I beg your pardon?' she asked, forcing herself to sound normal but her stomach was churning. 'And who are you?' She swung round to the other man, who was sidling up the steps. He stopped in his tracks and blushed a fine claret colour, which clashed alarmingly with his ginger hair.

'I think you heard me perfectly well the first time, Mrs Topsham.' Eldridge held out his hand to guide Esmeralda up the steps. At least she had the grace to look uncomfortable at the situation that was unfolding and less superior, Dolly thought.

'I heard what you said, Mr Eldridge, but I didn't understand what you meant ...' She paused, trying frantically to decide the best way to deal with him for she knew he would be a dangerous enemy. It would be expedient not to upset him – there was the matter of the money she still owed him, which she had been trying to ignore. However, since Esmeralda was with him he was unlikely to raise the subject. He must know that if he did, Dolly would let slip that he'd asked her to spy on his daughter.

'You had better come in and we can discuss any problem you imagine there is, in comfort.' She paused in the hall as one of the removal men appeared, puffing, with a heavy case. 'No, no!' Dolly waved her hands at him irritably. 'Not that one. Take those boxes up to the back bedroom with the blue curtains,' she ordered the carter, pointing at another pile, which contained the children's things. She had every intention of show-ing him she was in control.

'Stop.' This time Eldridge held up his hand to the men. 'Nothing else is to be moved into this house. Do you understand? Not as much as a teaspoon.'

'Papa ...' Esmeralda took his arm as if to restrain him.

'I'll deal with this, my dear.'

'Welcome,' Dolly said as, with an expansive gesture, she showed them into the drawing room. 'As you see, the views of the bay are far-reach-ing. Isn't it lovely even at this time of year? Just imagine what it will be like in summer. I shall ...' She continued to prattle for, in an odd way, she felt that if she kept talking he could not say what she feared he might be about to say. He watched her sardonically, reminding her of a black panther waiting to pounce.

Eventually she fell silent. Unsure that her legs would support her for much longer she sat down.

Stan Eldridge flicked up the tails of his elegant cashmere coat and sat opposite her. He placed his hands on top of the ornate silver cane, which stood between his legs. The other man moved the ottoman by the window and, from an attaché case, took out a sheaf of documents. He proceeded to check them. Dolly's nervousness grew.

Esmeralda was prowling round the room inspecting the objects and paintings on the walls. 'I do believe you have a Landseer here,' she called, but no one was listening to her.

'Perhaps, Mrs Topsham, you could begin by explaining what you're doing here and why your men are depositing your things in *my* house?' Eldridge began, in a tone that conveyed how little value he attached to her possessions.

'This bronze is superb, Papa. May I have it?' Esmeralda had picked up a heavy statue of a stag and was stumbling across the wide room with it. The other man leapt up to help her, his papers scattering.

This was too much for Dolly, who jumped smartly to her feet ready to protect what she had paid for. 'Excuse me!' She could not disguise her indignation. 'That is mine.' Even as she spoke, she knew her voice lacked conviction.

'Have what you want, my darling.' There was a hint of irritation in his voice.

'I'll take the painting too, if I may?'

'Of course – and then stop bothering me!' Eldridge snapped.

His daughter looked shocked. 'There's no need to be beastly,' she said, and to Dolly she seemed near to tears. Stupid creature, she thought. But Eldridge's reaction cheered her. It showed he was rattled, that he wasn't as confident as he appeared.

'Excuse me,' she ventured again. 'You don't have the right to give away *my* possessions willy-nilly.' She tried to instil firmness into her tone. 'You might claim to own this property but I'm afraid you are mistaken. I am the purchaser.'

Eldridge snorted derisively. 'You are at liberty to think you are but I can assure you that you are not. Henry, the papers.' He clicked his fingers and the young man riffled through the documents. 'Henry!'

The papers were laid out on an occasional table for Dolly to peruse. There was no doubting that they were the title deeds to a property, and different from the ones she had in the bank. For a start there were more of them, and they were yellowed with age. The script was strange and she found it hard to read, but she eventually made out that they referred to Trotters Mount. On the last page, sealed and witnessed, she saw

Eldridge's signature and beside it she recognized the hand of George Meopham.

'You claim to own this property, so where are your deeds?'

'I don't have them.' She could not disguise how despondent she felt.

'And why am I not surprised?' Eldridge sneered.

'Because they're in the damned bank,' she almost shouted.

'Mrs Topsham, I must object to your language in front of my daughter.'

'I'm sorry,' she said, but she wasn't. She fingered the documents. Her deeds were not like this. They were clean and white. She remembered now how George had explained them away, saying the originals had been lost in a fire and that these were certified copies and, sure enough, at the bottom there had been a shiny red seal. But it wasn't just Dolly who had swallowed the tale: her bank manager had too.

'Are you satisfied now? I purchased this property from Meopham's cousin as these deeds prove.'

'I have deeds. I told you, they are at the bank.'

'Fakes.'

Dolly could not bring herself to argue. All the fight seemed to have drained out of her. 'But I paid ...' Her voice faded away.

'Of course, George Meopham is a very plausible gentleman. Attractive too.' He smiled.

'What are you implying?' Dolly thanked God she was not the sort who blushed. She had a horrible conviction that Eldridge knew everything; she wondered if he had guessed or whether George had betrayed her. She felt vulnerable and alone.

'Nothing. But if you take my advice, you should be aware, Mrs Topsham, that all confidence tricksters are charming and credible – they have to be. And there are no real bargains in this world. If something is cheap you must ask yourself why.'

What an insufferable man. How dare he lecture her? He was the last person she would take advice from. He was rumoured to be a German – he should be locked up.

'Mrs Topsham ... Since Mr Eldridge has already mentioned bargains ...' There was a discreet cough.

The lawyer looking at her so kindly that tears pricked her eyes. She turned away. She couldn't afford to let him know she was weakening. 'Might I ask how much money you have paid?'

Should she tell them or not? What had she to lose? 'More than ninety-five pounds.'

At this Stan Eldridge laughed, jeeringly. When Dolly looked at him, he had the grace to stop. 'It was to be the first of five instalments, paid over five years.'

'And you thought the value of the house, with its contents, was a mere four hundred and seventy-five pounds?' Eldridge said, with amusement. 'If that were so I wouldn't have considered its purchase. I buy only the best.'

Dolly's hand itched to hit him. She didn't know how best to react. 'I have little experience of business,' she said, hoping modesty might help.

'Which is evident. Only a fool would have thought that sum a true value of this house *and* its contents.'

'If that is so, I agree. We cannot all be as clever as you.'

'I should point out that flattery will get you nowhere with me, Mrs Topsham.'

'I wasn't flattering you. I was speaking the truth.' She wished they would go so that she could be left alone to contemplate the muddle of her life. She knew how much the cottages and the inn were worth, why had she not thought the valuation too low? Because she had been greedy. And she had thought herself in love.

Tears welled, and her throat ached as she tried to control them. If she had nothing else, she still had her pride. She would not weep in front of this hard man and his frivolous daughter. At which point she broke down. A great gasp of misery escaped before she could stop it. She fumbled in her bag for a handkerchief. Suddenly she saw that Esmeralda had sunk to the floor beside her and was handing her one.

'Mrs Topsham, please don't cry so, you'll make yourself ill. And I shall cry, too, in sympathy.' Esmeralda fussed over her and briefly Dolly enjoyed it – who normally cared anything about her? The idea brought on another storm of tears.

'Can I be of assistance?' The man called Henry was kneeling beside her now. She blew her nose, then dabbed at her eyes, beginning to feel better – until she caught sight of Eldridge. He sat impassive, his lip curled in that cynical smile. That and his manifest coldness made her howl again.

'Papa, you have to help this poor woman,' Esmeralda appealed.

'How? Should I give her this house? It's hardly my fault that she has made this disastrous investment.'

'I acted in good faith …' She gulped.

'No one thinks you didn't, Mrs Topsham,' Henry put in.

She smiled gratefully at him. For the first time she noticed he was quite good-looking, even though she wasn't one for red hair. 'I'm ruined. I don't know what to do, who to turn to. What is the bank going to say?' And she had need of the handkerchief again.

'You appear to have a penchant for being in my debt, if I remember. A small matter but one not fulfilled,' Eldridge reminded her.

'I fully intended ...' What? She no longer knew.

'Tell me, Mrs Topsham. What were you intending to use this mansion for? I presume such a businesswoman as you are had plans.'

She could not make up her mind whether he was being sarcastic or if he meant it. But there was no point in trying to outsmart him now. 'I intended to create an exclusive hotel.'

'In Cress?'

'Yes. If this war continues, more and more officers will be sent to Cresswell Manor. There is no suitable hotel for the wives and parents of the patients. There is a need for a hotel here.'

Stan Eldridge tapped his cane on the floor in a tattoo. 'Excellent. Exactly what I thought and what I planned.'

'Then, Papa, the solution is simple ...'

'Thank you, Esmeralda, I can manage my own affairs. Now, Mrs Topsham, I have a suggestion ...'

Over the next half-hour he outlined his plans. At the end Dolly was in a whirl of delirious excitement. She had been created manageress of the planned hotel; she would not enjoy a salary until her debt to Eldridge was cleared. She was to liaise with Henry whose surname, she now knew, was Kempson, and was relieved to be dealing with him, not Eldridge. The less she saw of him the better.

'But what about the money I gave George?'

'Really, Mrs Topsham. You cannot expect everything in this life. I fear that remains your problem.' So saying, he got to his feet. 'There's just one other thing. You have children?'

'Two. Apollo and Cordelia.'

'What charming names. Their ages?'

'Thirteen and eleven.'

'I suggest you send them to boarding-school. You cannot concentrate adequately if they are here, needing your attention. I demand total commitment from those I employ.' He gave a slight bow, then swept from the room, the others following in his wake.

Dolly slumped back on the chair, part relieved, part still worried and afraid. She was also disappointed, furious – and determined to take her revenge on that arrogant man, though she had no idea how.

Chapter Five

Winter 1915-16

1

'When I think of the wonderful Christmases we enjoyed in the past, I could weep!' Eve Gilroy complained, as she continued to prepare the food. 'Fifty for Christmas luncheon one year – do you remember, Edward?'

'And you surpassed yourself, if I might say so, Eve.'

'That was the year we had three parties, not counting the staff knees-up.'

'I for one shall not miss *that* event.'

'There was certainly a lot of shenanigans went on. Still, it was only once a year.'

'I'm sure we'll make the best of it, as we always do.' Whitaker looked up from filling his pipe with tobacco. It was a new acquisition, a particularly fine meerschaum, one that, in Eve's opinion, made him seem even manlier. He gave her one of his rare smiles – which, as always, gladdened her heart. 'Miss Cresswell has told me there's to be no gathering of the staff this year for the family to give them presents. Now that does sadden me. It was always such a joyful occasion.'

'What they done that for? Saving money, I suppose.'

'I would hardly think it necessary for the Cresswells to economise, Eve.'

'Wouldn't you, Edward? I tell you, this family will be on its uppers within twenty years. If I was a betting woman I'd put a sovereign on it.'

'And what brought you to that conclusion, Eve?'

'When the gentry start selling land you know there's a problem. And Sir Mortie sold acres to that Stan Eldridge, didn't he? Never touch capital, and what's land but that? I've heard that said many a time.'

'I'm sure it's more that they think it would not be right for us to celebrate when our poor soldiers are being slaughtered.' He puffed at his pipe. 'It's seems a miracle to me that more men haven't gone from here, but it's just a matter of time,' he added dolefully.

'Don't think that, let alone say it. What would we do if Mr Morts and

Mr Oliver went? There would be such disorder here without them to run things. And how would poor Rowan manage?'

'She would deal with the situation as so many of our brave women do. Why, when I was in Barlton I came across a woman driving a grocery delivery cart and another on a butcher's bicycle. It doesn't seem right that the fair sex should be expected to perform such tasks.'

'I don't know. I'd quite like to ride around on a bicycle all day, out in the fresh air, meeting people. And it wouldn't be such hard work as this is.'

'Not much pleasure in the wind and the rain, though, Eve. But it struck me, seeing those women, that our world is being turned upside-down. Nothing is as it used to be and I find myself wondering if it will ever return to normal.'

'I don't know. When peace comes ... eventually ... we'll soon be back to how we were. At least, I hope I'll have enough kitchenmaids.' She sniffed the air. 'I like the smell of your baccy. Sweet and comfortable-smelling.'

'You don't object to me smoking in your kitchen? I do apologise – most remiss of me – I should have asked. I don't know what came over me ...' He began hurriedly to pack away the paraphernalia.

'Bless you. I don't mind. You smoke whenever you want. You need to relax when you can after the extra duties put on you these days.' Eve began to peel the onions for the forcemeats. 'I like a man who smokes a pipe. It reminds me of my father,' she said sentimentally. She liked to pretend she'd had a perfect upbringing in a respectable home but she didn't even know who her father was. That was a secret she would never divulge to a living soul lest the shame destroy her.

'I've had mixed news, Eve.'

She paused in her task to look at him enquiringly.

'Mrs Hamilton and the children are coming for Christmas.'

'Well, isn't that wonderful news? I like Miss Lettice. I know there are those who didn't approve of her running away from her husband as she did, but I've always had a soft spot for her. And to have little Georgia and Charlotte here. A house needs children at such a time.'

'I said it was mixed news, Eve. Sir Mortie and her ladyship are coming too.'

Eve laid down her vegetable knife with a clatter. 'But why? She hates it here. We were getting on so well without them.'

'As you know, they moved out of London in August. The zeppelin raids had become too much for them.'

'Cowardly.'

'I don't think we should judge them, Eve. After all, we don't know how bad it had become – going to bed at night not knowing if one was going to wake in the morning.'

'Why can't they stay at her father's estate instead of bothering us? It's very grand, I hear, much more so than Cresswell.'

'Unfortunately that has become a convalescent home too and I have heard a rumour, which, of course, I can't substantiate and which I would not like you to repeat to anyone ...'

'Of course I won't.' She tried not to sound fractious but there were times when he was a mite long-winded.

'Well, I heard that it's not exclusively for officers – that other ranks are admitted.'

Eve hacked viciously at the onion. 'Other ranks get wounded too, doesn't she know?' The pile of onions grew. 'But that explains everything. I'm surprised her ladyship doesn't fall over more often since her nose is stuck so high in the air. But tell me ...' She waved the knife in the air. '... how is everyone to fit in? Where will they all sleep? And if she thinks I'm going to prepare the meals I used to, well, she's got another think coming.'

'Miss Cresswell is arranging the accommodation. I wouldn't like to be in her shoes.' Whitaker laughed, an even rarer occurrence than his smile. It changed his face completely, softening the lines.

'What's the joke? Can anyone join in?' Sergeant Bob clattered into the kitchen.

Noisy oaf, thought Eve. It was no longer a secret that he was walking out with Lady Penelope's nurse, Betsy Winlock, a particularly crude woman, in Eve's opinion. As a consequence she rarely spoke to him other than to ensure the smooth running of the kitchen. However, he still chatted to her, even though she scarcely answered.

'Not good news, then,' he said, once Whitaker had explained about the impending visitors. 'Well, that'll make trouble. Change in the menus then, Eve. Expect that'll be the order of the day.'

Since this was a kitchen matter she allowed herself to respond. 'Most certainly not. Her ladyship will have the food I prepare for the officers and she can lump it.'

'That's my girl!'

'I'll have you know I'm *not* your girl, thanks be.'

'Need any help, Eve?'

'Potatoes,' she said shortly, and to emphasize her displeasure she marched off to her pantry. She paused at the door to listen but, to her disappointment they were not talking about her.

She leant against a sack of potatoes and, for a second, let the unhappiness she fought slither into her mind. She missed the old camaraderie they had once shared, the three of them in the kitchen. Sergeant Bob had hurt her. If only he had confided in her it might have been different. And Betsy Winlock was no beauty, which made her fret even more. Still, she told herself, what's done is done. She collected a basket of carrots, some curly kale and a Savoy cabbage. Feeling sorry for herself would never do.

When she returned it was to find Rowan at the table, talking seriously to Whitaker. 'Good morning. Have you heard the news?'

'Miss Cresswell told me earlier.'

'I expect it's upset you.'

'No, Mrs Gilroy, why should I be upset? It will be nice for my husband to have his parents back.'

Whitaker beamed at her response.

She's learning, thought Eve, but it was taking her further away from them – she had grown to like Rowan in the past few months. Lady Coral would make her life more than difficult.

'How's your mother? I haven't seen her for months.'

'I haven't seen much of her either. She's so busy, these days.'

'Moved back into the inn, hasn't she? In charge! Nice for some …'

'She's very content. She always loved working there. She enjoys the company, and it's better for her than when she was living in the cottage.' Rowan had an odd expression.

'That Dolly's sold her cottages. Did you know?'

'When?'

'Back in October, November time, wasn't it, Edward?'

'Nobody told me.'

'I doubt anyone would think you were interested, Rowan. Though who would be mad enough to buy them, given their condition – they need pulling down.' She noticed Rowan was frowning. Something afoot, she thought. 'Melanie Topsham must be spinning in her grave when you think how hard she worked to buy them in the first place. I sometimes thought she wouldn't rest until she owned the whole of Cress.' Eve laughed. 'Dolly's queening it, I'm told, up at Trotters Mount – only she calls it Topsham Manor. Have you ever heard anything so ridiculous? Rolls-Royce ideas and a push bike pocket, that one. You mark my words, she'll get herself into trouble.'

Rowan began to look uncomfortable with the conversation and asked permission to use the range, which Eve liked. Others just barged in and took over.

'Not that I like to gossip, but …' Whitaker began, in a whisper, now that Rowan was out of earshot. Eve leant forward. 'It seems the trouble has already come. There's something odd about the purchase of that house. I've been told Dolly lost a lot of money, that although she says she's the owner, she isn't. Mr Eldridge is.'

'Never! Makes you wonder what *is* going on there, doesn't it?'

'Poor Zeph's in for a shock when he gets back from the trenches and finds out what she's done. And rumour runs that the inn is up for sale too. That *will* cause ructions.'

'Zeph? Who's got an outlandish name like that?' Sergeant Bob asked.

'Zephaniah Topsham, to give him his rightful name,' Whitaker told him.

Despite her resolution never to speak to him about non-kitchen matters, Eve could not resist the opportunity to impart information. 'He owns the inn at Cress, not that you'd know it, the way his wife, Dolly, carries on. It was left to his mother by old Sir Mortimer – and very strange that was too …'

'Eve!' Whitaker nodded towards Rowan, who was making a jug of Bengers by the hob.

'She's not listening,' Eve whispered. 'Wrong side of the blanket, if you understand.' She winked to emphasize her meaning. 'His mother went in for peculiar names, called her daughter Xenia.'

'I wonder what's happened to her. I haven't heard anything about her for years. Beautiful woman,' Whitaker said thoughtfully.

'She'll turn up like the bad penny she is. We haven't seen the last of her, that's for sure.'

Rowan, her task complete, thanked Mrs Gilroy for the use of the stove and left.

'You shouldn't have said those things in front of her, Eve. It's not fair. It puts her in a difficult position.'

'Fiddlesticks, Edward. She wasn't listening. And, in any case, who started the conversation? Answer me that.'

He found it necessary to cough. 'I accept it was I, and I shouldn't have. We can't be sure she didn't hear, Eve. But I was impressed by her loyalty towards her mother-in-law.'

'Truth be told she must be quaking!' Eve looked forward to trouble. It was always more interesting than equilibrium in the house.

2

A ll the time she was working, Rowan was mulling over the gossip she had heard in the kitchen. She had not seen her mother since that awful day when Flossie had been so angry with her. But, hearing about Dolly's schemes, she had known that, once again, her family was at risk and she had no choice but to visit. Perhaps they could bury the hatchet.

As soon as her duties were over for the morning, Rowan arranged with Fanny to cover for her while she took an extra hour for lunch. It was bitterly cold so she wrapped up warm and decided to drive the governess cart rather than walk.

Strangely the stables were deserted. Normally all was bustle and noise, but today it was silent. She called but no one answered. Gingerly she pushed open the door to the tack room searching for a groom. Harold, the senior coachman, was sitting on a pile of horse blankets, a large red handkerchief clutched to his face. He was crying.

Rowan was unsure what she should do. She was embarrassed and puzzled to find a grown man weeping.

'Mrs Morts,' Harold scrambled to his feet. 'I'm sorry ... I didn't hear you.' He wiped his sleeve across his tear-stained face.

'I'm still Rowan to you, Mr Harold.' She smiled at the kind man she had known all her life. 'But what can be the matter?'

'It's the horses. Oh, Mrs ... They've taken the horses ...' He collapsed again on to the blankets as if his legs had given way.

'Who has taken them?'

'The army. They're to be shipped to France.' At this his massive shoulders slumped and he made a rasping noise as if he were fighting for breath. She waited patiently until he had controlled himself.

'Who gave permission?' she asked.

'I'm not sure. Mr Oliver, I presume. But how could they? Them hunters, they're like my children ... I was there when most of them were born ...'

Rowan was horrified. What hope was there for the horses to survive? 'The pony?'

'He's still here – too small, you see – and some of the old ones have been left but ... But they're pining, missing their stablemates. They'm left the shires for the field work, mind you.' He gave an almighty sniff. 'Are you wanting the pony harnessed?'

'No, thank you, not today. You stay where you are,' she said. 'Try not to worry, Mr Harold. I'm sure they'll come home safe and sound.' It had seemed the right thing to say but she didn't believe it.

Cold or not, she would have to walk. She set off at a cracking pace for time was of the essence. When she had set out she had been upset, but now she was even more so. Every day the news was worse. Now she refused even to look at a newspaper. It was, she had decided, best not to know. The world was too topsy-turvy.

On the way she kept meeting people she knew, but she could not stop to talk. Of course, this rush was her own fault. She should have known what was going on. She should have forgiven her mother months ago, but she had been so involved with her own problems that she had not had time for her family.

She should have known that Dolly had sold the cottage. How could the woman have done that and not told Rowan when she had paid a whole year's rent? It wasn't right. Worst of all, she had not known her mother was working at the inn again because she had cut herself off from everyone and concentrated on Morts.

'This is a surprise,' Flossie said, as Rowan entered the kitchen at the inn. 'I'd begun to forget what you looked like.'

The sarcasm put Rowan on her guard. 'You could come to me.'

'And how would I find the time?'

'Exactly. Then you'll understand my difficulty in getting here to see you.'

'You're not telling me you, of all people, couldn't get away if you wanted to.'

'I hear Dolly's sold the cottage you were living in, also, that you're in charge here.' She was determined not to be tied up with silly arguments about visits and lack of time.

'Fortunately it's turned out for the best. I was worried when Dolly told me her plans, but she offered me this position and I was happy to oblige. At least it gives us a roof over our heads.'

'How much is she paying you?'

Flossie folded her arms over her ample chest. 'I don't think that's any of your business.'

'I wouldn't ask, but I need to know.'

'Why?'

'Because I worry about you.'

'There's more to this than meets the eye. Why do you *need* to know?'

'I can't tell you.' Rowan felt the blood rushing to her face.

'Yes, you can. It's your duty to tell me.'

Suddenly Rowan was no longer a married woman with a new life. She was a little girl whose mother had caught her doing wrong. 'Please, Mum, don't make me.'

'You're not leaving here until you do.'

Rowan's heart sank. 'I paid a year's rent in advance for the cottage ... and for some repairs to it.'

Flossie sat down with a bump. 'You'd no right to do that.'

'I'm sorry.'

'You know how I feel about taking charity. You've shamed me.'

'For heaven's sake Mum, I'm your daughter.'

'All the more reason for you to understand my feelings and respect them.'

'I couldn't see you homeless.' She was close to tears.

'You should have told me.'

'You would not have let me do it.'

They sat in silence for a moment not looking at each other.

'Dolly should have told you about the cottages,' Flossie said eventually. 'I suppose you've a right to know – I work in return for a roof over our heads and our food.'

'No wage?'

'No wage.' Flossie seemed suddenly older and, Rowan feared, beaten.

'Oh, Mum.' She moved round the table and put her arms round Flossie. 'This isn't fair. That Dolly!'

At first she wasn't sure that she was hearing correctly, but she was. Flossie was laughing. 'In a way you've got to admire her ...' She was still chuckling. 'When she wants something she gets it.'

'She's greedy. I hate to think what Zeph would have to say.'

'Mind you, she got her comeuppance. She paid out money for that huge house on the hill but the man selling it to her was a confidence trickster. He scarpered with the lot.'

'They were saying in the kitchen that it belongs to Esmeralda's father.'

'That's right. He had sold it to both of them at the same time. I had to laugh. The silly woman pretends it belongs to her when everyone knows it's Stan Eldridge's. She's just the manageress. She's met her match with him. Imagine, working for a martinet like that. And your father reckons she must owe the bank a lot of money. Cuppa?'

For a moment they were silent. Then Flossie suddenly said, 'You were wrong to do what you did, Rowan. But I understand. It was kind of you.

I wish I could pay you back but I would never find the money. You're a good girl, Rowan.'

'Oh, Mum, I love you ...' Her mother's hug made her feel safe again. But she hadn't the heart to tell Flossie the latest rumour that Dolly was selling this inn.

Rowan was going to be late back on duty but it couldn't be helped. She was standing in the large bay window of the drawing room at Topsham Manor – Eve Gilroy was right. It *was* arrogant to have changed the name of the house.

'This is a surprise,' said Dolly, sounding like Flossie. 'Tea?'

Rowan did not have patience today for social niceties. 'I want you to pay my mother an adequate wage for the work she does. And I demand you return the money I paid you for the rent and repairs on the cottage they were living in,' she said, with no preamble.

Dolly laughed. 'If wishes were horses, beggars would ride.'

'I'm serious, Dolly.'

'Mrs Topsham to you.'

'What proposals do you have?'

'None. Why should I?'

'Because what you've done amounts to stealing.'

'How dare you accuse me of that?'

'You're using my mother, taking advantage of her situation.'

'And whose fault is it that she's got problems? Call yourself a daughter? You're a disgrace. I'm not a charity. You help her – you've money enough.'

'I'm warning you, Dolly. If you don't give me the money I shall make your life difficult.'

'Oh, really?' She laughed again. 'And how can you hurt me?'

'There is much I can do.' She ticked one finger. 'I shall tell Esmeralda that you're a cheat. I shall see her this evening. I'm sure she will find it necessary to warn her father of what a dishonest person he's in business with.'

'I don't know what you mean. This is my business.'

'You might pretend it is, but everyone knows who owns this house.' That was a shot in the dark. All she knew about it was based on rumour. She ticked a second finger. 'I shall also warn the officers I help care for not to let their loved ones stay here. I'm quite capable of doing so.' A third finger. 'I can tell your husband about a certain Mr Meopham. The list is endless ... *Dolly.*'

'You cunning little bitch. How dare you threaten me?'

'I would never normally do anything like this but I'm not willing to stand back and see my mother used by you or anyone else. The money, now.' She held out her hand. Dolly stalked out of the room. What was she planning? Rowan wondered. It was one thing to make threats, quite another to put them into practice.

She was picking up her bag when Dolly returned, an envelope in her hand. 'Here.'

Rowan took it. 'I'm glad you saw sense. And my mother's wage?'

'I'll pay her.'

'How much?'

'That's none of your business. What she used to be paid.'

'No. She's now not only the cook but the manageress and that is a big responsibility.'

'I'll give her a third more.'

'Thank you.' And Rowan, walking tall and straight, left the room.

As she ran down the hill, for she was now very late, she wondered if she was holding Dolly's money or Stan Eldridge's. The latter's, no doubt.

She felt elated until she was walking across the park and reached the paddock. It was empty, and the unhappiness returned.

3

The nation was embroiled in a cruel war. Men were dying in their thousands. Essentials were in short supply. Cresswell Manor was a convalescent home. Half of the staff had left and everyone was working twice as hard. However, none of this stopped Sir Mortie and Lady Coral arriving with their normal flurry, their retinue of servants and their usual mountain of luggage.

Standing on the steps watching the cavalcade of motors drawing up with maids and valets tumbling out, Hannah felt that trumpets and cymbals should have been sounding in welcome. The thought made her smile, which was as well for she was feeling particularly nervous at her sister-in-law's arrival. With luck they might think it was a smile of welcome. She moved down the steps, Cariad tottering behind her.

Then Coral's Pomeranian, decanting itself from the car, saw the Westie. It shot across the forecourt and bit Cariad's upright ear. Blood poured from the wound, splashing over the dog's white coat.

'Get away! Shoo! You horrible creature.' Hannah pushed at the Pomeranian, which growled at her as she bent down and swept Cariad into her arms.

'My dog is not a horrible anything. What sort of welcome is this, Hannah?' Coral's imperious tone rang out.

'Your dog went for mine. You should control it. Cariad was doing nothing.' Hannah was staunching the blood with her handkerchief and trying to soothe her trembling dog.

'That dog should have been shot years ago,' announced Coral, as she swept past.

Mortie, stouter than ever, bent and kissed his sister's cheek. 'Sorry about Cariad, Hannah. This one's a vicious little beast.' He aimed a kick at it, but missed. 'Are you all right?' Mortie's normally good-natured face looked worried. 'Not finding it all too much for you?'

'Working hard, but we manage – thank you for your concern. I'm so happy to see you, dear brother.' Hannah patted his arm.

'How's Mother?' He pulled a face – Mortie had a repertoire of funny faces. This one indicated a mixture of apprehension and dread. Mortie was a kindly man, but no one had thought Penelope could live much longer and, like most people, he was afraid of her.

'Surprisingly well. She has a new friend in young Rowan. The two are inseparable.'

'Really? How interesting. Coral won't like that one little bit.' Mortie chucked Cariad under the chin, which made the little dog snap at him.

'Cariad, how impolite.'

'Getting her own back, no doubt.' Mortie grinned as he stepped back to let Hannah precede him into the house. He ambled after her to her office.

'The house smells. You know I have a sensitive nose, Hannah.' Coral was waiting for them, ready to pounce. This was the first of what would be myriad complaints.

'I'm sorry, Coral. It's the disinfectant, and I'm afraid there's nothing we can do about it. It is, I admit, somewhat pervasive.'

'Then stop using it.'

'We can't.'

'Why not? Of course you can. My father's house doesn't smell, and they have patients too.'

'Perhaps not surgical cases. I doubt our medical officer would approve.'

'Whose house is it, may I ask?' Coral sat down, then immediately

180

stood up again. Like many nervous people, she was incapable of sitting still.

'The government's for the duration,' Mortie said, as he inspected an artificial leg, then held it against his own for comparison.

'Excuse me, my lady.' Coral's maid tapped on the door. 'Your room is occupied.' She looked flustered – as well she might, thought Hannah.

'What do you mean, occupied? Occupied by whom? Get them out.'

'We've a general in that room. I doubt the doctor would permit him to be moved. He's had double pneumonia.'

'It's not the doctor's business.'

'I'm afraid it is, Coral. The doctor's word is law here.'

'We shall soon see about that!'

'If the general is moved, the consequences could be dire,' Hannah said.

'So you're a doctor now, are you, Hannah?'

'No. I am repeating what the doctor told me when I was trying to arrange the accommodation.'

'Have you become my housekeeper too?' Coral's face was suffused with spite.

'The patients are my responsibility, not Mrs Herbert's.' For once Hannah stood firm. Though she had dreaded Coral's return she had vowed to herself that she would not let the woman bully her.

'Where are we to sleep if you *insist* this stranger occupies my room?' Coral demanded.

She had been in the house barely five minutes and already everyone was scuttling to her tune. She was now flouncing about in Hannah's office, picking up papers, throwing them down, ruining Hannah's system.

'Fortunately Esmeralda has offered to take Lettice and the children.'

'Why is *she* coming? She should be with her husband. Has she not caused problems enough?' Coral swung round. 'And stop fiddling with that disgusting thing.' Mortie ignored her.

'Her husband has rejoined the army. Naturally she wanted to come home.'

'This is no longer her home. Her husband's estate is her home now.'

'We've just been to your father's, and you often refer to his house as home,' Mortie pointed out, in a patient and reasonable tone. There were times when Hannah could have kissed her brother for being so calm, logical and tolerant with his wife.

'At least we shall be spared the children's noise. It's always so trying.' Coral returned to her inspection of Hannah's desk.

Hannah wished she could summon a bit more courage and tell her to stop, but none was forthcoming. She watched her snoop. She would never understand Coral. Had she been blessed with children and grandchildren Hannah knew she would want to spend every possible moment with them and never regard them as a nuisance.

'I trust this doesn't mean Lettice is planning to see the unspeakable Ramsey Poldown again.'

'I'm sure not.' Hannah was sure of no such thing, remembering the last time she had been to Esmeralda's for luncheon. Ramsey had been a guest even if she had not seen him and might still be there.

'I wouldn't put it past Oliver and his wife to take him in,' Coral announced.

'Oliver is far too honourable to do any such thing. He would never allow Lettice's position to be compromised, even if the man is homeless.'

'Still? He should have rebuilt his house by now.'

'Perhaps he hasn't the money to do so,' Mortie contributed, having now moved to inspect a large wicker wheelchair, which creaked alarmingly when he lowered his not inconsiderable bulk into it.

'The best thing Hugo Hamilton ever did was burn the man's house down.'

'Coral! It was dreadful that the poor man lost everything. In any case, we don't know that Hugo did it.'

'Hannah, you're so infuriatingly naïve at times.' Coral laughed, a hard, coarse sound. 'Of course dear Hugo had it set ablaze. And who can blame him? The Poldown man deserved to be punished for taking his wife from him.'

'I've often wondered why Lettice went to him. She is such a sweet and gentle person. It was unlike her ...' Hannah trailed off, frozen by the contempt on Coral's face. Hugo Hamilton, while charm personified, was also a bully and Coral, as far as she knew, was the only member of the family who still had a good word to say about him.

'Perhaps Lettice was badly hurt by Hugo. Could never stand the cove myself.' Mortie was now inspecting a new consignment of surgical instruments.

While Hannah could never condone her niece's adultery, if Lettice had been her child she might have been somewhat more sympathetic to her plight – but, then, she did not know, never having been a mother.

'Hannah, I don't think wicker is a good material to use for these chairs. What if bodily fluids got into it? Devil's own job to get rid of it.'

'Mortie! Do you have to be so disgusting?' Coral reprimanded him.

'A good point, Mortie. But only those with no dressings use them.'

'I might have a go at designing something better for them.' Mortie studied it seriously.

'By the time you'd invented something this war would be over and we'd probably be in the middle of another one.' Coral found this funny but Hannah saw the disappointment on her brother's face. 'So, which are to be our rooms – or are you not going to tell me where I should go?'

'I'm so sorry, Coral. There's so much to talk about,' Hannah said diplomatically. 'Morts has agreed to move out of his.'

'Morts's room? Don't be ridiculous, Hannah, it's far too small for the two of us.'

'He's in the blue room now on the south wing.'

'Why did he move?' Coral demanded.

'He needed much larger accommodation.'

'What on earth for?'

'Our son is married, Coral, or have you forgotten?' Mortie said.

But for the circumstances, Coral's horror might have been amusing. As it was, Mortie and Hannah held their breath, preparing themselves for what was certain to follow.

She stamped her foot, which was ineffectual on the thick rug, then thumped the desk with her fist making the pen-holder rock and the pens jangle. 'You do not expect me to sleep in that slut's bed?'

'The linen is new,' Hannah said.

'I want the furniture changed immediately.'

'But, Coral, that is impossible. We are so short-staffed and it will take too long.'

'The number of staff is irrelevant to me. I wish my instructions to be carried out. Speaking of which, I trust you are not sleeping here, Hannah. If you remember, I asked you never to set foot in this house again. If you thought I might have forgotten what you did to my darling Felix, I have not.' With this parting shot, Coral collected her bag to leave the room.

'I quite understand your feelings, Coral. If you so wish I will vacate this office immediately. No doubt you will enjoy taking over my duties.'

Coral paused in the doorway. 'No. You may continue, provided you don't live here. Come, Mortie, we shall go for a drive until our rooms are prepared for us.' She swept out.

'Sorry about that, Hannah, but you know how she is. She seems to blame you for Felix joining up – I must say, I'm rather proud of him.'

'It will be a great worry to her. He's only sixteen, after all.'

'Yes, but why blame you?'

'I've no idea,' she lied. 'Do you hear from him often? I think of him constantly.'

'Surprisingly, yes. He's a good letter-writer. From what I hear he's conducting himself well. If you ask me, it'll be the making of the boy.'

If he's not killed, Hannah thought sadly. 'Still, I mustn't keep you. I have to see to the room for you.'

'Tell you what, old girl. I'll take her for a long drive. Just rearrange it a bit. She won't know the difference. Sorry she's such a nuisance.'

'Bless you, Mortie.' Hannah stood on tiptoe and kissed his cheek.

'Best get the doc to look at old Cariad's ear. Sew it up a bit. Nice dog, that. Makes me think of Papa.' At which thought Mortie had to blow heartily into his handkerchief.

4

Two weeks ago Rowan and Morts had been lying in bed, cuddled close together, holding on to those precious moments, reluctant to get up and go to work.

'I've been thinking, with my family arriving soon, it might be better if we moved into the Cottage – you know, that old house over by Maiden's Wood. Would you mind?' Morts had said.

'Mind?' She had sat bolt upright and hugged him with joy.

'It's only temporary while the house is so full over Christmas,' Morts had said, but Rowan was already planning differently. 'You hate living here, don't you?' he had said, holding her at arm's length and looking her in the eye.

It was true, she did, and even more so with the arrival of her mother-in-law imminent. 'I love the house,' she had said, not wanting to hurt him since she knew what it meant to him – and it was not the house's fault, it was the people in it. 'Just think, Morts. It will be just you and me in our own house. At last I can be a proper wife to you.'

'But you are already the perfect wife.' He kissed the tip of her nose.

'No, I'm not. How can I be when I can't cook for you or wash and iron your shirts? Take care of you as I want to.' She had not known why she felt so shy saying these things, but she did.

He had laughed. 'You're such an original creature. Many women would sell their souls for the life I can give you.'

'But not me.' And she wasn't sure that she had liked what he had said.

It had been a wonderful surprise, though, especially because she had given up trying to persuade Morts to move. She wondered if she had Hannah to thank for his decision.

That afternoon he had taken her to inspect the house. Rowan had fallen in love with it the minute she had seen it – gabled, with mullioned windows and oak beams. It was set in a large garden grown wild from neglect, backed by Maiden's Wood, where Rowan had played as a child. From the windows in the front there was a fine view of Childer's Hill and the wishing tree on its summit.

It had once been the estate manager's home but since Oliver had taken over his duties, it had remained empty. Though it was called the Cottage it bore no relation to one: with four reception rooms and five bedrooms, it seemed huge to Rowan.

For her and Morts to have their own home was all Rowan had ever wanted. She would have moved in that day but she had to contain her impatience while some work was done on the house. She had spent any time she could snatch from work planning and finding things for it. During her precious hours off duty, she had scrubbed the Cottage from top to bottom, and although the weather was cold and damp she had opened every door and window to air it.

The first time she had climbed into the vast attics at the manor she had been astonished by the amount of furniture that lay there covered with layers of dust, ignored and unwanted. There was enough to furnish dozens of cottages and give pleasure and comfort to scores of people. How wasteful this family was. Hannah had told her to choose whatever she wanted from the heaps that were stored there. Rowan's problem was deciding what to take – everywhere she turned she saw items she liked.

She began by looking at beds. She would have preferred to take their own – she didn't like the idea of anyone else sleeping in it, least of all Coral Cresswell. But she felt too shy to ask. There were plenty to choose from – testers, four-posters, odd foreign-looking ones – and countless chairs, sofas, sideboards, tables, lamps, curtains by the trunkful and cupboards of linen. The sheets smelt musty, but after she'd washed them she'd have a linen cupboard with enough to last her all her life.

Among the bric-à-brac she found a neglected rocking-horse and included that. She knew it would lead to speculation that she was having a baby, which she was not, much as she longed for one, but she liked the horse and wanted to clean it, mend it and keep it in the hall of her new home.

The great day had arrived and Hannah had arranged for her not to work. Rowan was excited and content. She had been up at five and was hanging curtains by candlelight at six, wishing dawn would break.

When the cart arrived, Rowan had felt shy to be ordering men she had known all her life, but soon she was issuing instructions as to the manner born. As each piece was put in place the rooms sprang into life. Before her eyes the house changed. As the day wore on it became an elegant home, with its beams and inglenooks, and taught her that quality furniture brought with it a timeless grace.

As the evening drew in, she lit the fire and the oil lamps in the sitting room, then she stood back to admire her handiwork and tried to see it as Morts would. Was anything missing? Had she forgotten something? She wanted everything to be perfect on the first night that they would be alone.

She washed and changed into the simplest of her recently bought dresses. Then, she gazed at their new bedroom, which she had made so comfortable with an armchair for Morts, who loved to watch her dress. She had found a mirror with an ornate frame decorated with fat golden cherubs that she had put on a pretty serpentine mahogany table. The bed was covered with a fine lace counterpane that she had found in the bottom of a trunk – what a waste, she had thought.

Downstairs she just had time to lay the table. Their cutlery was not silver but plate – Whitaker had apologised but she hadn't minded. It shone like silver and was pretty with everything matching. Earlier she had had difficulty in lighting the range but eventually she had conquered it, and had just checked the roasting chicken when she felt Morts's arms slip round her waist. She slammed the oven door and turned, melting, into his arms, grasping the wonderful sense of security she always felt when he held her.

'You've found my old rocking-horse! You clever darling.'

'I was afraid it would look silly here.' They went into the small hall to admire the little piebald, his mane newly combed and his body polished to a shine.

'He looks perfect.' And he pulled her to him.

'Morts, the chicken! It'll burn ...' She disentangled herself, laughing at him, knowing what he was thinking.

'Darling, what do you mean? We're expected to dine at the manor.'

Rowan felt as if someone had thrown a bucket of cold water over her. 'But I'd planned our first dinner here.'

'I'm sorry, my darling, but we have to go. My parents arrived this afternoon and we have to be there on their first night, don't we? What would people say if we didn't go?' He was stroking her hair and she knew he was trying to comfort her, but she didn't want him to. She knew, from the tone of his voice, that there was no point in arguing with him. He had made up his mind. She went back into the kitchen, took the chicken out of the oven and began to put away the china and glass. She felt the old nervousness at the prospect of seeing Coral.

When she returned to the sitting room it was to find him in white tie and tails. 'But you've changed!'

'Of course.'

'We've been dining informally for months now.'

He laughed. 'Can you imagine my mother approving of the manner in which we have sat down to dine?'

'Then I must change.'

'We don't have time. In any case you look adorable.'

The beginning of the evening was not too onerous for Rowan because so many people were present. She was able to sit on the window-seat, at the edge of the group, and hope that no one noticed her.

At first Coral Cresswell was not present, and Rowan could almost pretend that she was enjoying herself as she noted the dresses of the other women – they were all in silks and satins and she saw that her plain blue linen outfit was not suitable: she should have insisted on changing. She saw how prettily they had arranged their hair with jewelled clips – one woman had gorgeous butterfly pins and when she moved her head they fluttered as if alive. She wondered where she had purchased them. She touched her own hair, wishing she had something like that to control it.

It was some time before she realized that Hannah was not in evidence and wondered why. The senior officers were drinking in one corner of the room; she knew them all but as an orderly was too shy to talk to them. To her disappointment she saw Sylvia Ferguson standing in the doorway, surveying the room, deciding, no doubt, which male to concentrate on. She reminded Rowan of a bird of prey about to swoop on its victim. She saw her make a beeline for Morts. She was less concerned, these days, but she could still wish that Sylvia did not admire her husband quite so much.

The vicar and his wife had been invited and the minute Oliver arrived he stopped to speak to Mrs Plunkett. Esmeralda fluttered over to Rowan, who moved up to make room for her.

'You always hide away, dear Rowan,' Esmeralda teased, having enveloped her in a fragrant embrace.

'I don't want to be seen.'

'Tsk. You're the loveliest woman here – except for me, of course!' She laughed at what she considered a joke but which Rowan thought was the truth.

'You're looking well.'

'I can't remember when I felt so happy.'

Rowan wondered if she was indeed happy. There was a brittleness about her and she had noticed that Esmeralda's hands were constantly fiddling. And she kept glancing at her husband. Suddenly Oliver laughed, which made them both look in his direction.

'I wonder what the joke was about,' Rowan said, for something to say.

'No doubt it was Oliver. I can't imagine Sorrel joking, can you?'

'I've not thought much about her at all. I do know that I don't like her.'

'Rowan! How honest you are, but how dangerous to say that! She might be my best friend.'

'But she isn't, is she?' Rowan was certain she wasn't.

Esmeralda did not reply but continued to look about the room. 'It's wonderful to have Lettice here – and the children are so adorable with Marigold. They amuse her all day long.'

She had purposely changed the subject.

So I was right, Rowan thought. 'Is Lettice coming tonight?' she asked.

'But of course! She's over there.' She gestured with her head. Rowan had learnt it was rude to point, another rule she found silly, like the one that forbade her to whistle. Why not? was her instinctive reaction.

'I can't see her.'

'There. Talking to Morts. No doubt she rescued him from the predatory Lady Sylvia.' And she laughed again, a joyous sound.

'That's not Lettice!'

'It is.'

'But it doesn't look like her. She's so thin and … Well, she looks …'

'So old? Was that what you were about to say?'

'Well, yes, but I didn't like to.'

Esmeralda leant towards her. 'That monster Hugo has been making her life misery. Never a day without him shouting at her and …' She moved even closer and murmured, 'It's worse than we thought. Lettice confided in me that he's now constantly beating her. He has broken her ribs twice ... but don't tell ...'

Rowan looked at Lettice with concern. Her shoulders were hunched as if she was trying to make herself smaller, less noticeable, and although she appeared to be listening her face was vacant, as if her mind was elsewhere. She looked defeated. 'Why doesn't she run away again?' she asked. So much for keeping secrets, she thought. Esmeralda should not have broken Lettice's confidence.

'How could she? The scandal.' Esmeralda fanned herself agitatedly at the very suggestion.

'If she stays he might kill her. Which is worse? Death or scandal?'

'You don't understand.'

'No, I don't,' Rowan said, quite sharply.

'She has to consider her girls. Who would want to marry them if their mother bolted? No one.'

'But she's already done it once,' Rowan pointed out.

'That's the past. We don't mention it, Rowan, my dear.'

'I don't understand. If Lettice ran away before, she's already damaged them. And if a man didn't want to marry them because of something their mother had done, he wouldn't be worth marrying in the first place,' she argued, with a logic that obviously confused Esmeralda. 'And surely they'd rather have a happy mother.'

Esmeralda frowned, thinking this over. 'I think it must be different for people of—' She stopped, her hand flying to her mouth as if to trap any further words.

Rowan smiled. 'My class, you mean? There's no need to be embarrassed – I am from a different class. But there is no difference. I know women who are beaten black and blue every Friday night, and they stay but only because they're trapped – they have no money, no education, and if they left they'd starve. But Lettice has money. She has a family who would care for her – you would, wouldn't you?'

'But she would lose her daughters.'

'They'd come and find her when they were older. Or else she could go to law ...' That was a weak argument to offer, she thought, since she had no idea what the law was and had a sneaking suspicion that it would not find in favour of poor Lettice.

'Perhaps her husband will be killed and that will solve everything,' Esmeralda said matter-of-factly.

'Esmeralda! What a wicked thing to say!'

But Esmeralda was laughing. 'Be careful, Lettice is coming over,' she warned.

'What makes you laugh so?' They tried not to seem startled as Lettice joined them, sitting down on the window-seat with them, kissing Rowan's cheek. 'Please tell me, I need to hear something funny.'

For the life of her, Rowan could think of nothing to fill the silence, which seemed to go on for ever.

Esmeralda gave a nervous little cough. 'It was a stupid joke.'

'About me?'

'My dear Lettice, of course not. But we're both worried about you. You look so sad.'

Lettice took Esmeralda's hand. 'I forbid you to be concerned. Now I'm here I'm happy. I shall stay as long as I'm permitted to.'

'You should run away and come here for ever,' Rowan said.

'My dear friend, you will never know how much I envy your contentment with my brother.'

'I'm so blessed,' Rowan said, happy and relaxed with Lettice and Esmeralda.

'And I hear you've moved house?' Lettice went on.

'Yes, isn't it wonderful? It's a good thing we did. There are so many people squashed into the manor now.'

'The fighting in France and Belgium worsens, doesn't it? Aunt Hannah was saying you now have thirty-five patients and there is talk of more coming.'

'Yes. We've had an extra doctor join us, and two new nurses. So more patients must be expected. It makes sense for Morts and me to move out ...' she trailed off as she saw her mother-in-law approaching.

'We dress for dinner in this house, Rowan. Surely somebody told you.' Disdainfully, Coral assessed Rowan's pale blue linen day-dress.

'I'm sorry. I didn't have time to change.'

'A lady makes time. What was your maid thinking?'

'I don't have a maid.'

'How ridiculous.'

'I don't need one.'

'Every lady needs a maid. But then, of course, I suppose you wouldn't, would you?' Coral flashed a supercilious smile. 'Well, you can't dine with us looking like that.'

'She looks lovely, Mama. What can the problem be?'

'I expect guests to be suitably attired at my dining table and *she* isn't. What will people think?'

'Her name is Rowan, Mama,' Lettice said firmly. 'Poor Rowan works all the hours of the day, she should be excused—'

'Please, Lettice. I don't particularly want to dine here in any case.' Rowan picked up her bag from the window-seat and went in search of Morts.

'I have to leave, Morts.'

'What on earth for?'

Should she say she had a headache? Why should she lie? 'Your mother has ordered me out. I am not suitably dressed.'

Morts looked at her dress. 'As I said, you look lovely to me.' Her heart lifted, then plummeted as he said, 'but I'm not surprised. We know how particular Mother is. Very well. I'll see you later ...' Even his kiss did not help.

She could not sleep but lay in the dark awaiting his return. It had promised to be such a perfect evening, just the two of them in their own little house. Now it was ruined. She kept thinking of Sylvia Ferguson, still there, gloating. Flirting.

Why had he not stood by her? Why had he not come with her?

It was long past midnight when he returned.

'We began to play billiards. I stayed longer than I intended but I won fifty pounds!' He threw the crisp white notes on to the chest of drawers and began to unbutton his dress shirt. 'I wish we had room for my valet.'

'Let me. I'll be your valet.' She knelt on the bed, and as she removed each stud, he kissed the top of her head. 'Fifty pounds!' she said. 'That's more than my family have to live on for a whole year.'

'Hardly my fault,' he said, his voice muffled as he took off his dress shirt. 'You know, Rowan, you can sometimes sound very pompous.'

He was grinning at her so she was not sure if he was being serious or not. She had almost decided not to say anything but then, if she didn't, she knew it would rankle within her. She took a deep breath. 'I wish you had defended me against your mother.'

'Why? You did have the wrong dress on. Such things matter to her.'

'And it mattered to me to be ordered out as if I was still in her employ.'

'Ignore her. I can't fight all your battles for you. Come here – I need you.'

She moved across the bed and into his arms but it was not the same. She felt too hurt and humiliated to be happy for him to take her.

'But this is delightful. I had no idea that these *little* houses could be made so sweet and cosy. Why, I could almost envy you living here.' Esmeralda was sweeping round Rowan's sitting room, like an exotic bird, inspecting the contents. In another, that might have been interpreted as nosiness. If she had been dressed in black, Rowan thought, she would have compared her to a jackdaw – loving shiny things and unable to help herself.

'*Almost*?' Rowan's voice betrayed her amusement.

'Oh dear, did I sound rude? I didn't mean to. You must forgive me. You see, I meant I'd need more space. It would be a little claustrophobic here for silly me.'

'It's what you are used to, isn't it? Compared to the poky cottages I've lived in this is huge.' Rowan swept her arm wide. 'And there's a dining room, a study for Morts and five bedrooms,' she added, with pride.

'As I said, minuscule.'

'Esmeralda, really! You'll upset Rowan,' Lettice chided her, but when she saw that Rowan was laughing, she subsided into the cushions of the couch on which she was half lying. It was as if she hadn't the energy to sit upright. 'I've always lived in mansions and I'd change places with Rowan tomorrow.'

'Can I get you something, Lettice? You look so tired. It's far too long a walk from Esmeralda's to here.'

'We enjoyed it. It did us good, didn't it, Esmeralda?'

Esmeralda pulled a face, which made Rowan laugh. 'A little sherry perhaps?' Rowan was unsure if she should offer it – was it too early? Was it correct for a lady to offer another a drink? It was such a confusing world she had joined, or, at least, was trying to.

'Tea would be lovely. You mustn't worry about me. I'm hardier than I look. The weather was cold but quite pleasant. My girls are longing for snow.' When Lettice smiled, as now, one could see a hint of the prettiness that had once been hers but was now sorely faded.

When Rowan returned from making the tea it was to find Esmeralda still flitting about the room.

'Just look at these birds. They must be Minton.' Esmeralda turned them over to look at the mark. She shrieked. 'No, I'm wrong. They're Spode – how exciting! Where did you get them?'

'Esmeralda, what a thing to ask! And did no one ever tell you it's rude to admire another's possessions?' Lettice was laughing, thus removing any sting from her remarks.

'I don't mind being asked, Lettice. They were a wedding present from Lady Prestwick. She's been so kind to me. But is it true that it's impolite to admire things? I do it all the time.'

'You shouldn't, really. There, Esmeralda, you see what a bad example you're setting our friend?'

'I think that, like so many of the rules you tell me about, it's silly. I'm happy when someone likes something of mine.'

'Sweet Rowan, when you're with friends, as now, nobody minds – I was teasing Esmeralda. But if you did it with others, when visiting socially, they wouldn't understand and might say unkind things about you.'

'Might? They undoubtedly would.' It was Esmeralda's turn to laugh.

'Then there is no problem, for no one in society will invite me, will they?'

'You're most fortunate, Rowan. Being in society is one hideous hurdle after another. And when you think you understand it all some other trap appears. At least, it does for silly me.'

'But people don't look down on you, Esmeralda, as they do me.'

'Rowan, my dear, I am *persona non grata* with half the county. My father is in *trade*! That is unforgivable to some. An aristocrat can be a criminal and still be invited. If you are besmirched by commerce, that's a different thing altogether.'

Although Esmeralda was smiling Rowan sensed that she suffered from a deep-rooted hurt because she'd said it to her before. 'That's not fair.'

'Much of life is unfair, Rowan.' Lettice seemed even sadder.

Esmeralda had stopped her inspection and had sat on the blue wing chair, Rowan's favourite. 'There's something else I've been meaning to tell you. It is regarded as impolite to comment on the quality of the food when dining. You did so, the other day, at Hannah's.'

'Of course I did. It was a lovely meal. What's wrong with that?' Rowan's face was creased in puzzlement.

'It's not as silly as it sounds. In congratulating them you're implying that you are *surprised* the food is good. Its excellence should be taken for granted.'

'That's tosh. In any case, Miss Cresswell always thanks Mrs Gilroy and tells her how splendid a meal was.'

'But Eve Gilroy is a servant so that is perfectly correct.'

'The more I hear about what is right and what is wrong the more stupid everything seems. Lady Penelope told me the other day that I must never wear diamonds before luncheon, that it was vulgar.'

'She's quite right. I wouldn't dream of doing such a thing and neither must you, Rowan.'

Rowan laughed. 'I don't possess any diamonds, but if I did I'd wear them morning, noon and night.' She leant forward towards the tea table, wishing she could sit on the floor – so much more convenient for pouring tea. 'More tea?' Taking the utmost care she poured it into the fine china cups; she was inordinately proud of her silver teapot, a present from Hannah, but she supposed that to them it was nothing out of the ordinary. 'Lettice, have some cake.' She cut a larger than normal slice of the sponge, which oozed jam and cream.

Lettice took the plate, cake fork and napkin. 'I find eating difficult.'

'As we see ...' Esmeralda said, with irony. Lettice was now so thin she might have had consumption. Rowan was not alone in fearing for her.

'But you must eat. Try a little ...' Rowan encouraged her and, much to her relief, Lettice nibbled a forkful.

'My congratulations, Rowan, on choosing such a competent cook.' To everyone's joy she took another bite as Rowan coloured.

'I suspect Rowan made it, Lettice.'

'Good gracious! Why on earth do that? Such drudgery.'

'I enjoy cooking. And you two should be careful – you congratulated me on the food.' Her smile was one of mischief.

'We didn't. We were complimenting you on your choice of servants. Had we known, we wouldn't have said anything.' Esmeralda seemed quite huffy, Rowan thought. 'What is more, I really think you should employ a cook. People might talk. I know of a good woman.'

'How could I have a cook? The kitchen is small and there's just the two of us. In any case I don't want anyone else living here.' All this was true but the main reason she did not want servants, which she could not admit to these two, was that she wouldn't know how to deal with them, and was sure that anyone she hired would sneer at her for who she was. 'And, in any case, what would people talk about?'

'They will think it very strange that a person in your position is her own skivvy,' Esmeralda explained.

'I hate that word. It's not a kind one.' It was Esmeralda's turn to blush. 'And I don't care if people talk about me. They already do.'

'But you should care. It's important that you don't create gossip, if not for your own sake then for Morts's.'

Rowan would never have thought that Esmeralda could be pompous, but she was now. And how could she have said that with Lettice sitting there? When she had run away from her husband and set up home with another man, the gossip had resounded for months. There were still whispers, and she had heard, too often, people arguing about the rights and wrongs of Lettice's actions. She wished Lettice would say something, but she lay there as if she was in her own little world.

'I'll make a fresh pot.' Suddenly Rowan wanted to leave the room and used the tea as an excuse. As she waited for the kettle to boil she gazed out of the window but she did not see the soil she had turned over in preparation for planting a small vegetable garden. Neither did she see the fine view across the park to the manor. She had thought those two were her friends but certain conversations, like the one they had just had, showed her that she and they were miles apart and, she feared, would never understand each other.

There was a loud knock on the front door. As Rowan passed the sitting-room she heard the two women whispering and giggling. About her? She shook her head. Why must she always think like that? She passed the rocking-horse, patting its mane as she always did, and opened the heavy front door.

'Mrs Morts Cresswell?' The man standing on her doorstep removed his hat and gave her a little bow. He had a kind face, rather than a handsome one, and was of modest build; he smiled, and Rowan was struck by the warmth that suffused his face. 'Is Mrs Hamilton with you?'

'Yes.' Rowan sounded cautious.

'She is expecting me.'

She held the door open for him to enter. 'Who shall I say is calling?' she asked, slipping seamlessly into servant mode.

'Ramsey Poldown.'

Rowan nearly fell over with shock. Then, 'This way,' she said, for lack of anything else.

When she opened the door to the sitting room Lettice's demeanour changed. She leapt up from the sofa and tripped across the room her arms held wide in greeting. 'My darling – at last!' She melted into him.

Rowan was not only embarrassed at this display by a married woman but confused too. It was not right that he was here, and witnessing their embrace made her feel she was part of a conspiracy. 'I'll see to the tea,' she said, as she slipped from the room but no one noticed her leave.

'Isn't it exciting?' Esmeralda fluttered into the kitchen. 'Darling Lettice has missed dear Ramsey so much. I thought I should leave the lovebirds alone – much more tactful, don't you think?'

But Rowan wasn't sure what she thought, except that it was wrong.

'It is so kind of you to let them use your house for their little tryst.'

'I wasn't aware that I had agreed to it.' She stood rigid. She didn't wish to offend Esmeralda but she did not want to be party to this clandestine reunion.

'Oh, Rowan, don't be such a fusspot. So disagreeable of you.'

'I'm sorry if you find me so but I can't be any other way ...' She would have liked to add 'just to please you', but she lacked the courage to do so.

'But they're so in love. Don't you want to help them? I do.' Esmeralda picked up a cucumber sandwich, looked at it with longing, then put it back on the plate.

'Why have they not met at your house?' Rowan asked, with unimpeachable logic.

'Oliver would never forgive me. I couldn't possibly.'

'And what about Morts?'

'That's different. Lettice is his sister. Surely he would want to help her. In any case he's younger and will understand.'

'Then why did you not ask him if they might meet here?'

'He might have said no and I didn't wish to compromise him.'

'But it doesn't matter about me?' Rowan wasn't sure what 'compromise' meant. The tea was made and she was uncertain now what to do.

'You won't tell?' Esmeralda leant forward and grabbed Rowan's hand. 'This is our secret. Promise?'

'You and I have secrets enough, Esmeralda. I don't want the burden of any more, thank you.' She picked up the tray.

'Don't take it through. Give them time.'

Rowan wavered. 'I'm sorry, I can't.'

'You're a spoilsport, Rowan.'

The unfair comment hurt. At the door to her sitting room she wondered if she should knock. Instead she coughed and hoped they'd heard. On entering the room she tried not to stare at the lovers but noticed how flushed they were. 'Fresh tea,' she said, and thought how inadequate that sounded.

As always, she had bathed and changed ready for Morts's return from London. This was to be his last visit to his office before Christmas. She would have him at home with her well into the New Year. She hugged herself with happiness at the prospect.

'Did you have a good journey?' she asked her husband, as she poured him a whisky and soda.

'Very, thank you. It was long, as always, but I met an interesting man on the train, which whiled away the time.'

'Why was he interesting?'

'He had innovative ideas on the economy.'

'What sort?' Rowan wished he would not use words whose meaning she did not know. She often had to guess at what he might be talking about as she had stopped asking when she realized her constant querying showed how uneducated she was. Her scheme for learning words, acquiring a new one every day, wasn't working fast enough. Perhaps she should aim to grasp three – or five? Or would that be too many? 'What ideas?' she asked, since he had not responded.

'Nothing you need bother your pretty head about.'

She hated it when he spoke to her like that. It was as if he was talking to a child rather than his wife.

'And you?' he said. 'How was your day?'

'Esmeralda and Lettice came to tea.'

'That was nice for you.'

She sat opposite him, wondering what to do. 'If I tell you something, will you promise not to tell anyone else?'

He laughed. 'You sound as if you were still in the nursery. Secrets? I promise.'

'Ramsey Poldown came too.'

Morts frowned and looked so angry that she wished she hadn't mentioned it. 'What did you do?' he asked eventually.

'I gave him a cup of tea.'

To her astonishment Morts slapped his thigh and roared with laughter. 'Oh, my darling, you're beyond price.' He leant forward and kissed the tip of her nose. She relaxed. 'It was wrong of Lettice to put you in such a position, and I shall have a word with her.'

'No, don't,' she said, alarmed. 'You promised.'

'But I didn't know that what you were about to tell me was so serious. You do understand he mustn't come here again?'

'Of course.'

'You shouldn't have let him in.'

'I had no choice.'

'Of course you had a choice. This is your house.'

'Would you like another drink?' She asked to cover how angry she felt at the injustice. Whatever she did, she'd be in the wrong for evermore, she was certain.

'There are two ... gentlemen asking for you, madam.' Milner, the butler, stood at the door of her boudoir. The masterly pause he had executed, embellished with a little cough, showed that, in his opinion, he was not dealing with gentlemen at all. 'They are awaiting you in the hall. Are you at home, madam?'

Milner's disapproval of these individuals had the reverse effect to that which he had intended – Esmeralda was intrigued. 'I shall be down in five minutes, Milner. Show them into the little sitting room.'

Alone, she sat at her untidy desk and watched the dial of the pretty clock, which stood to one side. She wasn't doing anything in particular but she had no intention of letting her guests surmise that. In delaying she liked to think she was creating the notion that she was busy.

The five minutes past, she checked herself in the looking-glass, patted her luxuriant hair, pinched her cheeks, moistened her lips, smoothed her fine linen skirt and sallied forth.

'How do you do?' she said, as she swept elegantly through the door. It was a particularly pretty room, simpler than the formal drawing room. She spent much of her time there.

The two men jumped to attention. Immediately she saw why Milner had registered that they were not men of standing. Both wore ill-fitting dark suits, and their stiff collars appeared to chafe their necks. One was stout and middle-aged, a cheap watch-chain spread almost to breaking-point across his rotund belly. The other was younger, with an unfortunate beaked nose and bad skin.

'Please be seated.' Esmeralda sank with her usual grace on to the sofa. Who were they? Perhaps she should have taken more notice of Milner's disapproval and not seen them alone. She smiled warmly, hoping to make them feel more comfortable as they looked about for somewhere to sit – which amused her as the room was full of chairs. They settled with much hitching of trousers and repositioning of booted feet. The way they sat, perched forward on the edge of their chairs, reminded her of ravens roosting. 'What can I do for you both?'

The older man coughed. 'Sergeant Burton, madam.'

'And why are you not in your uniform, Sergeant? Or are you on leave?'

Her questions appeared to confuse him for there was much rearranging of his collar. As he did so, she saw the angry weal on his neck and felt quite sorry for him.

'And this is Constable Rightway,' he said instead.

'Oh, silly me! You're policemen!' She laughed at her mistake. 'It's this wretched war. I hear "sergeant" and immediately think of soldiers. How intriguing.' Her face was alight with curiosity.

'We was wondering – Mrs Cresswell I'd be obliged if you could tell us if you knew a ...' At this point the man had to refer to his notebook, much to her frustration. 'Sorry, Mrs Cresswell. The old memory isn't what it was.' Esmeralda smiled. 'A Mr Petroc Cornish?'

It was fortunate that she was sitting down. At mention of the hated name she felt as if the walls of the room were caving in upon her. Had she been standing she was sure she would have fainted. As it was dizziness enveloped her and she was forced to take a deep breath. She hoped she had not gone as white as she felt she had.

'Petroc Cornish?' she managed. 'Cornish?' she repeated, playing for time. 'I can't say I do, Sergeant ... I would have remembered such an unusual name.' She smiled again – her glorious smile had got her out of trouble on many occasions.

The policeman smiled back and she began to relax.

'It is just that we found your name and address among his effects. And we were wondering why such a person should be in possession of your name, Mrs Cresswell.'

'As I said, I don't think I know him.' It amazed her that she could speak for her mouth was dry and her throat constricted. Every nerve in her body was alert, and she was astonished that she was not quivering all over. 'But, of course, I meet so many people socially and I can't remember all their names.' She leant forward. 'You see, Sergeant, I'm so silly – I can't remember names. It's embarrassing sometimes.' She laughed and hoped it didn't sound false. Panic was swamping her. If they asked more, what should she say?

'Mrs Burton is the same, Mrs Cresswell – she says her brain's like a sieve. I quite understand.'

Esmeralda managed not to sigh with relief. She wished they would go. What excuse could she make to leave the room? If she acted precipitately they might be suspicious.

'But, then, Mrs Burton's problem is when she meets someone, that's when she can't remember. She knows if she's heard a name or not.'

'Exactly, Sergeant. It is why Mrs Burton and I are *so* alike in this matter. I have not heard this man's name.' Silently she blessed the unknown

Mrs Burton. She did not attempt laughter this time, certain that it would sound insincere.

'Then why should a stranger have your name and address?'

It was her stomach this time that reflected her nerves. A dreadful pain stabbed at her and, for a moment, she thought she was about to lose control. 'I have no idea, Sergeant Burton ...' She was pleased with herself for remembering his name. She knew people liked to be acknowledged. 'Perhaps he was wanting to sell me something. Milner is always turning hawkers away. We have notices at the gates but they are regularly ignored. I say to my husband that we might as well take them down for the good they do.'

'That was the strange thing, Mrs Cresswell. He did not seem to have any occupation.'

'Why don't you ask him?' she asked baldly.

'We can't. He's deceased,' the sergeant replied, equally directly.

Before she could stop herself Esmeralda fanned herself with her handkerchief. She felt horror, but also immense relief. Then, realizing her agitation with the hankie might seem suspicious she forced herself to put it away. 'Oh, the poor man. How awful. I mean ...'

'I wonder if you remember him now, Mrs Cresswell?'

What to say? 'No. I can assure you, I know no one of that name.' There. The die was cast. But perhaps she should show more curiosity. Wouldn't an innocent person do so? 'Was he ill?'

'His body was washed up on a beach further down the coast.'

A squeal of horror escaped her and what little colour she had left fled. She knew she must be ashen now. Still, she told herself, wouldn't any lady react with horror? 'How dreadful. The poor man. Please, I beg you, tell me no more ... I simply couldn't listen.' She fluttered her handkerchief, its perfume flooding the room.

She needed time to think. How had they found her name if he'd been in the sea? What had the papers said?

The door opened and Oliver strode in. He regarded the men curiously. 'My darling, what has happened? You're so pale. And you are?' The policemen had scrabbled to their feet, incongruous with their big boots, in Esmeralda's pretty room.

Hurriedly she made the introductions. 'Oliver, they've been telling me such a horrible thing.'

'Perhaps you would be good enough to explain to me what you're doing here and why you're upsetting my wife.'

Esmeralda, though appalled that Oliver was there and would want his own explanations, could not help but feel enormous relief that he was in the room, protecting her.

Sergeant Burton explained in his ponderous manner.

'Let me be sure I understand, Sergeant. This man was found in the sea but his papers included my wife's name? Would not paper be destroyed by the sea?'

'Undoubtedly, but he had been reported missing by his landlady some months ago and we had access to the possessions in his room.'

'And he had been in the sea for some time?'

'That is so, sir.'

'Then how do you know it is him? Surely time, the water and the fish—'

Esmeralda squealed again. 'Oliver, please! You're frightening me.'

'A ring and a scar on his body identified him to our satisfaction, sir.'

'And why on earth do you think my wife should know anything about this mystery man?'

'Mr Cresswell, it was our duty to see your wife. It is not our intention to upset her. We needed to know why he should have her name in one of his jotters. And why he should have made a note about her in his diary.'

This was wrong, thought Esmeralda. The policemen, with their big feet, should be muddled, in awe of Oliver, leaving, apologising. Instead it was almost as if they were in control.

'What note in his diary?'

Burton took time to get out his pad, then thumbed slowly through the pages. 'It reads, "EC, North Gate. Noon." We wondered if this referred to your wife, sir, and if she understood what he meant.' Burton smiled, and Esmeralda saw he had two gold teeth. She wondered how he could afford such dentistry.

'It could mean anything.'

'Of course. But since the initials are the same it seemed to us an odd coincidence. I gather you have a lodge at what is referred to as the North Gate.'

'We do. Darling, do you know anything that will help these gentlemen?'

'Nothing. I told them I knew no one of that name.' Esmeralda longed for them to go.

'Well, there you are. She has told you she has no knowledge of the man. I had planned some building work to be done. Perhaps the note relates to it. That is the only assistance we can give you, so I would be obliged if you would now leave us.'

Esmeralda expected the policemen to refuse to go but to her joy they thanked her politely for her time and then, with a slight bow in her direction, left.

She had hoped the anxiety would disappear now that they had gone but, to her horror, it worsened.

'Why are you lying, Esmeralda?' Oliver said, without preamble.

She had been white, but she was now bright scarlet. She tried to smile but her face muscles would not obey her and she grimaced. 'I'm not. What an awful thing to say.'

'I know when you are, my dear wife. Now, tell me.'

Esmeralda tried frantically to marshal her thoughts. Could she wriggle out of this interrogation? She giggled but he frowned. 'I think he was a friend of my father,' she said lamely.

'Then why did you not say so?'

'How could I?'

'Because it was the truth, and you should have told the police what you knew.'

'And perhaps get my father into trouble? I may be stupid but I couldn't do that.'

'What trouble?'

'I don't know. But I was … Well, he could have … I just thought it was better …'

'Good God, you don't think your father killed him?'

'Gracious me, what an idea. Of course not.' But she had been thinking just that. She knew her father was a ruthless man, but murder? He wouldn't go that far.

'It's always your father, isn't it?'

'I don't know what you mean.'

'He causes problems between us. Would he kill someone? I doubt it, but he might if he thought they were harming you. Now I shall have to think what to do.'

'What do you mean? You'll tell the police I lied? How could you?' Tears welled in her eyes.

'No, that I think he knew your father.'

'This dratted war!' Esmeralda complained aloud, as she hitched up her skirt and began the laborious bicycle ride to her father's house at Courtney Lacey, four long miles away. It was insufferable that the horses had gone. Oliver should have kept at least one carriage horse, perhaps two, for her. But what did men think and talk about these days? War and then war.

A little later, soaked by a sudden downpour, chilled to the marrow, she was sitting in her father's study, rubbing her hands, trying to get the circulation back.

'You had to bicycle here. How can your husband allow it? And in this weather. You shall have a couple of my horses. I can't see my daughter so deprived.'

'Darling Papa, that is so kind. But won't they demand your horses too?'

He laughed. 'Not if you know the right people to reward. But, tell me, what is the urgency?'

Hardly stopping for breath, she told him of her visit by the police.

His expression darkened as the tale was told. 'Your husband is an insufferable prig. What business is it of his? You were right to deny you knew that evil creature, Cornish. And your thought for me shows me what a good daughter you are. I'm proud of you.'

'There is one thing, Papa. Please forgive me, but I have to ask you ...'

'My dear child, of course not.' He laughed, showing his fine white teeth. 'How could you even think I might kill somebody? Whatever next?' He slapped his hand on to the desk.

'I had to ask.'

'Of course you did. I understand. That doesn't mean I was incapable of wishing him dead. He was warned to leave you alone, to cease black-mailing you and leave the area ...' He stopped abruptly and gurgled with mirth. 'He certainly did that!'

'Papa, that's not a nice thing to say or think. The man is dead.'

'It's true, though,' he spluttered.

'But I've suddenly thought. If you went to see him for me you might have been noticed. Someone might remember you and tell the constabu-lary.' Her lovely face was creased with worry.

'Sweet one, there is nothing to fear. I did not see him, it was not necessary. I sent one of my associates.'

'Then he will be remembered and the connection to you will be found.'

'That will not happen. He lives in India now.'

'So far away?'

'Safely far away.'

The expression on his face made Esmeralda shiver. It could not be. Not her darling papa.

'I shall, of course, go to the police.'

'Papa, no!'

'Due to your husband's meddling it is far better that I do. And that I tell them before he does. I shall tell them that Petroc was an acquaintance, nothing more, and that you had not met him.'

'But he had written down my initials and the rendezvous I arranged at the North Gate. How can you explain that?'

'You forget, I, too, have a North Gate. He was to arrange some repairs for me. As for the initials I shall say I have no idea what they mean. You see? Nothing for you to worry about.'

She kissed him, relief flooding her soul. If he was going to do that, it proved his innocence.

7

The Madonna-blue gown was brand new and Rowan loved the feel of the satin on her skin. It was the first dress she had found the courage, on her own, to have made for her by the dressmaker in Barlton. With sapphires and diamonds sparkling at her neck, ears and wrists, Rowan hardly recognised herself in the long cheval mirror. Gently she touched the priceless jewels that Lady Cresswell had insisted on lending her – she hoped she wouldn't lose them – and wondered if they were not a little too sparkly and showy for someone like her. 'You look like a Christmas tree,' she said to her image. She twisted this way and that. With her hair arranged in an elegant chignon, she thought she looked older, more sophisticated. Her sister, Acacia had put it up for her, and she had been surprised by what a good job she had made of it.

While her sister had been doing her hair Rowan had wondered if Acacia might be the solution to a problem. Everyone was constantly telling her she should have a personal maid. She had resisted so far. First, she didn't need one but also she was afraid to employ one – the ladies' maids she had met in the servants' hall had been rather superior beings who had ignored the likes of her. Why should she inflict one on herself? But if she employed Acacia none of these problems would occur. What was more, the wage she would pay her would help their parents and, hopefully, her mother would not regard it as charity. Once Christmas was out of the way, she would raise the subject with Morts.

When they had arrived at the manor and Whitaker had taken her cloak, she was still glowing with the compliments Morts had showered on her. There had been so many, each followed by a kiss, that they had nearly been late. Each embrace had made them long for their bed and she had had to be quite firm with him. Still, she had told herself on the journey, if the evening was awful she could always think about the lovemaking that lay ahead. The thought gave her courage, as well as a delicious feeling of anticipation.

'I promised your grandmother I'd show her my gown,' she explained, leaving Morts to go into the drawing-room on his own. She had indeed made the promise but she had an ulterior motive. The longer she could stay with Lady Cresswell the less time she would have to spend with her mother-in-law. She already felt nervous at the prospect of Lady Coral's spiteful criticism.

'Here I am,' she called, as she entered Lady Cresswell's suite, confident she would be welcomed enthusiastically.

'Don't you look a picture? Perfect. I knew my sapphires would be ideal. Turn round – let me see the back.'

'You're dressed up too,' she said, as she twirled. 'I'm so proud of you for making the effort.' She would have liked to kiss her but Penelope was not a demonstrative woman.

Lady Penelope was sitting in her basket-weave wheelchair, resplendent in a magenta velvet evening dress. A set of rubies nestled on her wrinkled neck. On her feet were a pair of jewelled and satin evening shoes, whose effect was somewhat spoilt by the puffs of excess flesh that had escaped them; they reminded Rowan of the trimming on a pie.

'Those are pretty shoes.'

'They're too small. I used to have such nice feet. And look at my fingers.' Penelope held out her hands on which at least five rings sparkled. 'Like sausages.'

'No, they're not. I've always thought them rather fine. They're soft and white. If you'd mine you'd have reason to complain.' She held out her own, with their short nails and red, roughened skin.

'You shouldn't be doing such work. It's not suitable.'

'But I love helping the officers.'

'Flirting with them, more like. Now, call Colette. I need a last spray of perfume before I descend to dine.' She rubbed her hands with glee.

'You're going downstairs?' she asked, with astonishment, as she rang the bell to summon the maid.

'I'd hardly bother to dress up if I planned to dine alone. You can be so foolish at times, Rowan.'

'As can you …' Rowan laughed, at ease with the teasing.

'I am making this great effort for you.'

'Why?'

'Someone has to protect you from my hideous daughter-in-law. I sometimes think Mortie married Coral to annoy me. Come, girls.' She gestured grandly as if she were ordering slaves.

'How – I mean, which way should we go?' Rowan was appalled at the idea of herself and Colette trying to support the vast Penelope down the long staircase but was too polite to say it was impossible.

'The nursery dumb-waiter, of course,' Penelope said briskly.

With ample giggling, Rowan and Colette pushed the creaking chair along the corridors to the lift. It was not easy – its wheels were intent on going in opposite directions.

There, they helped Penelope from the chair and slid open the door. Rowan wondered if Penelope would fit into it. However, with judicious manoeuvring, they packed her in and, holding on to the rope for dear life, lowered her slowly to the ground floor.

'What if the rope should break?' asked Colette.

'It wouldn't dare.' Rowan laughed.

Eventually, certain that Penelope had arrived at her destination, they ran with the chair to the servants' staircase. Colette held the back and Rowan took the front. It was a perilous descent, not helped by several fits of giggling, but soon they were in the kitchen corridor.

'You took long enough,' Penelope greeted them, hunched in the dumb-waiter. 'Get me out of here. All circulation has ceased.' They repeated the necessary hauling and steadying required to get her back into the chair. Then Rowan pushed her along the corridor towards the dining room.

'No! We go to the great hall for the present-giving to the staff.'

'Not this year. It's been cancelled.'

'I've never heard such nonsense. What will they think? I insisted it be reinstated. I've never heard of such parsimonious behaviour.'

'I see.' Rowan's heart was sinking. At the same time she wondered what 'parsimonious' meant and made a mental note to look it up in her dictionary.

Whitaker and one of the remaining footmen came to her rescue and pushed the chair into position. Rowan, as instructed by Penelope, stood beside her at the front.

'I'd rather be at the back.'

'You'll stay there beside me. Don't move.'

As she waited for the ceremony to begin, Rowan looked about the great hall. How different it had been in previous years, with the wonderful decorations, a huge tree and a table piled high with beautifully wrapped presents, food and drink. This year there was a small tree and few baubles. Someone must have decided that it would be unseemly to decorate as usual in wartime. And this year since so many had enlisted and so many maids had left to work in the factories, the line of servants was much shorter than usual.

Rowan felt ill-at-ease on the family side of the hall when in spirit she felt she belonged on the servants' side. She wished she was not dressed up in her fine new gown and that she had resisted accepting Penelope's offer of her jewels. What must the staff be thinking of her? She wished herself anywhere but there.

'Grandmama, how wonderful to see you here.' Morts had arrived. Resplendent in white tie and tails, he leant forward and kissed her.

'Stand beside your wife,' she ordered.

'How did you get here, Grandmama?'

'Your remarkable Rowan arranged it. You've a gem there, my boy, and I trust you're aware of it.'

'Oh, I am, I am.' The look he gave Rowan made her catch her breath. It was so loving and full of longing that she blushed.

'Enjoy such expressions of love and lust, Rowan. A day will dawn when he looks at you and can't even see you.'

Penelope's words, so blunt, so personal, made the blush deepen. And then, in the strange way that sometimes happens, she became aware that someone was staring at her. She glanced about and, from the cluster of people greeting Penelope, Coral was regarding her with such hatred that the blush drained away until Rowan was as pale as ice.

The butler called the staff one by one to step forward. As they shuffled past to receive their gift from Penelope, Rowan could not bring herself to look at them. Her shame was illogical but she could not help it.

They filed past, the men bowing their heads, the women bobbing. They bobbed to her, which she found excruciating, and despite Penelope's instruction, she moved back until she was shielded by Oliver. There she skulked until the line had passed.

In other years the ceremony had taken a long time, but mercifully it was soon over. There were to be no carols from the church choir because the organist had been killed at Loos.

Later they made their way to the dining room, Morts having taken charge of the wheelchair. Rowan hung back nervously, as she did every time she had to dine formally.

As they walked along they were joined by Major Fellowes, and finally Hannah arrived, late as usual, still in her uniform. Rowan did not understand why she had not noticed before that the women were dressed fairly simply. Only she and Penelope looked sumptuous and only they were wearing jewels.

'I've made another mistake with my dress,' she whispered to Lettice. They were in the inner hall off which lay the dining room. 'Last time I was here I was in trouble for not dressing and tonight – well, just look at me.' She slid her hand down her dress, feeling stupid and a clown.

'Did you not get the message?'

'What message?' But even as she asked she knew what Lettice was about to tell her.

'Mother said we were to dress down.'

'I wasn't told.'

Lettice took her hand and squeezed it. 'How unkind of her. She did it on purpose to upset you. My mother can be so intolerably nasty.'

'Lettice, you speak of your mother!' Rowan was shocked.

'And when she deserves it I shall be critical of her.' She paused. 'And admit that I don't like her.'

Rowan's gasp was audible. She could never have said that of her own mother. Why, even though Flossie was distant at the moment she knew she could never think, let alone speak, ill of her. It was her turn to squeeze Lettice's hand. 'How sad you must feel to say that. I'm sorry.'

'My dear Rowan, you mustn't waste your sympathy on me.' She moved away sharply, as if she did not wish to pursue the conversation.

Lady Coral was bossily telling people where to sit, which was unnecessary since cards indicated everyone's place. Rowan hoped to slip past her to her own place. But it was not to be.

Lady Coral grasped her wrist. 'Everything is a muddle and it's your fault,' she whispered ominously. 'You should have told me *she* was coming.'

'You mean Lady Penelope?'

'Of course! Who else?' she snapped.

'I did not know myself until half an hour ago.'

'Don't argue with me.'

'I'm not arguing, just telling you the facts.'

To her relief, Morts was approaching them. 'Mama, I've put Grandmama beside Father.'

'Dearest Morts. Thank you.' She lavished a smile upon him that, because of its rarity, took Rowan by surprise. But it was far from genuine.

208

'Isn't it wonderful to see her down from her room and in such good spirits?' Morts added.

'Absolutely marvellous,' Lady Coral gushed, to Rowan's disgust. She took the opportunity to leave the danger zone and find her own seat. She'd been placed between a young captain who was about to be discharged and, to her dismay, Oliver Cresswell. Ever since Esmeralda had confided her fears in her she preferred to avoid him, always afraid she might say something to compromise her friend – that was one of her new words.

'We don't see Morts and you frequently enough,' Oliver said, as soon as they were seated.

'Life is such a rush and we're both so busy,' she explained.

'My sister says you're a stalwart of the convalescent-home staff.'

'Did she? That's nice.'

'It's most commendable of you.'

'I enjoy the work,' she answered, unsure if he meant it or if he was just being kind.

'I hear you're now living in the estate manager's house.'

'We are. It's lovely.'

'I quite envy you your simple life.'

Immediately she wondered if he was being sarcastic, then saw that he looked wistful. If he was discontented with his life, why didn't he change it? He was rich enough. 'I don't think we live simply,' she told him. 'It is luxury I never dreamt would be part of my life.'

'I stand – or, rather, sit – admonished.' He smiled and bowed to her.

'Oh, no, I didn't mean … What I was trying to say …' She waved her hand and clipped her glass, which went flying. 'Oh dear.' She stood up, frantically blotting the wine with her napkin, then sat, then stood again.

'What *are* you doing, Rowan?' Lady Coral's clipped voice rang out and everyone fell silent. 'Whitaker, do see to that mess Mrs Morts is making.'

'It's my fault, Coral. I spilt the wine,' Oliver lied.

'Then don't be so clumsy, Oliver dear.' She smiled broadly at her brother-in-law.

'Thank you, Mr Oliver,' Rowan whispered, once the butler had done as he had been asked.

'Don't let her bully you,' he said, in an undertone. 'She can't harm you, can she?'

'No, but being disapproved of constantly is very wearing,' she replied, unaware of how dignified she sounded.

Then she remembered the etiquette that Lettice and Esmeralda had taught her and turned to the officer on her left.

Dinner finished, the women had congregated in what had once been the morning room but was now the family drawing room. The large one had been converted into a ward.

Rowan had already made three journeys to Penelope's room to fetch things for her: a handkerchief, her lorgnette and finally a book that Penelope wished to lend Lettice. She did not mind: it took her out of the room and away from the gossip about people she had never met.

She had taken a seat as far away as possible from her mother-in-law and felt better for being hidden behind a large fern. She hoped Penelope would soon want to go back to her room so that she could excuse herself to escort her.

Esmeralda joined her. Rowan thought she seemed agitated, as though she was overexcited about something.

'I've been longing for a word with you,' she said quietly, as she sat down beside Rowan. 'I have wonderful news. Petroc is dead.'

'How awful. The poor man.'

'What do you mean? What about poor me?'

'Of course poor you. But dead? That's dreadful.'

'But it means I'm safe. Don't you see?'

'Of course. However ...'

'Oh, well,' Esmeralda stood up, 'I thought you'd be pleased.'

Rowan said nothing. There seemed little point. How could Esmeralda think that someone's death would please her? Now her friend moved away with a petulant expression.

'At least the poorly decorated Christmas tree was not so noticeable once Rowan entered the room,' Lady Coral said, in the manner of one who is bored and wants to create a diversion.

'What do you mean, Mama?' Lettice asked.

'Why, she is decorated like one, don't you think? So many jewels sparkling on her.' Lady Coral gave a supercilious smile.

'I think she looks perfectly lovely,' Lettice said.

Though grateful that Lettice had defended her, Rowan felt it might be better to ignore her mother-in-law. 'It doesn't matter, Lettice,' she said.

'La! There you are, Rowan. I thought you'd left and here I am talking about you.'

'Jealous, are you, Coral?' Penelope asked, from her wheelchair. Everyone in the room either stared at their hands or at some distant object, anywhere than at the protagonists. Rowan found herself standing, though she could not remember having got up.

'Jealous? Why should I be?' Lady Coral sat upright but Rowan noticed she was clenching her hands so tightly that the knuckles were white.

'Because she's young and pretty. You're not and never have been.'

'Really! How ridiculous!' She was twisting her handkerchief into knots.

'And because Morts loves her and you hate that!'

Lady Coral appeared to be fighting not to respond to this. Her back stiffened but she couldn't look at Penelope.

'And because I chose to *give* the sapphires to her.'

'What do you mean? *Gave!*' With each word Lady Coral's voice rose shrilly.

'That is correct. I gave them to her, and I think they look perfectly lovely on her.' Penelope was evidently enjoying herself.

'They are part of the Cresswell jewellery collection. You cannot do so.'

'No. They are mine. I may do as I wish with them.'

'You can't. I shall tell Mortie what you're doing. They are part of his inheritance. We shall go to law.'

'Go to law – go to hell, if you so wish. Rowan.' She twisted in her wheelchair. 'I wish to retire.' With an imperious wave she acknowledged the others, who scrambled to their feet, apart from Lady Coral.

Rowan spoke to no one. She was too upset and longed to be swallowed into a large hole.

Concentrating on the chair, and the need to keep it straight, distracted her from the hideous scene. She went to the servants' hall to find someone to help her and asked two men to haul on the dumb-waiter. It would be harder to get Penelope up than it had been to get her down.

Once in Penelope's room, she said, 'Lady Cresswell, you should not have done that.' As she was speaking, she was unclipping the necklace.

'And, pray, who are you to tell *me* what I can and cannot do? I want you to have the jewels. They suit you.'

'But Lady Coral was so cross. Thank you very much for the kind thought but I can't possibly accept them.'

'Rubbish! Your position calls for you to possess decorations of quality.'

'I thought you were lending them to me.'

'I was. I only decided latterly to give them to you.'

'Because of Lady Coral?'

'No. Because you look so lovely in them. They will be yours one day anyway, but by the time you inherit them you will probably be old and wrinkled. So you should have them now.'

'But I—'

Penelope held up her hand. 'No more. I'm tired. You must learn to be more gracious, my dear. If you refuse them I shall be insulted.'

Gently Rowan laid the necklace, bracelet and earrings in their box on the white velvet lining. 'You are very kind to me. Thank you,' she said quietly, but as she spoke she had to turn away. She did not want Penelope to see the tears in her eyes. She sensed that she would regard them as a sign of weakness rather than gratitude.

8

New Year's Eve was crisp and sunny, which broke the monotony of the damp, miserable days they had endured recently. Esmeralda needed fresh air after being indoors for so long. As she set off on a brisk walk with Blossom she met Oliver's Labrador, Nadger, who lolloped along with them.

The dogs were having such fun rootling in the undergrowth and playing with each other that she went further than she had intended. Soon they had reached the North Gate. The sight of the place made her shiver. She had been so nervous that day when she had waited for Petroc. Now she wondered if he had already been dead while she was waiting. The thought induced a shudder. She would go no nearer. 'Nadger,' she called.

These days, she hardly ever thought of the man and had not mentioned him again to her father. Her father had said that she was not to worry, that all had been resolved, so she had preferred to forget the entire incident. No doubt Papa had had to fill more brown envelopes with money to bribe. This thought made her smile. Her father was incorrigible.

'Nadger!' she called again. But the dog raced towards the lodge, followed by a puffing Blossom. The Labrador hurled himself at the front door and whined. What strange behaviour! Had he hurt himself? Oliver would be so cross if he had. 'Nadger. Here, boy.' He was clawing at the door. 'Nadger, stop that! You're such a bad dog.' Overcoming her fear of the place, Esmeralda approached it. Perhaps she could find some string or rope to use as a lead. Gingerly she opened the door and Nadger raced in, flinging himself at an inner door and whining.

'That's my Nadger,' she heard a voice say. Oliver! She was surprised. He had said he was going to Barlton. Perhaps he had changed his plans and was here with the builder for the improvements he'd been planning. How lovely. They could walk back together and at least Nadger would obey him. She pushed open the door. Immediately she wished she hadn't. Her husband was lying languidly on a pile of cushions, his clothes in disarray. Beside him totally naked, lay Sorrel Plunkett.

Her inclination was to run, but she couldn't move. She stood as if glued to the floor. Her face was distorted with the horror she felt. It took her a colossal effort, but finally she turned on her heel and ran from the room, the cottage and her husband's infidelity.

'Madam? What have you done to yourself? Your poor face,' Bridget fussed.

Esmeralda was tired. She had been running for some time, through the woods, across the park, trying to distance herself from what she had seen. She put up her hand to her cheek. When she brought it down it was covered with blood. 'I fell over.' At least, she presumed she had.

'What were you doing? Just look at your skirt – and those boots. You're soaked. We'd better get you into a nice bath.'

Esmeralda saw she had torn her skirt and that her kid boots were ruined. How strange. She had no recollection of any of this happening. 'Why am I wet?'

Bridget looked at her oddly. 'It's been raining for the past couple of hours.'

'Blossom?' She had suddenly remembered her pet.

'She came back a good hour ago. Sodden she was. Milner took her down to the kitchens to dry off. And the master's been asking for you.'

'I don't want to see him,' she almost shouted.

'Now, Mrs Oliver, sit down. Let me ...' As she would a child, the maid steered her mistress to an armchair and lowered her into it. 'We'll have you straight in no time.' Gently she bathed the graze. 'Does it hurt?'

Esmeralda sat mute. She was beyond pain.

'Should I call the doctor? Perhaps—'

The door burst open and Oliver strode into the room. 'Leave us, Bridget.'

'No, stay,' Esmeralda countered his order.

The maid looked from one to the other, unsure what to do.

'Out.' Oliver pointed to the door. Bridget needed no further bidding and scuttled from the room. 'Esmeralda, I don't know what to say ...'

He stood in front of her, hands outstretched, shrugging as if he was mystified.

'There is nothing *to* say. I shall be moving to my father's house later today.' She had made the decision without having to think.

'Please, Esmeralda, don't act hastily. You may do something you will regret.'

She could barely believe her ears. '*I* do something? *I* regret? You speak of yourself, not me. You have humiliated me beyond endurance.' She had to close her eyes. She couldn't bear to look at him. She loved him and she wanted to continue loving him … But she couldn't. Never! He had betrayed her, an inner voice screamed. 'And with the vicar's wife. You seem to have a fondness for them, don't you? Or have there been others who are not married to the cloth? I hope for your sake this one doesn't kill herself like the first.' She was surprised by how vocal she was and what strength she had acquired.

'That happened long ago.'

'Another fine scandal for tongues to wag about.'

'I beg you, Esmeralda, don't. She has children.'

'Then she should have thought of them before she committed adultery with you.' Abruptly, Esmeralda stood up and crossed to the looking-glass to inspect her face.

'Please, let us talk. We can resolve this.'

'I doubt it.'

'My darling, I don't know why I betrayed you. She means nothing to me.'

She swung round, her eyes blazing with anger. 'That she is nothing makes it worse. You would risk all for *nothing*! Love, I might understand. But this!' She sighed. 'And how long has *nothing* been occupying you?'

'Just this morning.'

'I don't believe you.'

He looked away, his guilt evident.

'That's why she came so far to my sewing bees, isn't it? Did you have assignations then?'

He did not answer. There was no need. She had been duped for nearly a year.

She opened a drawer of her dressing-table and began to snatch out the contents, which she threw on to the bed. Then she emptied the chest of drawers. From the cupboard she dragged a bag across the room, rejecting his offer of help. She piled her clothes into it.

'Don't go, Esmeralda. Stay here. Try to forgive me. I love you.'

He so rarely said those words and for him to use them now seemed more an insult than an endearment.

'I have no choice. This is your doing, Oliver. Not mine.'

He stood up straight, his expression hardening. 'Then perhaps I should warn you. If you go, you leave Marigold. You cannot take my daughter with you.'

She looked at him, her own expression a mixture of pain and fear. But, quickly, everything was doused by anger.

'She's my daughter, not yours. You did not father her.'

There. She had said it. The truth was out. No more pretending.

He swayed. The silence in the room appeared to last for ever. And then he hit her. She hardly felt it.

'You bitch!' he shouted. 'Is it the truth? Tell me! I demand to know!' His face was suffused with fury.

'Why should I say such a thing if it wasn't?' His wrath did not frighten her. She felt as if nothing mattered. But then she realized she was feeling another emotion – an overwhelming sense of relief.

He did not sit down but, rather, collapsed on to a chair. He put his head into his hands. She saw that his shoulders were shaking. He was weeping. Her strong, purposeful husband had broken down. At this she was engulfed with fear. If only she could wind back the clock. If only she had not said those words. If only she had not been so cruel ...

'Oliver, I'm sorry, I should not have told you.' How inadequate those words sounded.

'How can you blame me when you have done far worse?' he said, with such a bleakness in his face. 'I have a right to know who it was.'

'The man the police came about. I met him in Buxton ... But it is—'

'And you have lied to me all these months. With one adventure you have taken away all that is precious to me.'

'It was not an adventure! He attacked me!'

'Why? You must have done something. You must have provoked him.'

'Don't you understand? He violated me!' He had said what Esmeralda had always feared. That it had been her fault. Her wonderful world was at an end.

'I shall go to France,' he said.

'You must do as you wish.' She spoke as one who no longer cared, when every cell in her body was screaming for him to stay.

'Goodbye, then.'

She did not answer. But when the door slammed she allowed herself to cry. What had she done?

During the week between Christmas and the new year Rowan survived the close proximity of her mother-in-law by dint of keeping away from her. This was not difficult to achieve since there was an influx of wounded and Rowan was needed on the wards for as many hours as she could spare.

The pretence that Cresswell Manor was just a convalescent home had long passed. For several months now the racquet court had been an operating theatre. It had been intended that minor surgery would take place there, but the nurses soon found that far more serious procedures were undertaken. They were now admitting men who had been blinded by one gas and those who had been burnt by another. When they had started their patients had been cheerful and full of bravado. Now the officers were exhausted, wary and afraid.

The war was not going as they had been promised. The numbers of the dying were mounting daily.

There were times when Rowan, having finished her shift, was so tired she could barely put one foot in front of the other. She had hoped to be less drained tonight for it was New Year's Eve and, to her surprise and joy, Morts had suggested they spend the evening alone. She was excited even though she would have to cook their dinner, exhausted as she was.

Now in the manor's kitchen she was waiting for a large saucepan of milk to heat. She was preparing hot chocolate for the patients. 'That smells nice,' she said to Eve Gilroy, gesturing to an even larger pan on the range.

'It's beef stew ...' Eve paused. '... For the men.'

'Not for the family?'

'Her ladyship feels that stew is too common for her table.' Eve spoke in a tight-lipped manner that oozed disapproval. 'I am obliged to make a different dinner for her.' She threw a pheasant she had been dressing on to the pine table. 'Only six courses.' Disapproval had changed to sarcasm.

'I'm sorry.'

'Nothing to do with you, my dear.'

'No, but these are difficult times and sacrifices have to be made.' She wondered if she should have said that – but, then, why shouldn't she?

'Quite so.' Eve beamed. 'But you're in for a treat. One of my soufflés.'

'I love your soufflés but, sadly, not tonight. Morts and I are eating at home.'

'À deux!'

'I don't understand.' Rowan giggled.

'Just the two of you. It's French – not that I approve of the French but sometimes they say things in a nice way.'

'À deux,' Rowan repeated. 'I must remember it.'

'Young people shouldn't be burdened by family, especially when they've not been married long and in these uncertain times.' The spinster Eve spoke as if she was an expert on the subject. 'Will you be cooking?' Rowan nodded, and there must have been something in her expression for Eve added, 'Before you leave after work, pop down here, I'll have something ready for you.'

'Mrs Gilroy, how kind you are.' Impulsively she gave the astonished cook a hug and kiss.

'No need for that.' Eve was flustered and pleased at the same time. She reminded Rowan of her mother.

Rowan's Christmas present from Morts had been a bicycle with a large wicker basket on the front. He could not have found a better gift. Now she could be home from work in a matter of ten minutes. Also, she enjoyed the sense of freedom it gave her – she could go anywhere now without having to bother anyone. In the past week she had twice popped over to see her mother. There was still tension between them but Rowan hoped it was lessening.

At home, she had bathed and changed. The fire was burning well, the candles were lit and now she was in the kitchen, unpacking the basket Eve Gilroy had given her. No wonder it had been so heavy, she thought, as she lifted out a large container of the stew. There was a fish terrine, too, bread, two dishes of trifle, cheese and fruit. They were in for a treat.

She heard the front door open and Morts entering the hall. Immediately she went to meet him.

'My, that smells good.' He put his arms round her, and held her so tightly she could hardly breathe. 'I'm a lucky man.'

For a second she thought of pretending it was her own work, then said, 'Mrs Gilroy gave me a basket of lovely things for us. We shall eat in style tonight.'

The food was perfect, the wines lovely, and Morts so attentive. Rowan couldn't remember when everything had been so perfect.

Now they were sitting, holding each other, on the sofa in front of the fire. Rowan was watching the flickering light of the flames streaking across the ceiling for the candles had long burnt out. She was sleepy but didn't want the evening to end. She had never been happier.

'My darling, we must talk.'

His tone alerted her. He didn't sound himself at all. 'What about?'

'I have some papers I need to explain to you.'

'Yes?' She shifted as he rose from the sofa. He went to his study. While he was away she lit more candles and two of the oil lamps.

'Dearest, I am going away.'

She put her hands over her ears.

He smiled at her. 'Sweetheart, you must listen.'

'I don't want to.' She felt the muscles in her stomach tighten.

'You must – I'm relying on you. Look, this document … I have discussed everything with my partner, Alkie Sommerton. He will take care of most financial matters but I have arranged for Toby Rawlings, an old schoolfriend and a lawyer, to monitor things. I'm not too sure about Alkie, these days. Should there be any problem, Toby will be in touch …'

His voice droned on. She wasn't listening. He was going away, but he had not said where. Was he afraid to tell her? She feared she already knew. 'Why not ask your uncle Oliver to take care of things?'

He didn't answer. That could only mean Oliver was going with him. Her heart was pounding, her palms sweating.

'And this is my will …'

He didn't finish for she would not let him. She clung to him, felt for his mouth and put a finger over his lips, anything to stop him saying the words she feared were inevitable.

'My love, we leave for France.'

'No, no, no!' she shouted. She stood up. 'You said you'd never have to go. You said you'd be here. You promised you'd be looking after our defence.' She had dropped to her knees now.

'I know we did and that was what we thought. But no one knew the war would be so bad. Conscription is inevitable.'

She could barely see him through her tears. 'When?' she asked, with difficulty.

'Tomorrow.'

Rowan had been filled with dread but now she was overtaken by terror. Blackness encroached on her. She felt as if her soul was shrivelling. She couldn't let him see her like this. She put her head into her hands, trying to order her mind. She must control herself. She couldn't let him down.

'I love you,' she said simply. 'It won't be for long.' She smiled as her world shattered. 'How long have you known?'

'Three weeks.'

'And you didn't tell me?'

'I didn't want to ruin Christmas.'

'You should have. We should have shared this. Is everyone going?'

'Yes. We vowed to keep it secret from our families.'

'When do you think it will end?' Even as she asked she knew it was a pointless question but it was one that everyone was always asking everyone else.

'With General Haig in command from this month, not long, I'm sure.'

She nodded, clutching at this straw – the idea that one man could save them. 'Lucky Oliver. I should have married an older man,' she tried to joke.

'Oliver has chosen to come with us.' There was coldness in the way he spoke. She wondered why.

Later she lay in bed unable to sleep, listening to Morts's steady breathing. How calm he was. How accepting of his fate. Not she. She railed at the unfairness of it all.

She had felt safe in this house. She had lived her whole life on this estate. It was an oasis of tranquillity and peace. Now that had been assailed. The wall of the estate that protected them had, she felt, been breached.

Chapter Six

Summer 1916

1

Barlton railway station's Platform One was crowded with a moving, whirling mass of people. The noise as they chattered among themselves, calling to each other, the children squealing and shrieking, was deafening.

'You'd think it was a festival the way these people are behaving. It's so disrespectful. All it lacks is a brass band,' Hannah said, exasperated.

'It's always like this. They'll quieten down once the train comes. No one can be noisy then,' Rowan assured her.

'But they're ill-mannered. We must be rid of them.'

Rowan doubted she would get her wish.

'How many times have you done this, Rowan, dear?'

'I've lost count.'

'Too often, in other words. Perhaps it was remiss of me not to come too. I should have.' Hannah looked about her in a distracted way. 'I do wish Major Fellowes was here to maintain some order. Do you know where he is?'

'Not really.' She half lied because she'd seen him entering the saloon bar of the Station Arms but knew better than to say so.

'Let me see ... Who can help us? Ah, the very person. *Station-master*,' Hannah called loudly, waving her parasol imperiously in his direction. The man responded immediately. Rowan admired Hannah's natural authority. 'Mr Bootle, I need your assistance – this instant, please.'

'Yes, Miss Cresswell, of course. What help can I be to you?' He doffed his shiny top hat, beaming with pleasure that she should call him by his name.

'If you could ... Perhaps with the constable's assistance ...' She was dithering, thought Rowan. If she went on like this she'd be of little help when the train arrived. 'We need to clear the platform of these people,' Hannah said eventually.

'That might be quite difficult, Miss Cresswell. Perhaps you're not aware but most of these members of the public are meeting relatives and they've bought platform tickets.'

'Quite so. I hadn't thought. But we do not know who is on the train – there is no list – so if they're searching for their men the confusion will be even worse. Perhaps *I* should have a word with them. If you could help me...?' With Mr Bootle's assistance, Hannah clambered on to a luggage trolley, the better to be seen. 'Ladies and gentlemen,' she began, but nobody reacted because they couldn't hear her over the hubbub. 'Mr Bootle?'

With a flourish that reminded Rowan of a magician performing a trick, the station-master produced from an inner pocket a whistle attached to a chain that disappeared into the nether regions of his frock coat. The blast from it was mighty. There was a great deal of shushing but silence descended.

Clutching her large tapestry bag as if it were a lifebuoy, Hannah coughed, then took a deep breath. 'My friends, might I please request that you move from the platform and out into the station yard?'

There was an uncomfortable swell of disagreement. The crowd was in no mood to co-operate. 'It is essential ...' Hannah said sternly.

'Who do you think you are, telling us what to do? I'm not budging nowhere,' a rather short and belligerent-looking youth, with his cap at a jaunty angle and a cigarette in his mouth, shouted. Many agreed with him, which emboldened him. 'What right have you...?'

Hannah held up a hand to silence him. 'Please, if you don't mind ...' She glared at him. 'Manners,' she said, but wisely, Rowan thought, in such a low voice that the youth did not catch it.

Enough people wanted to hear her, though, that they quelled the more difficult with colourful language.

'I speak in my capacity as matron of the convalescent home at Cresswell Manor,' she went on. 'Of course, you are at liberty to remain where you are, but I should warn you that you will be impeding the work of my nurses and that you will undoubtedly delay the unloading of this train and your reunion with your loved one.' She had their full attention now. 'I am aware that, to be here, you have had to purchase platform tickets. If you surrender them to Mr Bootle you will be reimbursed.' She jumped down from the trolley with an agility that impressed Rowan – in whose eyes Hannah was so old. 'If you could collect the tickets, Mr Bootle, I shall settle with you later for your trouble.'

To everyone's surprise, the crowd formed an orderly queue to move out of the station and into the yard. The ominous muttering had ceased.

Once the throng had dispersed they could see two other groups of nurses waiting further along the platform.

'Barlton General and Newton Abbot,' said Hannah. 'We should join them.'

Rowan glanced over her shoulder to make sure the contingent from Cresswell Manor was following them. Evidently it had not struck Hannah that they might have difficulty keeping up, encumbered as they were with bags of equipment.

The talk among the other nurses about their own hospitals was unsettling. They spoke of increasing numbers of wounded, and said that the injuries they were seeing were of increasing severity. Everyone agreed that things were getting worse, not better, that they were overstretched, that they did not have enough beds. Rowan wanted to shout at them to stop. Such information fuelled her fears for Morts.

'Look! The train's coming.' She pointed, feeling a degree of relief that the doom-laden talk would cease.

Further along the line, the engine, quivering in the heat haze, steam pouring from its funnel, was approaching. 'They are such beautiful machines, are they not?'

'Rowan! They're hideous, noisy and dirty! Now, is everyone ready?' Hannah counted her staff.

As always, when meeting one of the trains, they wore anxious expressions for none knew what awaited them. The women clung to large canvas bags with bright red crosses on them while the men had the cumbersome wooden and canvas stretchers.

The train was shuddering to a halt, spewing steam so that everyone disappeared into the white cloud that ensued. Before the train had stopped, an officer jumped down on to the platform and marched smartly towards them, holding a file of papers. He gesticulated to the medical personnel who joined into one large group clustered round him.

'I've sixty-four wounded ...'

There was a communal sigh. 'So many?' Hannah looked worried.

'Barlton is almost full.' The senior nurse from the General spoke quickly and then, as if realizing her mistake, corrected herself. 'We haven't one spare bed.'

'You should make up your mind, Sister. Either you're full or *almost*.' The captain's voice was a mixture of sarcasm and irritation. 'We've all got to make sacrifices. Taunton and Exeter took as many as they could – well above the numbers they'd thought they were to be allocated.'

'It's not as simple as that, Captain, if you don't mind me saying so.

If we haven't got beds, we haven't and that's that. There's nothing—'
Hannah spoke up.

'Use corridors and outhouses. It's not as if it's winter,' he snapped,
and turned his back on her.

'How rude,' Hannah said to Rowan. She stepped forward and tapped
his shoulder. 'Excuse me, Captain, but I was speaking to you. Do have
the courtesy to listen.'

'I'm sorry.' He did not sound it as he returned to his list of names.

'I've room for six at the most. We're not a hospital but a private
house.'

'Are you representing Cresswell Manor?' He referred once more to
his papers. 'You're down here for ten. It would have been more but we
lost five.'

'Oh dear, how sad.' This information had taken the fight out of
Hannah for she sounded ashamed to have made a fuss.

Rowan found the soldier's matter-of-fact tone chilling, as if he no
longer cared who lived or died. No doubt the suffering he had seen had
hardened him; she hoped she never became inured to it.

At this point there was a clatter as the mortuary attendants filed on to
the platform pushing trolleys with purple canopies.

'Excuse me, but won't those trolleys upset the men?' Hannah asked
tentatively.

'They've seen worse than that,' was the captain's gruff reply. 'As I was
saying, I've a list here that says you're to take ten.'

Hannah looked harassed. She was clearly trying to work out where
she was going to put everyone. 'Oh, there you are, Major,' she said, for
Fellowes had appeared beside her. 'This young man is expecting us to
take ten patients and we don't have room for them all.'

'Then we shall have to make room, Miss Cresswell. It's our duty to do
so. Well, Captain, what have you for me today?'

How callous the major sounded – as if he was collecting his shopping,
thought Rowan. There were times, these days, when she did not like
Major Fellowes and yet she had at the beginning. She was sure it was he
who had changed, not her. He and the captain were discussing the list
in earnest now. She wondered if the major was choosing the best cases
for himself, for that was the impression he gave.

Suddenly an argument erupted with the nurses from Barlton. The
sister in charge was emphatic. They could not take thirty new patients.
Rowan wondered what would happen to those who were left behind.
Would they stay on the train going round and round for ever?

'Cresswell, when you've finished daydreaming perhaps you'd let me pass,' Sylvia Ferguson chivvied her.

Rowan stepped aside. She wondered why the woman was hurrying – she was always the last to put herself forward when work was in the offing. Then she saw a handsome young man with blond hair and the bluest eyes clambering off the train, with difficulty since he was on crutches. 'James Headington-Greene, how lovely to see you ...' she gushed – as if she was at a party. Poor man, she thought, which made her smile.

Within minutes the men were getting off the train. First came the walking wounded, who shuffled along as if they were no longer interested in where they were. Their uniforms were filthy and they wore bandages stained with mud and dried blood. They would smell, Rowan knew from past experience. What they needed was a hot bath as soon as possible. These men, she discovered, were to be billeted in private homes since their medical needs were less; she hoped those houses had bathrooms and endless hot water.

Next came those who needed assistance and had no crutches – she'd heard there was a shortage – and several in wheelchairs. They were the lucky ones. Despite their disabilities, most were smiling because they had already been in hospital and were happy to have escaped. They should be coming to Cresswell Manor, as convalescents, but then she saw far more injured men, on stretchers, and feared that they were the more likely patients. The major was waving his arms for them to join him.

'I think matters have been decided for us. I would have appreciated a measure of consultation,' Hannah said briskly. 'We had better join them, Rowan.'

Lugging her canvas bag, Rowan followed dutifully. Fanny Petty was close behind, guiding the younger girls who, since this was their first trip to an ambulance train, were strained and anxious.

The men were in a pitiful state. Some appeared unconscious or were they sleeping? Either way, they seemed to be the lucky ones. Many of those who were awake were groaning and one man turned away his face so that no one could see the tears that gushed from his eyes.

'It's just not possible and I won't.' Hannah was speaking stridently to the officer from the train. 'It wouldn't be right.' She and the captain were standing at either side of a stretcher on which lay a slim, undernourished man, his face grey with fatigue and pain, an expression of sadness in his eyes.

'I'm sorry, Miss Cresswell, but this is no time to be bothering about such niceties. You were informed that you might receive a mix of officers and non-commissioned men.'

'I most certainly was not.'

'Then you should have been.'

'Undoubtedly. And I suggest, Captain, that you stop using that hectoring tone with me.'

'I did not mean to, and if you feel I'm guilty of doing so, I apologize.' Although the captain was saying the right words he sounded as if he was having difficulty controlling himself.

'Very well. I accept your apology.' Hannah inclined her head graciously. 'But I'm sticking to my guns. We offered to take in officers. No one else.'

'If it's a matter of class—'

'Of course it's not,' Hannah snapped.

Rowan couldn't think what else it might be.

'Then what is it?'

Rowan was sure he spoke through gritted teeth for his speech was suddenly muffled.

'You must understand, Captain, it's my brother's house, not mine, and I have a responsibility to him.'

'I'm not going to nick the silver if that's what you're thinking.'

They both looked with astonishment at the man on the stretcher.

'And I'm not deaf,' he added.

Major Fellowes bustled up. 'Ah, you've met our star patient, Miss Cresswell. Splendid. Now, don't worry, Corporal, I shall soon have you right as rain.'

'A moment, Major,' Hannah said.

'There's a problem, Major,' the captain butted in, before Hannah had a chance to go on. He explained.

'Of course Miss Cresswell is right. It should be officers, as was originally arranged. However, these are exceptional times and this is an exceptional case. I would very much like to deal with it myself. I've arranged for us to take another corporal – company for him, don't you know?' Fellowes swung round, but before he did, Rowan glimpsed his expression and wondered if she had been wrong about him. He was anxious, she could see, despite his bombastic approach. If he was worried, why did he not say so? Pride, she supposed.

'Now, you, stretcher-bearers, carry this man gently and when you get to Cresswell Manor go to the stables. I've arranged accommodation there for him and the other corporal,' he barked.

'When did you make arrangements for the stables to be used?'

'This morning.'

'And you didn't think to consult me?' Hannah's back was ramrod straight with indignation.

'I thought you'd make a fuss. Evidently I was right.'

'I hardly think putting these men in the stables is acceptable.'

'Nonsense. With the horses at the front it's empty space needing to be used.' He touched his cap and swaggered off. The captain gave Hannah a cursory nod and followed him.

'Well, that's two of us been ignored and put in our place!' the corporal said, with a cheeky grin. He was older than most of the men, in his forties at least, Rowan thought.

'I like your spirit, Corporal,' Hannah said, looking at him with interest. 'Now, where was I? Make sure only men with "Cresswell" written on their papers accompany us,' she ordered her staff. 'Yes, well, we'd better be moving. No point in stopping here – goodness only knows what other sorts of patients the captain might decide to give us.'

Rowan felt so embarrassed that Hannah should speak thus in front of the corporal. She smiled at him in the hope of making him feel better, and he responded. When he smiled his whole face lit up and there was an endearing impudence about him.

'I'm Bert Banks.' He put out his hand to shake hers.

'Rowan Cresswell,' she replied.

'Crikey, you're not related to the stuck-up dragon, are you?'

'She's my aunt by marriage. And she's not really a dragon.' Even if she is a snob, she thought.

They carried him through the booking hall and out into the yard. The crowd had been silent but at the sight of them they began to call the names of their loved ones. It always upset Rowan when they did that – they sounded so plaintive. They surged forward, not in a menacing way but eagerly, peering at the faces. Many put cigarettes, chocolate and knitted socks on the corporal's stretcher. It was a touching ceremony, which she had witnessed each time she had done this duty.

'Crikey, you'd think it was blooming Christmas.' Bert clutched his gifts.

'What's wrong with you?' she asked, once they had reached the ambulance and he was safely loaded. It was called an ambulance but it was the local butcher's van, which he had donated and which had had a red cross painted on the outside. Inside it had been scrubbed and fitted with shelves for the stretchers.

226

'Got blown up. There's a lump of shrapnel in my spine. I've been promised a geezer who can remove it. Then I'll be able to walk again.'

'Major Fellowes?' How scandalous, thought Rowan. Up to now they had only performed minor operations in the converted racquet court. Or did the major have other plans? 'Where are you from?'

'Bibury, in Gloucestershire. A little village.'

'A long way off. They sent you because of the major?'

'I don't think so. I've only just heard about him. Several of my mates were on the train with me. And there's a group from Norfolk.'

Rowan frowned. The men were supposed to be sent to hospitals as close to home as possible. How could the authorities make such mistakes? No doubt men from Devon were being dispatched to Norfolk.

At the sound of her name she peered out of the ambulance. 'Here's another for Cresswell,' one of the stretcher-bearers called. She jumped down to welcome the man.

'Hello, my name is ... Good Lord!' she exclaimed. 'Zeph Topsham! What a surprise!'

They followed the ambulances in Hannah's Rolls-Royce. Rowan never enjoyed such trips when Hannah was driving because she went far too fast, and while Rowan wasn't frightened for her own safety she worried about passers-by.

'I don't know who that captain thought he was but I felt mortified! How dare he? I was within my rights too! I should have stood my ground. What do you think, Rowan?'

Oh dear. Whatever she said would be wrong. Still, she'd better say something and why not the truth? 'If they need us, I don't think it matters what rank they are.'

There, she'd said it.

'You think I was in the wrong?'

Worse! Now what? 'Yes, I do.' There was a long pause when neither said anything. 'As Mr Whitaker says, these are extraordinary times.'

'To my shame, Rowan, *I* think I behaved badly.'

When she spoke like that Rowan had nothing but admiration for her. 'It must be difficult for you,' she said.

'How lovely. You understand. My world is changing at such a speed that I have difficulty in keeping up with it.'

She stopped talking as she negotiated a sequence of sharp bends. Rowan closed her eyes.

'What do you think of Major Fellowes?'

Rowan thought. 'He's afraid.'

'Major Fellowes? What of?' Hannah laughed with apparent incredulity.

'Of the responsibility he's shouldering.'

'But he seems to be enjoying it.'

'Is he? I'm probably wrong.'

'I liked the corporal, didn't you? A jolly soul. I shouldn't have spoken as I did in front of him. I shall have to apologize to him.' She sighed. 'I've become an old dinosaur.'

Even though Rowan could only see her profile she knew Hannah was sad. 'Oh, I wouldn't go that far,' she said, and laughed. To her relief, Hannah joined in.

2

When the new hotel had opened, Dolly had not doubted that it would be a success. What had concerned her was how difficult working for Stan Eldridge might be.

When he had offered her the position of manageress of his new hotel – *his*, how that little word rankled – she had had no choice but to accept. There was the matter of her debt to him, which had to be repaid and, having lost her money to that crook, Meopham, there was also her debt to the bank. That day she had been at her wits' end and would have agreed to be Eldridge's washerwoman, had he asked.

Now she could laugh at the worries that, for weeks, had kept her awake at nights. She could not have been happier. Stan Eldridge rarely visited. He appeared to trust her. Mostly, over financial matters, she dealt with his assistant, Henry, with whom she enjoyed flirting. She was reaching the point at which she could wind him round her little finger.

The hotel had been busy from the minute its doors had opened to the public. She had been right. There had been need for such an hostelry for the families of wounded officers. Dolly was in her element welcoming the select clientele she had never dreamed of dealing with when she had been running the Cresswell Arms.

Best of all, she was fairly certain that no one knew she was not the owner. That was important to her. She had felt so foolish and ashamed upon discovering she had been duped. But, for reasons he had never explained, Mr Eldridge had told her he thought it was better this way.

'It gives you a better standing in the community. Let it be our secret, shall we?'

She was overjoyed when he agreed that the name she had chosen – Topsham Manor Hotel – should remain. It never crossed her mind to wonder why he should have agreed, or why he wished the secret to remain. Dolly lived for the moment.

If anything marred her contentment it was that she missed George. He was a crook and a scoundrel, but she had finally admitted to herself that she loved him and, if he ever turned up, she would take him back. She had learnt that his story of the house and his cousin in Australia was true. His crime had been to sell the property twice – but only one was legal. She had made discreet enquiries, but she had been unable to find out where he was.

There were those who longed for the war to end. Not Dolly. To her it was a Godsend. The longer it went on the better, as far as she was concerned. If hostilities ceased, so would her guests.

She was still toying with the idea of selling the Cresswell Arms. She rarely went there, these days. That was her past and this was her present. Flossie was reliable and grateful, and every day she toiled up the hill with the previous day's takings – Dolly always made a point of counting the money in front of her. There was nothing to be gained from the woman learning that she trusted her. She was thinking that if she sold the inn she might persuade Stan Eldridge to sell her his business – she would have to pay for it in instalments. It would take courage to ask him and, no doubt, he would expect a healthy profit. One day, she told herself.

Now she could hardly remember living at the inn, with the noise and smells. She couldn't imagine going back there to work, let alone live. She had become used to better things. If she was to sell, she had to do so before Zeph returned from the war and while she still had the power to run his affairs. She could imagine the fuss he would make about her plans – he had a strong sentimental attachment to the dreary place. But if the deed was done ... She found herself smiling.

'You're looking very happy with the world, Mrs Topsham?'

'Such a glorious day, Sir Benjamin.' She bestowed on him an even bigger smile. 'Good morning, Lady Bagshawe,' she said, to his somewhat stout wife, but there was no response. Ignorant old biddy, she thought. Dolly was not bothered by the woman's attitude. It was always the same. She had good relations with the men but most of the women treated her with disdain – I'll be able to buy and sell you one day, you fossil-eyed old trout, she thought. 'Visiting your son today, Lady Bagshawe?' she persisted; she liked showing up the old snobs. 'I trust he's recovering well.' Lady Bagshawe inclined her head and waddled off to the terrace, her large rear swaying. She reminded Dolly of an elephant she had once seen at a circus.

'He's to be discharged today. Too soon, in my opinion.' Sir Benjamin was laying out his cheque book on her desk.

'Oh, you should complain, Sir Benjamin, if you think he should be kept longer. A gentleman of your standing would be listened to.'

'I'm afraid you would be wrong, Mrs Topsham. No one listens to we civilians, these days. I have arranged for a nurse to move into our home to care for him. It would be too much for my wife.'

'But of course.' Lazy baggage, she thought, but still she smiled.

'So it's time for my account, I'm afraid, Mrs Topsham.'

'I always hate this moment. It seems wrong to ask for money from someone I now regard as a friend.' She lowered her head in a gesture of modesty.

Sir Benjamin rootled in his pocket and produced his card case. He took one out and laid it on her desk, coughed rather noisily, then glanced sheepishly over his shoulder and coughed again. 'If you are ever in London ... my card.' This involved more coughing. 'I would be honoured to escort you to dine.'

'Why, Sir Benjamin, how very dear of you.' She took the card and held it cupped in her hands and beamed at him. Discreetly she nudged towards him the silver salver on which she had put the account – padded out with a goodly sum because his wife had been so unpleasant.

The cheque written, she made a play of ignoring it. However, unnoticed to Sir Benjamin, she had watched him like a hawk while he had filled it in. One couldn't be too careful. That done, she accompanied him to the terrace to wave goodbye. She liked that bit best. It was as if she really was a gracious hostess seeing her guests off.

Back in her office, which she always referred to as her study, she put the card with the others she had been given. One day she might take the stupid old fools up on their offer. The cards were a comfort to her. If everything went wrong, she had an army of potential benefactors.

A noise in the hall alerted her. She went to investigate, bustling out in her best professional demeanour, then stopped dead in her tracks.

'How dare you come here?' she said.

May Snodland was standing, looking annoyingly pretty, in the middle of her exquisite hall. May might think Dolly had forgiven her for stealing her husband – but that was when Dolly had had need of her. She didn't now so she could show her true feeling. Unadulterated hatred.

'I'm sorry to bother you, Dolly. I didn't know what else to do. I'm worried about Zeph.'

'He is none of your business. He's *my* husband.' Dolly was inflated with indignation.

'I don't want to argue, Dolly—'

'Mrs Topsham to you.'

'Very well, Mrs Topsham. I haven't heard from Zeph for some time.'

'And why should a slut like you expect to hear from him?'

'Because he writes to me.'

'Oh, does he, now?'

'Yes. He asks after Charlie and—'

'Sends you money? Well, you can say goodbye to receiving any more. I'll see to that!'

'As is your right. I would never have come, or told you, but I haven't heard from him for more than a month. Have you?'

'Of course,' she lied. Zeph's letters had become sparse as the war had progressed. But she hardly wrote to him either so she was not unduly concerned.

'Thank goodness for that. I've been so worried. I feared he was wounded or worse.' May looked close to tears. Good, Dolly thought. 'I went to the barracks but they wouldn't tell me anything since I wasn't his wife. I couldn't think who else to ask other than you.'

'You've wasted your time, then, haven't you?' Dolly turned sharply on her heels and left May standing, wan and lonely. She went into her study and slammed the door.

The wretch! She'd kill him. How dare he humiliate her so? What attracted him to that whining, useless creature?

Her happy mood was totally dissipated. She was in a fury now. She went into the kitchens and took out her spite on the cook.

Hannah had been wrong. The stables, cleaned, scrubbed and repainted, made an ideal overflow ward for the non-commissioned officers. In the heat of summer they were cool and shady and the doors could be left open for a constant cooling draught.

'Zeph, are you in pain?' Standing in the doorway, Rowan had noted his grimace.

'Nothing I can't tolerate, Rowan. But it's kind of you to ask, and to visit this old crock. You must be tired out. I've watched how they work you nurses.'

'It's surprising what you can get used to. I was sent over to the racquet court with supplies and I thought no one would miss me for ten minutes if I popped in to see you.'

'I couldn't believe my luck when we arrived at Barlton station.'

'You *were* lucky. Most of the others, and that includes the officers, are miles from home. It's so silly. I don't understand the authorities. Poor women with children can't travel the length of the country to see their men, and how many can afford to stay in hotels?'

From the bed on the other side of the room came loud clapping. 'You never said a truer word, love. What you need is a soapbox, join the suffragettes.'

At this both Zeph and Rowan burst out laughing.

'What have I said?' Bert was clearly puzzled.

'This family's had enough of suffragettes, Bert,' Zeph called back. 'Miss Cresswell was locked up for brawling with a policeman on a suffragettes' march.'

'She's gone up in my estimation.' Bert was grinning.

'How *is* Miss Cresswell?' Zeph asked.

'She's wonderful at organizing everything, but there are times I think she's very lonely. Mind you, she still has her little dog, the one that belonged to her father.'

'Cariad? Still alive? She must be very old.'

'Esmeralda says she's dreading the day she dies. Miss Cresswell will go to pieces.'

'Some people do feel like that about their pets.' He moved awkwardly in the bed.

'What's wrong with you, Zeph?' she ventured to ask. How one changes, she thought. She would never have asked that question before, but now, with the war, so many inhibitions had disappeared.

'I was too close to a shell when it exploded. I copped a lot of shrapnel but it's all been taken out – at least, I think it has. I was in this hole, in the mud, for two days and my legs packed up. They don't think I'll walk again.'

'That makes me so sad for you. But you mustn't give up. They work near miracles here.'

'Do you see much of Dolly?' He changed the subject abruptly. She mustn't bother him again about his injuries, Rowan thought. Obviously he didn't like talking about them. She wasn't sure if it was her imagination but his voice had seemed strange when he'd asked about his wife.

'Not really,' was her non-committal reply. She wouldn't burden him with the details of her bother with Dolly. 'I gather she's very busy with the new hotel.'

'What new hotel?' He struggled to sit. She leant forward and, linking her arm through his, pulled him up the bed.

'Has she not been to see you?' She skirted the question.

'Perhaps she doesn't know I'm here.'

Rowan was embarrassed now, unsure what was going on.

She consulted her watch. 'Gracious, the time! Sister will grill me for tea. I'll come and see you tomorrow.' She moved away but at the end of the bed she stopped. 'Have you ...' She stopped, longing, but dreading, to ask the question.

'Seen Morts? No, I'm afraid not. But he'll be fine. I was wondering ...' He took a small leather case from his bedside table. 'I was wondering if perhaps you could post this for me.' He held up a letter.

'Of course.'

Outside, she glanced at the address and wished she hadn't. It was to a Mrs Snodland who lived in Barlton. She'd heard rumours about the woman and Zeph. 'Oh dear.' She sighed. What was it about her that she so often became tangled in other people's affairs?

3

As Rowan worked, she worried. Concern for Morts was, like her shadow, with her every hour of the day. At night those fears took on another life and her sleep was restless. Most nights she would wake drenched in sweat, the booming of the guns and the screams of terror that had disturbed her dreams following her into wakefulness.

'Rowan, forgive me for being so presumptuous ... but is all well? You look tired. I know you're worried about Morts – we all are. Perhaps you should let the doctor examine you.' Hannah's face was creased with concern.

'Really, Miss Cresswell, I can assure you there's nothing wrong. I haven't been sleeping well, that's all.' Rowan was touched by Hannah's anxiety.

'Perhaps a sleeping draught.'

'No, really. That would make me even more tired.' And it might make the dreams worse, she thought.

'I commend your good sense, Rowan. But perhaps a little brandy or whisky last thing might assist you into the Land of Nod. I shall let you into a secret. I have a tot every night. It helps relieve the pressures of the day.'

'I could try,' she said, not wishing to offend her. She didn't believe that even a whole bottle of whisky would release her from the terror she felt for her husband.

Each day he wrote to her, wonderful letters, full of his love for her, his plans for their future together. That frightened her because the gods might seek retribution for his confidence in his survival. He never wrote of the war and what was happening to him. She did not know whether or not to be grateful for that. If she knew what he endured would it make the waiting easier or even harder to bear? She was astonished how he filled the pages. When she replied, it was a laborious task. She did not tell him of the suffering she witnessed, or of her tiredness, or of the nightmares, but instead wrote of the plants and trees, the animals, local gossip. She was not to know that this was the best thing she could have done.

She cherished his letters. For some time she had kept them under her pillow until there were too many and they rustled as she turned or fell to the floor. To solve this problem she had devised a ritual. Each night she sat on her bed, and from her collection, which she kept in a lace-lined basket, she would read a selection, then choose three. Those, tied together for safety with a blue ribbon, she put beneath her pillow. Having them there made him seem closer to her, and also as if she was protecting him. Her mind told her this was nonsense. Her soul insisted that she persevere.

At night she went to bed clutching the shirt he had been wearing on the day he left. To her distress, as the weeks rolled by, the scent of him on the linen, which had been so strong, faded. But still she clasped it to her.

When he had first left to go to the front she had hoped to find that she was expecting a baby. That would have been some consolation. And her bleakest thought, which lingered deep, and which she feared to address, was that if he died he would have lived on in their child. But it was not to be.

When her fears for him were at their worst she would sneak off to the church. At first she had felt a hypocrite since, although she had a vague belief in God, she only attended the services when she had to. But she found peace there, which took her by surprise. As the days ticked by, her visits became more frequent.

She had another ritual. Every day, no matter the weather, she would climb the steep Childer's Hill to the ancient oak on its summit – the family's wishing tree. There, in the ancient tradition of the Cresswells, she would circle it three times and chant, 'Dear God, please don't let him die ...'

This morning she was already tired before she set off. It had been busy on the ward. The major had done three operations, mainly removing shrapnel and bullets from his patients. Rowan had nothing to do with the surgery since only qualified nurses could help him. But it was she, with a porter, who had to collect the men from the operating theatre in the racquet court, and push them over the cobbles to the back door. If they were still sleeping from the anaesthetic it was not too bad, but if they were awake they were likely to wince, scream or curse them for the pain.

To avoid carrying the men up the stairs after surgery to their rooms, the library, which initially had been used for relaxation, was now the post-operative ward. This was where Rowan spent her days. It was interesting work, and responsible too, for it necessitated close scrutiny of the men, for fear they might bleed or relapse.

The main problem was the men's reaction to the anaesthetic. Some sailed through, but they were in the minority. Others took a long time to wake up, which was always frightening – and she would watch them closely, always concerned that they were in a coma. A few came round quickly, then wished they hadn't as they vomited repeatedly. And then there were ones who had dreadful hallucinations, which terrified the nurses. But after a month she knew she didn't want to work anywhere else.

Her duties finished for the morning and free until four o'clock, Rowan set off on her daily pilgrimage. It was hot as she toiled up the hill and she could feel sweat trickling down her back. She was glad she had put on her battered straw hat, even though it looked incongruous with her uniform. As she climbed she was looking forward to the shade the large tree offered.

First she had to do the wishing. Three times round she went, repeating the mantra to the spirits who lived in the tree. 'Dear God, please don't let him die.' She never varied the chant for she feared that if she changed the wording he would be killed.

Her task finished, she slumped on to the ground, leaning against the gnarled tree-trunk. It was so old it had been mentioned in the Domesday Book. The heat, her fatigue, the shade and the peace conspired to make her fall asleep.

She woke with a start to the sound of sobbing, interspersed with muttering, so low that she couldn't catch the speaker's words. All she could see from her green canopy of leaves was a cream skirt and white kid boots marching round the tree.

Rowan did not know what to do. Should she stay where she was? Looking at her watch, she realized she had been asleep for some time and would soon have to leave. But if she got up now she would confront the person making the wish. It did not bother her that someone else would know she came here but she didn't want them to think her foolish for believing in the tree. She decided to give whoever it was another five minutes. Then she would have to confront her.

Patiently she waited. When the noise came, it chilled her to the bone. Suddenly the air was pierced by a high-pitched wail from which she knew she was listening to someone's secret terror. It rose in volume, an awful sound. It reminded Rowan of the cry of a mortally wounded animal. Then there was a silence.

Rowan sat so still that she could hear the tiny creatures who inhabited the grass scurrying by. From the woman there was no sound. She must have gone back down the hill, she decided. She eased herself to her feet and ventured out.

After the shelter of the tree, beneath which the light was soft, filtered by the branches, she blinked rapidly at the ferocious brightness of the sun. Temporarily blinded, she did not see the woman lying prostrate on the ground and tripped over her. 'I'm sorry,' she said. 'The sun … I couldn't see where I was going.' Then she saw who it was.

Lettice was looking up at her, her face streaked with tears.

'Oh Lettice, what is it?' She knelt beside her and took her hand, which, despite the extreme heat, was ice cold.

'Leave me alone. Don't be kind to me, Rowan. Never! I don't deserve it.' She was virtually shouting and her eyes were wild. She was shaking from head to toe.

'Of course you deserve it. You've always been kind to me.'

'I thought I was alone,' she said abruptly, as if in explanation. 'I wasn't aware that I was being listened to.'

'I went to sleep under the tree. I'm not sure how long I've been there.'

'You heard me?'

Rowan felt uneasy. Such intensity was not normal in Lettice. She was unsure how to answer but finally decided that the truth was best. 'Yes, I did. I heard your pain. I understand your suffering, Lettice.'

'You can't.'

'I suffer too.'

'But how can you understand? No one can. I'm so afraid.'

'I know how dreadful it is for you.' How could Lettice question her understanding? Why did she think she was the only one who feared? 'It's with me too and it haunts every second of my day,' she said quietly.

'And the nights ...' Although she was gazing down the hill at her family home Lettice had the look of someone who was seeing another view. 'It's the dread ... If anything ... If the worst happens ... If ...' she spoke in short, sharp bursts. 'Then ...' There was a longer pause, which Rowan thought would never end. 'Then it will be my fault. His death will have been my doing ...' She began to cry, not the noisy weeping of before, but silently as tears slid down her cheeks. She seemed oblivious to them for she made no attempt to wipe them away.

'You must not think like that, Lettice. Nothing will happen—'

She did not finish for Lettice had grabbed her hand. 'How dare you say such a thing? You tempt the gods.'

'What I meant was—' Again she stopped, for what did she mean? Who was she to be handing out advice when every day she herself bargained with God. 'I know how hard it is for you, Lettice, but you mustn't blame yourself.'

Lettice sat upright. 'Don't you understand? I must! It *is* my fault. Who else is there to blame?'

'I'm sure your husband—'

'Rowan, don't be foolish. Don't pretend. Don't be like the others. You know I don't speak of my husband. If he died I would not blame myself but rejoice. *Rejoice!*' she shouted at the sky, making the rooks wheel in the air. 'I would rejoice!'

Rowan put her hand over her mouth to cover the imminent gasp. 'But, Lettice, if you say such things ...' She did not know how to go on for she could not condone, let alone comprehend, such wickedness.

In a trice Lettice was on her feet. 'I forbid you to lecture me. How can you understand from your neat, tidy little world? No one does.'

'But I wanted you to see that if you say such things and anything did happen you—'

Lettice put her hands over her ears as if to shut out Rowan's voice. Then she began a tuneless song and took off down the hill. As she ran, Rowan could hear her screaming. She shook her head. She loved Morts, lived for him, would die for him but such frenzy as she had just witnessed would help no one. She must tell someone of her fears for

Lettice, whose nerves had given way. Was she going mad? Could the tree do that? Perhaps she should stop coming here.

4

It saddened Hannah that her friendship with the major was so changed. There had once been such a camaraderie between her and Frobisher Fellowes; they had found so much in common. She had enjoyed his company and their chats. But now there was this distance. Perhaps Rowan had been right when she had suggested he was overburdened with his responsibilities.

When he had first come here she had had such silly dreams about him, romantic fantasies that now she felt ashamed to admit to. They had gone, so perhaps she had imagined them. Had her longing for true companionship in her life distorted her judgement? There were days when she thought she didn't even like him any more – yet he was the same person.

'Do you like Major Fellowes, Fanny?' she found herself asking one day. That she was asking Fanny – a woman of a lower class – such a question would have shocked other members of the family. But Hannah knew her well. She was a good woman, and wise, too. They had suffered together as suffragettes – or, rather, Fanny had done the suffering, in being force-fed, while Hannah had inherited the guilt. But it had bonded them in a way that would have been unheard of a few years ago.

'You want me to answer honestly, Miss Cresswell?'

'But of course, Fanny.'

'He's too pompous for his own good. A bit of a know-all, if you ask me.'

'He's a good doctor.'

'He might be, but does he have to be an expert in everything else?'

Hannah had to hide a smile of agreement.

'And he doesn't seem to care much for the men.' Fanny was warming to the theme.

'Rowan thinks he's worried by the responsibility he has to shoulder.'

'Then he'd get more sympathy if he wasn't so gruff with everyone. Our Rowan's too sweet for her own good. He used to be all nice smiles but not any more, he isn't.'

Fanny had hit the nail on the head. It wasn't just Hannah. He had changed.

'And how are we today, Zeph?' Despite her earlier reservations, Hannah looked forward to visiting the men in the stables. She liked their spirit, their good humour and their jokes so much that now, rather than popping in for a few minutes, she was spending up to half an hour with them. She would go so far as to say their company cheered her, especially when she was down.

'Major Fellowes is going to have a go at my legs. He says there's no medical reason why I can't walk. He's to anaesthetize me and straighten them out.'

'How interesting,' she said, in her best evasive way.

'Shock – that's what he's got,' Bert Banks called, from his adjacent bed.

'You think so, Corporal Banks?'

'I do, Miss Cresswell. I've seen a lot of it. The body refuses to work even when there's no mark on it, like old Zeph's. Not a blemish remains, but his old pins won't do what God intended.'

'It's an interesting hypothesis.'

'And what might that be when it's translated into English for the ignorant likes of me?' Bert asked, with a broad grin.

Hannah liked it when he smiled.

'Forgive me, Corporal. Idea might be a better word.'

'I've no time for high-falutin' words I can't understand.'

'Yes, well …' Hannah felt oddly flummoxed. 'Has Dolly been to see you today, Zeph?'

'No, Miss Cresswell.'

'That's strange.'

'I reckon she hasn't been told he's here, miss.'

'But she must have been. Next of kin are always informed of injury. Of course, the letter might have gone to the inn and Flossie hasn't taken it to her …'

'Why? Where is she?'

'She's running the hotel, of course. And most successful it is too.'

'What hotel? There's no hotel in Cress, just the inn,' Zeph said, puzzled. 'Come to think of it, Rowan mentioned something about a hotel but I didn't take much notice. What's Dolly been up to, Miss Cresswell?'

Hannah wished she hadn't begun this conversation. The poor man knew nothing of what had gone on in his absence. She took a deep breath. He had to know some time and it might as well be her who told him as anyone else. 'Dolly's been very clever. She saw a need for a hotel and converted the large house at the top of the hill into one. People say it's lovely. I haven't been there myself.'

'And how did she pay for it?'

If he was upset by the information he was disguising it well. 'Some say it's hers and others that she's managing it.'

'And the children?'

'Zeph, you should speak to Dolly yourself. I had no idea she didn't know you were here. I shall contact her immediately. Now, don't worry … Come, Cariad,' she called, and left before he could ask any more questions.

As she hurried back to the house, Hannah worried. Rumour had it that the inn had been put up for sale just this week. Where that would leave Flossie, heaven only knew. But, then, there were always so many rumours doing the rounds in the village that it was often difficult to know what the truth was. And in this case it didn't help that Dolly had always been rather unpopular.

How embarrassing that scene had been, not just for her but for Zeph too – and in front of Bert. But he seemed a nice man, kind and considerate. If anything was amiss Zeph would have a friendly ear there. And she had to escape – next she would have had to tell him his children had been sent away to boarding school. Dolly was a law unto herself. Still, she must be doing well if she could afford the fees.

'Doris, if you could connect me with Cress two two, please,' Hannah said, loudly and distinctly, into the mouthpiece of the telephone, holding the earpiece close to her ear. She had found that not everyone spoke as clearly as she did when using the instrument. She listened patiently while Doris at the telephone exchange, not the brightest of souls, connected her. She had an uncomfortable feeling that Doris listened in on conversations when it suited her.

'Dolly, is that you? It's Miss Cresswell.'

'How nice to hear from you, Miss Cresswell. What can I do for you?'

'Have you been informed by the War Office of Zeph's whereabouts?'

There was a pause. 'No.'

The short answer alerted Hannah's suspicions. Dolly was lying. If she had not been told, surely she would be full of questions now – at least shown some concern.

'That is regrettable, Dolly. I can't imagine what has happened.' Still no response, no questions. 'Well, I'm afraid I have some unfortunate news.

Zeph is a patient here at the manor.' Dolly's silence persisted. 'Hello?' Hannah raised her voice. 'Are you there?' Dolly acknowledged that she was. 'I can reassure you that he is well, except for his legs. But, no doubt, he will be walking soon.'

'He's a cripple?'

'He can't walk for the moment but ...'

This was also greeted with silence.

'I'm sure you're aware you may visit in the afternoon, strictly between three and four. You are most welcome to come and see me to discuss ... Are you there?' Hannah shook the mouthpiece.

'Mrs Topsham has disconnected, Miss Cresswell,' she heard Doris say.

'Thank you, Doris,' she said. Dolly Topsham's manners were appalling.

It was the silence that woke her. She sat up in bed and held her breath to listen. She heard nothing. 'Cariad,' she called. The dog, old as she was, normally snuffled in her sleep ... And then she knew.

In the light filtering into the room from the rising sun she saw across the room her little dog, lying half in and half out of her basket.

'Cariad, my darling.' She wasn't sure if she had said the words or merely thought them. 'Cariad.'

She crossed the room, feeling sick, and knelt down by the little creature, who lay unnaturally still. Her body was warm, which gave Hannah hope. She patted the dog, urging her to wake, with building desperation.

But there was no life. Cariad's body was warm so she had only just died. Hannah scooped her into her arms, cuddling her, whispering her love, in the hope that she might still hear.

She had been expecting this for a long time. At first she had been grateful for each extra year, and then each extra week and finally for each extra day. She had prepared herself for the time when this link with her father would be no more. But all the preparation in the world could not help her now as she buried her face in the silky fur and wept for the creature she had loved with all her heart for so many long years.

5

'**I** was becoming concerned as to your whereabouts, Hannah. I was thinking of sending out a search-party, with entrenching tools to find you.' Major Fellowes smiled broadly, obviously pleased with his little joke, then continued to puff at his pipe. 'I was apprehensive that you wouldn't be here in time for coffee.'

There had been a time when his concern and teasing would have thrilled her. Now she barely noticed it. Instead she rang the bell for the maid. She wanted some coffee.

She removed her gloves, placed them neatly on a side table, then took off her hat. She placed the large hat-pins in the pin-cushion, shaped like a crown, which she kept in her office.

'Excuse my impertinence, Hannah. Is something wrong?'

Hannah didn't answer. She couldn't. She was sure that, if she tried, the mere forming of words would be too much for her and the tears, which had finally ceased half an hour ago, would return – with a vengeance. She feared sympathy more than anything.

The maid appeared with a tray of coffee and shortbread, which gave Hannah a few more moments to steel herself.

The maid gave a little bob. 'Miss Cresswell, I was so sorry to hear of your sad loss.'

'Thank you, Ruby. That is most kind of you ...' From her pocket she fished out her handkerchief and held it in readiness. She fought against weeping with such concentration that her throat ached.

The major puffed silently at his pipe. What a horrible smell, she thought. Had she once enjoyed it? Surely not.

As she began to pour the coffee the door flew open and Lettice rushed in. 'Aunt Hannah, is it true?'

'I'm afraid so. Last night ...'

'Oh, my dear, I'm so sorry. You must be bereft.' Lettice burst into tears. This was too much for Hannah and tears cascaded down her cheeks again.

'Could someone tell me what has happened?' The major sounded irritated. And as if to underline the fact he banged the bowl of his pipe against the side of the fireplace.

'It's Cariad, Major Fellowes. Aunt Hannah's dog has died.'

'She was very old, wasn't she? She'd had a good innings,' he said matter-of-factly, then loaded more tobacco into his pipe.

'Her age doesn't make a jot of difference to the grief my aunt is feel-ing.'

'Then get another.'

Both women looked at him with disbelief.

Now he compounded his error. 'Well, it was only a dog.'

At that, Hannah stood up abruptly.

'That was a hideous thing to say,' Lettice said, with spirit. 'How could you be so insensitive? Can't you see how upset she is?'

Handkerchief pressed to her face, Hannah rushed from the room.

Two hours later, her composure restored, Hannah had finished her ward round and was on her way to the stable block to see the corporals. It was essential to keep busy. Caring for others obliged her to control herself, and there had been moments when she had been able to forget her beloved dog. But it was hard now as she walked across the cobbled stones of the stableyard without the click-click-click of Cariad's claws behind her.

'Good morning, gentlemen,' she said, as brightly as she could.

'Miss Cresswell, what's wrong?' Bert asked immediately. 'Sit you down.' He patted the side of his bed.

'Why, nothing, Corporal Banks.' The smile slid from her face as wax down a candle. She began to cry as if she would never stop.

The corporal shrugged his shoulders in a gesture of bafflement but she couldn't explain – the sentences just wouldn't form in her mouth. He leant forward even though it must have hurt him, took her hand and pulled her gently towards the bed where she sank down on the coverlet.

'My dear lady ...' He patted her hand and mouthed to Zeph, 'Maybe she's had a bad telegram? Perhaps someone she knows has been killed ...'

Even though her vision was blurred Hannah made out what he had said. She dabbed her eyes, shook herself and sat up straight. 'There's no telegram ... It's my dog. She died in the night ...'

'Not the little Westie?'

Hannah nodded.

'Oh, Miss Cresswell, I can't tell you how sorry I am.'

'Thank you.' She looked down at her sodden handkerchief. 'She was nearly seventeen.'

'A great age for a dog. Mind you, that only makes the loss greater, doesn't it?'

'You understand?'

'That I do, Miss Cresswell. I'll let you into a secret. When my dog died, I cried more than I did when my old mum croaked it.'

'You were a child?'

'No, bless you. It was last year.'

'Corporal Banks, thank you.' Shyly she touched his hand. 'You have made me feel so much better. I'd begun to feel I was being silly. Out of control. Which is not like me at all.'

'Many people don't appreciate what a dog means. I don't bother with them, myself. In my life I've found that if a person doesn't like dogs I won't like them. Same thing goes for them as don't drink. Not to be trusted in my opinion.'

'Quite,' said Hannah, emphatically, with bitter memories of teetotal Agnes Beatty.

'What do you think, Zeph?'

'I run a public house, Bert. What else could I do but agree?'

Zeph seemed in much better spirits, Hannah noted. 'I'm so sorry about the little dog, Miss Cresswell,' he said. 'In a way she was a link with your father, wasn't she?'

'Do you know, Zeph, you're one of a very small band who remember that. When I stroked Cariad I was often aware that my father had done just that. Now the link is gone forever ...' She was talking about her dog and not weeping; perhaps it was because she was with people who understood how she felt. And if she wanted to cry they would find it perfectly normal.

Zeph, she became aware, was looking uncertain. 'Is there something you wish to discuss, Zeph?'

'I don't want to intrude ... not today ...'

'You're so considerate. But what is it, Zeph? Keeping busy distracts me.'

'I wonder if I might ask you something. I've been hearing talk and I don't know whether to believe it or not.'

Oh dear, what now? she thought. No doubt it would be about his wife and she didn't think she should be involved. 'I don't approve of gossip, Zeph. It can lead to so much trouble.'

'Nor I, Miss Cresswell. But this is important to me and my children. You see, I've heard that the Cresswell Arms has been put up for sale and I didn't give instructions for it to be sold. It's my livelihood but, apart from that, I shall never forget that your father bequeathed it to my mother. I would never let Sir Mortimer down.'

'I have to admit that I've heard the same news.' She hated to be the one to tell him but he needed to know. It was his source of income. 'There was an advertisement in the *Barlton Gazette* last week. Perhaps I should have mentioned it.'

'I should take advice.'

'That would be wise, Zeph.'

'Would you do me the favour of contacting my lawyer, Mr Henry Battle? There are matters I need to discuss – and quickly.'

'I shall do so this afternoon.' Inwardly she shuddered at the mention of Battle's name. When she had been arrested for demonstrating with the suffragettes, the solicitors had failed her miserably. 'Still, I must press on. Anything you gentlemen need?'

'A case of champagne and a lobster would go down a treat. And don't forget the cigars.' Bert Banks was grinning at her.

'Corporal Banks, what *would* the doctor say?'

Reluctantly she left the stables. There was an honesty about Zeph and Bert that many others lacked. And despite their injuries they were capable of having fun. She was now finding excuses to visit them.

As she crossed the yard, admiring the geraniums that always adorned the window-boxes in summer, she thought of how times had changed. Men were sleeping where once her father's hunters had pawed the ground; now the horses were gone, probably dead. Such a waste. She shook her head, wanting to rid herself of the image of their beautiful horses suffering in this hideous war.

And how strange that the simple corporal had understood so well how she felt about Cariad. How sensitive he had been. He, an uneducated man, had far more empathy than the major. Who would have thought it?

When she returned the major was standing in her office. 'I need some specialized equipment to operate on the two corporals.'

'Zeph Topsham and Bert Banks?'

'Their names are unimportant to me.'

'But not to them,' she said quietly. Even if Rowan was right about him, he should remember his patients' names. 'And what is it you need?'

He handed her a long list. She glanced at it, but the unfamiliar names of devices he wanted meant little to her.

'Is this operation on Banks wise? We seem to be poorly equipped for, I gather, such a difficult procedure.'

'If you place this order we shall be – And are you suggesting I'm not competent to perform it?'

'No, of course not. I meant no such thing. It has been suggested to me that perhaps Zeph is suffering from shock and that the feeling in his legs will return of its own accord.'

'Sometimes, Hannah, for an intelligent woman you have strange ideas.'

'I'll put the order through this afternoon. And if you could do me a favour, Major?'

He looked at her quizzically.

'When you are in my office I would appreciate it if you did not smoke your pipe. I find the fumes quite noxious.' To emphasize the point she flapped her hand.

6

'You shouldn't love Morts so much. It's dangerous. It makes the worry you have to endure far worse. Much better not to love your husband. Then, whatever happens, nothing would matter.' Lady Cresswell paused in the middle of her lunch to impart this wisdom to Rowan, who was sitting opposite. Recently she had been taking meals with the old lady. As she no longer lived in the big house, and was always rushed off her feet, she found it hard to visit the old woman at any other time.

'You loved Sir Mortimer.' She had been a small child when he had died and had never met him, but she had never heard a bad word spoken of him.

'I didn't, and he most certainly didn't love me. We had an arrangement. That is all that's needed in a marriage. Love muddles everything.'

'But surely that was when you were old. You loved him when you were young.'

'Why do you presume so? And you are wrong. I did not. I loved his title, his money and the position in society he could give me.'

'That's sad.'

'With such a statement you show your immaturity. It has always been thus.'

'Esmeralda and Oliver married for love. She told me so.'

'Silly child that she still is. My son felt he had compromised her reputation and had no choice in the matter. And what has happened shows only how right I am.'

'What *has* happened?' Rowan laid her knife and fork neatly on her plate, as she had learnt to do.

'Have you not heard? They are considering separating. Before he went to France my son confided that he feared his marriage was over. There'll be scandal for a while, but it will die down.'

'Never!' Had Morts known, and if he had, why had he not told her? 'I've heard nothing.'

'Nothing has been said because nothing is decided. Esmeralda was planning to move to her father's residence – the best place for her, in my opinion – but Oliver, stupidly, has insisted she remains at Lees Court. He will regret arranging it so. And then he went off to war when there was no need. I shall blame her if anything befalls him.'

At this echo of her own mother's words, Rowan shuddered.

'Have you a chill? Don't pass it to me.'

Despite the shocking news she had just heard she had to smile at Lady Cresswell thinking only of herself. 'No, I've no chill,' she reassured her. 'But this is dreadful news. I'd no idea. I wondered why I hadn't seen Esmeralda for … It must be months. But why?' She had a sinking feeling, sure she knew the reason.

'I know, of course, because Oliver confided in me, but I'm not at liberty to tell you. Being sworn to secrecy is such a dreadful bore. Do you think I can have two puddings? I've been so controlled in my eating recently.'

'No. You would undo all the good you have done. Poor Esmeralda.'

'A fig for that unspeakable creature …'

Rowan began to clear away the china to give herself time to think. There was only one explanation. Esmeralda had told Oliver about Marigold and her fears for her parentage. But why? How stupid of her. But perhaps that was right and Rowan was wrong in thinking it should have remained a secret. How confusing everything could be.

Rowan had presumed Esmeralda was still visiting the manor and that she had missed her because she was always working or at her own house. Perhaps, though, she had stopped coming altogether. But Lettice, who spent more time here, reading to the patients, had said nothing. Well, she probably didn't know that Esmeralda had confided in Rowan too. She would search her out and try to find out.

'Was Esmeralda the friend who, last year, had the terrible problem that got you into such trouble?' Penelope took her unawares with the question.

'No,' she lied.

'Hmph,' was Penelope's response.

'I must go.'

'You've only just got here.'

'I'm sorry. I'll try to return before I go home.' She leant forward and kissed Penelope's cheek – as she had been doing for the last two months.

She was halfway to the door when they heard a scream – so loud that it reverberated off the walls, echoing on the long staircase. It drenched the ancient rafters with its pain.

Rowan looked at Penelope. 'What on earth?' they said in unison.

'Go and see who it is!' Penelope ordered.

Rowan found clusters of people on the landing. Patients, visitors, nurses, orderlies – all were peering out of doors. No one knew what to do.

The screaming continued as Rowan ran down the staircase, skidding on the highly polished floor of the inner hall. She thrust open the doors of the great hall and saw a scene of disarray.

Lady Coral was screeching orders that no one was obeying. Sir Mortie was sitting down, his head in his hands, rocking back and forth. Something must have happened to Felix, Rowan thought, their younger son. But then, she realized, the screaming was louder now that she was close to it. An anxious-looking Whitaker, with Hannah in tow, was chasing a deranged Lettice, who was running round the hall smashing anything she could lift, pushing over suits of armour so that they hit the floor with a resounding clash.

'Get out! This is no business of yours,' Coral snapped, but Rowan ignored her. 'Go away!' she shouted, above the hullabaloo. But Rowan darted further into the room.

'Thank goodness you're here, Rowan! We can't calm her. She might listen to you.' Hannah was wringing her hands. 'I'm worried she'll harm herself.'

'Oh, Rowan,' Whitaker was close to tears, she saw, and, in the heat of the moment, forgetting how he should address her. 'We fear she's had bad news of her husband.'

Unlikely, thought Rowan. 'Lettice, stop it. We can't help you if you don't calm down.' She doubted that Lettice was even aware she was there. She was wrong.

'How dare you?' Lettice swung round. Her face was a mask of despair, yet her eyes blazed with fury. Rowan saw that her whole body was shaking, tremors racking her. 'Leave me alone – leave me *alone!*'

'I want to help.' Rowan put out her hands towards her.

'You ... help *me*?' The words were punctuated by heart-rending sobs. 'How?' She was swaying and seemed about to fall. 'I hate you. *Hate* you!' Her face was distorted with venom. 'You and your smug little life. I despise you!' This time a group of shields went flying. Rowan knew she had to act fast for swords and knives were displayed further along the wall. If Lettice got her hands on them ...

Rowan lunged at the fleeing figure, yanked her by the arm and stopped her. Then she slapped her face. From Coral there came a noisy objection, from Lettice a startled look and silence. Then quietly, almost in a whisper, she said, 'Rowan, I don't hate you. I love you ...'

'I know you do.' She put her arms round the tiny frame.

'He's dead, Rowan. My darling is dead ...'

'I'm so sorry ...'

Lettice slid to the floor, Rowan still holding her. There, she cradled Lettice, terribly aware of her frailty, and rocked her as she would a child, talking quietly, gently to her. She glanced up, saw Hannah's anxious face. 'The doctor, Miss Cresswell?'

'Of course. I'll fetch him.' She bustled off.

Lady Coral approached. 'That will be all,' she said, as if Rowan was still her maid. 'You can leave her with me.'

'I'm staying with her. She needs me.'

'Needs a skivvy like you? Don't be ridiculous.'

There was a roar from Mortie, who leapt off his chair, suddenly galvanized into unusually speedy motion. 'For the love of God, woman, leave her alone! Just for once stop your infernal nagging!'

'Well!' Lady Coral looked like an exotic bird whose feathers had been ruffled by the wind. 'How dare you speak to me in that tone?'

'Out daughter's heart is breaking and all you can do is criticize Rowan, who is the only one to help her.'

'How can her heart be breaking? She loathed Hugo.'

'Because it isn't her husband who is dead, you fool. It's Ramsey Poldown.'

'Well, in that case, good riddance.' Lady Coral, mustering a modicum of dignity, stalked out.

Rowan smiled her thanks at Mortie and continued to rock Lettice as they waited for the doctor.

Rowan was sitting beside Lettice, holding her hand. If she tried to move away, Lettice whimpered, so Rowan stayed where she was. Lettice had been put into the bedroom reserved for senior officers; fortunately a general had vacated it that morning – no others were free. The doctor had given her a sedative that should have sent her into a deep sleep, but it hadn't. She cried out, sobbed and moaned.

Rowan had sent a message of apology to Lady Penelope who, apparently, was unhappy to have been excluded from the drama. Her place on the ward had been filled and Hannah had told her to remain with Lettice until Esmeralda arrived or Lettice no longer needed her. Rowan was glad they had sent for Esmeralda, though in the circumstances she wondered if she would come.

There had been disdainful talk, which she had overheard, at Lettice's reaction to the telegram. 'Hysterical,' she'd heard the doctor say, and 'Self-indulgent,' from Sister Westall. But what did they know of grief? Had either of them been in love? Perhaps neither had known that glorious state.

How would she have reacted if it had been her? The very thought made Rowan's stomach clench, her nerves jangle, and she became so restless that she disturbed Lettice just as she had fallen asleep. She tried and failed to blank the idea from her mind. It was easy for her to imagine the pit of despair Lettice was in. The doctor might have given her a sedative now but what would happen when it wore off? She could not take opiates for the rest of her life.

She wondered what Lettice would do. Surely she wouldn't go back to the husband she loathed. But what about her dear little girls? What a tragedy. And what a muddle. At that she smiled to herself. Perhaps Lady Penelope had been right, after all.

There was a tap on the door. 'Oh, dearest Rowan, thank heavens it's you here. I feared my sister-in-law might be waiting to harangue me.' It was Esmeralda, beautiful as always but worried. 'Ah, there she is, the poor sweet.'

She fluttered across the room and gazed down at Lettice. 'What shall we do, the pair of us?' she said to her, in a half-whisper, a sad smile flitting across her face. 'Whitaker tells me she's dreadfully distressed.'

'It was awful to witness. She was mad with grief.'

'She loves him so deeply. I fear for her, Rowan. She has always said if he should die she would not want to live. I've thought for some time that she has been … a little deranged.'

'I've wondered too. I was going to talk to Miss Cresswell about it but in the end I didn't think it was my place to do so. She wouldn't do anything silly, would she? Not with the little girls?'

'Perhaps they'll keep her sane. We can but hope,' Esmeralda said, but without conviction. She glanced about her. 'This room was always so beautiful but now it looks awful.'

The way Esmeralda's mind jumped from one subject to another astonished Rowan. 'The general was only discharged this morning. I've forgotten what the room was like before.'

'It was old Sir Mortimer's. I don't think it was used after he died. You don't think Coral will come, do you? I couldn't tolerate one of her tirades.' She sighed.

'It seems ages since I last saw you.'

'I've neglected you dreadfully, but I've become quite a recluse. I'm sorry, I should have come to you and explained everything. I expect you know my situation.' She laughed weakly. 'I'm the wicked one.'

'I only learnt today. I was shocked when I was told that you and Oliver have, well ...'

'Separated. In a manner, yes.'

'You told him everything?'

'I had to, Rowan.' Esmeralda's lip trembled.

Oh, not more tears, thought Rowan.

'I had no choice,' Esmeralda went on shakily.

'Was it necessary? Poor Marigold, she loves her papa.'

'He says the child should not be punished.'

'How noble of him.'

'Noble!' A brittle laugh rang out.

'I don't understand. You've kept your secret for so long. Why now?'

'Rowan, don't be horrid to me. Don't judge me. I hate it when you're cross with me.' She pouted prettily. Rowan found she was irritated by the little-girl pose. It was silly in a woman of Esmeralda's age.

'He hurt me and I needed to hurt him back.'

'How could you? The poor man.'

'He is not a *poor* man. He was having an affair with Sorrel Plunkett.'

'No!'

'For a year he's been deceiving me. A *whole year*. I found them together.' She leant close to Rowan. 'In bed.'

'How awful for you and how sad. Is there no hope?'

'He rarely writes to me, so I doubt it.'

'Could you forgive him?'

'I already have.' Esmeralda buried her face in her handkerchief.

Lettice stirred.

'Your friend is here,' Rowan murmured to her.

'Hello, dear one ...'

At the sound of Esmeralda's voice Lettice's eyes opened. She let go of Rowan's hand and grabbed Esmeralda's. Rowan excused herself for a few minutes.

As she walked back to Lady Penelope's room she thought over what Esmeralda had told her. She felt desperately sorry for her and Lettice, but she would be lying to herself if she did not admit that she was hurt Esmeralda had not told her sooner. She had carried the burden of the secret and should have been told the consequence.

When she entered the room Lady Penelope was sitting up in bed.

'There! What did I tell you? The consequences of loving. Silly girls.'

7

Sitting at the kitchen table, with lunch for fifty still to be cooked, Eve Gilroy was not feeling right.

'Eve, you're so pale. Are you indisposed?' On entering the kitchen, Whitaker was concerned to see her wan, and was soon fussing over her.

'I don't know what's afoot, Edward. I came over all queer and had to sit down or I'd have fallen.' She laughed nervously. It was a new experience for her to feel poorly. Eve was never ill.

'You need help in the kitchen, Eve. Too much is expected of you.'

Eve felt almost overwhelmed by his sympathy. 'It's the worry, Edward. There are days when I'm engulfed by a feeling of doom.' And, to the astonishment of them both, she dissolved into tears.

'Eve, don't upset yourself. Don't cry.' Whitaker was horrified. He looked like a man facing a tiger. 'It's the war – the news gets us all down. Don't take on so.' He patted her shoulder ineffectually.

'I'm sorry, Edward. I don't know what's come over me.' And Eve trumpeted into her hanky, embarrassed now that she had allowed herself to break down in front of the butler. Whitaker, she knew, regarded the display of emotion as self-indulgence. What must he think of her?

'Let me get you a cup of tea. And what about a nice tot in it?'

Eve struggled to her feet. 'No, Edward, you can't do that – it wouldn't be right.'

'Now, Eve, you stay there. I'm quite capable of making us a pot of tea.'

He wasn't, she thought, as she watched him cross the kitchen for the umpteenth time, collecting cups, forgetting the teaspoons, then remembering the teapot. She could have done it in a trice – but in fact she couldn't. It was as if all the energy had drained out of her. To stand would take more effort than she could muster. She who was always upright slumped on the chair.

'Should I call the doctor?'

'No. I'll be right as rain in a minute.' She took a sip of the watery, oversweet tea but appreciated the whisky in it. 'Poor Miss Lettice – hearing her screaming, it's more than a body can stand. That's what's done me in.'

Whitaker set down his cup. Clearly he wasn't enjoying the tea either. 'It was a scene the like of which I never wish to witness again. And while I feel sorrow for her, I find I can't condone ...' He stopped.

'It's difficult, isn't it? I mean, on the one hand ...' Eve drew a sharp breath, as she always did when she didn't approve of something. 'But we've known her since she was a child and I'm that fond of her ... Yet to marry and then betray her husband ... It doesn't bear thinking about.' Eve nodded sagely. 'On the other hand ...'

'Yes, Eve?'

'If she was unhappy ...'

'Such thinking's too modern for me. It denotes a self-indulgence alien to my upbringing. But it's the lack of discretion, Eve, that bothers me. It would be naïve to think that the gentry have not misbehaved before, but nothing was blatant.'

Hypocrisy, Eve thought, but she wasn't about to argue with him. 'How is she today?'

'According to Rowan, she just lies there mute, staring into space.'

'Poor soul. But Rowan's come up trumps, hasn't she? Who'd have thought it?'

'Despite her background she has an inner strength I was not aware of.'

'Mind you, marrying into this family, she'd need it. Still, sitting around isn't going to feed everyone, is it?' Eve stood up and fainted on to the hard stone floor.

When she came to she was on the sofa in the housekeeper's sitting room. She was wrapped in a blanket, with Whitaker, Philomel Herbert, Hannah Cresswell and Rowan standing in an anxious semi-circle around her. As her eyes opened they all gave a sigh of relief.

'Mrs Gilroy, how are you feeling? I've sent for the doctor but he's operating at the moment and the other doctor's assisting him. Oh dear ...'

'Now, don't you fuss yourself, Miss Cresswell. I'll be right as rain in a moment. All I need is a few minutes ...'

'No! You must stay there.' Eve registered the concern in the butler's voice and settled back on the cushions.

'Mrs Gilroy's exhausted, Miss Cresswell. Too much is expected of her and since the sergeant left ...'

'Where is he? I haven't seen him for a good two weeks.'

'He was called back to his regiment. Off to Ireland, so I heard.'

'Ireland – oh, really ... Such a nuisance! As if we don't have enough problems in France ... Still, the troops there need feeding too. The news is not—'

'And good riddance, says I.' Eve managed a mischievous grin. Sergeant Bob had hurt her when he'd taken up with Lady Penelope's nurse – her with such big feet and a nose to match. Still, she thought, it hadn't lasted, which gave her a modicum of satisfaction. When he had begun to flirt with her again she had enjoyed freezing him out. However, she missed him and the capable pair of hands he had been in her kitchen – not that she would admit that to a living soul. She had hoped for so much from him. What was her future going to be? Alone, struggling on the small savings she'd put by. Thinking about him, and the future, to her horror, she began to cry.

'Oh, dear, it's started again,' she heard Whitaker say, but she couldn't see him for tears blinded her.

Rowan leant her bicycle against the wall of the inn and entered by the back door. As she walked along the corridor to the kitchen she detected the wonderful aroma of her mother's cooking. If only *she* had inherited that talent.

'Hello, mother. Sorry to bother you, but I'm on the cadge.'

Flossie looked up from the saucepan whose contents she was tending. 'You're tired,' she observed.

Rowan laughed. 'A welcome would be nice. Are those gingernuts? Can I have one?'

'Cuppa?'

'Please.' She watched her mother put the kettle on the old range. Although they were now speaking, Rowan felt that last year's terrible scene had changed their friendship for ever. She felt a wariness with Flossie that she couldn't erase, and the hurt lingered.

'What do you want?'

'Acacia and Cherry, to help in the kitchens. Mrs Gilroy has collapsed and the doctor says she has bronchitis. The army sergeant's left and Miss Cresswell's at her wits' end. I suggested our two might help out. Acacia's a good cook, thanks to you, and Cherry can be her kitchenmaid.'

'It'll be too much for her, all them numbers.'

'Fanny Petty's been taken off nursing to help, and Miss Cresswell's sent for Lavender Potts. We thought if they all worked together ...'

'Will they be paid?'

'Of course.'

'Then it's up to them. And what about you? Can't you do something?'

Rowan found herself counting to ten at the implied criticism. 'I have patients to care for and I'm also looking after Lettice.' As well as keeping Lady Penelope sweet, she thought.

'I heard about her. Brought it on herself.' Flossie sniffed. 'She needs to be told to pull herself together. There's many suffering more than she.'

Rowan was about to jump to Lettice's defence, then decided there was no point. But her mother had sounded so spiteful, so unlike her old self.

'Zeph had his legs seen to. He's much better and beginning to walk again. But did you know Dolly hasn't been to see him yet? Some wife she is.'

'I reckon that May Snodland's been, though. You can't blame Dolly.'

If only you knew what a cheat she was, Rowan thought, little better than a thief. 'Did you know she's put the inn up for sale?'

'Yes. And Zeph's taken it back. Dolly doesn't know and I'm not going to tell her. It's nothing to do with me.' She winked at her daughter. 'Zeph's a good man for all his waywardness.'

'I don't think I'd like to be married to Dolly, would you?'

Flossie thought about it for a moment, then burst out laughing. 'The honest truth, Rowan, is that I can't stand her. She's got so stuck-up. But I seem to spend my life defending her because she's my employer.'

'Not now Zeph's back.'

With an excited Acacia and Cherry in tow, Rowan walked back to the manor. She remembered how eager she had been when she first left home. It would be different for them, though. No servants' hall packed with handsome footmen flirting and laughing. Everyone was working harder at everything as the staff shortages worsened.

She showed her sisters to their rooms high in the attics. Since they shared one at home, they were thrilled to have one each. Then she reported to Mrs Gilroy that all was under control, her sisters were there to help and she needn't worry. Then she reassured Whitaker who seemed beside himself with worry about the cook.

She was about to check on Lady Penelope when she was told her father was waiting to see her in the servants' hall.

'Hello.' She kissed him. 'I've just been to see Mum. You could have saved yourself the journey.'

'I saw you bicycling along, but I wanted to talk to you here.' He spoke so seriously that she sat down on the bench. 'I've finally done it. I've enlisted.'

'No! Why? Oh, no, please don't go.'

'I have to.'

'Is it the money? Acacia said you could earn a lot as a driver.'

'No, though it'll be useful. It's just not right if I don't. All the able-bodied on the estate have gone and I'm ashamed to be left behind. I want to do my bit.'

'No one thought ill of you.'

'Maybe not, but I thought ill of myself.'

'Mum didn't say a word.'

'Because she doesn't know. I thought I'd tell you first.'

'Is there anything I can say that will dissuade you?'

'No. My mind is made up. And, in any case, I've signed.'

'You're very brave and I'm proud of you. You'll be the best ambulance driver ever.' She hugged him, hiding her face in his jacket, fighting the tears that she knew wouldn't help him.

When he had left, she had a little cry, then composed herself and went to Lady Penelope's room. She found her in a grand sulk because she felt neglected.

'I've no time for temper tantrums,' Rowan said, and left her to seethe with anger.

On the stairs she ignored her mother-in-law and went to Lettice.

Of whom there was no sign.

As Dolly hurried down Trotters Hill, she was rehearsing in her mind what she would say to Zeph. She didn't want to see him, not after the visit from May, but she had realized that if she did not go, people would look askance and she set great store by what everyone thought of her.

She had already made plans for their future. First, she would persuade Zeph that it was for the best that the children were away at school. At least he would write to them – she never had time or the inclination to do so. If she was clever enough she might get him to pay the fees instead of having to juggle the books of the hotel so that she could cream off the fees. There was no way she could have a cripple living at Topsham Manor. It might upset her guests and they had to come first. He could move into the inn and Flossie would look after him – she'd enjoy that. She paused. But what if she'd sold the inn?

Like a stroke of lightning, she had the solution. Flossie could move into Briar Cottage with him. Dolly never wanted to see the place again. It was where Zeph and May had fornicated. And he could keep an eye on the children in the school holidays. It was all working out well.

En route she called at the inn.

'I've come for the takings, Flossie. I thought I'd save you a journey up the hill. We're neither of us getting any younger,' she said, trying to appear friendly. Normally she would never compare herself to Flossie, who neglected her appearance and got fatter every year.

'But I've new instructions, Dolly. The money has to be paid into the bank each day.' Flossie gave what seemed suspiciously like a smirk.

'On whose instructions?'

'Zeph's, of course.'

'You've seen him?'

'The minute I heard he were here. In a lot of pain, he was. But you must have seen that yourself.' Another sly grin. 'I reckon he's one of the lucky ones. They won't be sending him back, thank God.'

More's the pity, thought Dolly. And she had not missed Flossie's implicit criticism. She must have known Dolly hadn't visited him. For one thing she hadn't had time – but for another she hadn't felt inclined to.

'There's a Mr Raymond coming to view the inn tomorrow. You must know by now that it's for sale. I'm not sure if he'll wish to keep you on, although I'll put in a good word for you, of course. But if he buys it, I'm afraid you'll have to leave, Flossie.'

Flossie continued to peel potatoes calmly. Dolly was perplexed. She should have been in hysterics, begging for help. 'Did you hear what I said? Or have you gone deaf all of a sudden?'

'I heard. But it's been cancelled.'

'No one told me. Is Mr Raymond coming another day?'

'No, Zeph's cancelled the sale. And he's assured me that I have a job and that there'll be a roof over our heads for as long as we want.'

Dolly felt an almost uncontrollable urge to slap Flossie across the face. 'Oh, he has, has he? We'll soon see about that.'

Dolly walked at a cracking pace, fuelled by anger. She barely acknowledged the greetings of villagers she knew. Humiliated – that was what she was. How dare he? But fear lurked behind the anger. How was she to pay her debts if she didn't have access to the money from the sale of the inn? The cash she was taking from the hotel would not cover everything, she didn't dare take more for she was afraid of Stan Eldridge's wrath. Henry Kempton, his assistant, was assiduous in his study of the books each week. She had tried to seduce him, but to no avail. He had blushed, his face as red as his hair, then rushed out of the room as if she were the devil.

She marched up the steps and banged on the front door, which she would never have dared do until now.

It was opened by Whitaker.

'I didn't expect you to be answering the door, Mr Whitaker. Where's the footman?'

'And I never expected to find you seeking entrance by the same.'

'Times change, Mr Whitaker.'

'Not that much.' He was barring her way.

Should she make a scene? Did he not know she was a woman of substance? The stupid old fossil wasn't moving with the times.

The decision was made for her when Hannah, hearing their voices, appeared and ordered the butler to let her in. She swept past him, tempted to poke out her tongue.

She felt triumphant as she walked across the hall – until she was told that Zeph was in the stables.

When she got there and found his bed, the first thing she said was 'I can't say I'm impressed with this accommodation.' She was looking about the stable critically. 'Shows what they think of you, Zeph.'

'We're very comfortable here and the ward sister's an old battleaxe, so we're spared her rules and regulations. Nice of you to come, Dolly.'

Was he being sarcastic? 'I've been very busy.'

'So I gather.'

'And what does that mean?'

'Nothing. But I heard about the hotel and a lot of other things, too.'

'I wrote to you explaining what I was doing,' she lied. He'd never know – letters to the front were always going missing.

'I never received it. Doesn't matter. I've seen the bank and the solicitor.'

'I thought I was doing things for the best.' She batted her eyelashes at him, and smiled her most coquettish smile.

'How could you think selling the inn my mother left me was for the best? You know how I feel about that place. It's more likely you need to pay off the debts you've run up.'

'I don't have debts. Who told you that?'

'The bank manager.'

'How dare he?'

'Of course he should. Your debts are mine too. It was his duty to inform me. And I gather you lied to him, forged documents. You shouldn't have done that, Dolly,' he said – quietly, which meant he was very angry.

'And you shouldn't be talking to me like this in front of strangers.' She nodded towards another man's bed.

'He's asleep.'

'I don't think so.'

The man opened his eyes and smiled at her. 'Sorry, Mrs Topsham, I'm sure, but unfortunately I can't get up and walk out. I'll try not to listen.'

Dolly glared at him with such ferocity that he put his hands up in surrender, but he was still grinning.

'You've the nerve to tell me I've done wrong but what about you? You shouldn't have given money to that whore May Snodland. You wrote to her but not to me, your wife.'

'She replied and you didn't.'

There was, of course, no defence to that. 'I can't look after a cripple – I might as well tell you that now,' she said instead. 'I've the hotel to run. I've responsibilities.' She tossed her head defiantly.

'I shan't be asking you to. I'm moving into Briar Cottage. I'll make my own arrangements.'

'May Snodland, I suppose?'

'Look, Dolly, I don't want to argue with you. Our marriage has been dead for some time. Why prolong the misery? I'll look after you, that goes without saying.'

'You're leaving me?' She was alarmed now. This was not how the conversation should be going. 'How could you?'

'But you've just said you couldn't look after me – the cripple.' His voice was too calm, too placid. 'Why not contact that George Meopham? I'm sure he'd be only too happy to oblige.'

Dolly didn't bother to argue. She knew the game was up. She turned on her heel and stalked out of the stable.

'Phew! she's a fiery one,' she heard the other man say.

'I know, Bert. But I can't help admiring her,' replied her husband. She liked that. But uppermost in her mind as she hurried over the cobbles was the thought that she needn't be afraid. He'd look after her. She had the hotel. But, best of all, she would soon be free of Zeph and the restriction he'd impose on her, and then there would be no stopping her.

8

It had taken Rowan some time to find Ruby, the maid, whom she had asked to sit with Lettice while she cycled into Cress to see her mother. 'Did you leave Mrs Hamilton alone?'

'I had to. Lady Coral sent for me to do some sewing.'

'Didn't you tell her you couldn't leave Mrs Hamilton?' Ruby snorted. She was right, Rowan thought. No one would argue with Lady Coral. 'And you didn't think to ask someone to take your place?'

'No, she was asleep. She wasn't going to come to any harm, was she? When I returned she'd gone.'

'Have you looked for her?'

'No one told me to.'

'Have you any idea where she might be?'

'I hardly know her! How should I know where she's gone?' Ruby snapped defiantly.

'I'd rather you didn't speak to me in that tone.' Rowan astonished herself by taking the maid to task. She'd never done anything like that before.

'Sorry, Mrs Morts.' Ruby looked downcast, and Rowan felt a shiver of triumph at having asserted herself. She couldn't bring herself to dismiss the maid, though, because she had no idea how to go about it. Instead, she walked out of the servants' hall.

She checked every room but Lettice was not in the house.

'Mr Whitaker, has Mrs Oliver been here to collect Mrs Hamilton?' she asked.

'Not that I'm aware of, Mrs Morts. And I'm sure I would have heard her.'

'She's probably gone for a walk,' she said to comfort him. Lettice was far too weak even to contemplate such a thing. Her hope had been Esmeralda.

She turned towards the stables. Perhaps Lettice had gone in search of Zeph. They'd all been friends as children. She lectured herself to stop worrying, but she had remembered Lettice saying when they were standing on Childer's Hill that if Ramsey should die it would be her fault.

Zeph was sitting up in bed, looking much more cheerful. The other corporal was fast asleep, with Hannah sitting beside him. She and Zeph were deep in conversation. When they saw her, Hannah broke off. 'You're back, Rowan. I trust your expedition was successful.'

'Acacia and Cherry are already in the kitchen.'

'It really is most kind of you and your family. The major is rather worried about Mrs Gilroy. If she doesn't rest he fears pneumonia might set in. Have you told her about the girls?'

'Yes, but I don't think she's happy at the idea of others in her kitchen. Miss Cresswell, I've been looking for Lettice for more than an hour. I hoped she was here, or had been here.'

Hannah was immediately on her feet. 'You don't think ... No! Whatever next?' She was plainly as anxious as Rowan felt.

'Did I hear you say you were looking for Lettice?' Zeph asked. 'She was here earlier, asking for a horse.'

'She must know they've gone. There's only the pony and the old shire horses that work the fields now.'

'But if she'd found one where would she have gone on it?' Rowan asked.

'I'll go and telephone Esmeralda. She might be there or Esmeralda may know where she'll be.'

Once Hannah had left, Rowan turned to Zeph. 'How are you? How are the poor old legs?'

'They hurt more now than they did before.'

'You know what they say – the more it hurts, the better you're getting. And your friend?'

'Bert? All he does is sleep. He was much more fun before his operation.'

'There should be a nurse here, looking after him.'

'There was, but they're rushed off their feet. Another train arrived unexpectedly. I'll keep an eye on him. He's a cracking chap.' As she was about to leave he called her back: 'It's probably not important but Lettice spent a long time in the tack room next door, which seemed odd when there are no horses to harness.'

When she returned to the house it was to discover that Lettice was back. 'She felt the need for some fresh air,' Hannah explained. 'She's much calmer. I suggested we bring the children over tomorrow and she said she'd look forward to that.'

'What a relief,' Rowan said, and the weight of worry disappeared.

It was past midnight when Rowan arrived home, so tired that, for the first time ever, she didn't go through her usual ritual with Morts's letters. She was asleep almost immediately.

When she woke again, she thought at first that she was dreaming but slowly she realized that the banging on the front door was real. Quickly she got out of bed, struggled into her dressing-gown and wondered what had happened on the ward that someone should be trying to wake her when it was still dark. Or, far worse, had something happened to Morts?

She hung out of the open window. 'Yes?' she called, into the gloom. Far to the east she saw a stream of light on the horizon. It must be about four, she thought.

'Miss Cresswell says can you come quick,' a disembodied man's voice called back.

'Why? It's the middle of the night.' She longed to get back into her bed.

'She didn't say, just that you were to hurry.'

She splashed cold water on her face and dressed rapidly. If Hannah was there at this time in the morning, it was serious. She cycled through the darkness to the house, which was ablaze with light. Something seriously bad had happened.

She went in by the back door, then sped along the empty corridors. Hannah was not in her office. And then she heard people whispering to each other. She took the stairs two at a time and found a gaggle of staff collected on the landing. 'Lettice,' she muttered. They were outside her door. 'Mr Whitaker, what's happened?'

'Mrs Morts, thank goodness you're here. Miss Cresswell is beside herself with concern.' Despite the hour the butler was smoothly shaven and impeccably dressed in pinstriped trousers and black jacket.

Without knocking, Rowan went into the room. It was unbearably hot. The windows were closed, trapping the acrid stench of vomit. Only one lamp was lit. In the gloom Rowan could see a huddle of people round the bed. Lettice was lying on the covers, fully dressed. One minute she was thrashing about, the next she lay quiet. Sometimes her hands were at her throat, the next clutching her stomach. Sweat glistened on her forehead and her skin was a sickly grey.

Rowan tiptoed closer and touched Hannah's arm.

'My dear, thank you for coming. I'm sorry I had to have you woken, but Lettice has been asking for you.'

'For me?' She could not think why. 'What has happened? Is it something she has eaten?'

'Mrs Hamilton, if you won't tell me what you have ingested, I cannot help you,' Major Fellowes was bellowing.

'Go away. Leave me alone ...' Lettice spoke quite distinctly but then, as if the effort had been too much for her, the next sentence was an incomprehensible mutter.

'What did she say?' the major barked.

'Perhaps if I sit her up she'll get more air into her lungs and we might hear better,' suggested Nurse Winlock, resplendent in a voluminous silk dressing-gown at least two sizes too big, her hair in rag curlers; at any other time the sight would have made Rowan laugh. The nurse didn't wait for an answer but leant down and hauled her up the bed. The scream that issued from Lettice chilled Rowan to the bones.

'Pull yourself together, Mrs Hamilton. I need to know if I'm to give you an antidote.'

Lettice laughed. Rowan did not know which was worse – the scream or that humourless laugh.

'Stop bullying her,' she said.

'I beg your pardon?'

'I'm sorry, Major, but your shouting is frightening her ...'

'Rowan ...' Lettice put out her hand. Rowan grasped it, appalled by how sweaty it was to her touch.

'Lettice, I'm here. I won't leave you ...'

'Tell them to go ...' she whispered. 'I want peace ... Tell them ...' With a supreme effort Lettice whispered in her ear, then began again to mutter. Rowan forced herself not to recoil from her friend's foetid breath.

'What is she saying?'

'She wants you to stop calling her "Hamilton". She doesn't like it.' Rowan reported.

'Oh, really! This is a waste of my time. I've better things to do than attend to a spoilt, petulant, stupid woman.' He snapped his medical bag shut.

'Frobisher, you can't go!'

'I most certainly can.' And with that he stalked noisily from the room.

'Oh dear! Now what can we do?'

'I suggest we call the local doctor.'

'He's enlisted. It's all very well being patriotic but leaving the community without medical help is, in my opinion, irresponsible.' Hannah was vexed.

'Then we should send someone to fetch Dr Bunting. Or does he have a telephone?'

'But he's been retired for years.'

'I'm sure he would come for you, Miss Cresswell.'

'We shall have to pray that Doris at the exchange hears the phone ringing. Or perhaps I should send ...' Hannah was talking to herself as she left the room.

'Can we not bathe her, make her more comfortable?' Rowan asked Nurse Winlock.

'She refuses.'

'What did she have for supper to make her so ill?'

'Mrs Morts, it has nothing to do with food. She's poisoned herself.' Nurse Winlock spoke in the brusque tone that her profession adopted when bad news had to be relayed. 'She is *in extremis*. Whatever she swallowed is highly corrosive and is destroying the lining of her gullet and stomach.'

Rowan recoiled. The sheer horror of the information made her feel faint. 'I can't believe that of her. She wouldn't. She has children.'

'Then you don't know your sister-in-law very well, if you don't mind me saying so. I don't blame the major for leaving. If she doesn't want help, that's her business. When it's all over the police will have to be informed, though.'

'Stop saying these things,' Rowan ordered. 'Especially in front of her – it makes it worse.' Gingerly, so she didn't hurt Lettice, she sat on the bed and took her hand. 'I suggest you go back to bed, if you can only be unhelpful.' And Rowan turned her back on the woman in a gesture of dismissal.

'Well!' exclaimed the nurse indignantly. She made a lot of noise as she left, but at least they were finally alone.

'Lettice, my dear, tell me it's not true.'

Lettice shook her head, and immediately retched. Rowan put her hand on her forehead to steady her. Once the vomiting had ceased, she sat down again.

'I'm sorry, but I can't live without him. I want to join him. I had to do it.' Lettice's voice was almost normal. 'When I'm sick the pain eases a little,' she explained, as if she wanted to fill the silence her confession had induced.

Rowan wanted to mention the children, but decided against it. She felt such sorrow for Lettice – but also found she was angry that she could have done such a wicked thing. It was incomprehensible.

'What have you taken?'

'It's unimportant. But before the pain returns, and while we are alone, I must talk to you. I want you to promise – for yourself and Morts – that you will take my children into your home and care for them.' As she spoke of Charlotte and Georgia, her eyes overflowed with tears.

'Of course. But don't speak of such things. We shall get you better. There must be an antidote, as the major said.'

'No ...' Lettice winced and lay back on the pillows. She was waiting for the pain, her face betraying its gathering intensity until she was consumed by it. Rowan waited, not knowing what to do for the best.

'It fades ...' Lettice relaxed a little.

'Hugo will never let them stay here.'

'Yes, he will. The shame of me killing myself will ensure that he won't want them. In any case, he might already be dead.'

'Don't say such things, Lettice, please ...' As before, her friend's words shocked Rowan to the core. And if Lettice was facing death, as she seemed to believe, they were even more wicked.

'I have made a will. It's in a drawer in my room at Esmeralda's. When the solicitor came to see Zeph, I had him arrange it for me. It's binding...'

As the door opened she stopped talking.

'I thought Doris would never respond but eventually she heard the bell in the exchange. Really, in these unsettled times there should be someone on duty through the night.' Hannah was twisting her hands as she spoke. Her nerves are in shreds, Rowan thought.

'I don't think I shall ever forgive the major for deserting us. He is so cold, so uncaring.' She patted Lettice's hand. 'The doctor's coming, dear,' she shouted, as so many did to the sick. 'He won't be long.'

Mention of Zeph had reminded Rowan of something. 'I'll be back soon,' she promised, and left Hannah with Lettice.

First she went to the coachman's house, which was in the stableyard. It took her some time to wake Harold who, judging by the smell of whisky on his breath, had been sleeping heavily but not just from fatigue.

'I'm so sorry to bother you at this hour, but it's important. Is there anything in the tack room someone could use if they wanted to harm themselves?' Why, she thought, was she beating about the bush? 'What I meant was …' she paused '… do themselves a mischief,' she finished lamely. She could not bring herself to use the fatal words – 'to kill'.

'Lawks, Mrs Morts, I hope that's not your manner of thinking.'

'Gracious, no. But it really is a matter of extreme urgency.'

'I'll just get my boots.'

Rowan waited impatiently for him, pacing up and down the cobbled yard watched by a curious cat. Lettice was so ill that every minute ticking away hastened her doom.

Although the horses had gone, some of the best tack remained so that the room looked as it always had. Nothing was out of place. The saddles hung on their wall pegs, immaculately polished; the reins were stored by size. The metal bits gleamed. The horse blankets were neatly folded.

'You keep all this beautifully, Harold. It's as if it's just waiting for the horses to return.'

'I live in hope, Mrs Morts.' Harold blew into a large red handkerchief.

He scanned the shelves where everything was equally well-ordered, then made a loud sucking noise. 'Someone's been at the tartar emetic.' He pointed to a jar of crystals. 'It's been moved.'

By the time Rowan returned to Lettice, the doctor had arrived. Sister Westall and Fanny Petty had been woken. The two women were sponging Lettice, who moaned pitifully. She looked worse, and Hannah appeared close to collapse.

'Miss Cresswell, it would be better if you retired,' the doctor was saying to Hannah.

'I can't leave her.'

'Your distress is upsetting her.' The doctor, who had known Hannah all her life, spoke kindly to her, then took her gently by the arm and led her from the bedside.

'I'll go with her.' Fanny stepped forward. 'We're in the way here, Miss Cresswell. It's best we go.'

Hannah allowed herself to be led away.

'Doctor, may I have a word? I might know what she has taken,' Rowan whispered.

Immediately she had his attention, which annoyed Sister Westall. She did not like the orderlies talking to doctors.

They moved away from the others.

'I remembered she'd been in the tack room yesterday. I asked the coachman if anything had been interfered with. He gave me this.' She handed the small jar to the doctor. 'He said he had it for worming the horses.'

The doctor frowned as he studied the bottle. 'This isn't good news, Mrs Morts. Certainly, antimony, or tartar emetic as it is sometimes called, would produce these symptoms. A few crystals induce sickness – I gather that ladies sometimes utilize them as an emetic to stop their husbands imbibing too much wine. But I fear Miss Lettice has ingested far more than a few crystals.'

'Miss Cresswell was talking of an antidote.' She wished he would stop talking and do something.

'Tannic acid followed by doses of opium.' He spoke more to himself than to her, as if he was reminding himself of what he should do. She wished he wasn't so old. 'But I fear she is too far gone.'

'Oh, Doctor, please don't say that.'

'All we can do is to make her as comfortable as possible until the end. I shall, of course, attempt ...' He opened a small wooden case in which nestled a row of cork-stoppered glass vials. He began to check them, searching for the right one, she assumed. 'I doubt that this will help. I shall try to relieve her pain as much as I can.'

An hour later Rowan felt ashamed that she had doubted the doctor. He was so gentle with Lettice compared with the major. As she had expected, Lettice refused the antidote, shaking her head from one side to the other.

'We could bind her arms,' Sister Westall suggested. 'Hold her firm.'

'I don't think so, Sister. She would only damage herself further.' Instead, promising Lettice that it would help the pain, the doctor managed to administer the opium between the bouts of sickness.

Mercifully, Lettice slept.

The agony continued. It was unbelievable that the body of one so frail could continue to survive. Rowan, while feeling such sadness for Lettice, also felt for Sir Mortie and Hannah. The anguish on their faces was hard to witness. Sir Mortie sat day and night beside his daughter. Lady Coral did not enter the room. Rowan heard several people saying how shocked she was. She thought differently. She was sure Lady Coral was keeping away because she could not bear to see her child *in extremis*.

With Lettice, her own patients and Zeph to visit, Rowan was constantly on the run. Zeph was upset about Lettice and waited eagerly for her visits.

'You look done in, Mrs Morts,' Bert Banks said. He was making reasonable progress now. 'Don't you worry about old Zeph here. I'll keep an eye on him and ring the old bell here if necessary.' He patted the hand bell which stood beside his bed.

The last two days she had missed her Childer's Hill ritual, which worried her. She had told herself that if she didn't wish, he would die. As soon as her shift ended, Rowan set for the wishing tree.

Soon she was walking round and round it, this time wishing not only for Morts but also for Lettice to live. She wondered if she shouldn't be wishing for her to die – the agony they were watching was unbearable.

Her task completed, she leant against the tree to gaze at the timeless beautiful view.

Then, toiling up the hill, she saw a figure. As he got nearer she had to rub her eyes. 'Morts.' Oh, my God, she thought, he's dead? This is his ghost. And then the ghost waved. Rowan hurled herself down the hill and into his arms.

'I knew I'd find you here,' he said, holding her as if he was afraid he might lose her.

'What are you doing here?'

'They gave me compassionate leave,' he said bleakly.

'I'm so sad for you and for poor Lettice.'

'I know you are. Thank God we have each other. Let's sit a moment.' They sank down on to the grass. 'Why has she done this?'

'She's punishing herself, Morts.'

'Those poor children …' He broke down. Rowan held him until the storm had passed.

'God, what use am I, crying like a baby?'

She kissed him. 'I understand.'

'Hannah's told me what a brick you've been. I can't thank you enough.'

'Lettice has always been kind to me. I needed to help.'

'You're a good woman, Rowan.'

She wasn't sure why but those words made her prouder than anything else he had ever said to her.

Lettice's agony finally ended on the fourth day. Her family were with her, not that she knew it. Each stood in a capsule of their own wretchedness, thoughts and memories. It was Rowan who put her arm round the sobbing Lady Coral to comfort her. Lettice's mother had finally summoned the courage to be present.

An hour later the telegram arrived informing Lettice that her husband had been killed on the Somme. No one, not even Lady Coral, could grieve for him.

Rowan looked at the buff telegram in her hand. How ironic. And how sad for Lettice when all she wanted, in the afterlife, was to be alone with her Ramsey.

9

'Suicide is such a selfish act. So unfair on those left behind. Everyone fretting that they should have known, or could have done more to stop it.' Lady Penelope popped a chocolate into her mouth. 'Why are you tutting?'

'That chocolate will ruin your luncheon,' Rowan told her.

'I thought you might be shocked by my opinion on suicide.' She raised an expressive eyebrow.

'No, you may think as you like.' Rowan had a suspicion that Penelope was bored and prodding her into an argument. She was confused about the whole sad business. Half of her agreed with Penelope, but the other half pitied poor Lettice.

'Suicide creates so many problems. Where is she to be buried? The Church won't have her. *And* it's a criminal act. No doubt the police will be involved and scandal will ensue. All too upsetting for everyone.'

'None of that will happen. It was an accidental death.'

'Accidental! Poppycock and fiddlesticks! Who has decided that?'

'The doctors. Who else?'

'Then they're lying.'

'Perhaps they're being kind.' Rowan inspected the seam she had been working on and pulled a face at the uneven stitches; she'd never been able to sew.

'And you're to be a mother to those two little ones. Hardly fair on you, is it? You see what I mean? Pure selfishness.'

'Morts and I are honoured that Lettice should choose us to care for Charlotte and Georgia.'

'How old are they?'

'Ten and eight.' How strange that Penelope did not know the ages of her own great-granddaughters.

'Impossible! Too demanding. Always wanting to know something or other. Too dull!' She put another chocolate into her mouth, no doubt to rouse Rowan, who ignored it.

'And what happens when your own children come? How do you think they will fare then?' Penelope went on. 'You'll favour your own. It's human nature to do so.'

'I won't. I love them already.'

'What about the work you claim to love so much?'

'I won't be able to carry on. But that will give me time to bring the girls to see you.'

'Don't! If there is one thing I can't abide it's children.' She shuddered in an exaggerated way that made Rowan laugh.

'You are incorrigible.' She said her latest new word with pride.

'Are they already here?'

'No, they're still at Esmeralda's. Morts wanted to get the funeral and the formalities out of the way first.'

'Sadly I shall miss the reading of the will. You can't imagine the fuss there was when my late husband's was read.'

Rowan had to concentrate on her sewing so that Penelope could not see her smile. From what she had heard, it was Penelope who had made the fuss when Sir Mortimer's will was read. 'I can't imagine why you would want to be there,' she said eventually. 'I said I didn't want to go but Morts says I must.'

'Quite right too. After all, who else is going to report back to me on the spats? The Cresswells can't make a will without there being a to-do.'

The funeral had been sparsely attended. Evidently the villagers agreed with Penelope on suicide for many stayed away. Rowan knew that the rumours about how Lettice had died would run rife. She was standing at an upstairs window, dressed in black, watching the cortège move across the park towards the church. The coffin was carried easily by the pall-bearers, who included Morts and his father, for Lettice had wasted away to almost nothing during her horrific ordeal. Rowan was concerned for Mortie; he walked like a broken man.

Lady Coral was already causing problems. She would not believe that Lettice had asked Rowan and Morts to be her children's guardians. 'We shall see when her will is read. I can't believe my daughter would entrust her children to you, of all people,' she told Rowan. 'In any case, Hugo will probably have left other instructions.'

This made Rowan wonder if she had understood Lettice correctly. And what if Coral was right about the children? She would be sad if they were not to have them.

There was to be no wake. In the circumstances, it was felt inappropriate.

When the funeral party returned, Rowan had butterflies in her stomach as the family took their places in the small sitting room for the reading.

The proceedings began with a letter, which had arrived that morning from Hugo's father. It was fulsomely apologetic, which did nothing to soften the blow that Hugo had cut not only his wife but his daughters out of his will.

'Scandalous!' Morts objected.

'How spiteful,' Hannah said.

'We shall fight it in the courts,' Lady Coral declared.

'No, we won't. I'm not begging for Hamilton money and that's that. Hugo's done enough damage to this family already. If she hadn't been unhappy ...' Mortie trailed off. Hannah, sitting beside her brother, squeezed his hand. Lady Coral sent him a look of unmitigated loathing.

'If we may proceed ...?' the solicitor requested.

To everyone's relief the will was short and precise. All of Lettice's capital was to go into a trust that would be set up for the girls. The income would be used for their upkeep and education. Morts and his uncle Oliver were to be the trustees. This occasioned a murmur of approval. Lettice had requested that the trustees ensure her daughters were given the best education available. At this, Hannah inadvertently applauded, then apologized to everyone. When the youngest reached twenty-one, the trust would be dissolved and the capital given to the girls.

'Far too early,' Lady Coral commented, interrupting the solicitor. 'They'll fritter it away.'

'You don't know that, Coral,' Sir Mortie admonished. 'Now, do let the poor man continue ...'

The details of the children's future were dealt with. It was as Rowan had said. She and Morts were joint guardians. In the event of Morts's death – Rowan had to clasp his hand tight – Rowan would have sole guardianship.

'Over my dead body!' Lady Coral was on her feet and interrupting again.

'Coral, please,' Sir Mortie begged.

'How can she, of all people, bring up our grandchildren, Mortie? For once try to think with what little brain you have. She cannot be entrusted with them. She knows nothing! We cannot contemplate a mere servant taking charge of them – it would make us a laughing-stock. It is insupportable! Lettice was mad when she wrote this travesty.'

'Mother ...' Morts tried to stand up, Rowan hoped to defend her, but she caught his hand and pulled him down.

'It doesn't matter, Morts. Not today of all days.'

Lettice had divided her jewellery between Charlotte and Georgia, detailing which piece was to go to which girl. She had so much it must have taken her ages, Rowan thought.

'My diamond tiara with the pearl droplets, in the certainty that she will care for me to the end, I bequeath to my sister-in-law, Rowan Cresswell ...'

Lady Coral leapt out of her seat. She was like a jack-in-the-box, thought Rowan.

'I have never heard such rubbish in my life,' Lady Coral began. 'That tiara is far too valuable to be given to *her*. She will undoubtedly sell it.'

The assembled company looked anywhere but at each other. Rowan wished the ground would open up and swallow her. This was awful. But as the woman continued to rant, Rowan became angry. Eventually she could take no more. It was her turn to stand.

'I might not know all the rules of etiquette, Lady Coral, but it strikes me I've better manners than you. How dare you speak of me in that manner and, what is more, on such a day as this?'

Lady Coral collapsed back on to her chair, gaping with astonishment. 'Be quiet,' she eventually managed.

'No. I will not be so insulted. Morts did me the honour of marrying me and making me a member of this family. You have done nothing but attempt to undermine me. I've had enough of your spite.' So incensed was she that nothing could stop her. 'I wouldn't dream of selling Lettice's tiara. I had thought I did not want it and that perhaps I would give it to the girls. But, thanks to you, I shall keep it now, as Lettice wanted.'

Rowan felt quite giddy. She was enjoying herself in a way she would never have thought possible. She was finally answering all the insults and snide remarks of the past two years.

'I am the first to admit that there is much for me to learn. I am also fully aware that I am of a lower class than you. But what you don't seem to understand is that I'm not ashamed of it. In fact, I'm proud to be working class. At least I'm not a parasite.' She shouldn't have said that, she thought, but it was too late. 'Since it is apparent that you cannot be civil to me, I think it is best if we have no more to do with each other.' She bent down to pick up her bag. 'Of course, my husband will do as he wishes but I shall not be dining here again while you are in residence.'

Rowan did not dare to look at anyone.

Lady Coral was taking enormous breaths as if she was trying to control herself. 'Mortie, do something!' she screeched.

Sir Mortie lumbered to his feet and applauded. 'Well said, Rowan, well said.'

Hannah was at her wits' end. There appeared to be no end to the stream of sorrow that flooded the old manor. When she heard the groans and curses of the men she wondered if the walls were absorbing their horror and pain to carry this new burden for ever. Trying to work out where to put people was a daily logistical nightmare.

'The two non-commissioned men in the stables may leave.' Major Fellowes was studying her bed chart with her.

'And where are they to go? Corporal Banks has no family and Gloucestershire is a long way off. Corporal Topsham is local, of course, and it won't be difficult to find someone to cook for him.'

'He should be up and walking by now. Idleness, if you ask me.'

'He is making good progress but, if you remember, you yourself said it would take at least six months.'

'Well, I leave it with you, Miss Cresswell. You had better decide what's to be done. I've work to do ...'

What an exasperating man he was, she thought, as she frowned over her charts. He had the knack of implying that he was the only one doing anything. Admittedly his was the most important job but without everyone else doing their bit his patients wouldn't survive. There were days when she wished he would be transferred somewhere else.

She began to make a list of things to do. Her whole life, these days, was controlled by lists.

In the stables she consulted the men. 'Zeph, I wondered if you could perhaps stay at the Cresswell Arms? Dear Flossie will look after you there.'

'I'd rather not, if you don't mind, Miss Cresswell. I have the cottage so I can go there.'

'But who will look after you?'

'I'll make my own arrangements.'

How satisfactory, thought Hannah. He must have made friends with Dolly. Mentally she ticked Dolly off her list.

'And what about you, Corporal Banks?' She stood beside his bed. Discharging him was a scandal when he was not fully recovered. Despite her reservations about the risks, the major had successfully removed the shrapnel from his spine, but he had reacted badly to the anaesthetic and was still weak, although he did his exercises assiduously. Where the incision had been made he had a nasty sore that nothing, it seemed, would heal.

'I was wondering, if I arrange transport, is there anyone in your village to care for you? Major Fellowes says it's time you moved on.' She was not sure why but as she spoke to him a lump came into her throat. She knew she would miss him and his cheerfulness.

Bert turned his face to the wall and said nothing. Then Hannah saw his shoulders were shaking.

'Corporal Banks, what is it? Oh dear. Oh, please ...' She sat on the edge of the bed and put her arm round him. 'My dear man. What is it?'

But Banks could not reply.

'He has no one, Miss Cresswell. He's been dreading this day.' Zeph advised.

It was as if Bert's barrier of good cheer had crumbled and all the pent-up pain and anxiety had been released.

'I have a solution,' she said. 'I can't think why I haven't suggested it before. I want no disagreements, Corporal. You shall come and stay with me. I have a large house with just me in it. I can hire a nurse to care for you. Yes, that is what we shall do. What do you say?'

There was a long silence. She noticed him wiping his nose on the back of his hand and handed him her handkerchief. 'Miss Cresswell, I don't know ... I've never met with such kindness before.'

She patted his hand – he was about to break down again.

'On one condition,' he said, 'that you call me Bert.'

Hannah laughed. 'Bert it is.' She did not understand why, suddenly, she felt so happy.

It was two weeks since Eve Gilroy had fallen ill. As Major Fellowes had feared the bronchitis had turned into pneumonia. For a week she had drifted in and out of consciousness. Twice she had nearly died and several times her coma was mistaken for death. So ill was she that she was unaware of the dramas swirling round her in the house. Neither did she know that, night after night, Edward Whitaker had sat with her and no one could persuade him otherwise.

Finally she was up, in her dressing-gown and sitting in a chair by the open window by Philomel Herbert's sitting room.

'It was kind of you to let me use your rooms, Philomel. I hate to think I put you out.'

'Eve, it was my pleasure. Having you on the ground floor made caring for you easier too. I'm so glad to see you've eaten your lunch all up.'

'I couldn't finish the stout.' The soufflé she had just eaten had been perfect but she wasn't about to say so. 'What's my kitchen like? No doubt it looks like one of them zeppelins has bombed it.'

'Everyone's been pulling their weight, Eve. And I must say young Acacia's a treasure. Cooks just like her mother. And Cherry's a hard worker too.'

Eve sniffed as if she didn't believe a word. 'I must get back to work.'

'You'll do no such thing. You need to rest and get your strength back.'

Eve lay back on the goosedown pillow with a contented sigh. 'It would be nice to take a little time, perhaps have a holiday.'

Something fishy was afoot. Eve couldn't put her finger on it but she felt there were secrets to which she was not privy. Her first fear was that the housekeeper had vamped Whitaker, taking advantage of her indisposition.

'Edward, are you keeping things from me?' she asked one evening, when he had popped in to see how she was.

'Yes, we have. Miss Cresswell and I thought it was better if you had your strength back before we burdened you.'

'You're worrying me, Edward.' She was almost panicking. Was she to be replaced by that slip of a girl, Acacia? She'd be cheaper to employ, of course.

'I'm sorry to tell you, Eve, but young Mrs Hamilton passed away ...'

'No! Never!'

'Unfortunately ...' And Whitaker told her of the awful dark days.

'The poor child. Why, I remember when she was a little girl coming into my kitchen, looking for jam tarts with her brothers. That *is* sad news.' She dabbed at her eyes, upset. After a good blow into her handkerchief, it had soon passed. 'Accidentally poisoned herself, you say. Well, I never! And Sir Mortie?'

'He's taken it bad.'

'Lady Coral?'

'There was, well ... a scene.' He recounted Rowan's stand.

'Good for her. And her ladyship's gone off in a huff?' Eve chortled at this.

'To her father's. Sir Mortie's stayed behind. We're all at sixes and sevens.'

'It's this wretched war. No one knows how to behave no more. Not like the good old days, Edward.'

For a while they sat in contented silence. 'Edward, I don't know where

I've been these last few weeks, but it's frightening all this going on and me not knowing.'

'You were so ill, Eve. I despaired of you ever recovering … I can tell you now, the doctor warned us to expect the worst.'

'Good gracious me!'

'You're not better yet either. You're going to need special care, that's for sure.'

It was almost worth being ill to hear him speak to her thus.

'I thought I was going to lose you, Eve,' he said, with a catch in his voice.

'You're not going to get rid of me as easy as that.' She laughed.

'What spirit! An example to us all.'

Eve glowed.

'I've been thinking, Eve … It's like this. Last year when the powers-that-be brought in compulsory registration, I thought it'd only be a matter of time and conscription would follow. Well, as you know, it has for men up to forty-one. How long will it be, with the losses we're suffering, before it's up to fifty-one, then sixty-one?'

'No. Not you,' she said. He was too old – and God help the country if it had to rely on old men. But fortunately she did not say this.

'I fear it's inevitable. And I worry about not doing and saying things I should have years ago. The last couple of weeks have been a shock to me … Mrs Hamilton, you. I was wondering …' He paused. 'I was wondering, Eve, if you would do me the honour of becoming my wife?'

It was fortunate that Eve was sitting down for had she not been she would have fallen over with astonishment. As it was, she had to suppress a triumphant squeal. Her dream had come true. It was worth having been at death's door.

'My dear Edward, you do *me* the greatest honour. And I happily accept.'

She leant back on the cushions. How many years had she been practising that speech?

'My cup runneth over,' she said, and fainted once more.

Chapter Seven

Early 1917

1

Despite the recent tragedies, Rowan had been happy over the past few months. Not that everything was perfect, it wasn't, but she had changed. Now she didn't expect to be happy all the time. And something else had happened. She had learnt not to get too upset. She was more patient and tolerant.

Georgia and Charlotte's arrival had been delayed for a few days after Lettice's funeral because they had both succumbed to German measles. Now, though, they had settled with their nanny into their new home, which meant that the house was full. Rowan loved their noise and clutter – she had lived there alone for too long.

When they had first arrived the girls had asked for their mother. Rowan had been dreading this since Morts had suggested she deal with it. He didn't know what to say. Gently she had explained their mother had gone to heaven. Then she had taken them into the garden, shown them the stars and told them that one was Lettice.

'Don't be silly. They're just stars,' Charlotte had said.

'She's dead, isn't she? Our ponies are dead too. Papa had them shot.'

'I'm sure he didn't,' Rowan countered, unsure how to handle this conversation.

'He did. It was horrible of him.' Georgia's eyes filled with tears. 'Is he still in France, fighting?'

She took a deep breath. She might as well get everything over in one fell swoop. 'I'm sorry, your papa died, too, on a battlefield.'

'Who died first?' Charlotte asked.

'I don't know.'

'Wouldn't it be funny if they died at the same time?' Georgia suggested.

'Where are we going to live?'

'Here, with Uncle Morts and me.'

'Good!' they shouted in unison, and did a little dance. 'What's for tea?'

A week later she found Georgia sobbing on the upstairs landing.

'Why are you crying, poppet?' She scooped the child into her arms, big as she was.

'Nanny said I was the most horrible child she had ever met.'

'I'm sure she didn't mean it.'

The crying stopped and Georgia looked at her, exasperated. 'Why don't grown-ups ever believe me? She *did* mean it. And I'm glad she's leaving us.'

The children's nanny had joined them and was watching the child with an aloof expression. Rowan did not like the woman's air of superiority. But when she had suggested to Morts that they didn't need her, he had decided it was better for the girls if she remained. 'I'd have died if Nanny Wishart had suddenly left me,' he had explained.

But, in Rowan's opinion, this was no Nanny Wishart.

'You're leaving?'.

'Yes, Mrs Morts. I told the girls this morning.' She spoke as if she had no regrets.

But then, thought Rowan, perhaps she was controlling herself. 'It might have been better if you'd told me and we could have planned how best to tell them.'

The nanny shrugged. 'They had to know some time.'

Evidently she had been wrong, Rowan thought. The nanny didn't care about them. 'Why are you leaving?'

'This is not the standard of establishment I'm used to.' The way she looked about her showed her disdain for Rowan's beloved house.

'Why? Are we too modest?' Or is it me? she wondered.

'I have no nurserymaid.'

'There's hardly need for one here. And where would we put her?'

'Exactly. I have been approached by a family of *high* standing. I shall, of course, remain in this position for the next month.'

'I would not wish you to *discommode* yourself.' That sounded wonderful, she decided. It was her latest word. 'You're free to go now. In fact, I would rather you did. Come, Georgia, let us go and find some sweeties.'

'Nanny says I shouldn't eat them.'

'Nanny doesn't know everything. I do.'

Holding the child's hand firmly, amused by the nanny's shocked face, they ran down the stairs and into the kitchen to find the bullseyes Rowan had bought that morning.

Their dinner over, Morts was seated at one side of the fireplace, reading, and Rowan at the other. She loved him so much, she thought, as she watched him, engrossed in his book.

Suddenly he looked up and smiled at her. 'What are you thinking?'

'If only we could stay like this for ever.'

'Dreams are lovely, but you must be brave. You know I return to the front next week.'

'I do, but I can pretend, can't I?'

Morts returned to his book, and Rowan gazed into the fire. She had better tell him but she wondered if he would be cross. 'Morts, the nanny has left.'

He closed the book, leaving one finger marking the page he had reached. She didn't like it when he did that – it made her feel he was impatient to get back to the book rather than talk to her.

'Why?'

'She didn't think we were grand enough.'

Morts laughed. 'Then we shall have to find another.'

'I'd rather we didn't. I think it would be best if I looked after them.'

'Don't be ridiculous. Women in your position have nannies.'

Rowan slipped off the chair and sat on the floor in front of him. 'I think it would be better for the girls, and blow my *position*!' She laughed. 'I'm worried about them. They haven't cried once and seem to have accepted too easily that their mother is dead. They showed no sorrow that their nanny was leaving.'

'Surely that's good. They can't be suffering.'

'It doesn't seem right to me. I think they feel unloved. No doubt Lettice saw them very little and the nanny was a cold fish.'

'What was Lettice supposed to do? Get down on all fours and play with them?' The idea amused him.

'Yes,' was her short answer. 'I shall teach them what it is to be loved.'

'When our baby arrives you'll need a nanny.'

'No, I won't. No one could look after our baby as I will.'

'But it will be too much for you.'

'My mother had eight children and each of us knew we were loved.'

It was at times like this that Rowan could see the differences that lay between her and Morts. And, being a worrier, she wondered if they would make difficulties for them or if they would surmount them?

*

The next day Rowan heard gleeful shouting and laughter coming from Morts's study.

'We're going to school, Aunt Rowan. Isn't that lovely?'

'When?'

'Tomorrow.' There was more dancing and clapping.

'You two, shoo! I can't hear myself speak with the noise you're making.' The children raced from the room seemingly incapable of moving slowly. 'I've arranged for them to go to St Margaret's, a girls' school, in Exeter. George is bringing a couple of trunks over from the big house. I've asked that the headmistress take them to Pinder and Tuckwell for their uniforms.'

'But how will they get home for tea?' Rowan asked, puzzled.

Morts laughed loudly. 'They won't. It's a boarding-school.'

Rowan was upset. Why send them away when they needed her and Morts? Why send them away at all? What was wrong with the village school? The questions had tumbled out of her.

He countered all of her arguments. 'My love, they have to go. It is what my sister would have wanted for them. Remember, she asked that they have a good education. The village school won't give them that.'

'But what if they miss us? What if they cry for us?'

'They won't. You heard how excited they are. Although their father disinherited them, they will both come into a lot of money when they grow up and make good marriages. They'll need their education to become good wives and know how to run their homes.'

It was a good thing that at that point he had looked back at the accounts on his desk and didn't see the horror on Rowan's face. She had had little education. All she had to be proud of was that she could read and write. Should she educate herself more? Learning new words was evidently not enough. Was he telling her that she was not a good wife because she had only been to the village school?

That day her confidence, which had been building, collapsed. She could not sleep, and worried. She had done so much, come so far. She'd show him, she said to herself. She'd teach herself lots of things.

She had cried when she saw them off to school because they suddenly looked so grown-up. She found a calendar and hung it in the kitchen so that she could see how long she had to wait for them to return for the holidays.

Then her wish that Morts need not go back to the death and destruction of the front was granted, albeit temporarily.

'Poor Morts, how is he? Would he mind me visiting him?' On hearing he had been taken ill Hannah had come over with a basket of fruit from the hot-house and some of Eve Gilroy's game soup.

'I'm sure he'd love to see you, but I should warn you, he's not the easiest of patients. Grumpy is the word I'd use.' She laughed. 'The doctor has visited. He says it's German measles, caught from the girls. He's far more ill than they were.'

'Childhood illnesses are often worse in adults. And naughty you, Rowan. It's no longer German measles, remember, but Belgian rash.'

'I do think that's silly.'

'I agree. You remember the phonograph machine I acquired for the officers? Well, the other day one objected to listening to Beethoven. The other men told him not to be stupid, but he wouldn't have it. He went to Major Fellowes, who agreed with him, so we can't play it. But, of course, the major *would* do that, small-minded as he is.'

'The war is hardly Beethoven's fault.' How sad, Rowan thought. Hannah must have fallen out with the major and she had hoped they would marry. Hannah should have a husband to love, she had decided long ago. She had learnt that Hannah had a lot of love to give.

'Precisely,' Hannah agreed, as she mounted the stairs.

No sooner had Morts recovered and was making plans to return to his regiment than he slipped on some ice and fell heavily. A water butt had overflowed and a sharp frost had followed. He had broken his right leg. While she regretted the pain he suffered, Rowan couldn't stop herself feeling relieved that she had him at home, safe, for a little longer.

It was a precious time and Rowan stored away every tiny detail so that she could think of it when he had gone. She had begun to keep a diary for the same reason, and soon discovered that it helped to write down anything that troubled her.

Twice a week they dined at the manor. Since Lady Coral was still away, Rowan was happy to go there and was growing close to her father-in-law, a man she had once thought stupid. Now she could acknowledge that, while not very clever, he had a big heart.

'There's just you and Morts now. I'm lucky to have you,' Sir Mortie said one night, almost tearfully, as he helped himself to more port. 'Everyone's gone.'

'I'm sure your wife will soon return,' she replied, thinking more's the pity.

'I didn't mean *her*.'

'And Felix will come back from the war.'

'If we're lucky.' He was taking the loss of Lettice hard.

Christmas had been quiet, they had decided to celebrate with just the two of them and the children. It was, Rowan decided, the best ever.

Although she tried to see her mother, she did not manage it nearly often enough, she knew. These days, she was torn between her duties, Morts and her family. It was hard for Flossie with no Alf to help her, and Rowan knew she pined for him. Nothing was ever said but she had the illogical feeling that Flossie blamed her for his enlisting. She often wondered if her father had made a dreadful mistake in telling her first.

Her anxiety over Morts's safety never left her. At night when he tossed and turned or, worse, screamed in terror, she would wonder what horrors he was revisiting and wished she could go there for him.

One particular night when the nightmare recurred he had sat bolt upright, his hands held out beseechingly. Then, covered with sweat, he had begun to weep. It was no ordinary crying for the sobs racked his body as if he were having a fit.

'Morts! You're here, safe with me.'

He had looked at her and, for a second, appeared not to recognize her. 'I don't want to die!' he had cried out, with such pain that she could no longer hold back her tears.

'You shan't die,' she said, holding him tight and praying that God would not think her presumptuous and punish them.

Finally he calmed down. 'I'm sorry,' he said.

'What have you to be sorry for? Nothing. I'm here for you. Do you want to tell me?'

'No.'

'It might help you.'

He laughed at this. 'Nothing can, my sweet one. I shall return to horror and inhumanity that beggars belief. I don't want to burden you with it.'

She kissed him. The trouble was, she was already burdened, but she wasn't going to tell him that.

The inevitable day arrived. They stood close together, holding each other in the January cold, as they waited for the train to arrive at Barlton. The station-master had made a fuss of Morts, and Rowan had wished he would leave them in peace for their last few precious moments together.

Morts caressed her stomach. 'Let's pray there's a baby in there. We tried hard enough.' He kissed her full on the lips. Once he would never have done so in front of strangers, but now everyone was kissing their loved ones goodbye and there was no one to notice. Another change.

The train arrived. Rowan felt sick in the pit of her stomach. What was there to say? How could she hide her fears? She must be brave.

'I adore you,' was all she said.

On the train he opened the window and they held hands. She would not let go as the train began to move and ran along the platform until she could no longer keep up.

Then she waved until she could no longer be sure that she could still see him. Eventually the train disappeared completely. She stood for a long time on the platform. To be there was a link, a pathetic one, to him. It was all she had.

2

Until Bert Banks had moved into her house, Hannah had not grasped how lonely she had been living there by herself. Now when she hurried home from work it was with a spring in her step and plans for what they would do that evening.

When she had first met Bert she had discovered he was clever, but undereducated and eager to learn. 'We didn't have books at home when I was a young 'un,' he explained.

'There must have been the library, though?'

'I wasn't allowed to use it. My old mother thought the books were dirty. I can hear her now, "You don't know where them books have been." Very particular my mum was,' he said, in an exaggerated West Country accent. He was a brilliant mimic, and his interpretation of Major Fellowes had Hannah holding her sides as she shrieked with laughter.

When she had suggested diffidently that she could draw up a reading list for him, he had responded with enthusiasm, devouring the books she chose. A few weeks later, she was teaching him Latin. He loved mythology, learnt poems with ease, and began to write them. 'You're opening a new world to me, Miss Cresswell.'

After a month, the nurse she had found to care for him was no longer needed because his wound had healed. Hannah had always felt that exercise, rather than languishing in bed, as the major advocated, would get Bert mobile again and she was right. In Barlton she had found a boxer who came every day and helped Bert rebuild his muscles.

From being bed-bound he had been promoted to a chair, and then progressed to crutches. Soon he used two walking-sticks. Now, after three months at Hannah's, he could walk fifty yards with one stick. He aimed to be walking unaided by February, and she had no doubt that he would achieve it.

Now, as she went into her house, she called, 'I've a new jigsaw.' Bert loved them. She began to divest herself of her outer garments. The weather was bitter and she was bundled up in jumpers, a long overcoat and a scarf she had knitted, which went round her neck at least twice. She wore earmuffs under her hat. 'Where are you?'

'In the kitchen.'

She was relieved to hear his voice. Every evening she expected him to be gone. Every day she prepared herself to be alone again.

'What are you doing?'

Bert was resplendent in one of the cook's capacious starched overalls. 'Cooking. What does it look like?' He waved a large metal spoon at her. 'The cook's brother's been killed, and I said she should go home. I hope that's all right but she was in such a hurry. Right old state she was in, too.'

'Poor Ethel. I do wish I'd been here. She's particularly close to her family. I must write to her. And of course you did the right thing.' She sat down, suddenly weary.

'Tired? Here you are, love.' He handed her a glass of sherry. 'You do too much. And that walk back of a night is the last straw. You should take the motor with you.'

'Oh, I couldn't do that. Remember, the government has asked us not to drive for pleasure and the King has set us such a good example.'

'Lawks, Miss Cresswell, you're such a stickler. You'd be driving back from work and, in my book, work isn't a pleasure.'

'It does me good. And it keeps me fit. But I'm not too tired. What I am is tired of worrying, Bert. Ethel losing her brother makes me worry more. The estate has been so lucky – we've not lost one man – but I fear this cannot go on for ever.'

'You really care about the estate workers, don't you?'

'But of course.'

'Not all landowners do. The old codger I worked for, he couldn't have cared less about us gardeners.'

'Then he was stupid. I think of our people as my friends – although I'm not sure they regard me in the same way.' She laughed. 'What are you cooking?'

'Steak, onions and chips.'

'How lovely. I'll just go and freshen up.'

An odd mix of food, she thought, as she climbed the stairs. She didn't think she'd had that combination before. It sounded rather heavy. She hoped it wouldn't bring on her indigestion.

Everyone's contentment couldn't last. Lady Coral suddenly returned to the manor and Hannah was the first victim of her wrath.

'Is it true that you're living with a peasant?'

'I beg your pardon?' Hannah was too shocked to sound indignant.

'I didn't know there was something wrong with your hearing as well as your senses. Have you no consideration for your family? First it was that unspeakable Sapphic creature, then your incarceration in prison and now this ludicrous arrangement.'

'But you—'

'He is half your age! Do you not realize how foolish that makes you seem? How can you live with the gossip? How can …' On and on she ranted. As usual her voice rose until she was screeching.

'Now what's afoot?' The door opened and Mortie strode into the room. His thunderous expression did not suit him – normally he looked pleasant and easy-going. 'You've only been here an hour, woman, and already there's trouble.'

'I would prefer you not to speak to me in that tone, Mortie. I'm not used to it.'

'Life has been so peaceful with you out of the way.'

Coral sank on to a sofa and began to cry. Mortie ignored her. Hannah was unsure what to do. Her innate kindness made her want to step forward and comfort her but after the conversation they had just had she wondered why she should bother.

'So, Hannah, what was that about?'

'Coral is under the impression that I am having a liaison with Bert Banks. It annoys you, doesn't it, Coral?'

'What business is it of hers if you are?' Mortie wondered.

'But I'm not. I've helped him because I like him and he's an interesting man. And, on top of everything else, he's a gardener.'

'Salt of the earth, if you ask me, Hannah. You don't want to let him slip through your fingers.'

At this Coral shrieked, 'Have we not enough peasants foisted on us already?'

'Don't you dare speak ill of Rowan. She's a damned asset to us. This family needs more like her.' Having made his feelings clear Mortie stamped out of the room.

'What has happened to him? He doesn't sound like Mortie any more,' Coral wailed.

'I think my brother might just have grown up. And I haven't time to stand here gossiping. I've far too much to do.'

Hannah found a marked degree of satisfaction in having the upper hand over her sister-in-law for once.

That conversation gave Hannah food for thought as she walked home. Were people gossiping about her? How unpleasant. But she should be used to that by now. When she'd been a suffragette the tittle-tattle had been incessant. Of course, she was unchaperoned with a man living under her roof but as she was fifty-three, and Bert ten years younger, she hadn't considered it a problem.

Should she ask him to leave? The idea filled her with dismay. At the moment they were planning the spring planting. 'But in these dreadful times should I be thinking of something as unimportant as my flower garden?' she had said, when he raised the subject.

'It's because of these dreadful times that you should. The soul needs beauty even more now than usual,' he had replied. Once again she had been amazed by how sensitive he was for one of his class.

At this thought she stopped in her tracks. Why did she always think in those terms? What had his class to do with how he thought? He was a good and perceptive man, whatever his background. 'You, Hannah Cresswell, are becoming a snobbish old woman,' she said aloud, her breath swirling like smoke in the bitter cold. '*Becoming*? Be honest with yourself, you have always been.'

She continued on her way home. But had it been her fault? Surely she came to instant, unthinking conclusions about people because of her background? Look at dear Rowan! Hannah had been wrong to think her unsuitable for Morts. Why, now she was of the opinion that Morts couldn't have found a better wife. People kept saying that times were changing. Well, it was about time Hannah changed with them.

Then a thought she would rather suppress snaked into her mind. Bert was a very attractive man. Sometimes she dreamt of him ... even when she wasn't asleep! Still, she thought, had she not done so all her adult life? She was always dreaming of the impossible, always longing for someone to love. What a joke she would be if anyone found out.

Hannah was always honest about herself. She wasn't stupid enough to imagine that Bert would find her attractive in *that* way – a ludicrous idea.

She had almost reached the house. Already she was worrying that he might not be there. How could she even consider asking him to leave? If only she could think of some way to invite him to stay for ever. Perhaps if she asked him to become her gardener ...

If she was to do anything it had to be soon. Bert, she knew from the papers she had seen, was soon to be discharged by the army. 'One of the lucky ones,' she muttered, as she opened the front door.

Ethel was still not back so she went straight to the kitchen where Bert was already at work on their dinner – she was learning to call it supper.

'Before you ask, it's lamb stew,' Bert said. Her sherry was waiting for her.

'You look after me so well,' she said.

'Someone's got to. Look at you! Done in again.'

'It has been a trying day.' She sat down heavily on one of the kitchen chairs, suddenly weary. She smiled to herself. Suppose Coral saw her now?

'What's the joke?' Satisfied that his stew could look after itself, he had joined her, a tankard of beer in hand.

'My sister-in-law has returned. She doesn't approve ...' Suddenly she found herself telling him about the unpleasant incident.

When she had finished, silence descended and she wished she hadn't been so stupid.

'Do you want me to go?'

'That's the last thing I want.'

'I will, though. I don't want to cause you unhappiness. I'd hate myself for ever more if I did that.'

'Coral is a difficult woman. No, she's an unpleasant, spiteful creature. I don't know why I let her upset me. She doesn't like to see me happy.'

'And are you happy?'

'Since you came here, yes. We have such good times together.'

'We do, don't we?' Bert took a long swig of his beer. 'But there's still the gossip.'

'I've learnt to ignore it.'

'I don't think you have. It upsets you.'

There was another long silence. Hannah was feeling wretched. She should never have told him. He'd go now.

'Miss Cresswell, what I'm about to say ... I don't want you to be insulted. It's been on my mind … The trouble is, I don't know quite how to put it. It's like this …' He looked at his hands.

Hannah wished he would speak up and get it over with.

Bert cleared his throat. 'It's like this, Miss Cresswell. I think I love you …' He stopped and blushed.

'I beg your pardon?'

'I knew you'd be upset. I shouldn't have said it.' He put his head into his hands. It was a gesture of despair.

'No, please!' Hannah cried. 'I didn't think I'd heard correctly. You see, I don't expect anyone to love me.'

'How can that be? You're the kindest, most thoughtful and wonderful woman I've ever met.'

'Oh!' Hannah was close to tears.

'It's true, but I shouldn't have said it. Only it would break my heart to leave here. It's like home to me now. And without you … Well, I'd be empty inside. But you're a grand lady and I'm nobody.'

'Don't ever say that again, Bert. I'm not a grand lady, simply a fortunate one. And you are a prince among men. You see, Bert, I *know* I love you.'

3

Esmeralda couldn't settle. She had had Marigold's clothes changed at least four times – much to the nanny's frustration. She had managed to restrict herself to three outfits.

Oliver was due home on leave. She would see him for the first time in a year.

For the umpteenth time she checked the accounts, which she had attempted to keep in neat order for him. This time they were better, she felt, with fewer mistakes than there had been when he had last left her in charge. As far as she could see, the books balanced – or nearly. She had thought of asking her father if one of his clerks might check them for her, then decided against it as the last person Oliver would want to see his finances was her father.

In any case Stan Eldridge was being difficult. It had been a mistake to ask him if she could return to his house, Courtney Lacy. When her plans had changed so that she and Marigold had stayed at Lees Court, her father had not been pleased. Every week he visited and every week he continued his campaign for her to leave.

'He doesn't deserve you. A second son! You could do better.' Her father was pacing the room, a sure sign that he was upset.

'Titles don't bring happiness.'

'They give you standing.'

'Who would want to marry a divorced woman?'

'With my money, lords aplenty.'

'Your money and not love?'

'Bah! Look what marrying for love has done for you.'

It was always the same.

'If you came to live with me you'd be better looked after, more comfortable. You have so few staff here.'

'Because of the war, Papa, and even you must admit the war is not Oliver's fault.' She smiled at him. 'It's probably the same with you.'

'There are always ways round these matters.'

'Large or small brown envelopes, Papa?' she teased. Her father always paid his bribes in the ubiquitous brown envelopes. 'In any case there's only Marigold and myself to care for. We don't need more staff. Stop being so grumpy.'

'I love you, Esmeralda,' he said simply.

'And I love you too, Papa, but I'm content here. Please believe me.'

It had been Lettice who, all those months ago, had solved the problem for her.

'He never took to Oliver and when all this drama happened no doubt he thought you would go home to him. You were supposed to be his little girl again. You've disappointed him.'

Dear Lettice. She grieved for her still. She knew she should have seen more of her when Ramsey had been killed. She had been to her bedside only once during her agony, and felt guilty for that.

Rowan had been wonderful, holding Lettice when she vomited, washing her, attending to her every need. Esmeralda shuddered. She couldn't have done that. The smell had been dreadful. At the time she'd thought that Rowan was used to such things – and, in any case, she hadn't expected Lettice to die. Optimist that she was, she had been sure her friend would recover. Now she still couldn't believe she was dead.

She missed going to Cresswell Manor. She had enjoyed helping the poor soldiers to write their letters. She liked and admired Hannah. But the disapproval she had to weather when she visited had been too much for her so she had stopped going. Why Oliver had told his family about her she didn't know. It should have been their secret. She was sure he hadn't mentioned his own misconduct. Then she brought herself up short. Was not she telling her father exactly the same?

Now she was waiting for Oliver to arrive. He had been on leave before, she knew. He had written and told her he was in Rouen and would be going to Paris. He had sent Marigold a miniature statue of the Eiffel Tower, but there had been nothing for her. She had been hurt and found herself wondering if he had sent a gift to Sorrel Plunkett. She hated that woman.

She had discussed her feelings for the vicar's wife with Lettice, and been shocked by her opinion.

'It would be sad to end your marriage and leave your home just because Oliver has been silly,' she had said.

'Humiliating me as he did is a little more than *silly*, Lettice.'

'He's a man. They're often silly.'

'Then why are you not at home with Hugo? Were you being *silly*?' she has answered sharply.

'No, I was not. I was in love. Oliver does not love this tedious woman.' Lettice had looked so sad that Esmeralda had hugged her, not wanting to argue with her.

'Oh, Lettice,' She sighed. 'If only you were here now.'

Esmeralda feared that Oliver would be cold towards her. She had thought long and hard about him and his betrayal. Had Lettice been right? Were men so different? How could he make love to someone if there was no love between them?

She should never have confessed her fears about Marigold to him. It had been cruel and, of course, she did not know the truth for certain. Anger had made her do it. She had so many regrets now.

As she waited she wandered aimlessly about the house, which she had grown to love. If he asked her to leave she didn't know what she would do or where she would go. She loved her father but she didn't want to live with him. He would expect her to do only as he wanted. Her year alone at Lees Court had made her value her new-found independence. She was not prepared to go back to being his child.

She heard a motor-car and glanced into the mirror. A year ago she would have lingered but now she ran out of the room and towards the door. 'It's all right, Milner. It's Mr Oliver.' She hurried to open it. He was climbing out of the car. Her heart jumped. He was leaner and his hair was greyer, but she knew she still loved him.

'Oliver! At last!' she said.

He raced up the steps two at a time. It's going to be all right, she thought. But when he reached her he held out his hand in such a formal gesture that she was sure she heard her heart crack.

'I've been so worried,' she said.

'That's kind of you.'

'Would you like tea?' It was the only thing she could think to say.

'No, thank you. Get Milner to open a bottle of claret. I want to see Marigold. I've a present for her.' He had dropped his bags and was already running up the long, cantilevered staircase.

Desolate, Esmeralda went to sit in the drawing room. How could they have come to this?

He seemed to have been gone for ages but when she peered at her watch, a mere half-hour had passed when she heard him returning. Marigold was chattering away and their progress was slow as he helped the two-year-old manoeuvre herself down the stairs. She was a determined child and wouldn't allow anyone to carry her.

'Goldie did it.' The little girl could not say her name and had christened herself Goldie.

As soon as they entered the room Marigold ran towards her, holding out an elaborate doll – French, from its ornate clothes. It was a Godsend for Esmeralda could admire it, and talk about it.

'Once you get away from the front line it's hard to realize there's a war on,' Oliver said.

'Is it bad?'

'Worse than you could imagine,' he said bleakly. She wished she hadn't asked.

'Your claret.' She was relieved to see Milner with the wine, and the champagne she had ordered for herself. She was in need of it. She did not want to be left alone with Oliver – it accentuated their awkwardness with each other.

'Sir, might I say on behalf of the staff how pleased we are to see you home, and safe?'

'That's very kind of you, Milner. I must say I'm happy to be here, even if only for a short time. How is everything?'

'Difficult, sir, but we manage. I don't know if you've been informed but we've lost three of the estate workers.'

'I had heard. How are the families?'

'Also managing, sir. And no one could have looked after them better than Mrs Oliver has.'

'That's good to hear.'

'We were sorry to learn of Miss Lettice's passing.'

'Yes, Milner. It was very sad ...'

The commiserations over, the wine served, Marigold once more with her nanny, the two of them were alone.

'Esmeralda, we must talk.'

She was unable to look at him. 'Yes ...'

'I've been wondering what you want to do. If you wish to continue living here.'

'I ... But it's your house. I don't wish to presume ...'

'Marigold is happy here. Perhaps it would be better if you stayed. I mean, it's up to you. I'll honour whatever you decide.'

'This house is all Marigold has ever known.'

'We must put our daughter's needs first.'

'Indeed we should.' He had said *our* daughter.

'Then you stay.'

'Thank you. We shall try not to inconvenience you.' She felt as if she was talking to a stranger. This was not how it should be.

'Esmeralda ...'

'Oliver ...' They spoke in unison, which made them laugh and relieved the tension a little.

'You wanted to say ...'

This was the moment. She clasped her hands. 'I'm sorry, Oliver. I am so ashamed of my behaviour. I should have been honest with you from the beginning.'

'How could you have told me something as awful as that?' he said. 'Perhaps it was a good thing you didn't. I would have searched him out and killed him, then been hanged for it.'

'Oh, Oliver.' Tears glistened in her eyes. 'What a muddle everything is.'

He gazed at her for what seemed a long time. 'She's my daughter, Esmeralda, of that I'm sure. I've given this matter a great deal of thought and I know that even if she wasn't it would make no difference. I would love her just the same.'

Esmeralda dabbed her eyes with her handkerchief.

'So it would please me if you both stayed here. I can find a room at the manor or eventually buy myself another house.'

'But I would hate that ...' She trailed off. How could she tell him she loved him when, no doubt, he no longer loved her?

'I have done you a great wrong, Esmeralda. All I can say is how sorry I am. You will never forgive me, but I wanted you to know how ashamed I am, and that I love you and always will.'

Esmeralda stared at him with disbelief. 'You still love me?'

'Yes. In the trenches it's easy to see what's right and what's wrong.'

'But, Oliver, I love you ...'

'You can forgive me?' He looked astonished.

'Well, men can be so silly at times.' ·

That night they made love with an intensity neither had known before. The long year of loneliness was over. And, unknown to them, a new life began during that time of tender reconciliation.

4

The banging on the door woke Rowan from a deep sleep. She was reminded of the night she had been woken to go to Lettice. But now she was assailed by a greater fear. Morts.

She grabbed a shawl and ran pell-mell down the stairs, feeling sick with apprehension. 'I'm coming!' she called, as she fought with the bolt, then flung open the door. 'Oak, what are you doing here?' Her brother was standing on the step, panting hard.

'You're to come quick! It's our Willow. I've got to get Acacia and Cherry.' Before she could ask any more, Oak was away, running through the darkness to the manor.

Rowan dressed in haste, tripping over her hem several times as she wrestled with her clothes. Then she could find only one shoe and lost time looking for the other. What time was it? It was pitch black outside. Her watch told her it was three o'clock. Something bad *had* happened.

Sick with apprehension, she pedalled as fast as she could across the park to Cress.

The Cresswell Arms was ablaze with light, which at this time in the morning was ominous – that was how the manor had looked on the night she had been summoned there. She rushed along the corridor to the kitchen.

'She's here,' Holly, her youngest sister, greeted her. 'Oh, Rowan, isn't it awful?' It was then that she noticed Holly had been crying.

'What's happened?' she asked, but she didn't really want to know.

'You took your time.' Flossie was standing in front of the range, arms folded across her chest in her usual stance, Acacia and Cherry beside her.

'I came as quickly as I could. What's happened? Is it father?'

Flossie didn't answer.

'There's been a big explosion where Willow works,' Holly said. 'A lot of people have been killed.'

Rowan felt her legs buckle and had to feel for a chair. She slumped on to it. 'And Willow?'

Flossie's mouth was set in a rigid line, as if she would never speak again.

'We don't know,' Holly told her. 'The policeman didn't know any more. Banging on the door he was, frightened us witless, didn't it, Mother?'

'When did he come?'

'This evening,' Holly said.

'Where's Oak?'

'He went on to Doris to send a telegram to Aspen and Maple – if he can waken her.'

'At this time of night?'

'You're not the only one with a right to know,' Flossie said. Why was her mother displeased with her this time? Rowan wondered, almost with resignation. It had been a perfectly reasonable question, and of course Aspen and Maple, both working in Exeter, should know.

There was a clatter in the corridor and the door opened. Oak had returned. He was no longer a child but had grown into a young man – too soon, she thought, from taking on too much responsibility. He was rubbing his hands, and made straight for the warmth of the range. Flossie smiled as she made room for him.

'Did you have any luck?' Rowan asked, having resolved not to let her mother upset her.

'Took a lot of banging but I woke Doris. None too pleased, she was, but she gets paid to do it so I didn't apologize.' He was still chafing his hands.

'Do we know what happened, Mother?' Acacia asked.

'It's a bit of a muddle.' It was Oak who answered. 'As far as the policeman could tell us, an explosion ripped through the works.'

'How could he be sure it was where Willow worked?' Cherry asked.

'I don't think they'd have woken us in the middle of the night unless they knew,' Flossie said kindly.

'But it could have been another munitions factory?' Oak suggested.

'It wasn't, Oak. It was the one at Crescent Wharf where Willow works. She should never have gone there,' Flossie said.

'I agree, Mother. But you know Willow – no one could stop her once she was set on something,' Acacia said, white-faced with anxiety.

'Even Mrs Gilroy failed,' Rowan said, in an attempt to lighten the atmosphere, but Flossie glared at her.

'Now, we've got to keep calm.' Oak sat down. 'It happened after the day-shift workers had left. Mum says Willow wrote a week or two back that she finished work quite early. We must hope she'd left for her lodgings.'

Rowan was impressed by her brother's common sense, which was exactly what was needed. She had registered that his voice had broken – he even spoke like a man.

'I hope it wasn't our Willow blew the place up.' Cherry giggled.

'Cherry!' Oak said, so sternly that his sister blushed.

'I wish she'd never gone.' Rowan sighed.

'And why did she go? Tell me that! But I doubt you will – you'll blame someone else like you always do.' Flossie pointed accusingly at her.

'I don't know what you mean.' Rowan's voice wavered.

'Because of you. That's why she went. To get away from *you*.'

'That's not true.' Rowan stood up to face her mother.

'Isn't it? She told me. Sat where you are now, she was. How could she be in service there and you queening it over her? That's what she said.'

'Mum, that's not fair!' Oak stepped in.

'It's the truth! She'd never have gone but for Lady Muck over there.' Flossie moved forward and, for a second, Rowan thought she was going to hit her. She was rigid with shock, and the others were stunned into silence. Flossie leant on the pine table that separated them, thrusting her head forward aggressively. 'And your father too. Why did he go? Because he lost his job and it was your fault.'

'That's not why he went. He told me. He felt ashamed not to have gone before. He felt it was his duty,' Rowan defended herself.

'Don't you lie to me. If he'd still had his job with the Cresswells, he'd be here safe and sound. As Willow would be, but for you.'

'I'm sorry they're not here, but this isn't fair. It's not my fault.'

'Fair? What's fair? Why couldn't it have been you? Why aren't you blown to pieces?'

Rowan reeled back from the onslaught as her siblings gasped. She opened her mouth as if to argue, but then she stood up and left the room.

'Rowan!' she heard her brother call. She quickened her pace. She didn't want to talk to him or anyone else. 'Rowan!'

'Not now, Oak.' She brushed aside his hand and climbed on to her bicycle. It was a good thing she knew the road for, blinded with tears, she couldn't see where she was going.

'What's the matter? You look as if you have all the cares in the world on your shoulders.' Lady Penelope was walking round her bedroom with the aid of a stick. 'Am I not doing well?' She beamed at Rowan.

'Indeed you are. I'm proud of you.' She tried to smile but she couldn't. Her spirits were too low.

'It's thanks to you – I'd never have bothered if you hadn't badgered me. Oops!' Penelope grabbed the back of a chair to steady herself.

'My grandmother used to say Oops-a-daisy,' Rowan told her.

'Stupid expression. Whoever tripped over a daisy?'

'You should concentrate on what you're doing.'

'There you are, bossing me again! But I must do more. I'm determined to be at Mrs Gilroy's wedding. Wouldn't miss it for the world. Mind you, it's a strange world we live in. In my day the butler didn't marry the cook. Butlers and cooks didn't marry anyone. Just another example of the disintegration of our society.'

Rowan would normally have been amused by this but not today.

'Move that chair here, Rowan. I should rest.'

As she helped Penelope into a chair Rowan was reminded of a large bird settling on to its nest.

'You didn't answer my question,' Penelope said.

'Have you ordered your luncheon?' Rowan didn't want to talk about the hideous scene, the hurt her mother had inflicted, to anyone.

'You can't fool me. Something dreadful's happened to you. It's not Morts, so what is it? Must be your family.'

'I'd rather not talk about it.' She busied herself folding some clothes.

'Stop fiddling. Come here and sit down. Don't be coy. You know you'll feel better if you tell me. I'm a *marvellous* person to talk to.'

'And modest.'

'Just look at you! You have the face of someone who's lost a hundred pounds and found a dead fish. You're deeply hurt, I can see. You need to talk to someone ...'

'My mother wished me dead ...' As Rowan recounted the story, her sense of injustice grew stronger.

'What a sorry tale, and how stupid of your mother. Why should she be so unkind to you?'

'I just said – she blames me for Willow and my father going.' She was as close to snapping as she had ever been with Penelope.

'There must be something else. Perhaps, in a clumsy way, she's trying to protect the others who have not had your good fortune. How old is she? Could it be the change of life? My mother went most peculiar. Father had her locked away, the best place for her.'

'I don't think so, though Acacia wondered that. She's never told me her age but I think she's too young.'

'And is there news of Willow, the cause of all this drama?'

'I don't believe she said those horrible things about me. We've always got on well. She's alive, thank God. Fortunately she'd left work before the explosion. Sixty-nine were killed and hundreds were injured. Some aren't expected to live.'

'No doubt a German spy was behind it. Hateful Huns!'

'Do you think so? That would make it better in a way, wouldn't it, than if an Englishman had made a mistake? Willow's badly shocked – well, you would be, wouldn't you? Acacia says she's coming home today.'

'I hope your mother has the grace to make an apology to you.'

'I think it's too late. And I'm not sure I could accept it.' She felt so sad. 'My marrying into your family will continue to be a problem for mine, whatever I do. I can't seem to do anything right.'

'Poor you, with a mother wishing you dead and a mother-in-law who undoubtedly agrees with her.'

'What bothers me, Lady Penelope, is that, to a certain extent, my mother was right. It must have been difficult for Willow working in the kitchens and me married to Morts. I didn't think. I was selfish.'

'Of course you weren't. You've hardly lived a life of luxury since you married my grandson, have you? Your duties as an orderly are menial. I'm sure you saw little difference between your work and Willow's. No, the problem lies with your mother. She had no right to say that to you. It was unforgivable. But you will weather this. You're strong.'

Rowan wished she had Penelope's confidence.

'How is Coral with you?'

'We ignore each other. It's better that way. But I don't dine here.'

'You've heard about Hannah?'

'No?'

'She hasn't told you? Too embarrassed, I should think. Coral, of course, is having the vapours. But what else would one expect from her?'

For the first time that day Rowan was interested in something other than her family concerns. 'Do tell.'

'She's getting married.'

'What wonderful news. When?' She even smiled.

'March, I gather.'

'Who to?'

'Therein lies the problem. To a corporal, no less. I find it so funny.'

'Not Bert Banks?'

'I'm not privy to his name. Sadly, Hannah and I have never been the best of friends. I always felt she was jealous of me and the great love I had for her father.'

Should Rowan point out that that was a lie? Only a few months ago Penelope had told her the exact opposite. Still, thought Rowan, she supposed it was one of the privileges of age to rewrite history when one felt like it. 'He's a lovely man,' she said, 'and a gardener by profession. It's a perfect match.'

'I doubt we shall ever persuade Coral to agree! Perhaps if hell freezes over.'

5

The telegram came, as Rowan had always known it would. It was Whitaker who gave it to her. As she accepted it, her hand was shaking so much it was as if she had the palsy.

'Shall I open it for you, Mrs Morts?' he asked kindly.

'No, thank you. I must do it myself.' At the sight of the envelope and Whitaker's sombre expression, the whole ward had lapsed into an uncomfortable silence. Fanny Petty was clutching a urine bottle to her ample chest. Even Sister Westall was regarding her with a sympathetic expression. Only Lady Sylvia continued to chatter – until Ella told her to be quiet.

'Excuse me,' Rowan said thickly. She walked out of the ward and ran along the corridor as if she were fleeing demons. She burst into Lady Cresswell's room without knocking. 'It's come. Oh, dear God, I'm so afraid.' She collapsed on to the floor beside the chair on which Penelope sat, all the strength in her legs deserting her. She thrust the telegram at her.

'Why has she got a telegram and not me?' She heard Lady Coral's shrill voice. She hadn't even noticed she was there.

'Because she's his wife. Don't start, Coral.'

'Give it to me! I want to open it!' She stamped her foot and lunged at Rowan to snatch the envelope.

'Calm down, for heaven's sake. You can't have it. Go away,' said Penelope.

Lady Coral had no intention of leaving. Rowan felt faint. She couldn't deal with any more scenes. Not now.

'Get out, Coral,' Penelope ordered her.

'I'm staying.'

'If you were not such an unpleasant creature I would agree that you should. But you make this child's life such a misery that you lost that right.' With superhuman effort, Penelope rose to her feet. A good four inches taller and no doubt weighing three times as much, she loomed over her daughter-in-law and raised her hand as if to hit her.

Lady Coral didn't stop to argue but ran from the room screaming, 'Mortie!'

'Now, my dear child, are you going to open this or shall I?' asked Penelope, as she lowered herself back into the chair.

'I can't! I simply can't do it!' Rowan was gasping for breath. She shut her eyes as Penelope tore open the envelope.

'He's wounded.'

Had she dreamt Penelope had said that?

'You can breathe, my dear. He's not dead.'

At this Rowan crumpled on to the floor and cried for sheer relief. She cried, too, for those who had died and for those who would die, she wept for the injustice of war and the pain it caused.

Penelope sat and waited, not touching her, unaware that tears rolled down her own face.

A fortnight later Rowan, accompanied by Hannah, was on her way to the railway station. Morts was coming home.

Surreptitiously she looked at her watch. Today Hannah, who normally drove too fast, was driving too slowly. 'You're not as speedy as usual,' she said, afraid that they would be late.

'Dear Bert was horrified by my driving. He said I must calm down.'

'I'm so happy for you, Miss Cresswell. He's a lovely man.'

'Thank you, my dear. I'm truly blessed.'

They lapsed into silence. If only she knew the extent of his injuries, Rowan thought, how long he would be in hospital or when he would have to go back to the front, she would not be in such a state.

As if she had read her mind, Hannah said, 'I tried to get more information for you about Morts. I asked Major Fellowes, but sometimes I think he enjoys being in a powerful position. Such an unattractive quality.' Hannah swerved violently. 'Did you see that cat?'

'No – was there one? What did the major say?' Rowan was sure there had been no animal.

'That it would not be fair to others if he found out about Morts for us.'

'That wasn't very friendly of him,' Rowan said.

'I'm disappointed in him. But generally the lack of information is a scandal. And how is Willow?'

'Much better.'

'Is she returning to London?'

'No.'

'It was sad that young Freddie was killed. Such a waste.'

Rowan willed her to stop talking. She knew that Hannah was trying to distract her from the fears that tormented her, but she wanted peace and quiet. She needed time to compose herself.

'Oh, look at all those women. What are they doing?' Hannah exclaimed.

They were passing Barlton's post office. Outside a crowd was jostling for position. Some were crying, and others laughing.

'They're looking at the lists of those killed,' Rowan told her.

'Why make such an exhibition of themselves? They would be notified by telegram in private.'

'It's only the officers' families who get the telegrams.' Whenever Rowan thought that Hannah's attitude was improving she would say something dreadful again.

Hannah grated the gears. 'Is that so? But Mrs Fisher in Cress received one and her son was a private.'

'Most aren't so lucky.' Oh, do be quiet, she thought. She wished she had gone in one of the ambulances now, but she hadn't wanted to hurt Hannah's feelings.

At last they were at the station. The train had arrived and the usual chaos of pushing, shoving and shouting had ensued. Not waiting for Hannah, Rowan jumped out of the car and ran on to the platform where several stretchers were already set out in lines. She went to the major, who was walking up and down the line, ticking off names on a sheet of paper.

'Major Fellowes, have you seen my husband?'

He pointed to the end of the platform.

The crowd parted briefly and Rowan saw him. He was standing! Her joy in that was marred quickly by the knowledge that he would have to return to the fighting. Slipping through the crowds, she darted towards him. 'Morts!' she called. 'Oh, my darling!' She didn't care who heard her. 'Morts!' Then she was beside him.

'My love.' He held out his arms to her. She could feel him. She could smell him. He was home. She would never let him go again. 'My darling, I've dreamt of this moment. Oh, how I love you. And even better! You called me "darling".'

'Did I? I must be learning!'

As they made their way to Hannah's motor, it was apparent that he was having difficulty in walking despite his crutches. His face was contorted with pain and he kept having to stop and rest.

'Morts, let me get you a wheelchair. It's too much for you.'

'No, that would be giving in and I won't do that.' His face was set so she didn't argue with him.

Rowan cooked their supper with care, his favourite game pie. She'd got the recipe from Eve Gilroy who had offered to cook it for her but she'd wanted to do it herself.

She banked up the fire in the sitting room, then lit the lamps and candles. How lovely their house looked.

Later she sat down to wait. Morts was still at the manor. He had to be assessed by the major and, she supposed, the all-important decisions would be made about his future. When Morts had announced he wanted to sleep at his home the major had not been happy. But Morts had argued that he would recover faster there than he would in the convalescent home. Recover from what, Rowan still did not know for she had left at that point. What little she had asked him, about his pain and his limp, had made him a little impatient with her.

'I'm in here,' she called, as she heard him enter the hall. 'Is it still as cold?' she asked, as he entered the room. 'Morts, what is it?'

He stood in the doorway, leaning against the jamb, pallid with fatigue. 'I'll be fine in a minute, but a whisky and soda might help.' He tried to grin.

'Did you walk back? You shouldn't have. It's too far. We've still got the pony and governess cart – I'd have come to get you,' she prattled, as she prepared his drink. 'Did you see the major?'

Morts lowered himself on to the sofa. She would have liked to help him and knew she was hovering, but she had to resist. She was sure he wanted to do everything for himself.

'He's not the most charming of men, is he?' she said.

'He can be gruff.' He lay back on the cushions, his eyes closed, exhaustion etched on his face. She was worried. He shouldn't look like that. She waited, holding his glass. When he opened his eyes and saw her standing there, he smiled with such sweetness.

'You're in a lot of pain, aren't you?' she asked.

'The doctor has given me an opiate, but at this moment I'd rather have the whisky.'

She handed it to him, then returned to the table to pour some for herself. 'Have they decided when you must go back?' she asked tentatively, afraid of the answer.

'I'm not going back.'

In her excitement Rowan spilt the soda. 'That's wonderful news.' But then she realized that there had to be a *why*. 'I mean ...' She was flustered now.

'My darling, I know what you mean. And the news is not all good.' His tone was so serious that Rowan's heart began to pound. 'I don't want to destroy your happiness.' Now her stomach turned. He patted the cushion beside him.

'I've not been entirely honest with you but I thought it was for the best.' She nodded for she could not speak. 'I was wounded several weeks ago – in fact, the day after I returned to the front.'

'I don't understand.'

'I didn't want to worry you and hoped I'd heal so you need never know. But now there's no escape. I have to tell you.'

She was hanging on his every word, wanting to hear what he had to say yet afraid of what it might be. 'Yes?' she whispered.

'I was shot ...' He pointed to his upper thigh. 'The bullet went straight through. It was a miracle that it didn't shatter the bone.'

'A miracle,' she echoed.

'The problem is, the doctors are not sure and I can't find one who will commit himself, but there is a possibility we may not now be able to have children.'

She was aware that he was watching her intently and knew that her response would be of crucial importance to their future. 'It won't matter. We have each other.' It was true, but she felt an enveloping sadness for the children who would never be born.

'I don't think you mean that.'

'It makes me sad, but it's not the end of the world,' she said firmly to make certain he would believe her.

'There's something else ...'

His words hung in the air. Instinctively she knew what he was unable to say. 'You cannot make love to me?' she asked, in a quiet, measured way.

'At the moment it's impossible and the doctors say it could remain so. On the other hand the feeling may return. No one can be certain.' He took a deep swallow of his whisky.

Was there more? she thought.

'If you want us to divorce I shall quite understand. It would not be fair of me to expect you to stay with me when I know how much you want children and how much ...' He couldn't continue.

'You don't understand me very well, do you, Morts?'

'I think I do.'

'You're very wrong.' She took his hand. 'When we married I had nothing to bring to our union but my love. It was and is the most precious gift I can give you. And I made my vows, remember, for better or worse.'

'But it wouldn't be fair.'

'I shall decide what is and isn't fair. We've had so much of the *better* that now it is time for the *worse*. Don't you ever mention divorce to me again.'

'It's easy to say that but it will be hard to live with it.'

'I want to be with you. And you see, my darling, we have our love. And that is our strength. It will see us through.' She kissed him.

As she did so she knew, with an unswerving conviction, that they would be all right. It would be hard, she knew, for theirs had been such a physical passion, and no doubt they would both shed many tears. But their love would sustain them.

'You see, my darling, you're alive and that is all that matters to me.'

'You called me "darling" again.' For the first time since his return he was laughing. It was going to be all right.

6

Hannah Cresswell sat in the family pew at Cresswell Church. As always, she felt that strange comfort in knowing that her ancestors were lying close by. She glanced up at the stained-glass windows behind the marble and alabaster altar. They needed cleaning. With the men away, it was jobs like that which never got done now. Looking at the modest brass plaque that commemorated her father, she wondered what he would think of Bert. She had a notion that he would have liked him, approved, and been pleased that she had eventually found happiness.

As was her habit, she was early. She liked to watch everyone take their seats. When she saw Bert enter and pause, she waved. 'Over here, Bert,' she called, and he moved towards her as fast as he could.

'I can't sit here. It's too grand for the likes of me.'

'You're marrying into my family and this is your rightful place.'

'If you insist, but don't complain to me about the gossip.'

'I'm not ashamed of letting the whole world know I love you.' She smiled shyly. It still surprised her that she could say such things. She tweaked her fur, then straightened the skirt of the blue dress she was wearing under her coat. Once she had worn mostly grey and black; since Bert's proposal she had branched out into colours.

She pulled her coat closer. It was a bitterly cold February day, and the coal shortage meant that the church was not heated. Perhaps they should have made an exception today.

Slowly the pews filled. It was a good opportunity for her to point out to Bert who everyone was. 'Those are the Marshalls, Rowan's family. They're all named after trees. Isn't that droll?'

'I think it's nice. A handsome-looking bunch. What's wrong with the one whose face is yellow?' he whispered.

She wished she hadn't said that about their names now. She didn't want him to think she was spiteful. Still, it was too late now. 'That's Willow. She's been working in munitions. Apparently they go that colour. Hardly healthy, is it? It's something to do with the cordite. It's a shame because, after Rowan, she was the best-looking.' She glanced round again. 'As usual, there are several Peppers. That's Polly over there. She helps with the nursing. Quite a difficult family. Opinionated. I should think this war will make them even more so. Who else? Oh, good gracious me, no one told me *she* was coming. That's my stepmother, Lady Cresswell.'

'Good job she's in a wheelchair. It would be a bit difficult if she wanted to join us, her being on the large size.'

'She's lost a good third of her weight.'

Hannah smiled at Penelope. She had realized recently that she was no longer afraid of her. Was that because the woman was such a sad wreck of what she had once been or was it because she had Bert beside her? She hoped it was the latter. She took his arm and gave it a little squeeze.

Penelope was having an altercation with the churchwarden. Young

Oak was summoned. The two, with difficulty, lifted the wheelchair up the step and pushed her towards the pew. There, Penelope struggled out of it – the congregation held its breath – and manoeuvred herself on to the seat. Hannah and Bert had to shuffle along. Bert had been wrong. There was enough space for her.

'Mother, might I introduce you to Mr Banks? Bert, this is Lady Cresswell.'

'I gather I'm to congratulate you, Mr Banks. I trust you will be happy and that you will take care of my daughter. She's a dear soul.'

Hannah's mouth dropped open. She thought she must be dreaming. Had Penelope really said that? It was the nicest thing she had uttered in all the years they had known each other. Bert had stood up and was leaning across her shaking Penelope's hand.

'I'd die for her, Lady Cresswell,' he said, which brought a tear to Hannah's eyes.

'I do hope that won't be necessary,' Penelope declared, which made Hannah laugh and the tear disappear.

'That poor boy. Do you think he'll ever be right again?' Penelope spoke of Morts, who, on Rowan's arm, was making his slow progress up the aisle.

'Rowan will make him better. She's such a fighter.'

'She needs to be, with a mother like hers.' And Penelope glared at Flossie, who, unaware that she was privy to Rowan's affairs, looked as perplexed as Hannah did, since she, too, was ignorant of what had happened between Rowan and her mother. Though she did notice that Rowan did not even glance at Flossie.

'I was so wrong about Rowan. She has more natural dignity than many I know,' Hannah observed.

'Speak of the devil ...' Penelope chuckled as Coral entered the church, with Mortie in tow. 'I hope this war has taught us to be more tolerant of our fellows.'

'I quite agree.' Now Hannah was stupefied. Was this Rowan's good work? 'Morts, you're looking so much better.' She was lying, but what else could she say?

'I'm feeling as right as rain,' he said, as he and Rowan slipped into the pew. She wondered why she didn't believe him.

It was unfortunate that Coral should end up sitting beside Rowan, but Hannah saw the magnanimous smile Rowan bestowed on her.

As more people arrived, the chatter increased. 'Noisy lot, aren't they?' said Bert.

As she watched them Hannah thought how dear they were to her, these families she had known all her life. They were a unit that stretched back hundreds of years. They cared for the Cresswells and the Cresswells cared for them. It was an obligation on both their sides. Would this war change everything? Would the old order disappear with the new independence she saw every day? She wanted things to be better for them, but she did not want anything to change for her family. And there was the dichotomy. If one changed it was inevitable that the other would too.

All of the Cresswells smiled encouragingly as a nervous-looking Whitaker arrived. Even Coral, who had noisily listed her objections to the marriage of her cook and butler, managed a wintry smile.

Oliver, on the last day of his leave, was standing as Whitaker's best man. It was such a relief to see him and Esmeralda happy together again, thought Hannah. She had not liked that period when she was supposed to dislike Esmeralda. Of course, she had not arrived yet – she seemed incapable of being on time.

The vicar appeared and had a word with Whitaker. Hannah quite liked the new man. When the Plunketts had left in such an unseemly hurry – admittedly, in the circumstances, it was for the best – she had had the task of choosing him in the absence of her brothers. A bachelor seemed to her a much more sensible choice, given Oliver's weakness.

She frowned when Zeph arrived with May Snodland. She wasn't sure how she felt about him and his unconventional domestic arrangements. On the one hand she liked and admired him, and Dolly, apparently, was not the best of wives, but to flaunt May! Oh dear! While she was prepared for change Hannah wondered if this one wasn't a little too much for her. Bert waved cheerily at Zeph, so it certainly didn't bother him. She'd discuss it with him later. He was so wise, far wiser than she.

The organ wheezed into life, and Hannah winced at the wrong notes. Doris should stick to running the telephone exchange. She lacked finesse in her playing. She made a mental note to find a new organist as quickly as possible.

The churchwarden waved his arm from the west door. The Wedding March – or an approximation of it – rang out in the ancient church. Everyone stood up – except Penelope. Just in time, Esmeralda appeared. She walked quickly down the aisle towards them, not in her usual giggling flurry but with a new, mature dignity. Well, thought Hannah, changes were afoot there, too.

Doris paused briefly and, for a moment, there was silence. Then the music thundered out again.

Attractive in a suit of cream silk, clutching her bouquet tightly, Eve Gilroy, smiling like a Cheshire cat, walked down the aisle on the arm of her cousin. There was, thought Hannah, an air of triumph about her. And what a nice touch to have Gussie Fuller as her matron-of-honour, even if she looked like a cat too, but one whose cream had been stolen.

As the service began, Hannah thought how lucky and blessed they were. Just a stretch of water away soldiers were dying in their thousands, men from this estate among them. Lucky? So far. Blessed? Only time would tell.